SLOW RIVER

NICOLA
GRIFFITH

SLOW
RIVER〜

DEL
REY

A DEL REY® BOOK

BALLANTINE BOOKS • NEW YORK

A Del Rey® Book
Published by Ballantine Books

Copyright © 1995 by Nicola Griffith

LIBRARY OF CONGRESS CATALOGING-IN-PUBLICATION DATA
Griffith, Nicola.
   Slow river / Nicola Griffith.—1st ed.
      p.   cm.
   "A Del Rey Book."
   ISBN 0-345-39165-9
   I. Title.
PR6057.R49S58   1995
823'.914—dc20   95-1720 CIP

Manufactured in the United States of America

First Edition: August 1995

10 9 8 7 6 5 4 3 2 1

For Kelley, my hoard.

SLOW RIVER

ONE

AT THE heart of the city was a river. At four in the morning its cold, deep scent seeped through deserted streets and settled in the shadows between warehouses. I walked carefully, unwilling to disturb the quiet. The smell of the river thickened as I headed deeper into the warehouse district, the Old Town, where the street names changed: Dagger Lane, Silver Street, The Land of Green Ginger; the fifteenth century still echoing through the beginnings of the twenty-first.

Then there were no more buildings, no more alleys, only the river, sliding slow and wide under a bare sky. I stepped cautiously into the open, like a small mammal leaving the shelter of the trees for the exposed bank.

Rivers were the source of civilization, the scenes of all beginnings and endings in ancient times. Babies were carried to the banks to be washed, bodies were laid on biers and floated away. Births and deaths were usually communal affairs, but I was here alone.

I sat on the massive wharf timbers—black with age and slick with algae—and let my fingers trail in the water.

In the last two or three months I had come here often, usually after twilight, when the tourists no longer posed by ancient bale chains and the striped awnings of lunchtime bistros were furled for the night. At dusk the river was sleek and implacable, a black so deep it was almost purple. I watched it in silence. It had seen Romans, Vikings, and medieval kings. When I sat beside it, it didn't matter that I was alone. We sat companionably, the river and I, and watched the stars turn overhead.

I could see the stars because I had got into the habit of lifting the grating set discreetly in the pavement and cracking open the dark blue box that controlled the street lighting. It pleased me to turn off the deliberately old-fashioned wrought-iron lamps whose rich, orangy light pooled on the cobbles and turned six centuries of brutal history into a cozy fireside tale. So few people strolled this way at night that it was usually a couple of days, sometimes as many as ten, before the malfunction was reported, and another week or so before it was fixed. Then I left the lights on for some random length of time before killing them again. The High Street, the city workers had begun to whisper, was haunted.

And perhaps it was. Perhaps I was a ghost. There were those who thought I was dead, and my identity, when I had one, was constructed of that most modern of ectoplasms: electrons and photons that flitted silently across the data nets of the world.

The hand I had dipped in the river was drying. It itched. I rubbed the web between my thumb and forefinger, the scar there. Tomorrow, if all went well, if Ruth would help me one last time, a tadpole-sized implant would be placed under the scar. And I would become someone else. Again. Only this time I hoped it would be permanent. Next time I dipped my hand in the river it would be as someone le-

gitimate, reborn three years after arriving naked and nameless in the city.

~~~~ THE FIRST thing she thought when she woke naked on the cobbles was: *Don't roll onto your back.*
She lay very still and tried to concentrate on the cold stones
under hip and cheek, on the strange taste in her mouth.
Drugs, they had given her drugs to make her stop struggling, after she had . . .

Don't think about it.

She could not afford to remember now. She would think
about it later, when she was safe. The memory of what had
happened shrank safely back into a tight bubble.

She raised her head, felt the great, open slash across her
trapezoid muscles pull and stretch. Nausea forced her to
breathe shallowly for a moment, but then she lifted her head
again and looked about: night, in some strange city. And it
was cold.

She was curled in a fetal position around some rubbish
on a silent, cobbled street. More like an alley. Somewhere
at the edge of her peripheral vision the colors of a newstank flashed silently. She closed her eyes again, trying to
think. *Lore. My name is Lore.* A wind was blowing now, and
paper, a news printout, flapped in her face. She pushed it
away, then changed her mind and pulled it to her. Paper,
she had read, had insulating qualities.

The odd, metallic taste in her mouth was fading, and her
head cleared a little. She had to find somewhere to hide.
And she had to get warm.

Rain fell on her lip and she licked it off automatically,
feeling confused. *Why* should she hide? Surely there were
people who would love her and care for her, tend her
gently and clean her wounds, if she just let them know

where she was. But *Hide,* said the voice from her crocodile brain, *Hide!,* and her muscles jumped and sweat started on her flanks, and the slick gray memory like a balloon in her head swelled and threatened to burst.

She crawled toward the newstank because its lurid colors, the series of news pictures flashing over and over in its endless cycle, imitated life. She sat on the road in the rain in the middle of the night, naked, and bathed in the colors as if they were filtered sunlight, warm and safe.

It took her a while to realize what she was seeing: herself. Herself sitting naked on a chair, blindfolded, begging her family to please, please pay what her kidnappers wanted.

The pictures were like a can opener, ripping open the bubble in her head, drenching her with images: the kidnap, the humiliation, the camera filming it all. "So your family will see we're serious," he had said. Day after day of it. An eighteenth birthday spent huddled naked in a tent in the middle of a room, with nothing but a plastic slop bucket for company. And here it was, in color: her naked and weeping, a man ranting at the camera, demanding more money. Her tied to a chair, begging for food. Begging . . .

And the whole world had seen this. The whole world had seen her naked, physically and mentally, while they ate their breakfast or took the passenger slide to work. Or maybe drinking coffee at home they had been caught by the cleverly put-together images and decided, What the hell, may as well pay to download the whole story. And she remembered her kidnappers, one who had always smelled of frying fish, half leading, half carrying her out into the barnyard because she was supposed to be dopey with the drugs she had palmed, the other one rolling new transparent plasthene out on the floor of the open van. She remembered the smell of rain on the farm implements rusting by a wall, and the panic. The panic as she thought, *This is it. They're going to kill me.* And the absolute determination to fight one last time, the way the metallic blanket had felt as it slid off her shoulders, how she pushed the man by her side, dropped the cold, thin spike of metal into her palm and turned. Remembered the look on his face as his eyes met hers, as he *knew* she was going to kill him, as she *knew* she was going to shove the sharp metal into his throat, and she did. She remembered the tight gurgle as he fell, pulling her with him, crashing into a pile of metal. The ancient plough blade opening her own back from shoulder to lumbar vertebrae. The shouting of the other man as he jumped from the van, stumbling on the cobbles, pulling her up, checking the man on the ground, shouting, "You killed him you stupid bitch, you killed him!" The way her body would not work, would not obey her urge to run; how he pushed her roughly into the van and slammed the doors. And her blood, dripping on the plasthene sheet; thinking, *Oh, so that's what it's for.* Remembered him telling the van where to go, the blood on his hands. The way he cursed her for a fool: hadn't she known they were letting her go? But she hadn't. She thought they were going to kill her. And then the sad look, the way he shook his head and said: Sorry, but you've forced me to do this and at least you won't feel any pain . . . And the panic again; scrabbling blindly at the handle behind her; the door falling open. She remembered beginning the slow tumble backward, the simultaneous flooding sting of the nasal drug that should have been fatal . . .

But she was alive. Alive enough to sit in the rain, skin stained with pictures of herself, and remember everything.

A taxi hummed past.

She did not call out, but she was not sure if that was because she was too weak, or because she was afraid. The taxi driver might recognize her. He would know what they had done to her. He would have seen it. Everyone would have seen it. They would look at her and know. She could not call her family. They had all seen her suffer, too. Every time they looked at her they would see the pictures, and she would see them seeing it, and she would wonder why they had not paid her ransom.

Her hair was plastered to her head. The rain sheeted down. She crawled into a doorway, realized she was whimpering. She had to be quiet, she had to hide. She had to lose herself. Think. What would give her away? She pulled herself up to her knees and tried to look at her reflection in the shop window, but the rain made it impossible. She scrabbled around in the corners of the doorway until the dirt there turned to mud on her wet hands. She smeared the mud onto her hair. After thirty days, the nanomechs coloring her head and body hair would be dying off and the natural gray would be showing. Only the very few, the very rich wore naturally gray hair. What else? Her Personal Identity, DNA and Account insert. But when she held out her left hand to the flickers of light flashing in the doorway she saw the angry red scar on the webbing between her thumb and index finger. Of course—the kidnappers would have removed the PIDA on the first day to prevent a trace.

She was alone, hurt, and moneyless. She needed help but was afraid to find it.

It was almost dawn before she heard footsteps. She peered around the doorway. A woman, with dark blond hair tucked into the collar of a big coat, walking with a night step: easy, but wary. One hand in her pocket.

"Help me."

Her voice was just a whisper and Lore thought the woman had not heard, but she slowed, then stopped. "Come out where I can see you." The kind of voice Lore had never heard before: light and quick and probably dangerous.

"Help me." It came out sounding like a command, and Lore heard for the first time the rounded plumminess of her own voice, and knew that she would have to learn to change it.

This time the woman heard, and turned toward the doorway. "Why, what's wrong with you?" The hand shifted in its pocket, and Lore wondered if the woman had a weapon of some kind. "Stand up so I can see you."

"I can't." Trying to imitate the slippery street vowels.

"Then I'll just walk along home." She sounded as though she meant it.

"No." Lore tried again. "Please. I need your help."

The woman in the long coat seemed suddenly to shrug off her caution. "Let's have a look at you, then." When she stepped closer to the doorway and saw Lore's muddy hair and nakedness, she grinned. "You need to get rid of the boyfriend or girlfriend that did this to you." But when the light fell on Lore's bloody back, the woman's face tightened into old lines, and her eyes flashed yellow and wise in the sodium light. She fished something out of her coat pocket, slid it inside her shirt, and took off her coat. She held it out. "This might hurt your back, but it'll keep you warm until I can get you home."

Lore pulled herself up the metal and glass corner of the doorway, and stood. The woman caught her arm as she nearly fell.

"Hurt?"

"No." It was numb now.

"It will." That sounded as though it came from experience. "It's too cold to stand around. Just put this on and walk."

Lore took the coat. It was heavy, old wool. The lining was dark silk, still warm. "It smells of summer," and there were tears in her eyes as she remembered the smells of sunshine on bruised grass, a long, long time before this nightmare began.

"Put it on." The woman sounded impatient. She was glancing about: quick flicks of her head this way and that. Her hair, free of the coat collar now, swung from side to side.

Lore struggled with the coat. She flinched when the warm silk touched her back, but all she felt was a kind of stretched numbness like the opening of a vast tunnel. "My name . . ." Shock made her dizzy and vague. "Who . . ."

"Spanner." Spanner was scanning the street again. It was noticeably lighter. Another taxi skimmed by. "Fasten the damn thing up. And hurry."

On that first night it seemed to Lore to be miles and miles from the city center to Spanner's flat. She learned later that it was barely a mile and a half. It was not that she had a hard time moving—on the contrary, she seemed to skim along the pavement without effort—it was more that the journey stretched endlessly and the false dawn blended with the sodium streetlamps to form a light like wet orange sherbet that always seemed just a moment away from fizzing, boiling off, leaving no oxygen. Lore knew she was ill. She remembered the blood, hers and his, the sharp plastic *tick* as it dripped onto the plasthene.

She had a vague impression of a shop window and railings, and then stone steps. The stairwell was made of unfinished brick. The mortar looked old. Spanner must have opened the door then, because she found herself inside.

Spanner did not turn on any lights; it was bright enough with the streetlights washing in through unshuttered windows. Lore swayed in the middle of an enormous L-shaped room. Several power points glowed at one end, like red eyes.

"You need to sleep," Spanner said, "not talk. Here's some water. Some painkillers." Her voice sounded different in her own room, and she seemed to appear and disappear, reappearing with things—a glass, some pills; showing Lore the bathroom. It was like watching a jerky, badly edited film. "Here's the mat." A judo mat, by the west wall, under the windows opposite the curtained opening to the short limb of the L, the bedroom. "I'll turn up the heat. You won't be able to bear anything on that back for a while. I don't think we can do much about it tonight. Looks like it's scabbing over. I'll get a medic for you in the morning, and we'll talk then."

Lore knew she must be saying things, responding in some way she assumed reassured Spanner, but she was not aware of it. Spanner touched a pad of buttons on the wall. "I've set the alarm. If you need anything, or want to leave, wake me."

Then Spanner went into the bedroom and closed the curtain behind her.

Lore was alone. Alone in a room filled with shadows of furniture she had never seen before, things that belonged to a woman she did not know, in a city that was strange to her. Alone. A nobody with nothing, not even clothes. It was like being kidnapped again, but this time she had no escape to dream of, nowhere to run to. Her sister had killed herself. Her father was a monster who had lied to her, year after year after year.

She stood in the middle of the room, aware of the strange smells and temperature, and knew clearly that she needed this woman, Spanner; depended upon her, in a way that was shocking. Lore's fear was sharp, undeniable as a knife pressed against her cheek. It woke her up a little from her dreamy shock state. She was thirsty.

The bathroom was enormous, its window bare. It was too dark outside to see much, but she thought there were perhaps walls, and the remains of a path. She did not want to put the light on, but she could make out a yellowing, old-fashioned tub and huge, cracked black and white tiles. The water ran from the bulbous taps under low pressure, twisting like crossed fingers. She let it pour over her fingers automatically, tasted with the tip of her tongue. Salty. Ions: probably chloride and fluoride and bromide . . . and suddenly she was crying.

Her fingers turned cold under the tap as she wept. She would have to drink this water that wheezed out from old lead pipes, would have to accept what she was given from now on, and she would have to like it.

When she had finished crying, she splashed her face with

water and dried herself with a towel—*Spanner's water, Spanner's towel*—and went back into the living room.

In the street twenty feet below, a freight slide rumbled to a stop but everything else was quiet. She looked down at the judo mat and imagined trying to sleep on it, facedown, back toward the closed curtains of Spanner's bedroom. Horribly vulnerable.

The judo mat probably weighed less than twenty pounds but it was awkward to handle. In the end she had to drag it behind her like a travois. Several things fell as she barged fifteen feet over to the east wall. She lay on her stomach facing the shadows. The freighter moved off again. She counted to two hundred and fifty-one before another passed. In the silence, she heard the creak of a tree limb rubbing up against the bricks of the outside wall.

As the streetlights faded and the sun came up, the red eyes glowed less insistently and the shadows before her shifted. An electronics workbench, she thought, and tools . . .

Lore dozed on and off until around ten in the morning, when the noise of passenger slides and people passing by on the street filled the room with a bright hum. There was no sound from the bedroom.

The living room was big, twenty by twenty-five at least. The centerpiece of the shorter south wall was an elaborate fireplace, cold and empty now. A variety of leafy green plants stood on the hearth and on a low tin-topped table nearby. There were some books, but not many. A rug. Then the couch and coffee table, all well used, not exactly clean. The carpet was rucked up where she had dragged the mat over it last night in the dark. Squares of bright sunlight pointed up the wear in its red and blue pattern. The tree outside cast shadows of branches and shivering leaves over the wall behind her. From this angle, all she could see of it was the glint of low morning sun through leaves already beginning to turn orange and red, but the leaves looked big and raggedy, like hands. Maybe a chestnut. She lay under its shadow and tried to imagine she was at Ratnapida, lying on the grass. The birdsong was all wrong.

A large proportion of the room at the north end was taken by two tables and a workbench, all covered with screens, data-retrieval banks, a keyboard and headset, input panel, and what looked like some kind of radio and several haphazard chipstacks, all connected together by a maze of cable.

She could not figure out what it was all for.

In what Lore would come to realize was a pattern, Spanner woke up around midday. She went straight from bed to the connecting bathroom, and about twenty minutes later emerged into the living room via the kitchen door, carrying two white mugs of some aromatic tea. The silk robe she wore had seen better days, and in the daylight her hair was the color of antique brass. "Jasmine," she said as she held out a mug.

Lore reached for the tea. The red scar between her thumb and forefinger showed up clearly against the white ceramic. Moving hurt. Spanner nodded to herself. "I called the medic. He's on his way. And don't worry. He won't report this. Or you."

Lore felt as though she should say something, but she had no idea what. She sipped at the tea, trying to ignore the pain.

"I know who you are," Spanner said softly. "You were all over the net." Lore said nothing. "I don't understand why you're not screaming for Mummy and Daddy."

"I'll never go back."

"Why?"

Lore stayed silent. She needed Spanner, but she did not have to give her more ammunition.

Spanner shrugged. "If that's the way you want it. Can you get any money from them?"

"No." Lore hoped that sounded as final as she felt.

"Then I don't see how you're going to repay me. For the medic. For the care you look like you're going to need for a while. Do you have any skills?"

Yes, Lore wanted to say, but then she saw once again the red scar on the hand wrapped around her teacup. How would she get a job designing remediation systems, how would she prove her experience, without an identity? "My identity . . ."

"That's another question. You want to get a copy of your old PIDA?"

"No." The pain was hot and round and tight. The infection must be spreading. Again, she thought of his blood mingling with hers.

"Then you'll need a new one. That costs, too. And what do you want me to call you? I can't go around calling you Frances Lorien van de Oest."

"Lore. Call me Lore."

"Well, Lore, if you want my help then you'll have to pay for it. You'll have to work for me."

"Legally?"

Spanner laughed. "No. Not even remotely. But I've never been caught, and what I do is low down on the police list—victimless crime. Or nearly so."

The only "victimless" crimes Lore could think of were prostitution and personal drug use.

Spanner stood up, went to her workbench, brought back a slate. "Here. Take a look."

Lore, moving her arms slowly and carefully, turned it over, switched it on. Wrote on it, queried it, turned it off. She handed it back. "It's an ordinary slate."

"Exactly. A slate stuffed with information. What do you use your slate for?"

Lore thought about it. "Making memos. Sending messages. Net codes and addresses. Ordering specialty merchandise. Appointments. Receiving messages. Keeping a balance of accounts . . ." She began to see where this was leading. "But it's all protected by my security code."

"That's what most people think. But it's not difficult to break it. It just takes time and a good program. Nothing glamorous. This one . . ." Spanner smiled. "Well, let's see." She sat down at her bench, connected the slate to a couple of jacks, flipped some switches. "Can you see from down there?" Lore nodded. On a readout facing Spanner numbers began to flicker faster than Lore could read them. "Depending on the complexity of the code, it takes anywhere from half a minute to an hour." Lore watched, mesmerized. "I've yet to come across one that—" The numbers stopped. "Ah. An easy one." She touched another button and the red FEED light on the slate lit up. "It's downloading everything: account numbers, the net numbers of people called in the last few months, name, address, occupation, DNA codes of the owner . . . everything." She was smiling to herself.

"What do you use it for?"

"Depends. Some slates are useless to us. We just ransom them back to their owners for a modest fee. No one gets hurt. Often we couch things in terms of a reward for the finder. No police involvement. Nothing to worry about."

"And other times?"

Someone banged on the door, two short, two long taps.

"That's the medic." But Spanner did not get up to let him in. "Better make up your mind."

"What?"

"Do you want to work with me or not? Even if I don't let him in, there'll be a small fee for call-out, nothing you couldn't repay when you're able. But if he comes in here and works on you, then you'll owe me."

The medic banged on the door again, faster this time.

"Sounds like he's getting impatient."

Lore had no clothes and no ID; she doubted she could stand. "I'll do it."

Spanner went to the door.

The medic was not what Lore had expected. He was middle-aged, well dressed and very gentle. And fast. He ran a scanner down her back. "Some infection. It'll need cleaning." He pulled out a wand-sized subcutaneous injector.

"No," Lore said. "I'm allergic."

"Patches, too?"

She nodded. He sighed. "Well, that's an inconvenience." He rummaged in his bag. Lore heard a light hiss, felt a cool mist on her back, tasted a faint antiseptic tang. The pain disappeared in a vast numbness. She knew he was swabbing out her wound but all she felt was a vague tugging. "Clean enough for now." This time he took a roll of some white material from his bag. She shuddered, remembering the plasthene. He paused a moment, then unwrapped a couple of feet and cut it. It glinted. Some kind of metallic threads.

"What's that?"

"You've never seen this before?" Spanner asked. Lore shook her head. The numbness was wearing off. "Here." Spanner passed her a hand mirror. "Watch. It's interesting."

The medic, who did not seem to resent being cast as entertainment, was smearing the edges of her wound with a cold jelly and carefully laying the light material over it. Then he unwrapped a few feet of electrical wire, attached it with crocodile clips to the material.

"What—"

"Stretch as much as you can."

"It hurts."

"Do the best you can. When this sets, it sets."

She did.

He plugged in the wires. Lore felt a quick, tingling shock around her wound, and the gauzy material leapt up from her back and formed a flexible, rigid cage over the gash, still attached to her skin where the medic had applied the cold jelly. He put away the roll and the wires, took something else out of his bag. She watched him carefully in the mirror. He held it up. "Plaskin." This time the spray was throatier, lasted longer. When he was done, the raised white material, the jelly, and a two-inch strip of skin around the wound were all that pinkish bandage color that marketers called "flesh." She looked as though she had a fat pink snake lying diagonally along her spine. He tapped it experimentally, nodded in satisfaction. "You won't be able to lie down on it or lean against it, but you should be able to wear clothes in an hour or two, and the wound can breathe. For the next ten days bathe as normal. The plaskin will protect it. I'll come back to take it off, make sure everything's all right." He put two vials of pills on the floor by her face. "This is all I have for now in the way of antibiotics and antivirals in pill form." She could feel the drying plaskin begin to tug at the healthy skin on her back. "Is the pain very bad?"

"Yes."

He knelt and Lore felt a cold wipe, then the sliding pinch of a needle in the muscle at her shoulder. She could feel the drug spreading under her skin, like butter. He stood and said to Spanner, "This cream is for when the plas comes off. It'll need rubbing into the scar three times a day to keep it supple. I don't have any painkillers at all in pill form."

"I've used needles before."

Lore wondered how Spanner knew about needles, but it did not seem to worry the medic. He pulled out his slate. "What name do you want to use?" He looked from one to the other.

"Lore Smith," Spanner said.

He scribbled. "This prescription is for the drug and disposable needles." He looked up. "Which pharmacy—the Shu chain do?" Spanner nodded, and he pressed the SEND button, tucked the slate back in his pocket. "They'll keep it on file for seven days; after that it's invalid. Keep the dosage down if you can. And don't give it to her more than every six hours."

Lore did not like being discussed as though she were not

there, but the painkiller was coating her face with ice and her brain with cobwebs. She lay in a daze as they moved off toward the door, still talking. He seemed unsurprised by her injury. She wondered what kinds of trauma he was used to dealing with, and how people usually got the kind of hurts that they did not want disclosing. Knife wounds, gunshots . . .

She fell asleep, woke up to swallow the two pills Spanner held out; a needle, in her buttock this time. She slept again. When she woke properly it was dark and she was covered with a soft quilt. She breathed quietly. Where the cloth touched the plaskin covering her wound, it did not hurt. She smiled at that. Such a simple thing, to not hurt.

Spanner was working at her bench, sharp halogen light pooling in front of her. She reached out, took a data slate from the pile in the shadow, hooked it up to a small gray box, read something from the screen, laid it aside, took another slate.

Lore watched her for a while. This woman knew all about her: her name, age, family. If she cared to check, she could get information on education, hobbies, friends. Yet Lore knew nothing about her, did not even know if she had had any school, if she had ever been hurt, ever seen a medic under her real name. If she even had a real name. Some people, she knew, were illegitimate from birth—the fact of their existence not recorded anywhere. But that line of thought was too frightening. She yawned loudly.

Spanner swung round in her chair. "I was beginning to wonder if I'd given you too many pills. How do you feel?"

"Thirsty. And I need some clothes."

"Both easily fixed." She stood up and disappeared into the shadow. Red power points glowed from the dark. She brought back an old, soft shirt, some underwear, trousers. No shoes, Lore noticed, but then she doubted she would be going anywhere for a while.

"We're about the same size, I think." Spanner went into the kitchen.

Lore sat up, sucked her cheeks in at the pain but made no noise. She pulled on the clothes.

Spanner brought back water and coffee. She set Lore's by the judo mat, took her own back to the bench.

Lore watched her awhile.

Spanner turned partway back toward her, impatient now. "What?" Her face glowed oddly in the white halogen and red power indicators. Like one of those late-sixties paintings that looked like a vase and then turned out to be two faces, Lore thought. She shook her head. Probably the drugs.

"If stealing from slates is so easy, then don't you worry someone will do the same to yours?"

Spanner made a huffing sound, halfway between amusement and cynicism. "I don't often carry one. Or a phone."

The only time Lore had not carried a slate was on the grounds at Ratnapida. Even then, it had made her feel naked: unable to reach or be reached. Also untraceable. Probably what Spanner liked. "But when you do," she persisted.

"Then I use this." She slid open a drawer and pulled out an ordinary-looking slate. "It's almost empty. I clean it every time I get back here. Take a look." She extended her hand. Lore had to drag herself up from her mat.

She looked it over, spotted the metal and ceramic protuberance immediately. "What's this?"

"A lock."

"But you said any code could—"

"It's not a code. It's an old-fashioned insert-key-and-turn lock. No one knows how they work anymore. Safe as the most modern encryption. For most people."

"Most?"

"Hyn and Zimmer are so old that they remember some things. And they've taught them to me. But that's all beside the point. This lock is like my tracking device. If someone is sharp enough, but dumb enough, to steal a slate that belongs to me, I'll want to know who they are. After they've tried to puzzle out this monster, they'll assume—wrongly, of course—that there must be some fabulous secrets on here, so sooner or later they'll start asking around for anyone who knows anything about locks. And I'll track them down. And then we'll have a little chat."

Lore looked at the bump of metal and ceramic on the plastic slate. *A little chat.* She thought of the medic who patched up ragged wounds without comment.

WHEN IT got too cold by the river I walked to the city mortuary and leaned against the wall, just outside the circle of heavy, yellowish-orange street light, and waited for Ruth. Dawn was well enough along to turn the lights into unpleasant turmeric stains on the pavement by the time Ruth stepped through the gates. I was shocked at how tired she looked.

"You look as though you could do with some coffee."

"No. I just want to get home." Her voice was listless. She handed me a thin box. "Her name and details are in there, too. She's a bit old but otherwise she's a very good match. From Immingham. Anyway, it's the best I could do."

It was a small box. I rattled it dubiously. "Everything's there?"

Ruth nodded. "Though it's not a full set of fingers. The corpse was missing thumb and index from her right hand, but then I remembered you were left-handed, so it shouldn't matter too much." She hesitated. "Lore, this has to be the last time."

I understood, of course. Between us, Spanner and I had done some pretty low things. Some of them to Ruth. I tucked the box into an inside pocket. "How have you been?"

"We're managing. I go back on days soon. I'll be glad when I've finished with nights. I feel as though I haven't seen Ellen for weeks. She's just leaving as I get home."

I envied them even that. "When you're back on the day shift it would be nice if you both came over for an evening."

"If you like." Ruth was too tired to hide her indifference. She turned to go.

"Ruth . . ." Maybe it was something in my voice, but Ruth stopped. "I mean it. I'd really like you to come. Just to talk. No favors. That other thing, the film. It's not . . . it won't . . ." I took a deep breath. "Things are different now. I'm not with Spanner anymore."

For the first time since she had walked out of the morgue gates, Ruth looked at me, really looked at me. I don't know what she saw, but she nodded. "We'll come. I'll call you."

At the river-taxi wharf, it was too early for the usual tourist hubbub so I took my coffee to a private corner table. The sun was coming up behind me, slicking the black-paned privacy windows and newly pointed brickwork of renovated dockside buildings bloody orange, like overripe fruit. Copters buzzed and alighted like wasps.

I slid open the box and took out the neatly printed flimsy. *Bird, Sal. Female. Caucasian. Blood type A positive. DOB* . . . Twenty-five. Four years older than me. It could have been worse. And all the other details could be fixed. In time.

The tiny black PIDA was in a sealed bag with a note attached in Ruth's handwriting. *Already sterile.* Next to it was a plaskin pouch the size of a pink cockroach. *Frozen blood for DNA tests.* It did not feel cold. I slid the box open further, wondering if Ruth had forgotten the print molds, and then smiled.

"Bless you, Ruth." Inside, instead of the print molds I had expected, there were eight glistening plaskin finger gloves. Ready to wear. I could get started today. If Spanner would help.

. . .

Spanner never got up until after noon. I went home and slept for four hours. I had bad dreams: sweating bodies, moving limbs, blood and plasthene. I woke up just before midday and stared at the angle of green-painted rafters over my bed. The room was long and narrow: bed at one end, under the rafter; matting in the middle, underneath the heavy old couch and spindly card table; larger table with gouged veneer at the other end, under the wide window. A ficus tree in a pot by the table. Beyond, sky.

I had to walk through the tiny kitchenette to get to the bathroom. I almost banged my head on the rafter over the tub. As usual, I felt dislocated. It was odd, to wake up alone and nameless.

Not for much longer.

It was midafternoon by the time I got out to look for Spanner.

Springbank, the road that had once groaned under a thousand rubber tires a minute, was now bobbled with gray vehicle ID sensors and laced with silvery slider rails that glistened like snail tracks in the late-September sunshine. It was the first day in two weeks I had not had to wear a coat. Foot traffic was heavy, and sliders hissed to a stop at almost every pole to pick up or drop off passengers. The occasional smaller, private car hummed and dodged impatiently around the tubelike sliders.

The building, old and massive, was built of sandstone. The sign over the entrance was a picture of a polar bear. Inside, it was the same as all bars.

Spanner was there. I threaded my way through the smell of stale beer and newly washed floors toward the fall of dark gold hair, and slid onto the stool next to her.

Spanner lifted her head. We looked at each other a moment. It was strange to not touch. "It's been a while."

"Yes." It felt like a year, or an hour. It had been just over four months. I beckoned the bartender and nodded at the glass Spanner nursed between her hands. "A beer and . . ."

"Tonic for me."

There had to be a reason she wasn't drinking. People changed, but not that much. I tried to keep the tone light. "Waiting for anyone in particular?"

"Just sitting."

She knew I knew she was lying, but I had gone past the stage of being angry, of facing her with it. It was Spanner's life, Spanner's body.

In here, the bright sunshine was filtered by old beveled glass and well-polished mahogany to a rich, dim glow, but it was enough to see the glitter in Spanner's eyes, the way she kept glancing up at the mirror behind the bar to see who came in the door. Her skin looked bad and she had lost weight. I paid for the drinks.

She sipped at hers. "How have you been?" She sounded as though she did not really care about the answer.

"Well enough." I hesitated. "Spanner, I've found some work, a job I might take. I need your help."

She finally dragged her attention away from the mirror and looked at me. "What happened to all your noble ideas about an honest living?" There was no mistaking the edge of contempt in her voice.

I had not expected this to be easy. "This is the last time. I want a new ID, a permanent one. I want to work, get an honest job."

"Ah. You need my dishonest help so you can make an honest living."

I looked at Spanner's face, at the hard, grooved lines by mouth and eyes that belonged to all those who had lived on their wits too long, and wanted to take her face between my hands, wanted to make her face her own reflection, and shout, *Look, look at yourself! Do you blame me for wanting to earn my living in a way that's not dangerous? In a way that no one*

23

will ever be able to use to make me feel ashamed? But it had never done any good before.

"I've found a PIDA that might make a match. I need help with it."

"Well, as you always said, I'll do anything for money."

"Spanner . . ." Even though I had tried to prepare for this, the pain of reopening old wounds was sharp and bright. I took a deep breath. "What's your price?"

"Let me think about it awhile."

We both knew what she would ask, eventually. "Fine, you do that, but I need the preliminary work completed now, within the next couple of days."

Spanner glanced in the mirror again, then at her wrist. She was getting nervous.

"I have an interview today," I pressed. "I should be starting work tomorrow, or the day after."

"Fine, fine. Come by the flat tomorrow." Her attention was beginning to drift.

I sighed and stood. "Your flat, then, tomorrow." But she wasn't listening anymore.

When I reached the street door, a couple were just coming in. They were laughing, wore expensive clothes, good jewelry. I glanced back. Spanner was rising to meet them.

Outside, adjusting to the bright afternoon after the dim warmth of the bar, I hesitated. Those two were trouble. Maybe Spanner was too desperate for what they were offering to notice the casual hardness of their faces, the way their eyes had flickered automatically over the room looking for exits, checking for weapons.

I waited outside for nearly ten minutes before I realized I could do nothing to help. I left reluctantly, wondering why—after all she had done—I still cared.

TWO

LORE IS five. Tok and Stella, the twins, are nine. They have been playing in the fountain in an Amsterdam neighbor's gardens. Lore has tried to catch the up-spouting water in her mouth.

Tok is shouting at her. "Don't you want to know what it is that you're drinking?"

"It's water," she says, puzzled.

"How do you know it's clean?"

"But it's always clean."

"This is clean," he says, "but it isn't everywhere." Lore hardly listens at first. His eyes are bright and fierce, an almost turquoise blue, like the sky first thing in the morning when the day will be burning hot. Like the eyes of their father, Oster, when he is excited. But then Tok pulls up facts and figures on water contamination incidents over the last thirty years and Lore listens in horror. "All it takes is one sip of some of this stuff, Lore, and then when you're grown up, or as old as me, it's leukemia, which means your blood goes yucky, or renal failure, that's when your kidneys rot and don't work anymore . . ."

She is frightened, but refuses to cry. Stella would mock her for weeks. "Does it hurt?"

"Of course it hurts!"

Lore does not go back to play in the fountain and that night she has nightmares of drinking swamp water full of dead rats, and she never forgets to test the water again. Even in the water- and air-filtered surrounds of the family holdings. Even on trips to luxury resorts in Belize and Australia. Even bottled water, because all it takes is one chemical spill in the groundwater table and the eau de source can be full of benzene—there and gone again in the blink of an eye, missed by the random testing. *Never take anything for granted,* her mother often says, and Lore never does. None of the family ever do. It is the company motto when Lore's greatuncle patents the hundreds of genetically engineered microorganisms that now are indispensable in the world's attempt to clean up its own mess. It is what prompts the ever-careful van de Oests to guarantee future monopoly and profit by making sure their patented, proprietary bugs need their patented, proprietary bug nutrients. And *Never take anything for granted* prompts them to use the first gouts of cash to corner a piece of the nanomechanical remediation technology market, a corner that grows steadily for the next fifteen years.

THREE

THE HEDON Road wastewater-treatment plant was on the east side of the river, the part of the city that grew during the Victorian era. The buildings were big and ugly: limestone, and sandstone partially eaten away by the corrosives in industrial soot.

I turned up at seven in the evening, and after a few perfunctory questions about name, age, and experience, the flunky showed me into a tiled locker room. He handed me a skinnysuit. "Get changed while I pull your record for Hepple."

"But I've only come here for an interview."

"You want the job, you talk to Hepple. You want to talk to Hepple, you wear this." He left with a shrug that indicated he did not care, one way or the other. At least I didn't have to worry about the records. Sal Bird's employment history was good enough for this job.

It was an hour after the change of shift and the room was

empty, though from somewhere down a corridor I heard the beating slush of a shower. I wondered if they used water from the mains, or siphoned off their own effluent. I smelled chlorine. The mains, then.

I stripped to my underwear, then sat on the wooden bench and pulled the skinny from its package. I was expecting cheap government issue and was pleasantly surprised by the slick gray plasthene. It was about a millimeter and a half thick—well within the necessary tolerances—and the seams were well made. I stepped into it, spent a couple of minutes wriggling my toes to get them in the right place, then hauled it over my hips and up to my shoulders. The smell of new plasthene on my skin reminded me of the sheet in the van, of dreams of blood and suffocation.

There was no easy way to skinny into these suits. You just had to squirm until everything was in the right place. I flexed my plasthene-covered hands, checked to make sure the roughed patches were at the tips of my fingers and thumbs. There were seals above the wrist for those jobs that needed the extra protection of gauntlets. I did a couple of deep knee bends to see if the neck seal would choke me.

It had been a while since I'd worn one of these, and then it had been specially made. I was surprised at how well this one fit.

No one had said anything about a locker so I settled for folding my street clothes into a neat pile on the bench. They were probably not worth stealing, and I had not brought a slate or a phone extension. They couldn't trace you from what you didn't carry. Old habits learned from Spanner.

A man wearing a tailored gray cliptogether over his skinny entered through the door marked EXECUTIVE PERSONNEL ONLY. His face was young and bland. A pair of dark goggles hung loose around his neck and his name tag read JONHE HEPPLE. He checked his hand slate. "Ms. Bird? Sal Bird?"

I stood. "Yes."

He looked me over. "Well, you know how to put on a suit, at least. I'm the acting shift supervisor." He handed me a magnetized name tag. "You must wear this at all times. It's also a miniature GC."

I slapped it onto the magnet over my left breast. Sal Bird, age twenty-five, with two years' experience at the wastewater depot of Immingham Petroleum Refinery, would know that a GC was a gas chromatograph, and what it was for. Jonhe Hepple, though, was taking no chances.

"It'll let you know if the atmosphere is contaminated to dangerous levels by changing color."

"Industry standard?"

Hepple looked confused for a moment, then adjusted his expression to one of superior amusement. "Superior to standard, as is all the equipment used here."

I nodded politely but mentally rolled my eyes. For now I'd just have to assume it used the standard color system, but if I got the job I'd make sure I asked another worker. If there was any kind of leak, I wanted to know exactly what I would be dealing with.

Hepple talked as we toured the plant. "The six city stations process more than twenty million gallons of household wastewater per day. The Hedon Road plant is the biggest, at between four and four and a half mgd."

"Just household?"

He gave me a long look. "Of course."

I nodded, trying to look satisfied. I just hoped that his reticence came from a feeling of superiority and not from ignorance. *Household wastewater* was anything but. It also included the runoff from storm drains. Which were prime sites for both deliberate dumping by waste-generating companies—large and small—and accidental spillage. Even if there was a spill in Dane Forest, forty miles from here, the contaminated water would find its way through underground aquifers to the city system. And those spills could be anything. Literally anything. I was glad that plants like these always had a large, specifically designed overcapacity. With people like Hepple in charge, we'd need it.

We climbed onto a catwalk over a hangarlike area where huge plastic troughs lined with gravel stretched into the distance. Bulrushes rocked and swayed in the water below. The air was snaky with aromatics and aliphatics. The workers below were not wearing masks but I said nothing. Sal Bird would not.

"This is the initial treatment phase where influent goes through simulated tidal marshes. The influent point itself is at the far end, housed in the concrete bunker." He pointed, but then we got off the catwalk in the opposite direction and went through an access corridor. It was noticeably warmer. "We have eighty parallel treatment trains here, and an impressive record. The Water Authority mandates less than thirty parts per million total suspended solids; we average eight. The biological oxygen demand needs only be reduced to twelve ppm, but even with extremely polluted influent, our effluent rarely tests out at over seven."

I had learned at age twelve, from my uncle Willem, that in a properly run plant the average BOD should never be higher than two ppm, but I didn't say anything. Hepple hadn't mentioned heavy metals or any of the volatile organic compounds, either, and I wondered what the plant's record was like on those.

We walked among enormous translucent vats filled with swimming fish and floating duckweed. Pipes ran everywhere: transparent and opaque, plastic and metallic, finger-thin and bigger around than a human torso. I could feel the vibration of larger pipes running under our feet.

"The fish graze on this weed," he said, "and if we have overgrowth we can harvest for animal feed. Further on we grow the lilies that are the real commercial backbone. But nothing, nothing at all, is wasted." He came to an abrupt halt.

"According to your employment file you've worked at the Immingham Petroleum Refinery. What was your speciality?"

"Continuous emission monitoring," I said, knowing full well that in this solar aquatics and bioremediation wastewater plant there was no such job.

"You'll be assigned something suitable, of course, but whatever your role, the one thing to bear in mind is that this plant—the four and a half million gallons coming in, the thirty-five million gallons on the premises, and the four and a half million going out—is one giant homeostatic system." He waited for me to nod. Probably wondered if I knew what *homeostatic* meant. "The more polluted the influent, the more plants we grow and the more fish we harvest, but the effluent is always the same: clean, clean, clean. The only way this can be achieved is through attention to detail. As you're used to a monitoring post, we might start you off in TOC analysis."

I asked, because Sal Bird would have. "What's TOC?"

"Total organic carbon analysis. Of the influent."

At the initial stage, where none of the workers wore masks. One of the dirty jobs.

We stepped through what looked like an airlock into another closed corridor. Hepple fussed with the seals and we started walking again. "It's not for you to worry about what a given reading may mean, but you'd better know what the parameters of any substrate are, and know what to do if they rise above or fall below that level. When you're assigned, your section supervisor will give you more precise details." We stopped at another air-sealed door. Hepple opened a panel in the corridor wall and took out a pair of dark goggles for me. He pulled up his own pair. "Goggles must be worn in the tertiary sector at all times." With his eyes covered, his mouth seemed plump and soft. "Even though you will not be assigned to the tertiary sector immediately, the possession of eye protection is mandatory." He ticked something off his chart. "The cost of those will come out of your first wage credit."

It seemed I had the job. I pulled on the goggles.

Hepple opened the door. The light was blinding: huge arc lights hung from a metal latticework near the glass roof; bank after bank of full-spectrum spots shone from upright partitions between vats. It was incredibly hot and the air was full of the hiss of aerators and mixers and the rich aroma of green growing things. I had forgotten how much a person sweated in a skinny. "This is where the heavy metals are taken out by the moss." I watched as a man and a woman lifted a sieved tray out of a vat and scraped off the greenery. "It's recycled, of course." A woman carrying a heavy-looking tray of tiny snails walked toward us. I started to move aside to let her pass, but Hepple pretended not to notice and the woman had to detour. A little tin god, lording it over his tiny domain. He wouldn't have lasted more than a day on one of my projects.

"Zooplankton and snails do a lot of cleaning up at this stage, along with the algae, of course." Women and men moved back and forth, harvesting zooplankton; checking nitrogen levels; monitoring fecal coliforms. Hard and busy work in the tertiary sector, but not dangerous.

We climbed up to a moving walkway that ran twenty feet above the floor. As we moved farther downstream and the water became progressively more clean, the heat lessened, as did the light, and the smell got better. "Our main sources of income at this stage are the bass and trout, and the lilies." As we glided past the hydroponic growth, the smell of flowers was almost overpowering. "We're planning to convert to thirty percent bald cypress next month."

That was ambitious, but I said nothing.

"Ah, here we are." We stepped down from the walkway. It was a plain white room, full of thick pipes. One had a spigot. I recognized a pressure reduction setup. Hepple pulled a paper cup from a stack and held it under the spigot, turned the tap. The cup filled with clear water. He drank some. "Here, taste it. Cleaner than what comes out of your tap at home. Pure. And that's our effluent."

I sipped, to show I was willing.

He slapped a pipe. "This is it. From here the water is no longer our responsibility."

He seemed to expect some admiring questions. "Where does it go from here? Out to sea?"

"Not so long ago, it did. And then we realized we had a practically foolproof system and started simply piping it back to the watertable." I nodded. Standard practice. "Now, though, even that's not necessary."

I couldn't quite believe what I was hearing. "The water goes straight back into the mains?"

He looked amused. "Certainly. We avoid all that unnecessary transport of water, cut out the waste of time and energy and worker hours. Productivity has gone up twenty-three percent."

I tried not to look as horrified as I felt. My half sister, Greta—a lot older than me—had told me, "Lore, there's no system on earth that's foolproof. One mistake with a wastewater plant and without that vital break in the cycle, you could have PCBs and lead and DDT running free in our water system. No matter how many redundancies there are, no matter how many backups, things go wrong." Hepple, obviously, had never heard that bit of wisdom. There wasn't even a last-line human observer here in the release room. One major spillage upstream at the same time as a computer failure here and there would be thousands of immediate deaths due to central-nervous-system toxicity, followed twenty years later by hundreds of thousands of premature deaths from various cancers. The implications were dizzying.

He looked at his wrist. "Time's getting on." He stared abstractedly into space a moment. "We're shorthanded

in three sections this month but I think, with your experience ... I imagine the Immingham plant gave you some
ideas of nitrification and denitrification processes?"

I tried to work out how much Sal Bird would understand of this conversation. "You mean the tidal marshes?"

"Just temporarily, of course." That translated to *Just until
you're no longer at the bottom of the heap.* Shit work. "The salary is scale, Grade Two, with an additional percentage for
the unsocial hours. You'll be paid monthly, in arrears.
Questions?"

I was just glad I still had a lump of money left. How did
other people manage without pay for a month?

"Good. I'm sure you'll enjoy working with Cherry
Magyar, your section supervisor. You should find her understanding. She's new at her job, too. I promoted her myself, just two weeks ago."

We did not shake hands. No welcome-aboard speech.
He just nodded, told me to get myself assigned a locker for
the skinny and goggles, and to report back at 6 P.M. sharp
tomorrow.

It was cool outside. I walked the mile and a half back to
my fifth-floor flat, trying to sort out how I felt about starting a job as a menial in a plant I could have run in my sleep.

I didn't expect to get much sleep tonight. That direct
mains release setup would give me nightmares.

WHILE HER back healed, Lore's days passed in a
haze of drugs and conversations at odd times of
the day or night. Spanner would disappear some evenings
and not return until the following afternoon. On the morn-
ings she was alone, Lore had nothing to do but watch the
window. There was always the tree, of course. Even when
she could not see it, she could hear it. The leaves hung
down like dead things now, and when people walked past,

she heard their feet crunching on those that had already
fallen. She spent hours watching the sun travel across the
warm sandstone of the building opposite. When she got
well enough, she sat up against the window. When the sun
was at just the right angle, she could see where layers of
sandstone had been blasted away to cleanse it of the soot:
acid, black effluvium from generations of factories, coal-
burning fires and, later, combustion engines. The sandstone
shone a deep, buttery yellow early in the morning, bleach-
ing to lemon and then bone as the light increased. She
guessed at the shape of the building she lived in by the
shadow it cast on the one opposite.

She listened to the morning chorus of sparrows and the
evening calls of thrushes as people came and went in algal
tides. She liked to drowse while the pigeons on the window
sill cooed and whirred their wings. The sill was white with
their excrement. She wondered what they found to eat in
the city. Once, waking from a thick, Technicolor afternoon
dream, she found a squirrel on the cable outside, watching
her. She could see the muscles and tendons of its haunches
as it gripped the thick cable with tiny claws. It had eyes like
apple pips, hard and opaque. Then it ran off, tail twitching.

But the window could not keep her occupied all the
time, and then Lore would wonder if the man, the kidnapper she knew only as Fishface, had really died, if the police
were still looking for her. Perhaps the other one, Crablegs,
had confessed, or been found. Maybe Tok had already de-
nounced Oster.

Once she tried to access the net, to check back on the
news, see if any bodies had been discovered, what the police
were doing about finding her, but she was locked out. The
keyboard was dead, and voice commands resulted in nothing but a flat, still screen. She did not mention her attempt
to Spanner. She wasn't ready. Not yet. She began to wonder
if this whole episode was a drug-induced nightmare, some
scheme of her supposedly loving father.

35

But then Spanner would return from her jaunts crackling with manic energy and a restlessness that did not disguise her fatigue, and Lore would understand that it was all too real.

Lore never asked where Spanner had been, but she wondered what she did in those hours that made her so tense. Business, she supposed, though she wondered why Spanner had to get so wired to transact a supposed victimless, low-priority crime. Sometimes it would be two or three hours before Spanner's deep blue eyes stopped their constant roving around the room, alighting on windows, doors: checking, always checking, as if for reassurance, the exits.

After a week, when Lore could get around the flat a little, Spanner called her over to the screen. "Sit," she said. Lore sat on the couch.

"It's me," Spanner told the terminal. The screen lit to light gray. "It's voice-coded. Won't even display the message-waiting light unless I tell it to. I'm going to set it up to accept certain commands from you." Lore felt herself being studied but she refused to give Spanner any idea of how it made her feel to be controlled like this. She said nothing.

Spanner sighed. "This is just a precaution on my part. I want you to understand why I'm doing this. I don't want you calling Mummy and Daddy when those painkillers start to wear off and you realize what a mess you're in. I can't afford any kind of notice, never mind the kind of wrong conclusion the authorities might jump to if they find you here, injured, and half out of your mind on drugs."

Lore kept her face still, but she remembered a tent, drugs, being naked. Was this any different?

"I'll allow any passive use. That means you can listen to my messages. Or some of them. You can access news. But you can't interact: no talking, no sending messages, no shopping. I'll bring you anything you need. At least for now."

"I'm not a child."

"No," Spanner agreed. "But this is the way it has to be."

. . .

The first time the screen bleeped when she was alone, it was a man's face that appeared: black spiky hair, blue eyes, thin eyebrows, smile like a cherub. "Remember those chicken hawks we came across last month? If you're still interested, get in touch."

That was it. Even with all Spanner's precautions the message had not said much. But Lore knew about chicken hawks. That was not victimless crime.

When Spanner got home, she went straight to the screen, took the message, called back. "Me. Yeah, I'm still interested. Usual place? Fine."

Lore waited for an explanation.

"Billy," Spanner said. "Business."

"I thought you said your business was victimless."

"Yes."

"Where there are chicken hawks, there are chickens getting hurt."

"You know more than I thought you might." Lore just nodded, and waited. Spanner sighed. "We got the information from some straight-looking punter's slate: he runs a daisy chain."

"Daisy chain?"

"A ring of fresh young faces. Younger than chickens. This one and his friends like them younger than four."

Lore felt her cheeks pulling away from her teeth in disgust.

"It's not much to my taste, either. So what Billy and I do is put a tap on him. Blackmail," she amplified. "A certain rough justice to it, don't you think? Those who hurt others get a taste of how it feels to be powerless, and we make money. All very neat."

Lore stared at her. Spanner thought she was some kind of Robin Hood. "But the kids still get hurt."

"Often they stop molesting them, once they've been burned."

"Often isn't always."

Spanner shrugged.

"You don't care, do you?"

"It's business. We can't go to the police because they'll want to know where we got our information. Besides, it could get dangerous if we meddled too far."

Lore remembered Spanner coming home with flushed cheeks; the hectic eyes, the sharp jaw where her teeth were clenched together and could not or would not let go, not for hours. Blackmail. "And who else do you blackmail?"

"No one who doesn't deserve it."

No one who can't pay. Lore thought about chicken hawks and daisy chains. "You could send an anonymous tip to the police."

"We've done that. Now and then. When we think the situation warrants. But without solid evidence, they don't usually take any action."

Lore saw that the lack of police action suited Spanner just fine. If the men who ran the chains weren't making money, they couldn't pay quiet fees to insure silence.

Lore dreamed that night of being rolled, dead-eyed, into a plasthene sheet and tipped into a grave. On the lip of the grave, throwing shovelfuls of wet mud, were cherubs called Billy, laughing, and Spanner holding something out of reach, saying, *When you're all grown up,* and Lore, who could not close her eyes because she was dead, saw that what Spanner held were manacles.

She woke up gasping and clutching her throat, remembering her lungs fighting the plasthene for air, a cupful, a spoonful, a thimbleful. It was morning. Spanner was gone, but the screen was lit to a sunburst of color and a cartoon of a rabbit with a thought balloon saying, *Call who you want. It's open to your voice.* Lore stared at the screen a long, long time. She would not call the police. She wondered how Spanner had known that. She did not feel too good about it.

Spanner was still out when the medic returned in the early evening. He pronounced Lore's back to be healing well and left her a tape-on plaskin sheath to wear when she was in the bath or shower. "The rest of the time, let the wound breathe. You won't need any more injectable painkillers. These distalgesics should do." He handed her a bottle of brightly colored caplets. "You need anything else?"

He seemed in a hurry, and Lore wondered what mayhem or despair he was rushing to. "Do you ever wonder where your patients get their injuries?" She thought of a three-year-old, and what injury an adult might do her or him in the name of need.

He looked at her with sad eyes. "There's no point. I just do my best to heal what I find."

When he had gone, she went into the bathroom to look at her back. It hurt to twist and turn, but she looked at the scar in the flyblown mirror as best she could. It stretched diagonally from her right shoulder blade to the lower ribs on her left side. At the top, it was nearly an inch wide. She could not bear to look at it. She stared out of the window into the backyard instead. It looked as forlorn and closed in as she felt: a fifteen-by-forty patch of rubble and weeds and what might be scrap metal, surrounded by a six-foot-high brick wall; barren and broken and played out. The walls were topped with broken glass set in cement.

The door banged open. Lore pulled on Spanner's robe, tied the slippery silk belt, and went into the living room. Spanner was snapping on switches, humming. She looked up at Lore and smiled. "I've got something for you. Be ready in just a minute." She punched a couple of buttons, read the bright figures that came up on her screen, then, satisfied with whatever the machine was doing, she popped something small out of one of her decks. "There." She held out her hand. On her palm was a round black metallic button. A PIDA. "It's for you. Just a temporary, of course."

Lore pulled her robe tighter with her right hand and looked at the slick black button. Her new identity. She was not sure if she wanted it. "Where did you get it?"

"Friend of mine works for the city morgue. Once they've been through official identification, and embalmed, corpses aren't too particular about their PIDAs. Don't worry. Ruth's a stickler for hygiene. It's probably cleaner than you are and, anyway, this one won't be going under the skin. Well? Don't just stand there, hold out your hand and I'll put it on for you."

Lore held out her left hand.

"You'll need to hold it in place for me."

"Let me sit down." She had to let go of the robe to keep the PIDA in place on the scar that was fading to pink. Spanner used a pair of scissors to cut a square of plaskin to shape.

"Not as fancy as the medic's spray, but this kind has one advantage." She pulled off the backing, carefully laid it over the PIDA. "It says your name is Kim Yeau. I've added the middle initial L., but just the initial. Less is better. The PIDAs will change, but as you get to know people, you'll have to have a stable name, one we can call you by. You have forty-three credits. You're eighteen." She looked up at Lore. "That's right, isn't it?"

Spanner knew damn well how old she was; this was just her way of reminding Lore how much she knew, that knowledge equals power. Lore didn't say anything, but the muscles in her forearm tightened.

"Hold still."

Lore stared at the top of the head bent over her hand. Spanner's scalp was creamy white, untouched by UV. Lore wondered how long she had been living a nocturnal existence, how long she had been rifling corpses and blackmailing and stealing. What did that do to a person? And yet Spanner did not seem bad. Just interested in looking out for herself. Maybe because no one else had ever been there to do it.

"You'll have to be careful how you use this. It's just a superficial job—it'll get you on and off the slides, pay for groceries or a download from a newstank, but that's it. Avoid the police. Don't try to get any licenses or whatever." Spanner squeezed the skin around the PIDA and the webbing, and straightened. "There. Should hold for a couple of weeks. The plaskin will match your natural skin color in an hour or so." She held Lore's arm up to the light, admiring her handiwork.

Lore could feel Spanner's breath on her skin, the robe slipping open, revealing her breasts.

"Beautiful," Spanner said.

Lore looked at herself in the bathroom mirror. Her hair was wholly gray now, and grown past her ears.

"Can you cut hair?" she called, but Spanner was working and did not hear. She opened the medicine cabinet, looking for scissors. There was a tube of dye on the top shelf. Brown. She tapped it thoughtfully against her palm. The sooner she could change the way she looked, the sooner she could get outside the flat, feel less . . . dependent. Brown would do to start with.

"Can I use this?"

"Um?"

She stepped into the living room. "This dye. Can I use it?" Spanner did not look up from the screen. "If you like." "I can't imagine you with brown hair."

"It's not mine."

The dye around the top of the tube was not crusted and dry. It had been used fairly recently. Lore stared at it for a while.

In the bathroom, she read the instructions. *Wet hair. Apply generously with comb. Wipe off any excess from skin. Leave for ten minutes.* It seemed simple enough, though not as easy as the way she was used to, when all she had to do was run a bath, pour in the nanomechs, and submerge herself for thirty seconds. With nano dyes and antinano lube, one could layer different colors on body hair, like silkscreening, and the results were clear, clean, and crisp. But nano dyes were for the rich.

This dye was a sticky paste. It was not brown, as she had expected, but a curious greenish yellow. It smelled like rotting leaves and had the texture of mud. She massaged it into her scalp, remembering to do her eyebrows and eyelashes.

When she had rinsed and dried, the mirror showed a strong chestnut. It suited her, suited her eyes, her mouth. She liked it. She turned this way and that, letting the cool northern light that seeped into the bathroom and reflected from the tiles play over the hair. It looked so good it was probably pretty close to her natural color. She smiled at her reflection: disguising herself by making her hair her real color had a certain ironic appeal.

She walked into the living room. "What do you think?"

Spanner turned after a moment. Said nothing.

"What's the matter?"

"I'm not sure brown is the right color."

Lore flushed. "I don't understand."

"Come into the bathroom with me." Spanner positioned Lore in front of the mirror, hands on her shoulders. Lore did not like the possessive feel of those hands, but it was Spanner's bathroom, Spanner's mirror. "Now, take a look at yourself, a really good look. Then look at me."

Lore studied herself. Brown hair, straight brown eyebrows, clear gray eyes, skin a little paler than usual but still tight-pored and healthy. Thinner than she used to be. Even teeth. She thought she looked remarkably good, considering what she had been through. "I think I look fine."

"Now look at me."

Spanner's skin was big-pored over her nose and cheekbones. There was a tiny scar by her mouth. Her teeth were uneven, her neck thin. Her complexion had a grayish tinge, like meat left just a little too long. Lore thought she looked a lot better than Spanner.

Spanner was nodding at her in the mirror. "Exactly. You

see the difference? You're too damn . . . glossy. Like a race-horse. Look at your eyes, and your teeth. They're perfect. And your skin: not a single pimple and no scars. Everything's symmetrical. You're bursting with health. Go out in this neighborhood, even in rags, and you'll shine like a lighthouse."

Lore looked at herself again. It was true. Eighteen years of uninterrupted health care and nutritious food on top of three generations of good breeding had given her that unmistakable sheen of the hereditary rich. She was suddenly aware of the cold tile under her feet, of the cracks she could feel between her toes. It was not yet winter. She wondered what it would be like to be cold involuntarily. She touched her eyebrows, her nose. How strange to discover something about oneself in a stranger's bathroom. "I assume it can be fixed."

Spanner dipped her hand into a pocket and pulled out a stubby buzz razor. Lore backed away from the flickering hum of its blade, remembering blood, the plasthene sheet. Spanner laughed, lightly enough, but Lore heard the cruelty in it: Spanner knew Lore had been scared, and enjoyed it. "It's for your eyebrows. Cut them a bit, make them uneven." Lore took the sleek black razor, not taking her eyes off Spanner. "I'm going to get a different dye, one that doesn't suit you as much."

Spanner brought back red dye and some peroxide. "And here." Spanner gave her a tube of depilatory cream. "Get rid of the rest of your body hair, unless you want to dye it strand by strand."

In the shower, her hair and the cream washed away in gelatinous clumps, leaving Lore as smooth and bare as a baby. Naked in a new way.

Spanner wiped the mirror free of condensation and Lore, still dripping, looked at her new self. The red hair made her face pale, pinched and hungry as a fox. Spanner stood behind her and stroked her hair. "Red was the right choice," she whispered, and kissed Lore's left shoulder blade. Her hand ran down Lore's ribs, over her hip, up her belly. "So smooth." She kissed the back of her neck. "Lift your arms." Spanner ran her palms over the hairless armpits, down over the hairless breasts. Lore could feel Spanner's nipples pebbling through her shirt up against her shoulder blades. Condensation ran in streaks down the mirror. Lore watched Spanner's hand reach down and cup her naked vulva. She closed her eyes, listened to Spanner's hoarse breath in her ear.

I am hairless and newly born.

It did not matter that Spanner might have seen her helpless and naked on the newstanks, because this was not the real Lore. This was someone different, someone's creation. A construct. One she could hide behind. One that would make her safe. Just as she thought she had been with her father, Oster. Only this time, she was aware.

She opened her eyes again and watched.

CHERRY MAGYAR turned out to be young, about twenty-three, with hair as thick and wiry as a wolfhound's, and hard brown eyes with a hint of epicanthic fold. Her skinny was deep green. Her thigh-high waders, fastened with webbing straps and Velcro cuffs over her hips and waist, were black. The six-inch-wide stomach and back support was bright red. "We're three shorthanded, so I hope you learn fast." Her voice was coarse and vivid.

"Yes."

"Well, we'll see."

I had to work at not wrinkling my face at the smell down here: raw sewage, volatile hydrocarbons, and something acrid that I couldn't place. If there were any air strippers installed, they were not working. I was not surprised. The space was at least as big as a city block, and sixty feet high or more. I couldn't even see the far wall. But the wall nearest to me was brilliant with safety equipment: the bright yellow of emergency showers, drench hoses, and eye baths every thirty yards; fire-engine-red metal poles that were in reality fire-blanket dispensers; the green-and-white-checkered first-aid stations; hard aquamarine for breathing gear . . .

"I'm going to put you on a combination TOC/nitro analysis and basic maintenance. They're both full-time positions, but we don't have enough people. I've been doing the TOC myself the last two weeks. Hepple says you're experienced. I need someone who knows what they're doing. You've done TOC analysis before?"

Sal Bird had not, but I doubted Magyar would have the time or inclination to backcheck her records. "Yes."

We walked for a few minutes along the cement apron that ran in front of the huge troughs that lay parallel with each other, numbered from left to right, one to eighty. If I was expected to work here and oversee the maintenance of one or more troughs, I'd wear myself out just walking to and fro. She opened the heavy, soundproofed door of a concrete bunker and motioned me ahead of her.

Inside was a vast, white space threaded through with silvery pipes. Four and a half million gallons a day thundered through those pipes, and the noise was a full-throated roar. Magyar leaned toward my ear and shouted, "Think this is loud?"

I nodded. She grinned and gestured for me to follow her. We went through a narrow doorway into what looked like an empty room. She hit a button on a plastic panel and a ten-by-ten section of the floor slid back.

The roar became a bellow, a deep chasm of noise, old and ugly, big enough to grind its way through the crust of the world. I clapped my hands over my ears, but the noise was a living thing, battering at my ribs, vibrating my skull. We stood at the edge of a pit where water rushed past, twisting and boiling. It was like standing on the edge of creation. Magyar was laughing. I was, too. That kind of noise puts a fizz in your bones.

Magyar hit the button again and the floor slid back into place. My ears rang with the relative quiet. "The only reason I like getting trainees is the excuse to open that thing up."

We went through another doorway, but this time the door slid shut behind us, cutting off the noise entirely.

It was a small room, faced with banks of digital readouts, and the same spigot and pressure-reduction setup I had seen for testing the effluent. Magyar became all brisk efficiency.

"The equipment is two years old. These readouts here are for your TCEs and PCEs. This one's nitrogens. Keep an eye on that. We get a fair amount of HNO_3—that's nitric acid—but the bugs break it down to nitrate and nitrite. Got to watch those levels, and the difference is important. Nitrate's what the bugs use as an oxidizing agent, turning it to nitrite, then nitrogen gas. But watch the nitrite. If levels get too high, the bugs die off and all we get is nitrate and nitrite instead of nitrogen gas. But if we get rid of it all, then the duckweed downstream's got nothing to feed on."

"What bugs are you using?"

"The OT-1000 series."

I nodded. The van de Oest OT-1000 series was tried and true. A strain, mainly *Pseudomonas paudimobilis*, for the BTEX and high-molecular-weight alkanes; B strain for chlorinated hydrocarbons; and probably by now the C strain that had been new when . . . before . . . I stopped thinking about it and looked instead at the readout for vinyl chloride, a vicious carcinogen. That was the red flag as far as I was concerned. VC levels told an observer a lot about the health and ratios between aerobic and anaerobic, methanotrophic and heterotrophic bacteria.

Magyar was still talking. "Here's your methane. Other volatiles like toluene and xylene. Biological oxygen demand, but don't worry about that, BOD's not our problem. Though if it goes much above the indicated range"—she pointed to a metal plate inset above the station, inscribed with chemicals and their safe ranges—"pass it along to me. My call code's written up there, too. Beginning and end of each shift I'll want a thumbprinted report. The slates are here." She pulled one down from a shelf and handed it to me. "Everything clear enough?"

She seemed a bit muddled, conflating more than one process, but I just nodded. "I think so."

"Good. These readouts over here are remotes from the dedicated vapor points, but they're often swamped during a big influx. And these two figures, in green, are the combined remotes from the on-line turbidimeter. The top one is NTU. Last but not least—" We walked three paces to a readout in red. "—the water temperature." Magyar stopped. "What does it say?"

"Twenty-seven point three degrees. Celsius."

"That's what it should always say. Always. Not twenty-seven point six or twenty-seven point one. Twenty-seven point three. That's what the bacteria need."

For a denitrification-nitrification process, heterotrophic facultative bacteria were usually comfortable anywhere between twenty-five and thirty degrees, but I just nodded. "What about emergency procedures?"

"That should have been on the orientation disk."

"I haven't seen an orientation disk."

Magyar swore. "Hepple said . . . Never mind. I'll see what I can do. Meanwhile, anything comes up that looks out of place, call me. Immediately. If your GC goes pink, find one of these red studs—" She pointed to what looked like red plastic mushrooms that bloomed every five meters from walls and floors and ceilings. "—twist it through three-sixty, push it all the way down, and get out ASAP. But make good and sure that your GC really is pink. The buttons shut down the whole system. That costs enough to mean that you'll be out of a job instantly if you make a mistake. You got that?"

I nodded.

"Good. Then we'll move on."

We went back to the troughs. "One worker for every two troughs according to the original design, but we operate on three per, and some are having to handle four." She pulled the slate off her belt, scrolled through a list, replaced it. "I'll assign you two, numbers forty-one and forty-two, while you're working TOC analysis."

I opened my mouth, changed my mind, and shut it again. She lifted an eyebrow. "Something to say about that, Bird?"

"TOC and nitrogen analysis is pretty important at this stage?" I knew damn well it was. Magyar nodded. "I'm just not sure that it's possible to keep a close eye on the readouts as well as maintaining two troughs."

"Then you'll just have to try extra hard. Any other questions?"

Does anyone here know what they're doing? "What about masks?"

"Do you see anyone else wearing a mask?"

"No . . ."

"Masks are available on request. But they'll slow you down, and if you can't keep up you'll be fired." Magyar's voice seemed almost kindly, but her eyes were flat and hard. "You'll soon get used to the smell. Besides, management doesn't take kindly to agitating for more so-called safety rules."

"I understand." Health and Safety regulations mandated the wearing of respiratory protective devices in the presence of short-chain aliphatics like 1,1,2-trichloroethane and aromatics such as 1,4-dichlorobenzene, but I wasn't going to argue the point here and lose my job on the first day for being a suspected union organizer. If I lost this job, my Sal Bird identity would be useless. Ruth would not help me again, and I did not want to have to ask Spanner. I said nothing.

Magyar nodded and left me to it.

The first thing I did was find the schematic handbook. It

was tucked behind the slates at the readout station. At the first break, I looked it over.

The plant was well designed: good automatic monitoring and lock systems. In the event of a massive spill, all pipes would shut down, the plantwide alarm sound, and the alert sent out to county emergency-response teams. An expert system then decided how far the pollution had spread and the pipes and tanks would be pumped out into massive holding tanks. I checked the capacity. Six hundred thousand gallons. Adequate. Even better, the whole system could be overridden on the side of caution and shut down by hand. There was a first-response team structure outlined. I examined it with interest. Apparently, we should all know about it, and how to access self-contained breathing apparatus and other protective gear.

It was hard looking for the gear without appearing to be poking into others' areas of work, but eventually I found it. There were only four sets of SCBA where there should be more than two dozen, and just two moon suits. A pile of EEBA—emergency escape breathing apparatus—all tangled together. I wasn't surprised. No one ever expected to have to use the lifeboats.

The schematics for the sensors and chemical controls looked good, but the maintenance schedule told another story: there was plenty of water, of course, for the sprinkler system, and plenty of regular foam, but someone had decided not to bother replacing the alcohol-resistant foam canisters. That smelt of Hepple: ARF had a short shelf life, and was expensive. Ketone spills were very rare. It probably seemed like a reasonable risk.

Air scrubbers; multilevel valves for sampling vapors and liquids heavier than air and water; incident control procedures . . . They were all there. I wondered how familiar Magyar was with all this. I hoped I would never have to find out.

FOUR

LORE IS seven. Her father, Oster, is brushing her hair. It is high summer. Outside, the buildings are washed gold by the sinking sun, but inside Lore's bedroom the ancient wooden paneling sucks in what light manages to get through the tiny window set deep in the thick fifteenth-century walls. Oster has almost finished with her hair, but Lore wants him to stay longer with her instead of running off and talking to Tok about his stupid pictures, or playing with Stella's hair, which she has just started dyeing yellow. Lore thinks about Stella's yellow hair. Lore's hair—and Oster's and Katerine's, and Tok's and Willem's and Greta's—is gray, like Lore's eyes. Gray all over.

"Why is our hair gray?"

Oster puts the hairbrush down, pulls back the bedcovers, and motions for her to climb in. "You won't let me go until I explain everything, will you?"

"No," she says seriously.

"A long time ago, in a fit of ostentation—" Lore frowns

at *ostentation* but does not interrupt. "—your grandmother had the color-producing allele turned off. She was rich—"

"As rich as we are?"

"No, but rich enough to be stupid. Anyway, she was so rich she did not know what to spend her money on. Doctors had just discovered that those people with pigmentless hair—gray with age, or white-haired albinos—got a lot of cancer in the scalp. That's because without pigment, the hair acts like a fiber-optic cable, conducting ultraviolet from sunlight straight to our follicles, bombarding them with mutagenic radiation." She frowns and he sighs, tries again. "Like the telephone wire brings your mother's voice and picture to you when she's out in the field." Katerine never calls her when she goes away to strange places to work, but Lore says nothing. It would only upset Oster.

"So when people get old and their hair turns gray, they get cancer?"

"No. They just dye their hair black or brown or dark red or whatever, or wear a hat."

"Is that why Stella dyes her hair? To stop the cancer?"

"No. Stel changes her colors because she wants to. Like your mother changes the color of her contact lenses." He smiles and ruffles her hair, the hair he has just brushed. Lore pats it back down. "She doesn't have to, none of our family do, because Grandmama van de Oest was so rich she could have genetic treatment—do you understand what genetic treatment is?" Lore nods, even though she doesn't. He is crossing and uncrossing his legs, which means he is getting restless. "She had genetic treatment against cancer. It's very, very expensive, and it takes a long time, and it hurts."

"Then why did she do it?"

"Because she was stupid and too rich. She—"

"Does that mean we're too rich?"

He looks at her for a long moment, his blue eyes still. "I suppose it does."

He doesn't say anything for a minute, and Lore has to

prompt him. "So Grandmama pays a lot of money for the cancer stuff . . ."

"Yes. And then she paid a lot more money to have her genes fixed so that all her children would have gray hair and the anticancer protection. Her way of saying to the world, look, I'm so rich I can afford to have this expensive anticancer treatment so I don't need to care about having gray hair. And, like a lot of stupid and wasteful things, it became fashionable. Which is why your mother has gray hair, too."

Lore sits up in bed so she can see herself in the mirror on the dresser. She turns her head this way and that, touches her gray hair. "Can we turn the gene back on?"

"Yes, but it won't make any difference to you. Only your children." He holds the covers, waiting for her to slide back down.

"Why didn't you turn it back on?"

"I did, but your mother didn't. She wanted you to have all the visible trappings of the rich and powerful. As she said to me at the time, you can always dye it. Now lie down."

Lore does. "What color am I supposed to dye it?"

"Any color you like." He goes to the window and pulls the curtains closed.

Lore frowns at his back. "But how will I know which color is the right one?"

Right, wrong; on, off; yes, no. She is used to black-and-whites, but at seven Lore is suddenly realizing she can make of herself what she wills. When she is old enough she can have red hair or golden eyebrows or hot, dark lashes like spiders' legs. And no one will tell her she is wrong, because no one will know. She could become anyone she wishes. But how will she know she is still herself?

She stays awake a long time, thinking about it. How does Stel know who she is if every time she stands in front of a mirror, she looks different? Before she falls asleep, Lore resolves that she will never, ever dye her hair.

FIVE

I KNOCKED, the two short, three long taps we used to use. Spanner opened the door. Her eyes were gummy and vague.

"We agreed I'd come here. Yesterday. In the bar."

"Right." She let me in.

I noticed the changes immediately. It was not just that someone else had been living there for a time—the different smells of soap and shampoo left behind in the bathroom, the exotic spices half-used on the shelf over the microwave—it was other things. We had never kept the place scrupulously tidy but it had felt alive and cared for. Now the worn places in the rug were dark with ground-in dirt and several plants were brown and curling. The plastic eyes of the power points were dull and cold and the equipment on the bench was covered in dust. I tried not to think about how she must have been supporting herself the last few months.

I couldn't help glancing at the bench again. She noticed, of course, and laughed the laugh I had first heard a few months before I left, the ugly one. "Don't worry. I haven't lost my touch." She ran her fingers through her hair, and the familiarity of the gesture here, in this flat, almost gave me vertigo.

"Let me see the PIDA."

I handed over the baggie. "It's sterile."

Spanner carried it over to the bench. She took off covers, flipped a couple of switches, then pulled on a pair of white cotton gloves, took the PIDA out of the bag, and slid it into the reader. She scanned the information that came on-screen. "How much detail do you want?"

"Not much for now. Change the fingerprint ID and physical description to start with. And add my middle name, of course."

She nodded. "Less is better."

It was as though that single sentence had been echoing in the flat for nearly three years, as though I had somehow just stepped out for a while and stepped back in to hear it once again. *Less is better.* If only she had kept to that axiom. I wanted to grab the PIDA, leave the flat, and never come back, but I did not know anyone else who could do this for me. At least, not anyone as good as Spanner. As Spanner used to be. "I have the fingerprints ready to go."

"Let's have those, too. You've used them to open an account?"

"Not yet."

"Good. You remember some things, then, despite your distaste."

I sighed and pulled a list from my pocket. "Here are the things I want. Her education and employment background are fine for now—unless someone wants to pay for an extensive backcheck."

Spanner just nodded for me to put the paper down on the tabletop by the screen. "You could make us some coffee."

I went into the kitchen, put on the coffee, and opened the cupboard under the sink. The watering can was still there.

Most of the plants around the flat were beyond revival. I watered them anyway. I stopped by one pot for a long time. When I had bought the cheese plant for her it had been just over four feet tall. When I left it had been nearly six, the leaves as big and glossy as heavily glazed dinner plates. And now the cheese plant was dying, the edges of its leaves yellow and parchment thin, the trailing aerial roots hanging like the shriveled skins of snakes.

"Put it on the table," she said when I brought out the coffee. "I'm just about done here."

I sat, and after a minute she joined me. It felt very strange to be sharing the same couch.

"So. Payment."

"Yes," I said, and waited.

"That scam you were so keen on a few months ago. The net ads for charity. Think it's still possible?"

"I can make the film, and it'll bring in money. Can you do the rest?" I deliberately didn't look at the dust on the bench.

"No problem." She made a dismissive gesture. "The hard part is going to be start-up costs."

"I've got nothing left. Not to speak of." I wondered briefly what it would be like to get a paycheck. Another three weeks to wait for that.

"I'll provide start-up, then, on condition that it comes out of the pot before we divide it."

"Fifty-fifty?"

She laughed. "You already owe me, remember? Seventy-thirty."

"Sixty-forty." I didn't care about the money. All I wanted was the PIDA. I was bargaining because Spanner would think me weak if I didn't. I wondered how dangerous her creditors were, and how much she owed them.

"Sixty-forty, then." She didn't bother to hold out her hand. I wasn't sure what I would have done if she had.

"How long?"

"I'll need to work out what equipment we need. And then I'll have to find it. Hyn and Zimmer should be able to help."

I stood. There was no point talking further until we found out about equipment. "I know the way out."

I walked back to my flat, thinking about Spanner and her dying plants.

Trees are not delicate. You can do all kinds of things to a fully grown tree—drench it in acid rain and infest it with parasites, carve initials in its bark and split branch from trunk—and it will survive. It is not presence but absence that will kill a tree. Take away its sunshine and it will stretch vainly upward, groping, growing etiolated, spindly beyond belief, and die. Take away its water and its leaves wrinkle, become transparent, and fall.

I tilted the watering can into the pot of my ficus tree, watching the brown, granular soil darken and smooth out as it absorbed the water. I sprayed the leaves, wondering when the light green of the leaves grown in the summer, summer when I had left Spanner, had blended with the seasoned, deeper green of all the others. And then I cried.

I was still crying when I went into the bathroom. It was small, painted peach and cream, and everything in it was clean, but somehow it still reminded me of the bathroom Spanner and I had shared. Even the mirror, which was new and square.

I turned the cold tap, splashed my face. Enough, I told myself sternly. But how could it be *enough* when even the clear, cold water streaming into the sink reminded me of the first time I went into Spanner's bathroom? How could it be *enough* when I looked into the mirror and even the hair framing my face was the fox red Spanner had chosen?

I looked at my hair more closely and sighed. The gray

roots were beginning to show again. That would have to be fixed before I went to my new job.

I had never liked red. I would buy some brown dye, and I would let my eyebrows grow back. Symmetrically.

〰〰 LORE'S BACK was healed and her hair was a different color. She was as disguised as she was going to get. She was getting restless.

She had been inside the flat for several weeks and, before that, the kidnappers' tent. Now she was afraid to go outside. She sat by the living-room window and watched the sky as it turned to November gray, and shuddered. It was so big, so open. She tried to imagine being out under the whipping clouds, among the people who all seemed to be hurrying toward destinations she could only guess at. But she had nowhere to head for. And she would be without a slate, without a real identity, with no one to call if she found herself in trouble. And people might recognize her, might stare and point . . .

She went into the kitchen to make coffee, try and distract herself. The weeds down in the back garden were turning yellow. She stared at them while the coffee bubbled. Weeds, interlopers, were always the last to die. They started small, but after a year or two they made themselves belong, put down strong roots.

Trying not to think about what she was doing—or she would panic—Lore went into the tiny hallway and pulled on one of Spanner's jackets. She did not pause to zip it up. She had to think for a moment before she could remember the door code Spanner had given her three weeks ago; then she opened it and went out.

The stairwell was damp, and funneled the cold November wind right through her thin jacket. But it was still enclosed. The hard part was reaching the street. People passed her, not looking, but she still felt horribly exposed. She was breathing hard.

The cut-through was five yards to her left. She ran. It was a brick-lined tunnel under the overhanging flat, about eight feet high and less than a yard wide. Her footsteps echoed.

At the other end was a gate. It was shut. She rattled the door. The knob came off in her hand, the wood was so rotten. She kicked it. The door split open. The wood smelled fruity and spoiled. She went through and lifted it back into place as well as she could. She was probably the first person to set foot back here in years.

It was hard to tell what had once grown here a hundred, maybe a hundred and fifty years ago when the row of large houses had originally been built. It looked as though no one had cultivated the place for a long, long time. Judging by the assortment of ancient appliances and precode concrete rubble, the place had been used as a tip for the last two or three decades. But everywhere—by the rusting washing machine, between the old tires, in between the broken paving stones—sprung weeds and small saplings. There were brambles and the remnants of what might once have been a rose garden. She squatted down by the tangle of thorns. They might be the variety that bloomed at midwinter.

This close to the ground she could smell the dark, cold, loamy dirt, a clean smell, one that reminded her of being small, watching while one of the van de Oest gardeners planted tulip bulbs. She dug her fingers into the leaf mold. It felt just the same.

There was a rotted-out lean-to by one wall. She poked at it, looked at the hole in the roof. It wouldn't be too hard to waterproof it enough for gardening tools.

She stood in the middle of the barren garden, surrounded by walls and broken glass, and smiled. She felt safe here. Many of the windows of the surrounding commercial buildings had been bricked up. Unless someone looked down from Spanner's bathroom or kitchen, no one could see her. She looked up at the windows. They were blank, reflecting only the scudding sky.

She waited until Spanner had taken off her shoes, then told her she wanted to do something with the garden.

"Like what?"

"Clear it first. Then see."

"You'll need all kinds of equipment."

"Not as much as you think. And besides, you said you'd get me anything I needed." It was a challenge. Lore remembered the weeds.

Spanner smiled and pulled a slate to her. "Give me your shopping list, then."

"A shovel, spade, rake, trowel." Lore pictured the gardeners at Ratnapida. "A wheelbarrow. Heavy gloves. Some shears. Grass seed. Other things when I'm ready to plant."

THE HEDON Road night shift ended at two in the morning. I was exhausted, so tired I could barely manage to unstrap my back support and the wrist and forearm splints. My arms felt leaden as I stripped off my skinny and showered. I was too tired to bother drying my hair. I regretted it as soon as I stepped out of the ugly pseudo-Victorian plant gates.

It was cold, and mist made the streetlights smeary; the kind of night that reminded me that in this northern city, autumn was just an eyeblink between summer and winter. At this time in the morning, all the passenger slides would be garaged at the far end of town. I would probably freeze if I had to wait for one to answer a request tapped in at a roadside pole. Besides, until I got paid—until I was sure my records would hold long enough to get paid—I would have to be careful with my money. A special call-out would mean a large debit from my PIDA. Six months ago I would just have jumped a ride on a freight slide. I knew all the times and delivery routes—Hedon Road, then Springbank, then Princes Avenue—but with my new PIDA it was no longer worth the risk. If I got caught, there would be a blemish on my record that could cost me my job. That would mean a new PIDA . . . and where would it ever end?

I was tired, but there was something about walking at night, when the streets were empty: my strides felt longer, stronger, and the cold made even my breath tangible. I was real. I was here. Nothing was complicated anymore. I no longer had to be ashamed. I was Sal Bird, aged twenty-five, and I worked for a living.

But when I got back to the flat I had to climb five flights of stairs, and when I opened the three locks on my door and turned on the lights, one of the first things I saw was my Hammex 20 camera and the edit box, and I remembered it wasn't over yet, that Spanner still wanted payment.

In the kitchen I snipped the corner off a plastic bag and poured half a pound of soybeans into a pan. They smelled of dust, and rattled on the metal as I filled the pan with water. As the water heated, the bean skins suddenly wrinkled, as though the outside absorbed water faster than the rest. The water boiled, and the beans began to rock, and some swelled before others, so it looked as though they were crawling over each other. In the space of minutes what had been hard, shiny ivory ball bearings plumped out into sleek alien ovoids curled up like so many fetuses. Like frog eggs in the desert hatching in a sudden downpour. And I laughed.

I ate well, and slept better, and didn't remember any dreams.

The mobile rake was churning up gravel and detritus and trying to dig its way through the trough's concrete bottom; even in the din of rushing water and pumps, I could hear its electric hum turn to an overstressed whine. I swore, pulled on my waders and went after it. The troughs were directly under the high, dirty glass of the roof. It was getting dark outside, and the light that made it through turned the choppy surface the color of zinc and pewter, like the North Sea before a storm. The water stank of shit and pollution and rot, and as the trough deepened toward the center, so did the smell of volatile organic compounds. Fourteen feet out, foul, warmish water spilled over the top of my thigh-high waders. It made no difference that nothing would get through my skinny; I felt soiled. And I could almost feel the hydrocarbons easing down my throat, smearing my lungs with filth. I was angry. Magyar had no right to deny basic safety precautions and procedures to her shift.

But Magyar had not written the rules, she merely had to follow them to meet the almost impossible productivity standards Hepple had set. And I doubted she knew any other way. She was smart, yes, and seemed to have good instincts, but she was untrained and unsupported. Hepple had no business appointing her to a supervisory position without even going through the motions of teaching her what she needed to know. No doubt he thought she would make him look good by comparison.

Even the orientation procedures were disorganized and sloppy. Magyar had surprised me on my second day by digging up a copy of the orientation disk. "Watch it in the breakroom," she said. "It runs forty minutes. I want you back on station in forty-five."

The carpets and walls of the breakroom were done in white and teal, and there were about twenty uncomfortable chairs and two screens, one tuned to the net—usually the news—the other to a video loop of swimming fish. There was a PIDA reader under each screen, but I didn't have to V-hand it to run the disk.

The video was terrible. It wasn't just the production values that were bad; there were several major errors in the procedures described, errors that would continue to echo down the line, like Magyar's insistence that the bugs could not tolerate even the slightest deviation in temperature. The information was simplistic at best: "In the primary section, specially tailored bacteria break down some of the more toxic compounds. Think of them eating ammonia and excreting other, less toxic chemicals, like nitrite . . ." Worse, there were half a dozen blatant edits where worker safety information had been taken out, probably by Hepple. No details about warning signs of the deadly chlorine gases that could build up, or methane explosions like the one that had killed four hundred workers in Raleigh, North Carolina, six or seven years ago, even though I had seen the red methane-release handles at the emergency station. The simple evacuation drill was clear—use this exit, not that; turn this off, not that—but unexplained. More worryingly, there was no mention of the stakes, the regional impact of polluted water if someone really screwed up their job: nothing about spontaneous abortion and convulsions, or violent dehydrating dysentery, spinal meningitis or central-nervous-system collapse.

"I hope you got something out of it," Magyar had said when I gave it back. "You need to look out for yourself in a place like this. Pay attention to the machines. They can be dangerous."

I had not known what to say. The machines in and of themselves were not dangerous—if you followed safety procedures. But you could not follow safety procedures that you were not told about. I wondered how much Magyar herself knew, how much she pretended not to know in order to keep her job. I had contented myself with a nod and a thank-you.

I circled the rake, which was still madly trying to dig its way to Australia. The month before I started this job, another worker had his left leg torn up by a mobile rake that had got stuck. Statutory regulations stated that a machine should never be approached while in operation; that it should be deactivated by remote, then towed out of the water and examined by a qualified technician. At Hedon Road, there was never time: turning the machine off and then on again in less than thirty minutes damaged it. The rakes were temperamental enough without adding to their unreliability, and we were so shorthanded that the unwritten rule was: Shove it out of the hole and keep it going. Once in the clear, whatever was clogging its tines usually got whirled off. If you couldn't find and retrieve what it was that fouled the blades in the first place, you just hoped that the next time the machine encountered it, it wasn't your shift.

It looked as though the right front tines were jammed. I stepped carefully in front of the stilled metal, hoping it wouldn't restart on its own, and leaned in and pushed. The rake chugged, sputtered, then moved sluggishly on its way. A two-foot length of bulrush floated to the surface.

Until I had started work at Hedon Road, I had not cared one way or another about bulrushes. After ten days on the job, I hated them. They were good at what they were intended for—facilitating the anaerobic and aerobic cycles of denitrification and nitrification, and buffering the rest of the system against toxic shock—but they were incredibly difficult to manage. Their tough, fibrous stalks fouled all the maintenance equipment and their fluffy cotton seed heads clogged air intakes. The rakes, of course, were designed to cut the rushes before the heads ripened, but because they had about thirty percent downtime—most of it, of course, during the night shift—we were always behind schedule.

When Magyar had walked by three days ago and seen me pruning the rush heads by hand, she had said nothing, but the next night the other workers had been issued with shears, and instructions to work out their own system for keeping the rushes trimmed. She may have been poorly trained but she was not stupid. She had nodded at me afterward, but said nothing. I found myself liking her.

I pulled down the record slate and started to check the readouts. Smart or not, good instincts or not, Magyar wouldn't take kindly to being shown too many times how to improve things by a new worker. I could not blame her for that. I wondered how my father would have handled the situation in my place . . .

And then I was standing staring at the slate without seeing it, tears rolling down my face. What was I doing here? I didn't belong. I could run this place in my sleep. I shouldn't be waist-deep in other people's shit. I could be back on Ratnapida, lying on my back in the sun-warmed grass watching the clouds, making up stories with Tok about industrial counterespionage . . . And we would eat dinner with Oster and Katerine, and Greta and Stella; Willem and Marley would be staying for the week . . .

But Stella was dead, Oster was not who he had pretended to be for all those years, and my family had refused to pay my ransom. There was no going back because what I wanted to return to had never existed, except in my Oster-woven version of reality.

I shoved the slate back on the shelf, angry for letting self-pity distort everything. Reality at Ratnapida would more likely be the family sitting at the table, pretending not to see me, pretending that the kidnap and abuse had never happened, that they had not received, not watched—over and over—the tapes my abductors had made for the net. My reality and theirs were different. Looking back, they always had been. The family had refused to hand over the money quickly enough for my abductors, but I doubted they would see it that way. Some might say it was their fault I had been subjected to such public humiliation, their fault I had ended up killing. But if I went back now they would just sip pinot grigio from crystal glasses, eat salad from Noritake china, and pretend that I had not been treated as a thing, had not had to scrabble to survive, that nothing had changed. And I would have to look at Oster and wonder if the decision not to pay had been deliberate, because I knew too much.

No. There was no going back. I had known that when I lifted the rusty nail and stabbed it into Fishface's neck. That part of my life was over.

I breathed hard, and clenched and relaxed my face muscles. Self-pity could creep up on anyone, but I would not let it happen again.

A flickering readout caught my eye. Readouts were not supposed to flicker. Another flashed from 20.7 to 5 to 87 and back again. That made no sense at all. Then all the readouts went berserk.

I lifted the phone, tapped in Magyar's call code. "This is station four, primary sector." I had to shout over the trilling station alarms.

"What is it, Bird?"

"I have readout anomalies."

"Which ones?"

"The whole bank. Going wild. Nothing makes any sense." Magyar did not reply immediately. She probably did not know what to do. "I need your authorization to cut the flow to the secondary sector."

"But we don't know that there's anything wrong with our stream . . ." She sounded scared.

"We don't know that there isn't, either, and they don't have the sensors we do."

"It's probably computer failure. Or maybe the monitors have gone down because of backflow. Flooding."

"The flood warning didn't go off. We have to—" I broke off. Judging from the entire bank of instruments going crazy, it probably *was* simple computer failure. There was another way. "Look, I think there's a way I can cut the stream temporarily and divert it to the holding tanks. Fifteen minutes won't do anyone any harm. Secondary sector might not even notice. And I can take some readings manually, if you have a handheld photoionization detector around."

There was a moment of silence. "There's one in the

locker that's about knee height. In front of you. Get me your results ASAP."

The PD turned out to be an old-fashioned portable of a kind I had not seen since I was a child. It was calibrated in parts per trillion. I lugged the case out of the influent bunker and along to my trough. It took me a while to remember how to assemble it. Thigh-deep in water, I hoped I would not stumble into one of the irregular gouges the rake had torn in the gravel. With the weight of the PD I would overbalance and I had no barrier protection for my face. The machine bleeped softly in my hand. Everything looked good so far.

It was full dark outside now, and the water, under its surface of reflected bright white, looked black, like ink. If the lights here went out, I wondered, would I be able to see the stars reflected in the troughs? Only if someone went onto the roof and cleaned off years' worth of grime.

Ten minutes later, when I waded out, Magyar was waiting, thumbs hooked in her belt.

"The readings are fine. Dead on normal."

"Good." I waited for her to say *I told you so.* The holding tanks would now have to be pumped out and cleaned. A lot of extra work for a shorthanded shift. She just nodded at the PD. "That's not a handheld."

"It's all there was."

"Looks heavy."

"It's not so bad when you're in the water. And, anyway, it feels a lot lighter than they used to when I was thirteen."

She gave me a strange look. "I'll have to take your word for that."

I pretended not to notice her surprise, but I was disgusted with myself. First self-pity, now nostalgia. It led to slips I could not afford.

SIX

Lore is nearly seven and a half. The family is staying with friends in Venezuela for month or so over Christmas. Greta is there, too.

The only image Lore really has of her half sister, Greta, is grayness: gray hair, gray eyes, and a gray kind of attitude to life. She is almost always away somewhere looking after the family interests. She is much older, of course—twenty-five now—and Lore tends to treat her more like an aunt than a sister, partly because Greta, even when she's around, seems so distant, withdrawn. Not unkind, just preoccupied with whatever it is that always makes her look stooped and check around corners before turning them. Lore has never seen her laugh, though sometimes she does smile. At those times Lore thinks she looks beautiful: her face stretches sideways a little, shortening it, taking away the grooves and hollows and shadows, changing it from gray to gold.

Lore's most vivid memory of Greta has to do with the
Dream Monster.

Lore is asleep on her stomach with the covers thrown off
the bed—how she always sleeps in a hot climate—when
suddenly she is woken up by the monster. It has her pinned
down and is breathing hot fire on her neck and groaning
like a beast. She shrieks, and pushes, and doors bang open
down the corridor, lights come on, and she must have
blanked out for a minute or two, or maybe she really was
dreaming, because then Katerine is sitting next to her on
the bed, still dressed, and Greta is in the doorway, with
Oster pulling on pajama trousers.

"A dream," Katerine is saying to Lore. She turns to Greta
and Oster. "Just a dream."

But Lore is still shaking and realizes she is crying.

"What is it?" Oster says, and kneels by the bed. He
takes her hand. "If you tell me what you're afraid of, we'll
fix it."

"Wasn't a dream," she hiccoughs. She has to make them
understand. "It was a monster."

"Of course it was a dream, love," Katerine says with a
smile. "How could it have got in?"

"Through the door."

Oster makes a shushing gesture at his wife. "A monster?
Well, I don't much like the idea of a monster being loose
when we're all trying to sleep, so you tell me all about him,
and then we can keep a look out." He ruffles her hair,
which she carefully smooths down.

She knows he is humoring her, but it doesn't matter, because at least he will listen. "It was big and heavy, only not
heavy like a rock, heavy like . . ." She doesn't know how to
describe it. *Heavy like the end of everything.* "Very heavy, anyway. It made monster noises. And breathed hot air." She
shudders. That air had felt so bad, like the breath of something dead.

"Well, the solution seems easy enough. If it came through the door, we'll give you a lock. A special lock that monsters can't open. Only people. Will that do?"

She considers it, then nods. By this time, Katerine is looking at the time display on the ceiling. "It can wait until tomorrow. It's past three already and I have that net conference at nine."

Lore is not sure whether her mother is talking to Oster, or to Greta who is still and silent by the door, or to her. She turns a mute look of appeal to her father.

He sighs. "I'll deal with it, Kat. You and Greta get to bed." They do. "I think we'll be lucky to find a lock at this hour. But there might be a place . . . Will you be all right on your own for half an hour?"

In answer Lore climbs down from the bed, puts on her slippers, and tucks her hand into his. He looks at her, then smiles. "Together it is, then."

In the end, they take the lock from the pantry door. It is an old-fashioned thing, attached by magnet to jamb and door, the mechanism a crude combination lock. But when they get it onto her bedroom door, and Lore wraps the combination cylinder with her hand so that even Oster can't see what number she chooses, she feels better. Oster tucks her up, kisses her forehead, and when the door closes behind him, she hears the satisfying *click* that means no one can ever come in here again until she rolls each of the white counters to its proper number.

She is getting dressed the next morning when Greta knocks at the door. She opens it proudly. Greta seems awkward. "Did you sleep better, later?"

Lore nods, then shows Greta her lock. Greta frowns. "This isn't good enough."

"But—"

"No, it's not good enough. Lock the door behind me and watch."

Lore, mystified as usual by Greta and her ways, does so. Twenty seconds later, the lock clicks back and the door swings open. Lore is suddenly terrified. She doesn't care that it is Greta who went out of the door, she is sure it is the monster coming back in. She runs to the bed intending to climb under it, forgetting that it is a futon and not her own, high bed in Amsterdam. The door closes again and Lore opens her mouth to scream.

"It's just me," Greta says. But she seems distracted. "We're going to do something about that lock." And she sits down on the futon right there and starts contacting people on her slate. "There. Now let's go eat breakfast."

They are the only ones at breakfast and though the maid drops Greta's croissant, Greta does not seem to notice. Lore nibbles at her own food and watches her sister surreptitiously over the rim of her juice glass. *Where does she go all the time?* she wonders. Wherever it is, it does not seem very pleasant.

The locksmith arrives only forty minutes later, and the three of them troop upstairs, again in silence. Greta simply points at the door and the locksmith nods.

It takes five minutes. Lore watches, fascinated, as the old lock is removed with something that looks like a cooking spatula, and a creamy ceramic square with a glossy black face replaces it. Lore thinks he has finished until he fishes a second from his pocket and fits it over the door and jamb on the hinge side. He doesn't look Venezuelan. When the locksmith is finished, he pulls out a white key remote the size of a rabbit's foot. He presses a button, and the black face turns to deep blue. "All yours." He starts to hand the key to Greta but she nods in Lore's direction and he gives it to her instead. He leaves.

"It's a special lock system," Greta says. "No one, and I mean no one, will ever be able to get through that lock. And because there are two, they can't just take the door off its hinges, or knock it down. They'd have to cut a hole through the middle. And the monster can't do that."

Lore looks down at the fat white key in her hand and wonders about monsters in the Netherlands.

"You can remove the locks and take them with you, wherever you go. I'll download all the operating instructions to your slate later. You'd better choose the code when I'm gone. Anything you like. You can even make them different for each side. And you can use algorithms to make sure it's never the same twice." She taps the key in Lore's hand. "Don't lose that."

After she goes, Lore sits on her bed, turning the locks on and off, listening to them thunk competently open and closed.

Greta leaves again the next day, and Lore develops a habit of reaching into her pocket to check she has her key whenever she is nervous.

SEVEN

I WAS surprised when Magyar somehow managed to get hold of a combination of handheld and portable PDs. She piled them up on the gangway and called the section, some twenty-odd men and women, together.

"You already know that the computer's down. It's going to stay down for at least a day. Systems want to dump the whole program, plus backups, to make sure there aren't any other viruses. Meanwhile, these are handheld detectors. I'll want readings every half hour—"

"There won't be time!" a red-haired man called. He worked two troughs down from me. He was flexing his right arm, over and over, testing his new neoprene and webbing elbow support, making it creak. His name was Kinnis.

"Shut up and let me finish. And try to keep still while I'm talking to you." The creaking noise stopped. "I'm not asking you to read every single trough every half hour—I only want readings from one trough per person. But make sure it's the same trough, and make sure it's from the middle. We want an idea of changes, got that? Good. Questions?"

"How long are we going to be doing this?"

"As long as it takes. Systems say they can't guarantee they'll have everything clean and back up in less than three days, but you know how much they overcompensate. It might only take a day. There again, it might not."

"But how do these things work?" Kinnis asked, looking dubiously at the pile of equipment.

"Ask Bird. She seems to be an expert." They all turned to look at me. I felt my blanket of anonymity evaporating, but it was my own fault. I managed to nod. What did Magyar suspect? Next time I would keep my mouth shut.

A big, rawboned woman called Cel looked at her waterproof watch, and said in a Jamaican accent, "We've another six hours of the shift to go tonight."

"Yes," agreed Magyar, "and those holding tanks have to be pumped out as well, so let's not waste any more of it, shall we?" She strode off, leaving the workers to look at each other, then back to me.

I shrugged, picked up one of the smaller handheld PDs. "This is a photoionization device. It's calibrated in parts per billion. The bigger ones there, the portables, are in parts per trillion. They're heavy, so maybe we can take it in turns."

"I don't mind heavy," Kinnis said.

"You wouldn't," Cel said. "What do they measure?"

"Volatile organics. Totals only, I'm afraid."

"That doesn't sound too bad." Kinnis picked up a portable, hefted it. "Easy." He frowned, turning it around, looking at the case. "There's no jack. How do you input the readings to Magyar's master board?"

"You don't. They're old. The readings will have to be input manually." They looked at me in disgust, as though it were my fault. "I know." The job was hard enough without the extra work. I hesitated. I was no longer anonymous; I might as well be liked. "Look, seeing as I'm already familiar with these things, why don't I come round the first time or two and collect your readings? It'll save you some time."

Cel looked at me suspiciously, as though trying to figure out what possible advantage I could gain from this. Then she nodded reluctantly.

I spent the next hour trotting from trough to trough, collecting readouts. Once I had everything, I saw we had a problem. The source of the problem was obvious. The solution wasn't. If I called Magyar and explained, she would have even more reason to suspect me. Would Sal Bird have been able to work out what was going on—and if she had, would she have cared? I didn't know. But if I ignored it, the whole system would gradually fall out of sync, and that could lead to danger for other workers in other sections.

I called Magyar. "Can you come down here?"

"I'm in a meeting with Hepple, Bird. Can it wait?"

I leaned against the readout console, trying to rest my legs a little. "Not for too long."

"I'll be there in fifteen minutes." She was. "This better be good."

I handed her the record slate. "Take a look."

Magyar glanced over them, frowned. "Lower than I expected." Her skin stretched tight over high cheekbones when she narrowed her eyes. "How come you're checking up on them?"

What would Sal Bird say? "I just thought it would save time if I went and collected the data, rather than everyone coming to the control center, one after another." And it meant someone was on top of the subtle changes, minute to minute. Someone had to be. The dangers here were real. I thought about Hepple happily releasing our stream into the mains and what could have happened if there'd been a spill while Magyar had been debating whether or not to close down for a few minutes.

Magyar moved her shoulders, easing tension. "You think there's something wrong with the PDs?"

I should have said I didn't know, let her figure it out, but I didn't know how long that would take, and I couldn't bear to see a system fail due to simple ignorance. "No. Just the way people are using them. The highest concentration of airborne volatiles is at the center of the trough. Where the water is deepest."

Magyar understood at once. "And those soft bastards don't want to get wet."

"You can't blame them," I said tiredly.

"Yes, I can."

All of a sudden, I saw how young-looking that stretched skin was, how her anger covered vulnerability. She didn't know what to do. I felt sorry for her. "If you wanted, I could probably come up with a formula to calculate the real concentrations, assuming they all go to about eight feet out."

The muscles around Magyar's eyes and mouth tightened even more. She looked as though maybe her ancestors had ridden horses on the Mongol steppes. "That won't be necessary." She looked at her watch. "I'll talk to you about this later."

Stupid. That was so stupid. Why was I risking myself like this?

I never much enjoyed the forty-five minutes midway through the night when, by law, the section took a break. I managed by being amiable and guarded to those I could not avoid, and then taking a chair out of the way, near the screen showing the tape loop of fish. Watching the endless play of light on water, the dance of angelfish and eel, was the only time I allowed myself to indulge in memories of the past. The tape reminded me of the reefs of Belize, where I had swum at fifteen. I could ignore the sweat and the stink as twenty-some people stripped their skinnies to the waist to free their hands to eat.

Usually I was left alone to eat the food I brought with me, while the rest of the shift complained about work, argued about the net channel, and played rough, incomprehensible practical jokes on each other. This time, Magyar was waiting for us.

"Turn that thing off," she said. "You people get paid to do a job. I'm paid to make sure you do. Sometimes both our jobs are easier than others. Now is one of the hard times. I've been looking over the readings you've given me in the last two hours, and they're no good." There were groans and one or two angry protests. "Oh, be quiet. If you'd walked those extra few feet into the middle of the troughs as you were supposed to then I wouldn't have to say all this." She looked at them one by one. "I've requisitioned chest-highs instead of the thigh waders, but they won't be available until tomorrow. I've also asked for hazard pay for the whole of this shift." There were a few smiles at that. "Don't get your hopes up. You know management."

Now the smiles were knowing. I could not help admiring the way Magyar manipulated her audience.

"One more thing, people. From now until the program is back on-line, I'll be checking readings personally, at random. Anyone who is more than five percent out will be fired on the spot. Now get back out there and do your job."

The workload, which had been hard and dirty, became almost unbearable. When we stripped and showered at the end of the shift, there was a lot of muttering about taking sick days. I just kept my head down and tried not to think about the fact that I seemed to be the only one there who really knew anything about the system.

My dreams were bad that night. Long, tangled images of plastic sheets and blood, and lying on my stomach, face in a pillow, choking while whoever was on top of me humped up and down and breathed in my ear. I woke up drenched in sweat, tight and heavy with need. I knew if I tried to do something about that need it would fade away into mocking memories of Spanner holding up the vial of oily drug and laughing.

I got to work a few minutes early. The computer was still down but there had been no emergencies during the afternoon.

When we were dressing for the shift, Magyar and two new men came into the locker room. One was wizened and bowlegged but seemed spry enough. He flashed a grin at the shift. The other one was just a teenager, with jet black hair and brown eyes. Something about the way he held himself, a strange mix of ramrod back and careless limbs, bothered me.

"This is Nathan Meisener"—the older man nodded— "and Paolo Cruz. I made Hepple pull his finger out on those vacancies. I thought you might appreciate the help."

There were one or two laughs but I wanted to yell at everyone: *You think two extra people will make a difference if a fireball rips through here?* Kinnis slapped Meisener on the back and Cel called out, "Hope you can swim," as she pulled on her waders.

"Right, people. Time to get to work." They began to file past Magyar. For all her apparent joviality, I could tell by the flush in her cheeks and line of her jaw that she was angry about something. Magyar pulled aside Kinnis and then me before we could walk past. "Kinnis, you take Meisener here. He has some experience, but it was a while back." She watched as Meisener followed Kinnis down the corridor. I could feel the other one, the teenager, looking at me. "Cruz, you'll be following Bird around for a day or two. She knows a lot more about the way things work around here than you might think."

It was impossible to miss the bite behind those words. I did not like that. Was she suspicious enough yet to backcheck Bird's records? As if I didn't have enough to worry about.

I shepherded the new man ahead of me and felt Magyar's hard, bright eyes boring into my back all the way down the corridor. Paolo, though he must have noticed, said nothing.

During the next couple of hours, as I showed him the ropes, pointed out that his back support had the over-shoulder cross straps for a reason, he hardly spoke at all. Something about him still bothered me. I watched him as he walked out into the trough, PD held at waist level.

"Not the talkative type, is he?" Cel said from behind me.

"No."

"Not like that Meisener. Talking a mile a minute." She lifted the PD she was holding. "How do you reset these things again?" I showed her. Cel clipped the PD to her belt, then nodded at Paolo, waist-deep in the water. "Let me know if you need me to take him off your hands for a while."

I was surprised at her friendliness. "Thanks. I might."

"New ones are always a pain." She looked at me assess-ingly. "Usually, anyhow." She waved, and moved off back to her own troughs. I returned my attention to Paolo.

Water sloshed as he strode another couple of feet deeper. I had watched several people taking their readings by now, and the one thing they all had in common was the gingerly way they walked through the polluted wastes. I did it my-self. It was not just the possibility of overbalancing; you never knew what you were about to step on, or through. It was hard not to imagine the floating feces or lumps of glu-tinous matter, the variety of things, organic and nonorganic, that people flushed down their toilets or that wriggled their own way through the municipal drains. It did not matter that your legs were protected by a double layer of polyurethane and plasthene; you could still feel the slimy things that bumped against you.

Paolo waded to the edge of the trough, seemingly un-concerned by what he might be treading on. He held out the PD. I waved it away. "Just read them out, it's quicker."

He did. Every fourth or fifth word, I caught an accent; not the softened consonants of Castilian, or the nasal vowels of Central American Spanish. Something else. Like the way he waded through the foul water unconcerned, it felt as though it should be familiar, and it bothered me. I shook my head at my own imagination.

"You want me to stop?" He was looking at me anxiously.

"No. You're doing fine."

When he finished with the readings, I held out my gloved hand to help haul him out of the trough. He pre-tended not to see it, and climbed out unaided. I could tell by the hunch of his shoulders that he was embarrassed about deliberately avoiding my hand, and wondered why. I did not ask.

I watched Paolo on and off until the break, and it was when I was handing him the scrape, a short metal tool for unclogging the rake tines, that I realized he had not refused my help—he had refused my touch. Oh, he was very adept, graceful even, but he always made sure his hand never touched mine, or my foot his, when we were thigh-deep in the water, me holding back the bulrushes for him to clip the heads.

While I finished up the rushes I sent him back into the trough to do the next reading, and this time, when he waded out to the edge, I made sure I held out the clipper handle for him to grab. He accepted without hesitation. His smile was warm and very young-looking, completely at odds with the message sent by his stiff, almost disdainful body language.

That stiffness reminded me of something, but when I

tried to remember, all I could conjure up was a vague memory of Katerine, years ago, grinning in triumph at something on the net. That was it. I went back to work.

Magyar was waiting for us again in the breakroom. Kinnis turned off the net without being asked.

Magyar smiled, but it was not pleasant. "Some of you will be pleased to hear that, as of twenty hours today, all personnel on this shift who spend time in the water, which is to say all of you, will wear masks and full-body barrier protection at all times. As mandated by Health and Safety regulations. You never know when we could get an unexpected visit from an inspector." She looked directly at me and it wasn't hard to tell she was angry. I had a bad feeling I knew why.

"Some of you, of course, will not be pleased at the cost, which will come out of your next salary credit, and all of you will no doubt be annoyed at the reduction in productivity and subsequent reduction in salary. But blame that on those that make the rules and regulations." Her voice was husky with anger. She looked at me again, and I understood: she thought she was preempting me. She thought I was a Health and Safety inspector. *She* was implementing these changes, to save her job. No wonder she was angry. Productivity would go down, and soon Hepple would be on her back. And she blamed me. "Questions?"

No one was about to ask her questions when she was in this kind of mood.

"Well, then. I'll expect you back on shift, with masks, in exactly—" She looked at her watch. "—forty-two minutes."

On her way out, she gave me a tight, matte-eyed nod. It was impossible to mistake the direct challenge. Cel noticed, and turned, puzzled. I managed to shrug and look surprised, but underneath my skinny I was slippery with sweat.

"Why's she got it in for you?" Kinnis asked, but he looked wary, as though wondering if talking to me was a mistake.

"No idea." My heart felt cold and dense and suddenly I wondered if my accent sounded right, if the quick, liquid syllables were thickening, if just by listening to me everyone would know who I was. I felt dizzy and horribly exposed. At least Magyar hadn't actually checked my records yet, or I wouldn't still be here. But it was only a matter of time. I had to get Spanner to speed things up. I fumbled my way to my locker and took out my food, trying to seem unconcerned. My hands were shaking. I needed to sit down.

Paolo was already sitting near the fish screen. I sat next to him, but not too close. I said nothing for a moment, not trusting my voice. He sat quietly, watching the screen. He was not eating.

"Here." I held out half my food, then remembered and put it on the table next to him instead. "You can bring enough for two tomorrow."

"I thought . . ."

"There is a cafeteria, but you have to scrub down and change before they'll let you in. And the food takes a long time and costs a lot. And it's full of executives and supervisors who'll stare at you like you're a bug."

"Thank you." He bit into the sandwich hungrily. I made a mental note to bring food tomorrow, anyway. He looked as though he needed to eat as much as he could afford to buy.

Kinnis and Meisener sat down opposite us. They must have decided it was safe to talk to me, after all. "So, Paolo, where're you from?"

"I've lived here since I was two years old." The words themselves were neutral enough, but I could hear the tension behind them. He didn't want to say any more.

Kinnis opened his mouth to ask another question, but Meisener was already talking.

"I was born here, but I've not spent much time in the city the last twenty years," he said. "Been all over the world. Army for a while, then mechanic for EnSyTec. Went everywhere. Then I got fed up of traveling, wanted to settle down, have kids. Took a job in Sarajevo, working the sewage lines. Got married."

"You have any kids, then?" Kinnis asked, forgetting Paolo.

"Two." And then they were pulling out pictures, talking about their children.

Paolo seemed to enjoy being included in their conversation without having to contribute. I was left to wonder how to deal with Magyar.

When I got home that night the message light was blinking on my screen. I hit PLAY before I took my jacket off; maybe it was Ruth and Ellen, inviting me round.

It was Spanner. "Hyn and Zimmer will be at the Polar Bear tomorrow night. Meet me there."

It turned itself off. I had not realized how much I'd been hoping for Ruth to call. I sat by the blank screen for a long time, listening to the deep, three-in-the-morning quiet.

I woke several times during the night, my heart beating too fast, wondering whether I should call the regional Health and Safety Council about Hedon Road.

LORE FOLLOWED Spanner down the dark stairwell and into the warm night. She kept her eyes down, fixed on Spanner's feet, refusing to look at the emptiness of outside. The wet asphalt sparkled in the sodium streetlights. She managed to get to the bar across the road without sweating too much.

The Polar Bear was dim and warm and no one looked up when they entered.

Lore had never been in a place like it. The casual bars and open-air cafés of Europe, the restaurants of Australia and tea rooms of India had not prepared her for this fecund, dark place, rich with the fruity scents of beer and layered with muted conversation. The wooden floors and bar surface were highly polished; the bar itself bellied out in biscuit-colored porcelain molded with grapes and leaves and bottles.

"It looks pregnant," she said, fascinated, wanting to go up and touch it, but Spanner was walking toward a table in the corner, and she followed.

An elderly couple were already seated. Spanner pulled out a chair. "This is Lore."

"I'm Hyn and he's Zimmer, but don't worry if you get us mixed up, a lot of people do."

Spanner went to the bar to get the drinks and Lore was left at the table with a man and a woman who looked like dried tobacco leaves with berries for eyes. Hyn and Zimmer. These were the people who knew something about locks.

They seemed utterly at home in this setting, but Lore suspected they might blend as easily with the woods as this urban nightscape. She wondered if they were brother and sister, or whether they had just grown to resemble each other in the bizarre way of some couples. She searched for something to say. Her early training, the endless meetings with local and national dignitaries, took over. "It's an un-usual name, the Polar Bear."

"Legend has it that a polar bear escaped from the zoo three hundred years ago, and was shot on this site." Zimmer sipped his dark brown beer. They seemed to find her amusing.

"What do you do?"

Zimmer laughed, a robust bouncing laugh that surprised Lore. "We're fences, my dear. And very good ones. And you?"

"I don't know."

"Don't worry. Spanner will soon fix that."

Spanner will fix that . . . She looked at her tiny, faraway image in the mirror behind the bar and touched her red hair.

Spanner came back with beer. "Make it last. After this we're heading uptown. You'll need a clear head. Time to start paying me back."

. . .

Lore discovered that they worked well as a team. One would smile and take a drink to a table near a small group. The other watched from the bar. The rich, confident people found in the bars Spanner chose could not resist a woman on her own, whether from bad intent or the best of motives.

"Come sit with us," one would say, if it was Lore's turn to sit by them, and offer her a drink, which she always took. And she would talk, and then maybe get hysterical with laughter, or cry, whichever would get the most attention, and perhaps spin them a story about being down on her luck, which was easy to do, with her accent and her bearing, and then Spanner would slide up behind them while they were fussing with handkerchiefs or orders for more drinks, and take one slate, or two. Rich people, Spanner said—and it seemed to be true—always left their slates in their jacket pockets, jackets that they hung over the backs of their chairs as though no one would dare to steal anything of theirs. Which, probably, no one had before. After all, what good was a slate to someone else? And after a while Lore would recover, and thank them decorously, and leave. She and Spanner would leap on the nearest slide or, if it was after two or three in the morning, swing onto the carapace of a beetling freighter, clutching hold of the emergency door release with their right hands—keeping their left hands, their PIDAs, shielded from the antenna on the top, because if the tiny beetle brain of a freighter sensed a human aboard, it would stop dead in its tracks. Freighters could be dangerous, but Spanner—and, soon, Lore—knew all the routes, all the stops, all the timetables.

Sometimes they would giggle uproariously, especially when it had been Spanner doing the poor-wee-thing-all-alone, because as they slid through the deserted city she would recount at the top of her lungs the outrageous stories she had spun for the rich and gullible victims. Sometimes,

if it had been dangerous work, or the alarm had gone out
just minutes after they had left the bar and they had had to
run, leap from one freighter to another, they would open a
bottle of champagne at home and watch the pale liquid fizz
like their adrenaline-rushing blood, and they would laugh
again, and drink, and tear off each other's clothes and fuck
like wild animals on a pile of slippery gray slates.

It seemed to Lore on nights like this that she had had no
other life before right now, here, every pore open to the
wild night's feel, every follicle attuned to changes in the air,
every taste bud and nerve cell hot and fluttering. She knew
that sometimes Spanner made money from other people's
suffering, but she did not have to see that, and she had suffered, too. Everyone suffered. It was just a question of making sure she was using them, and not the other way around.
She would not be fooled again, not the way Oster had
fooled her. Never again. And in the middle of sex she
would look up at Spanner moving over her and wonder if
those half-closed eyes were laying the newstank images of a
naked, weeping Lore on top of the real Lore.

On nights like that, too, when Lore slept she often
dreamed of being back in the bar, only now when she cried
for these strangers it was for good reason, and she would
wake up sweating in the hollow of the brightly colored
quilt, remembering Tok, or Crablegs; her mother; Stella
screaming in the fountain; and she would wonder which
parts of her life were real.

Sometimes, Spanner still went out on her own. Lore
pressed her face against the glass, watching until Spanner was
out of sight, and wondered where she went. Although it was
getting easier to go out with Spanner at night, she still did
not have the courage to do it on her own. And when they
were out, it was Spanner who dealt with the world. Lore hid
behind her: not literally, of course, but behind a cloud of
aloof silence. It had always worked when she was a child, a

van de Oest. It never occurred to her that it might not work now, when no one knew or cared who she was. Spanner had snapped at her a couple of times to not stand up so bloody straight, she was drawing attention. So she learned how to move like Spanner, alert and upright, but withdrawn, ready and wary. She learned how to slide together the beginning and ending of her words, to cut out the crystal pronunciation of her childhood. She gradually learned to become someone else, someone who recognized the thin, hungry face in the mirror, the red hair and naked vulva. But she still never went out into the open on her own.

There was nothing specific of which she was afraid, just . . . everything, as though the world were a gelatinous beast that would fall upon her and suffocate her. The open spaces, the feeling that her back was naked, that people could see through her clothes; that someone would recognize her as that heiress who was kidnapped three or four months ago. And her heart would kick under her ribs, and the muscles behind her jaw and in her throat would tighten as though someone had a thick, soft ribbon around her neck and was pulling very, very slowly.

On good days, she managed to get out into the garden. The hard part was getting past the front door. She would put her hand to the wood, and suddenly think, *Have I got my gloves?* And so she would check her coat pockets. Yes. She had her gloves. She would open the door a crack, think, *Are my roots showing?* and have to close it again, go to the bathroom and check her hair. And then she would have to stand by the door, breathing deep, telling herself it was *only a few seconds* on the street. *Only a few seconds.* Sometimes she hated herself for this fear. But then, if it was a good day, she would rip open the door in a rush and shut it and run down the steps, into the passageway, through the wooden gate that now had a new, shiny lock and a bolt she could push from the inside, and she would be safe.

Sometimes she spent hours in the garden, breaking concrete with a pick, hauling it into the barrow, sorting the bricks by hand into two piles: one to throw away, one to keep to make a raised flower bed. Many of the weeds she left alone. They had fought to be there; she wasn't going to be the one to pull them out. Besides, they were green and growing, and most of them would flower in spring and summer.

Today she took a spade and started turning over the hard dirt. She leaned her weight into the spade, enjoying the way the steel bit into the black dirt, trying hard not to slice any worms.

Something rustled in the undergrowth by the west wall.

Lore went still. Listened. Nothing. She must have imagined it. She bent to her digging. Heard it again.

She put her spade down carefully, not wanting to startle whatever it was, but when she got near the tangle of weeds and dead wood and what looked like it might once have been a bicycle frame, there was a flurry of movement. She squatted down, peered under the foliage. An eye gleamed, and a tail lashed in the shadows. A cat.

They stared at each other. The cat was not pretty. Its ribs were showing, and one eye was closed, probably missing altogether. She could smell its breath, a thick, hot stink as though it had been chewing on dead things.

Lore backed away carefully. It needed feeding, that was obvious, but if she left now, would it ever come back? And if it did, did she really want the responsibility of caring for a verminous, ill animal? It was probably dying. And if she went inside to get food, she would have to come out again. Run the gauntlet twice in one day.

The cat was pushed as far back against the wall as it could get. It hissed, hissed again. Its upper right canine was missing. Maybe it was old, and had come here to die. It moved its head back and forth, looking for a way past Lore.

She wondered what was in the kitchen that a cat might like to eat, and visions of the poor starved thing wolfing down cold rice, or scraps of two-day-old sushi or beans, trying to lick its whiskers afterward, made her sigh. Now she would have to feed it.

She brought out two saucers, one with raw egg, the other with defrosted ground veal. The cat was gone. She put the dishes down in the undergrowth anyway, and went back to her spade. She did not see the cat again that afternoon.

When it got dark, she went out one more time. The plates were empty. She smiled.

She watched the net but there was never anything about her kidnapping, no stories about bodies. Not surprising. She was old news: she had been taken at the end of August and it was now December. What was unusual was the absence of information about the van de Oests. Nothing. She scanned the business then environmental sections—still nothing. It did not make sense.

And then one day, on the news, there were her father and Tok, standing shoulder to shoulder by the fountain at Ratnapida. Tok, she noticed, was taller than her father now.

"We know she's out there somewhere," Oster was saying, "and we want her to come home."

Tok, circles under his eyes and a broken air to his stance, nodded. "Please," he said directly to the camera, "Lore, come home. It's . . . Everything's sorted out." He looked utterly defeated.

Four months ago, Tok, with just a few breathless sentences about why Stella had killed herself, had destroyed the image Lore had built of Oster over the years. She had loved her father; she had thought he loved her. But he was a monster. It had all been a lie. And now Tok—Tok, her brother, Stella's twin—was siding with him, telling her to come home, it was all *sorted out*. She did not understand.

• • •

Although she and Spanner slept together, although she
might owe her life to Spanner, Lore knew instinctively that
letting Spanner see chinks in her armor was dangerous. So
the afternoon Spanner called from the kitchen that they had
run out of bread, and suggested that Lore go to the market
because they needed some other things, too, Lore knew she
would have to go, would have to conceal her fear and saun-
ter casually out into the daylight on her own.

The day was thinly overcast. The clouds spread the light
into an eye-aching blanket that made her wince. It was
colder than it looked. Her breath, coming in great panicky
gusts, froze like gauzy sheets in front of her face. She wished
she had worn a hat. She did not go back for one; she knew
she would not be able to leave again.

The market sign flashed three hundred yards away. Lore
started walking. If she kept her eyes on the sign, she would
be all right. She crossed at the ceramic safeway she and
Spanner always used when going to the Polar Bear. Safe territory. Known. But then she was walking north along the
pavement and people were walking in front of her and
across her path and toward her. There was nowhere she
could look where they would not be able to see her face.
She walked faster.

The market was strange: small, but with that cavernous
feel of tight-margin enterprise. She picked up a basket and
wandered down the first aisle, trying hard to not look as bewildered as she felt. To look vulnerable was to be vulnerable.
It was all bar codes and machine voices calling out prices as
her basket passed. The only people she saw were shoppers.

She picked up a head of lettuce and turned it in her
hand. There was dirt on the underside. She put it back on
the piles of lettuces, picked up another. They were all dirty.
She chose one that seemed less grubby than the others, and
moved on to the carrots. It was peculiar to see them all

lined up on their sides and tied together in bunches. On the rare occasions she had shopped in the past, the vegetable section in Auckland had been a series of gleaming white vats, where the lettuces and dwarf radicchio, the spinach and bok choy grew hydroponically, right there in front of you. If you wanted something, you picked it yourself. You knew it was fresh, you knew where it had been, where it had come from. These vegetables seemed . . . dead. Not like real vegetables at all. Where had they been grown, and how? And how did you get them clean?

She laid the carrots alongside the lettuce. The aisles did not seem very well organized. After she had walked up and down them all twice, she found the bread next to the entrance.

She joined the lines at the checkout, realized that the woman in front of her, and the man next to her in another line, both had their vegetables in plastic bags. She wondered if they brought the bags with them. The line was the worst part. People in front of her, beside her, behind her, breathing her air, all comfortable, assured, confident through having undergone this simple procedure a hundred times, a thousand times. Natives in this particular stratum of culture. In a strange country, all Lore would have to do was smile and shrug, and say loudly in English or Dutch or French that she did not understand what she should do: foreigners were allowed to make mistakes. Natives were not.

She moved one step closer to the checkout. The woman in front of her turned casually, nodded, looked at her basket, turned back to the front. Lore almost panicked and threw down her bread and vegetables. Did normal people only buy vegetables and bread? Would the woman think she was strange because her things were not in plastic bags?

In her imagination that one casual glance became a searching stare, the nod a sharp gesture of condemnation.

Was it her hair? Her clothes? But then the woman was checking her goods through the scanner, V-handing her PIDA into the metal-and-ceramic jaws of the debit counter, packing her things—canned goods mostly—into a plastic string bag and leaving. The scanner bleeped at her softly. "Next customer, please. Next customer, please."

Lore waved her lettuce and carrots and bread through the scanner one by one, as she had seen the woman do. Then she stuck the V of her hand into the debit counter. It clicked green. The man behind her cleared his throat impatiently. She scooped her things up and walked quickly out of the door. Eyes followed her as she almost ran back down Springbank, across the safeway.

Spanner was working when she got back, frowning over a pile of slates. Lore's hands shook as she put the lettuce in the refrigerator. It was two days before she went back out into the garden.

One day Spanner came home around noon and announced that they would go to the park. To Lore's relief, they took back streets and cut-throughs and crossed the long-abandoned railway line to enter the park from the side.

Pearson Park was a pocket-sized patch of green in the middle of the west side of the city. Once, it had been part of the estate of some rich Victorian family. The statues they had erected at the jubilee of Victoria, Queen of Great Britain and Empress of India, remained untouched. Victoria herself, her white marble jowls turning slightly green with moss—like the shadow of a beard—graced a plinth in the rose garden. Albert, Prince Consort, lorded it over the pond and its score of mallards and moorhens and muddy-looking geese. Most of the birds were now asleep on the tiny island, head under wing, or begging scraps of bread or rice from the few hardy souls, well-wrapped against the cold, who were eating lunch away from the office. An oak tree, probably not much younger than the statues, Lore thought, had been half pulled up, pushed sideways, and trained to grow across the pond: a gnarled, moss-slippery bridge. Its roots were dug like long, bony fingers into the asphalt of the path.

Lore shivered.

"You'll be warm where we're going," Spanner said. She led Lore around the pond toward a Victorian conservatory, all white wood and glass greenhouse, with clouds in every shade of gray scudding along its panes. Lore followed Spanner past the little window where a bored employee sold seedlings and saplings, and inside.

It was like walking into a line of hanging laundry, still hot and wet and smelling of earth and sunshine and fresh rain. She felt as though she had stepped through a mirror into another world, where the ash and charcoal, the grim mercury and zinc and lithium vanished into the living colors of the tropics. A bird shrieked. The light was bright, and reflected from the vivid orange of half fruits at the bottom of the aviary cages, on the flash of a purple-throated hummingbird, on huge, blowsy red flowers.

"Heliconia . . ." Lore said, in wonder, and lifted her face to smell. The ceiling was three stories high, and the whole space was lush with greenery.

"How the hell did you know that?"

"I've been in the jungle. Before." Before all this.

She felt suddenly that her carapace had been ripped off, like a shiny scab, and she was open, raw and pink, to everything: the brilliant sherbet green of a parakeet's tail; to a dozen variations on brown—leaf mold, dead moss, peat, bark, beetles; to the crunch of their feet on the gravel paths that wound between the vines and palms and trailers that spanned the fifty or sixty feet from loam to glass ceiling. It was these plants that seemed to interest Spanner.

Spanner stopped in front of an enormous green tower

with trailing aerial roots and leaves that were fringed and full of natural holes. Lore tilted her head up, up, and was lost in the soaring spindle-weave of foliage, the tracery of different greens overhead, the architectural density of it all, like a great, Gothic cathedral.

She wondered why Spanner had brought her here.

"*Monstera deliciosa*, that's its Latin name," Spanner said. "The people who first brought it back from the jungle called it the fruit salad plant, because that's what the fruit tastes like." Her face was tilted up at forty-five degrees, and Lore could imagine her tramping through the tropics, braving unknown hazards to collect specimens, just to say she'd *been* there, a new place. But there were no more new places. Lore suddenly thought of Stella. Her sister and Spanner were very alike. They were the people who suffered because they were made for exploring the edges, pushing the boundaries. But the only boundaries left were inside.

She wanted to ask Spanner why she was letting down her barriers. Why now? She asked, instead: "Where does it come from?"

Spanner shrugged. "Nowhere, now, except hothouses." She lifted up her face again. "I've been coming here for six years, watching for fruit. I wonder what they'd really taste like—what *kind* of fruit salad? Once I dreamt I found a pineapple as big as a barrel on the floor. When I ate a bit, it tasted like strawberries." Her smile twisted at the last minute. "Imagine calling something that grows fruit salad a *cheese plant*."

Later, as they walked the half mile home, coats wrapped tight against the winter chill, Lore silent and waiting, Spanner suddenly said, "It's my birthday tomorrow."

Lore looked at Spanner's inwardly focused eyes and knew it would be pointless to ask her how old she was.

When they got back to the flat, Lore took off her jacket and went into the kitchen to make coffee. When it was done, she headed back to the living room but paused in the doorway. Spanner, still in her coat, was staring into empty space. Lore had never seen her look so vulnerable. She didn't think she had made a sound, but Spanner's gaze came back to the room, and focused on her. "I'm going out."

"But—"

"What?" Spanner's voice was harsh.

Lore looked at the cup in her hand. "Nothing."

"Don't wait up."

Lore stood where she was until the front door closed; then she went back into the kitchen and carefully poured Spanner's coffee down the drain. After a moment, she poured her own away, too.

Moving slowly, numbly, trying not to think, not to let in the pictures of Stella and Spanner, their loneliness—no, their *emptiness*—she picked up her coat. She buttoned it deliberately.

Don't think about it, she told herself again, only this time it was the outside she was trying not to think about, the big wide world full of open sky and strangers who might take a casual look at her, then look again, then open their mouths to shout, to point . . . She opened the door and headed back to the conservatory.

It was four in the morning and all the lights in the flat were off when Spanner got back. Lore heard the chink of a bottle against the wall. "Put the light on before you kill yourself," she called. Then she got out of bed and watched from the doorway as Spanner tugged off her jacket, tripped over the rug, saw the four-foot cheese plant, and stopped.

Lore walked barefoot into the living room. "Happy birthday."

Spanner started to cry. Lore held her.

WHEN THE shift finally ended I was almost glad I had to go to the Polar Bear to meet Spanner. At least while I was worrying about her and my PIDA, about Magyar checking up on Bird's records, I wouldn't be sweating over the score of things that could go wrong at the plant.

Outside it was cold and clear. Winter was coming.

When I got to the Polar Bear my face was red and my hands tingled with cold. Hyn and Zimmer were already there, with Spanner. I got myself a drink before sitting down. I took off my jacket and nodded at them.

Zimmer nodded back. "Spanner tells me what you want. We don't get requests like that very often."

"It's rare," Hyn agreed.

"And we don't know of anyone who's holding what you need."

"But you could find out," Spanner said.

"Oh, yes," Hyn said, "but do you really want us to?" I took a sip of my beer. It was cool and nutty. "They're not the kind of people it's wise to know."

Spanner laughed. "Nor am I. Nor are you, not really." No one said anything about me.

Hyn and Zimmer looked at each other. They seemed troubled. "Do you really need this equipment?"

"Yes."

Zimmer touched my wrist with one brown gnarled finger. "And you?" His eyes looked more like berries than ever, and still bright, but older somehow.

I nodded reluctantly. "Yes."

Hyn sighed. "Then we'll do it. But it'll be expensive." We all knew she was talking about more than money.

"How much?"

Hyn shrugged, looked at Zimmer. "Fifteen thousand? Maybe more."

That was more than I had expected. "I'm not—"

"We'll get the money."

I looked at her. "Spanner, I don't—"

"We'll have the money," Spanner repeated to Hyn and Zimmer. "Just let us know when and where, and you'll have it."

I had never seen them look so unhappy, but they nodded and stood. They left their unfinished drinks on the table.

Hyn and Zimmer were scared, but danger was just an adventure to Spanner. It put her in a good mood. We sipped at our beer in silence. This was not the only kind of danger I was in. If Magyar decided to use some budget on a back-check of Bird's record, she would see straightaway that I knew more than I had a right to. And then she might be able to justify a deeper search. And that meant she would find out Bird had died a while ago. And then I was in real trouble. Might as well take advantage of Spanner's good mood.

"I changed my mind about the PIDA records. I need that information substituting as soon as possible."

"When?"

"Yesterday."

"No problem."

Silence again. This time it lengthened until I couldn't bear it any longer. "Where will you get the money?"

"Does it matter?"

No, not really. I already knew.

When I got back to my flat, the air seemed stale and lifeless. There was no message from Ruth.

I heated soup, glad of the machine sounds and the occasional soft pop as the liquid bubbled. I ate slowly.

Once the bowl was empty and washed, I had to face the silent, empty flat. I could sleep, of course, but then what would I do in the morning? I sat in front of the screen, checked to make sure that a power hit had not wiped out any message that might have been left. I drummed my fingers on the desk, then pulled up my projects file.

When I first left Spanner I had spent days at the keyboard, inputting all I could remember about the Kirghizi project, then triple-copied the file, and extrapolated from each: one was the perfect scenario, with no setbacks of any kind; one involved random minor difficulties—a failing of one of Marley's bugs, the occasional breakage of the UV pipeline; the third was the catastrophe file—every breakdown, human, environmental, and mechanical, that I could envisage. It was the one I played with most. It usually reached the point of no return after about three months simulated time—two hours realtime. When that happened I wiped it back to the point where I had left it, nearly three years ago.

Tonight, when I pulled up the digital image of the pipeline stretched like a blazing crystal snake across the desert, I knew that was not what I wanted to see.

I changed the image to night, the perspective to the view a small nocturnal rodent might have from the desert floor. The ceramic support pylons and the vitrine troughs became huge, menacing. I darkened the sky to an eerie indigo-black, brought out the stars. Northern constellations burned like specks of magnesium. Better. I added cloud cover. The smeary, milky hint of a moon. I wondered what it would be like to sit out there, with the water overhead hissing endlessly. I wondered if a small rodent might mistake the hissing for the rasp of scale against sand, run terrified into the night from a snake that was not there. The whole world changed if you just altered your perspective a little.

I shook my head. For all I knew, the pipelines could lie like a broken dinosaur skeleton, crashed onto the sand, dry as dust, the victim of some interethnic conflict or other. For the hundredth time I contemplated, then rejected, calling up information on the project from the net. There was always the possibility of someone smart—my family, or the kidnappers—having a trace out for that kind of inquiry. I had no doubt that they were still looking for me.

I turned the screen off and went to the fridge. I pulled a beer free of the four-pack, then changed my mind and dragged the whole thing from the fridge.

One of the reasons I had taken this flat was because the living-room window opened outward onto the fire escape. From the fire escape, I could get to the roof. It was an old building, with a complicated roofline. There was one place, near the middle chimney stack—which had been blocked off years ago and served now to vent gas appliances—where the roofs rose in steep pitches on either side and I could lie on my back, face to the sky, hidden from the world. I had built six big planters up there, and filled them with dirt. One of these days I would get around to planting something in them.

That was where I took my beer.

Every city has a different-colored sky. In Amsterdam, the only city I had known until I was five, it had been gray-blue, a particular low-country Protestant shade that spoke of cheeses and oil paintings and grassy dikes. On Ratnapida it had been like light, clear glass. This city's sky made me ache. It could have been so beautiful: full of reflected river light and that soft, clear ambience that you only get near a northern sea. But the city glow stained the atmosphere like a muddy footprint.

I propped myself up by the chimney stack and opened the first can. The beer tasted cold and bitter, like the winter-morning frost I used to scrape from the old iron railings outside the family home in Amsterdam. The night was very clear. It was freezing up here. I shuddered, forced myself to drink down more frost and iron. Halfway down the can, I started to warm up.

About five miles away I could see the twinkling night lights of the bridge—the largest single-span suspension bridge in the world. And the owners were still in debt, even thirty years after opening it to paying traffic. They always would be. There weren't that many private cars anymore, and the local government had negotiated an annual fee for the slides that crossed and recrossed the river. The national government, of course, and ultimately the taxpayer were the big losers: the government had fronted the money, the contractors had spent it, and now the taxpayers were paying again, this time in local taxes for the slides.

I crumpled my can, opened another.

Corruption. It all stank of corruption. As did anything connected with any kind of government. There were layers upon layers upon layers. I thought about Kirghizia: the minister for labor and the commissar of the treasury whom I had wined and dined and eventually bought off. All so van de Oest Enterprises could make more money.

But that wasn't strictly true. It would also benefit the Kirghizians in the end. They would have clean water again. I sucked at the can. It was empty already. The third one was difficult to open. My hands were cold. I looked out at the bridge. Maybe the builders had told themselves that the local people would benefit in the end—after all, they would now be free to travel straight across the huge river instead of detouring fifty miles or more. But no one had asked the people. It had all been decided by those who met over white linen and flashing crystal, who chatted over the wine and shook hands over coffee. And took home hundreds, thousands, millions. And probably slept tranquilly every night.

I remembered the woman, the city executive who had taken Spanner and me to her flat in her private car; the heat; the film; what we had done . . . Local government. She hadn't been hurting for money. I wonder if she even knew how corrupt she was.

Did I know how corrupt I was? What did "corrupt" mean, anyway? I had never set out to hurt anyone, but I was wearing the PIDA of a dead woman. Bird was now nothing more than a plume of greasy smoke easing up into the night sky and being torn apart by the wind. I wondered what Sal Bird, aged twenty-five, had been like. Whether she had loved or been loved. If she liked her food, or smoked. What her favorite films had been. Whether she shouted out loud when she came. I wondered if anyone had grieved for Sal Bird.

I wondered if anyone had grieved for the man I had killed. I didn't even know his name. And he had been kind to me, in his way. I remembered his eyes as he knew I was going to kill him. I pushed that thought away.

I wondered if anyone grieved for me.

So, was I corrupt? I had killed a man. I was hiding from my family and living a lie. And everyone I met shied away from me. Ruth. Now Magyar. Everyone except Spanner.

When I was finishing the fourth can, I realized I was standing at the edge of the roof. My toes poked over the gutter. One more step. No more Sal Bird, aged twenty-five. No more fear about being found out; no more worries about dangerous people coming looking for me or Spanner; no more responsibility, feeling like I was the thin human wall between an unsuspecting city and an accident waiting to happen. It could all just stop. Here. Now. After all, Frances Lorien van de Oest had died a long time ago.

Dawn was breaking.

I stepped carefully back from the edge.

EIGHT

Lore is eight. One afternoon she sits with Oster in his office, watching patiently while he scrolls through several résumés. Her parents are just starting the cycle of argument and recrimination that will end in divorce a dozen years later, but Lore does not yet know this. All she knows is that her mother has accused her father of being out of touch with the workings of the vast organization of which he is the titular head, and her father has decided to take an interest in one of the van de Oest company's new ventures—the commercial production of fuel-grade ethanol.

He is talking half to himself and half to Lore as he works. "Now, do I choose this woman, the gene splicer, or should I go with James here, who performed so well on our Australian project?" Lore cranes over his shoulder, trying hard to understand exactly what her father is getting at. "Or maybe Carmen Torini?" He smiles at Lore then. "Stop peering from behind me like that. Get your own chair. Pull it up." Lore does, feeling very grown-up at the sight of their two gray heads reflected side by side in the computer screen, like equals.

He pulls up the three résumés. "Here we have three people who might do. This one is a researcher. They think in a certain way. They like elegance, theories. For this project we need someone different, someone who can smile and say, 'Well, that didn't work. Let's try again.' So then we come to James. He can make people work beyond themselves—look at what he did in Bulgaria last year when what we thought would be a simple bioremediation of a phenol spill turned so complicated." Lore loves it that he does not turn to her and ask if she knows what phenol is, or what bioremediation means. He trusts her to ask, or to look it up later. "But they were all tried-and-tested techniques. Nothing new or innovative there."

Lore frowns. "But if what he did worked, why isn't that good enough?"

"You could ask your mother that." He shakes his head. "Sorry." He taps the screen. "It's not so much what he did, it's what he didn't do. No brilliant shortcuts. No new high-efficiency methods. No record of him even contemplating anything not already done."

"Not everyone can think of new things."

"No, and there's a place for good, steady people like James. Our business is built on them. But the reason we're a leader, the reason we're so rich, little one, is that your grandmother, and your great-great-uncle before her, *did* think of new things, and were smart enough to patent them." He smiles gently. "And I was smart enough to marry your mother."

Lore says nothing to that. She senses that there is a great sadness in her father, but she knows, somehow, that it is not something she can fix. She does not want to think about it. "Who's Carmen?"

He pulls up a picture of a woman of about thirty: black curls, brown eyes, a touch of arrogance. The picture shifts to the corner of the screen and three text boxes appear. "She hasn't been with us long. Joined up from EnSyTec four years ago. Started as a quality control manager. Moved up to assistant project manager. Then your mother chose her to head that project in Caracas." He frowns. "Lots of innovation there."

Her father stares at the screen for a long time. Lore wonders what he is thinking about. He looks sad again.

He switches the terminal off abruptly and turns to face Lore. "I'm not like your mother. She always has to be doing, always in control. That's good, in its way, but it's not my way."

Lore nods, wondering if he expects her to take sides. He sees her wariness.

He ruffles her hair, laughs. "Don't look so serious, little one. People are allowed to be different." Lore wonders if her mother knows that. "Shall I tell you why this organization works so well without me? I understand good management. Some people would rather hire people less intelligent than themselves, thinking that in comparison they will look great. But that's not the way it really works. The secret of good management is to appoint smart people to work for you. It makes you look good, and it means you don't have to do so much work. Remember that." Then he looks very sad and says in a low voice that Lore is not supposed to hear, "And if you're as good at it as I am, you become redundant."

Lore is ten when the family moves. The company is not the same as the family, Lore's father is fond of saying, and it is time they had a place where they can put down roots, where Tok and Greta and Katerine can come home from their various projects and rest; where Stella can join them if she chooses; where Oster himself can stop off on the way to and from meetings in Beijing and Singapore, and Lore can come during school holidays. Where they can learn to be a family again.

Katerine leaves all the details to Oster. "Just make sure it's finished—" She checks her schedule. "—by early March. I have a window then."

The Buccaneer Archipelago lies off the northern coast of Western Australia. Cicely Island, near the southern tip of the chain, is all black rock, lush tropical foliage, and white beach. Oster buys it, renames it Ratnapida, Island of Gems, and builds a house.

Lore is the first to see it. Oster comes to her school in Auckland three days before the end of term. "I want you to see it fresh, as it's supposed to be." And though they fly from Auckland to Perth, then take a copter from Perth to Beagle Bay, Oster insists they travel the last ninety miles to Ratnapida, Island of Gems, by boat.

"The key to this place is leisure. It has to be approached in the right spirit. You and I can appreciate that."

The boat is a two-masted yacht but the wind is in the wrong direction so the captain uses the silent magnetic water propulsion. The noise of the sea is eerie.

It is mild for the subtropics, eighty degrees, and Oster wears shorts and a life jacket. They head northwest along the coast and the afternoon sun shines directly on his chest. The wiry gray body hair is almost golden in this light, and all of a sudden Lore knows what color his hair would be if his mother had not turned off her color-producing allele. She wonders idly what color hair her mother would have. One could often tell natural hair color from a person's eyes . . . She has seen her mother with brown eyes and black, violet and deep blue, green and hazel, but realizes with a shock that she does not know their real color. She has no idea of the color of her mother's eyes. She nearly asks her father, but does not: she is scared he might not know.

The boat docks at a wood and stone quay in a bay that has been scooped out of the black, volcanic rock. The island ascends in tiers of path and step and miniature waterfall to the house. When Lore sees it she understands immediately that this is her father's way of proclaiming who he is. His way of dyeing his hair. She also knows her mother will hate it.

"It's beautiful!"

Oster smiles.

It takes them more than an hour to climb to the house because Oster wants to show her every pond, every silent carp and lily, every arrangement of stone and water and hidden grotto. Lore follows him from pool to bench to bright bloom, laughs when a huge blue butterfly lifts from a purple flower by her feet. The gardens are very like him: playful, rich, and secret. Eventually they reach the top of the rise, where the secret places give way to formal grounds which give way to patio, then porch, then the house itself, almost as if there is no dividing line between inside and out.

The house is based on Indonesian styles: polished wood, high ceilings and low, stone sculpture, water, cool rooms. The gates are old iron filigree, the doors imported from a recently demolished temple. Lore is walking through her third room of wood and screen and slowly moving ceiling fans when she realizes she has not seen a single net terminal.

"Where are they?"

"There aren't any. Not in these rooms." He leads her through to the south side of the house. The change is subtle but definite. The curves of polished wood become more angular, the ceilings brighter, the air more brisk. Huge windows open to a long, long lawn with an intricate, tiled area at the far end. "I tried to disguise it a little." Lore looks more closely at the lawn, at the tiles, and notices the discreet gray stubs of sensors and sound controls. A copter pad. "When we're in a hurry, we can fly out."

Neither of them mentions Lore's mother.

.   .   .

For the first few months, the house on Ratnapida seems to be doing the job Oster intends. He always makes sure he is at the house a few days before Lore arrives at the end of the school term from Auckland. Sometimes Uncle Willem and his husband Marley are there; sometimes they can only fly in for a day or two. Tok, now a tall, serious fourteen-year-old, comes home from his school in Amsterdam, and Greta flies in from the field. Stella, who seems more like seventeen than fourteen, is there at odd times; sometimes she is sent home from school in disgrace in the middle of term, sometimes she spends the holidays with friends. Her hair is always a different color and her accent changes depending upon fashion.

Lore sees more of her mother than ever before. Perhaps under pressure from Oster, perhaps due to some last vestige of maternal feeling, Katerine makes sure that if she is not already there when Lore arrives, she turns up within a day or two. And Lore, nearly eleven, is allowed to stay up long after dinner, sipping water while the others drink coffee and wine, talking of projects, and work, and new techniques. Her eyes glaze with fatigue long before the talk winds down, and more than once she wakes up in bed and knows that her father has carried her there after she has fallen asleep at the table. But every night she struggles to stay awake, to listen to her family talk, afraid that if she falls asleep she will miss the rare and wonderful feeling that her mother, her father, her stepsister and twins and uncles all love the same thing. For a while she can believe that there is nothing wrong, that she is safe and loved and protected by a family that is whole.

One night, after dessert is just a trace of cream in her glass and the wine is gone and even Tok seems glazed and heavy-eyed, Willem pauses in the middle of filling his coffee cup and looks directly at Lore. "You're almost eleven."

Lore is startled, unused to being noticed in the evening. "Day after tomorrow."

"And I haven't got you a present yet. Is there anything special you want?"

I want to be grown-up, and then I'll be safe. Safe from what, exactly, she does not know. That confuses her, so she seizes on the symbol of adulthood closest to hand. "I want some coffee."

Willem turns to Katerine and raises an eyebrow. "Not very ambitious."

Even at ten, Lore knows when she is being patronized, and one of her father's favorite sayings pops into her head. "Sometimes the little things are harder to achieve than lofty goals."

Marley bursts out laughing. "Give her the coffee and just be thankful she didn't ask for brandy."

Lore glances at her mother, who is smiling at Marley, and at Oster, who is smiling also, but shaking his head. "Sorry, little one," he says, "I have a special surprise for you tomorrow for which you need to be up bright and early."

This is fine with Lore, who is not entirely sure she wants the coffee anyway, but before she can speak, her mother says lightly, "Oh, let the child have some coffee, Oster. Even if it keeps her up half the night, she'll be game for whatever you have planned at the crack of dawn. She takes after me in that respect. The more she does, the more she can do."

There is a silence at the table and from that silence Lore understands that she is the chosen battleground of her parents, that whatever she does, however hard she tries, one of them will feel betrayed. But she is not even eleven, and she cannot help but try. So she drinks the coffee, and gets up the next day before dawn to go fish with Oster. The night of her birthday she is included for the first time in her mother's and Greta's discussion on a reclamation project in Longzhou; she swims the following day with Oster and

Tok. She never complains and never says she is not interested when Katerine scribbles some catalytic reaction equation on a napkin, or Oster suggests they go look for some tree frogs, but by the end of the holiday, for the first time she is glad to get back to school.

At school, the principal, Mr. Achwabe, makes a comment about the fact that she has lost weight, but she just smiles and determines privately to eat more. In the evenings she reads the case studies her mother sends over the net, and talks to her father about the new species of carp he plans to introduce at Ratnapida before she comes home again.

The time she spends with her friends is almost desperate. She wants to shout to them, *Help me! Make them stop,* but she does not know how. They are her parents. They love her. She loves them.

NINE

As I walked back to the flat with my sack of flower bulbs, I wondered why autumn sunshine hurt the eyes more than sun in spring or summer. Probably something to do with refraction, with the fact that the October sky was a hard, arcing blue and the air was drier than a good gin. Whatever the reason, the slanting eleven-in-the-morning sunshine was smeared gaudily all over the remains of the night frost on rooftiles and guttering, bouncing off the front windows of passenger slides, even reflecting sharply from the lenses of one shopper's ski glasses. Everyone was wearing bright colors, their cheeks red and eyes sparkling. I doubted they were as cheerful as they looked.

Despite my hangover, I did feel cheerful, and it was somehow related to last night, my time on the roof. I felt different. Nothing miraculous ... more as though something tangled up inside me had begun to resolve itself.

My first thoughts this morning when I woke had not

been about how I had nearly fallen to my death, or the various diseases and corruptions of a city, but of the planters. Of how I had painstakingly built them, carried them onto the roof, filled them with good, black dirt. Of how they were empty. *That,* I had thought as I drank hot tea and got dressed, *is something I can fix.*

And I felt absurdly pleased with the bulbs I had selected, all locally grown: crocuses and tulips, snowdrops and marigolds, iris and verbena and salvia. Rich, bright colors that would last from the end of January up until midsummer. Maybe the scents and colors would bring bees. I tried to imagine lying on the sun-warmed tiles, smelling flowers, listening to the hum of bees, but I realized I was also hearing imaginary fountains plashing softly and the sough of wind in trees, and under all those the bone-deep vibration of sea against rock: Ratnapida.

I had to stop in the middle of the street for a man with three children who was trying to get on a slide. One of the children was refusing to budge and the man—the father, I assumed—was forced to drag him, wailing. The father shot me an embarrassed smile; I nodded as though I understood he had no other choice, but the truth was, I didn't know. Had Oster ever taken us three—Tok and Stella and me—out by himself? Even if he had, and even if one of us had had the bad manners to pull a tantrum, the family car would not have been far away to whisk us all off to luxurious privacy. I started walking again. One of these days I would be able to see flowers without thinking of family, or Ratnapida, its grass and fountains and low trees.

Maybe a tree wouldn't be a bad idea. A sapling wouldn't need too big a planter to start with, and I could get something that blossomed in spring: apple, maybe, or pear. But the wood, and the dirt, and the tree itself would all cost, and the money I took when I left Spanner was running low. I crossed the road on the ceramic safeway opposite my building, trying to work out how much I would get paid at the end of the week and, if I budgeted properly, whether or not I would have enough extra for a tree.

An old man was dragging a small shopping cart into my doorway. I had seen him before. He lived on the third or fourth floor. The cart looked heavy.

"Can I help you with that?"

He looked at me. His cheeks were sunken and his eyes filmy but his voice was robust. "Bird, isn't it? Sal Bird?" I nodded. He thought for a moment. "Fifth floor," he said, evidently satisfied with his knowledge.

I looked at the nameplates in neat rows by the ancient intercom. I had no idea which was his. He laughed at my expression.

"Tom Wilson, third floor. And yes, I'd count it a great favor if you'd help a tired old man with his groceries."

His suit jacket hung from broad shoulders; he would have been a big man thirty years ago. I wondered what it must be like to get old.

I balanced my sack on top of his groceries, and he talked as I humped the cart, one tread at a time, up the three flights of stairs. "What have you got in here?"

The look on his face was interesting: unsure whether or not it was polite to be offended at this invasion of privacy by a Good Samaritan. In the end, he grinned and said slyly, "That's for me to know and you to find out."

I smiled wryly. He was right. I shouldn't have asked. "It's heavy, whatever it is."

"Do you good." He held open a door for me and I pulled the cart gratefully onto the landing.

"Can you manage from here?"

"Didn't think you had to set off for your job for hours yet." That sly grin again. "I thought you might like to share a cup of tea with a lonely old man."

I couldn't think of any reason to refuse him, so I followed him into his flat.

It was bigger than mine, and cozy, filled with Scandinavian furniture, the blond wood and gray-nubbed fabrics of twenty or thirty years ago. Everything was very clean. He watched me take it all in. "Nicer than that tomb of a room the landlord gave you upstairs. Warmer, too. How strong do you like it?"

"What?"

"Your tea. I'm partial to strong tea myself."

"Oh. Whatever you're having."

"You won't ever get what you want unless you know. And unless you tell those who ask. I'll ask you again: How do you like your tea?"

I closed my eyes, thought back to other times. "Lapsang souchong, no milk, no sugar, no lemon, three heaped teaspoons in a pot big enough for two. And hot, not lukewarm. Served in bone china—the old kind, wafer thin, so you can see the color of the tea through the white—with a silver spoon. Steel spoils the taste." I opened my eyes. "Well, you asked."

"I did, I did. And thank you for sharing that with me." He nodded at me seriously, and disappeared into the kitchen.

He brought out a tray and took it over to the table by the window: two pots, two cups. One of the cups was Wedgwood. It had a tiny chip on the rim. He took it over to the table by the window which, unlike mine, looked out onto the street. "For you," he said, handing me the Wedgwood cup, and pointing to one of the pots. "Right out of Lapsang souchong and silver teaspoons. But I found some Earl Grey." I poured for both of us. My tea was that lovely light brown gray of undyed fine tea. His looked like treacle.

He sipped and smacked his lips. "Strong enough to stand a spoon up in."

I sipped mine. It was delicate and deliciously hot. I smiled and nodded. "Very nice."

"A simple pleasure, tea. Doesn't matter how rich or poor a person might be, good tea is good tea." He looked at me over the rim of his cup. His eyes were gray as a winter sea.

"Lot of simple pleasures are very important. Take that window, now. I can sit by it when I'm too stiff to get up and down the stairs, and watch the world. I know every one of the tenants in this building by sight. I know what time they go to work, or not, as the case may be. I know who visits them, and for how long."

I know you're lonely, he seemed to be saying. *I am, too. If you talk to me I won't pry for more, and I won't tell anyone else.* I didn't say anything.

"For example, I know that Mr. Rachmindi is moving out next month. His place is nicer than yours, and not much more a month."

"I'm happy where I am."

"Maybe you are, but think about the weather as the winter gets on. You'll be mewling with cold come January. And his window looks out onto the trees at the back, if that's what you'll miss."

"It's not that." He just waited. "It's . . ." I stood up, found my sack of bulbs, brought them back. I rolled one onto my palm. "Jonquil. In April that'll be a flower the color of hot sun on white sand." I put it on the table and took out another. "Bluebell. Like soft babies' eyes. Freesias, violets, crocuses, verbena . . ." They rolled out of the sack like toy trucks. "I took my flat because I can get onto the roof. I'm going to grow these." Where the squirrels could not get at them. "It will be a place of wild things, natural things. I need them." A tear dripped onto the lacy brown and beige wrinkles of the bulb in my palm.

Tom Wilson's papery hands reached out and folded my fingers over the bulb. "Best keep it dry," he said, and produced a large white handkerchief from somewhere. He watched silently as I wiped my face, then my nose, and put the bulbs back into the bag.

"This garden of yours . . . Will you invite me up to see it, when it starts to bloom?"

I opened my mouth to say, *I'd love to, but how will you get*

your old bones out onto the roof? and said, instead, "Yes." If he
wanted to see the flowers, we'd find a way.

I spent two hours with Tom Wilson and afterward
climbed the stairs to my flat thoughtfully.

When I got in I called Spanner. She answered immediately. "Did you get those changes made on my PIDA?"

"Last night."

"All of it?" I needed to feel safe from Magyar.

"Everything. You are now a fully three-dimensional par-
agon of virtue." She was still in that expansive, good mood.
"I was tempted to add a police record, something along the
lines of swimming naked in the docks as a protest for, oh,
animal rights or something." She grinned. "But I decided
against it."

I couldn't help it—I grinned back. She could be so
charming when she wanted. "I'm glad to hear it." Even
more glad to hear that the work was done. Now Magyar
could check all she liked.

"About that equipment," she said. "You available late tonight for a meeting? Good. I'll see you here after work."

The screen went blank.

THE MORNING of Spanner's birthday they stayed
in bed all day, eating, drinking, sometimes unbut-
toning their shirts to make love, sometimes buttoning them
again to sit up and talk. Lore told Spanner about Belize,
about the Heliconias with their leaves the size of canoe paddles, the Santa Maria pine and black poisonwood; Spanner
told her about forests she had seen on the net. While Spanner talked, Lore wondered if she had ever been outside the
city. She thought of her visit on her own to the park yesterday, how she had found a hidden corner where no one

seemed to go. She had stepped over a formal border, following a squirrel, and found herself among the dark and secret greenery of a classical Victorian shrubbery—bay and laurel and yew. Under the waxy leaves of a rhododendron she had come across a female mallard, its feathers a ruffled mix of tawny browns and beige and cream, asleep with its head under a wing. In the spring, she suspected the shrubbery would glimmer with pearly snowdrops and crocuses the color of March sunshine. Like lemon drops against the black, bitter dirt.

Spanner paused, wine bottle halfway to her mouth. "Are you listening?"

"Yes." And she was, sort of.

"Good. We're the same, you and I. We understand each other."

All Lore understood about Spanner was that whenever Lore reached for her, she wavered and was gone, like the shimmering reflection on the oily surface of the river.

"You know what it's like. To have someone kill herself. You know how it feels. Because of your sister, your sister . . ."

"Stella." It was hard to say her name aloud. Her sister's suicide was public property. She supposed it had been all over the net. "Who do you know that killed themselves?"

Spanner ignored her. "You know what that's like. How hard it is to explain to people. You can say, I saw it coming. You can say, It was only a matter of time. You can say, There was nothing I could do. And they don't believe you. Did you find that?"

"I didn't know Stella was going to kill herself."

Spanner squinted at her. "Yes, you did. She was unhappy, wasn't she?"

Lore nodded because she couldn't speak. She tried not to think about Stella and why she killed herself, because then she would have to think about Tok, about her father, about herself. "Leave some of that wine for me."

But Spanner was leaning down out of bed, bottom flashing as her shirt rode up to her waist. She seemed to be tugging on something under the bed.

"What are you doing?"

"Box." She heaved, and an ancient cardboard box slid out onto the carpet. She got out of bed and sat cross-legged by it. "There's a picture of my mother in here, somewhere." Her mother . . . Spanner scrabbled about in the box, which Lore could not see. She knew better than to try and look.

"Here." Spanner handed Lore an old-fashioned CD-ROM disk, poked about some more and came up with a flat gray drive case and some cable. She shoved the box back under the bed and stood up. "Bring the wine."

Lore followed her into the living room.

"I made the drive when I was fifteen," Spanner said as she plugged it into her system and ran a couple of tests. "Give me the disk. There."

The first picture that came up on the screen was a dog, an impossibly elegant whippet with a patch of black fur over one eye. "That's Anne Bonny. My dog, when I was nine. Looks like a pirate, doesn't she."

"What happened to her?"

Spanner ignored that. Several pictures flipped by too fast for Lore to follow. She tried to remember if whippets were expensive, what kind of money Spanner's family might have had.

"My mother." She had blond hair, lighter than Spanner's, and her face was thinner, almost hollow. She looked as though she had bird bones; one hard squeeze would crumple her like paper. Lore could not tell how old she was, but she thought she might have been around forty. She was wearing a dress of some kind of silky material, the kind that had been popular on soap operas fifteen years ago.

Lore wanted to know more about her. She was desperate to learn about Spanner. But she knew what kind of questions Spanner would ignore. "Did you take the photograph? Looks like it might have been a new dress."

"It was. She got it for her birthday. We all clubbed together for it." Not rich, then. But who did she mean by *we*? "She said she loved that dress. I looked for it, after she died. I thought I'd keep it, keep something that had meant a lot to her, you know, something that we had had between us. But it wasn't hanging in her wardrobe. I had to search the whole house. It was in a bag full of rubbish, old tat that was going to go to charity that Christmas. It was all wrinkled. Smelled like it had been in the bag for months. I threw it away." Spanner held out her hand for the wine bottle, took a long gulp, then wiped her mouth with her hand. "It was then that I realized that everyone lies. About everything. She must have hated that dress, must have been laughing at us all the time she wore it. And then she just left us. Like that. Didn't even leave a note." Spanner ejected the disk and hurled it against the east wall so hard that it chipped away a lump of plaster.

Lore took Spanner's hand. "I'm not lying. I'm not laughing at you. I want you to have a happy birthday. If you don't like the cheese plant, you don't have to pretend. If you buy me presents, I won't pretend."

She could not heal all of Spanner's hurt, she could not even offer the kind of love she thought Spanner might want, but she could offer the beginnings of trust. She hoped Spanner would know what to do with it. She thought about bulbs unfolding in the cold and dark, reaching up through the soil in blind faith.

Winter had come slowly and gently Lore's first year in the city, but the soft grays of December changed suddenly to an iron frost in January. The sun no longer reached high enough to coat the sandstone of the Polar Bear with gold. In the morning, the light was lemony-gray, like a falsely tinted black and white photograph. People walking stiffly in the cold on their way to the slide poles squinted against the long, slanting sunshine, the occasional glitter of frost on the pavement. A squirrel, its thick winter coat making it comical, like a furry dumpling, looked up at the ice-slicked cable that ran past the second-floor window, and stayed on the ground. It scrabbled halfheartedly at the frozen dirt around the roots of the tree outside. Lore wondered why it wasn't hibernating.

Outside, the temperature plummeted. Spanner went out less frequently to do business—"People don't go out as much in this weather." And Lore, who had now cleared most of the debris from the back garden and planted her spring bulbs more than a month ago, only went out to leave plates of leftovers for the cat she had seen that once.

They were watching the news and drinking loc—a hot, chocolate liqueur—when they heard about a fire in the warehouse district.

"Get your coat on."

By the time they got there, the firefighters were gone and all that was left was the stink of charred three-hundred-year-old timbers and bricks cracked open by the heat. The warehouse was still dripping, but icicles were forming, and the lake of hose water was turning to sheet ice. There was no one about; it was too cold for sightseeing. In the orangy street light, Lore's breath cloud looked like a bizarre special effect.

"Keep your eyes open."

"What—" But Spanner was already bending down, levering up what looked like a section of pavement but which turned out to be a two-foot-square panel of plastone.

"What are you doing?"

"This is the master switch"—she pointed at a red panel—"but we don't want them all." She flipped up the lid of the nearest of a row of squat gray boxes and touched something. Four streetlights went dark. She opened a second box. More lights went out.

"Come on." She pulled a hand light from her pocket. Its

blue-white beam licked at the rubble. She scrambled up over a pile of bricks and pipe. The flashlight whipped around as she turned. "What's the matter?"

Lore shaded her eyes with her hand, spoke to a silhouette. "It won't be safe. Why don't we just wait for the firefighters to come back when it's light and flatten everything. Then we could take our time."

"Five minutes after the building is safe, there won't be anything left. And there are some good timbers here."

There were. There were so many that once Spanner had a pile of what she wanted—which had cost Lore a burned finger and several scares as rafters sagged, suddenly, and floor timbers shifted—she called Billy and Ann, who brought a van. Obviously stolen for the occasion.

"But what do we want wood for?" Lore asked.

"A new front door."

"What's wrong with the one we have?"

"Does it matter? Maybe I just want a new one."

Lore eyed the beams warily. Risking their lives, just because Spanner wanted something to do.

Lore and Spanner spent nine days building a new door from the thick, old timbers they had scavenged. They took down the old door and hung the new one the afternoon the rain turned to a thin gray snow.

Lore stretched her back and kicked the old door. "I don't relish hauling it about in this weather."

"We could break it up for firewood."

"We don't need a fire. It's already hot in here." The flat was stifling. Spanner ran illegal spurs from the power lines and was as profligate with heat as with everything else: food, sex, promises.

But Spanner had disappeared into the hallway and come back with a sledgehammer. She hefted it a couple of times. Lore stepped out of the way and Spanner swung. The old door splintered with a satisfying *crack!*

"I said, we don't need a fire. It's—"

"If you're hot, open the windows. Fresh air's good for you." She swung again.

Lore did not understand Spanner when she got in these moods. She had no point of reference for the frenzy, the constant urge to do, to use, to experience that often lasted for several days at a time. So she tried to remember what she knew about open fires, and peered as best she could up the chimney to see if the flue was clear. There was no ash in the grate. "Have you had a fire here before?"

"I'm sure I must have." Rip. Splinter.

Lore moved the plants. "We'll need some paper, and kindling. I think." She rummaged around. "We don't have any paper."

Spanner paused, breathing heavily. "Look under the bed."

Lore trooped into the bedroom. Looked. "There's only your box."

"Then we'll use some of that stuff."

"No. We can—"

"Bring it," Spanner yelled. Lore sighed, and did.

"Open it." Crunch, splinter.

It was full of old photographs and documents. What looked like a birth certificate from the middle of the last century. "I don't think you'll want to use this." She started to put the lid back on, uncomfortable with the idea that she had been wrist-deep in Spanner's private family history.

Spanner dropped the sledgehammer and squatted down by Lore. She took a random handful of papers from the box, screwed them up, and tossed them on the grate.

"But don't you want—"

Spanner ignored her and kept taking handfuls from the box, occasionally tearing a large piece into shreds. "Should burn well enough."

Lore grabbed her hands. "Stop. Stop just a minute. We

120

can go buy some paper if you like. You don't have to use these." Spanner shrugged her off, hands already moving again. "Or we could use something flammable. Alcohol, maybe."

"It's just paper."

They were Spanner's memories. "Why are you doing this?" Why now, after all these years of hoarding them, keeping them safe? Spanner said nothing, but Lore thought she knew: because now that Spanner had started to talk about them—the memories, the pictures—they were a point of vulnerability for her. Get rid of the pictures, get rid of the memories. No more vulnerability. No more weak points. The armor would be smooth again. "I won't help you burn them."

Lore walked into the kitchen and filled the kettle. Instead of putting it on the burner, she stared outside. Once she could see past her own reflection, she saw there was a squirrel in the garden, digging. Digging up her bulbs, eating them one by one. All that work, gone in an afternoon. She felt bitter. There did not seem to be any point in trying.

Back in the living room Spanner laid the paper in the grate, followed by some of the smaller splinters from the door, then some larger boards. Lore watched as Spanner plugged in her soldering iron and used that to set alight the paper. Watched as a wisp of smoke turned into a river flowing upward, and the paper seemed to disappear.

"It's not working." Spanner poked at the burning mess with the sledgehammer handle. The bits of broken door were blackening, but not catching. "Why isn't it working?" She screwed up more paper, threw it on. A ball of burning paper roared up the chimney, borne on hot air.

Lore plucked a large splinter from the rug, examined it. "It's not wood," she said. "I mean, it is, but it's that pressed stuff. It's not going to burn."

"Fuck it!" Spanner threw the sledgehammer into the fire. Burning scraps of paper went everywhere. "Let's go get a drink."

They went out and drank too much and came back to hard, sweaty sex and fitful sleep. At least Lore slept. When she woke up, Spanner was pacing around the bed, talking about the projects she wanted to start on: relaying the floor, decorating, maybe rewiring the place. She had obviously been up all night, working herself up to this pitch. Lore let the talk flow over her as she got dressed.

". . . and here, I went out and got you some presents." Spanner dragged three bags into the bedroom. "Open them."

They were clothes. Some of them the kind she would wear, others not. They were all expensive.

"Pick out something nice for now and then we'll go out. We'll go shopping, buy you some other stuff if you don't like this—"

"This is just fine."

"—or we could just look around. I want to get out. I need to have some fun."

She would not stop talking. Could not. Her eyes glittered and she seemed jerky and tense. Lore chose something at random; then, seeing Spanner's eyes, she remembered her promise and chose a moss-green chenille tunic and matching leggings. "I'll wear these. They're lovely."

"And the black dress? You like the black dress?"

"I don't wear dresses much but, yes, if I wear a dress soon, this is exactly the kind of thing I would choose."

"You're not lying? You like it?"

"I'm not lying. I really like it. It's too cold to wear it today, though. I'll wear this." She lifted her original choices. "Where are we going?"

〜〜 At Hedon Road, the mood in the locker room 〜〜 was mixed: face masks had arrived, but the systems were back up.

I pulled on my mask: neoprene and plastex with knobby filters on each side of the mouth gasket. I fit-tested the mask with negative and positive pressure, tightened the strap at the back of my head. It felt strange and primitive to wear a breathing mask again. I was used to either nose filters and automatic, trained nasal breathing, or the full-face mask and air tank of an SCBA. These masks were no good if something splashed on your face, but enough to keep out most vapors and particulates—if the filters were changed every week or so.

I showed Paolo how to pull the seals tight across cheekbones and jaw. It was hard, helping him fit it without touching his hands.

As we walked into the primary sector to relieve the day shift, Kinnis clowned around in his mask, making bug-eyed-monster noises. Lots of people laughed. We were all relieved that the systems were back up. If someone or something slipped now, it was up to the machines to catch it, not us. Not me. And the system was good enough to stop most things, except the unk-unks: the unknown unknowns for which it was impossible to plan.

But Magyar did not give me time to worry about unk-unks.

We'd been on-shift about twenty minutes and one of the rakes had already jammed. Paolo and I had freed it and were just climbing out of the trough when Magyar, mask loose around her neck, walked over.

"It's against regs to free those by hand, Bird. Could be dangerous. Paolo doesn't know any better, of course, but consider yourself under verbal warning. Further infractions of Health and Safety regulations will result in a formal written warning. A third infraction will mean dismissal." Her eyes were hard and pleased.

A few troughs down, Meisener and Kinnis were wrestling with a stalled rake. I didn't need to be afraid. My records were airtight, now. I looked over at them deliberately, back to Magyar.

"Do you understand, Bird?"

Behind me I could hear the damn rake whining as it caught on something again. I pulled my mask off, jerked a thumb over my shoulder. "What do you want me to do about that?"

"Follow the regs, Bird. And don't let your productivity drop."

I think I surprised us both by laughing. "I'm good, Magyar, but not that good. Make up your mind: the regs, or productivity. Your choice. Doesn't matter much to me." I looked sideways at Paolo. "Why don't you go check on that rake while the shift supervisor and I have a little talk."

He retreated obediently.

Magyar was furious. "I could have you fired!"

"Then why don't you?" She couldn't, we both knew that. I was the best worker she had. She looked as though she was going to say more but I was tired of this, and my PIDA was safe. "Go harass someone else. Let me do my job." I pulled my mask back up and waded out to help Paolo. I just hoped Spanner had not lost any of her skill, or I would be out of a job by midnight.

The rest of the shift was hard, but I felt curiously light. Whatever I had started on the roof last night and continued at Tom Wilson's was still going on.

At the shift break I left Paolo with Kinnis and Cel, and took my egg rolls into a corner. I wanted to think.

I felt good. I was beginning to stand up for myself. I felt a little nervous, maybe. This was, after all, uncharted territory. Before, I could do or say anything I wanted: I was a van de Oest, with name, power, money, and education behind me. Now, though, it was just me speaking as me. The name didn't matter.

I listened to the rain that was now pounding down on the glass roof, and smiled. I was finding I was maybe more than who I had thought. It pleased me.

I still felt good as I left the plant, even when a truck pulling into the yard drove right through a puddle and drenched me with cold, muddy water.

The truck pulled up, the window wound down. "Sorry about that!" the driver shouted. We both looked at my dripping coat. I was wet through.

"I thought I'd missed the rain," I said, and smiled to show I knew it wasn't his fault. He waved and the truck moved another twenty yards to the unloading bay. The logo read BioSystems. I didn't think anything more of it.

When Spanner opened the door and motioned me in, I was grateful for the stifling heat. My wet clothes began to steam gently.

"I thought it had stopped raining."

"Careless driver." I was glad she was still in a good mood.

"Ah. Well, give me your coat. My robe's in the bathroom if you want to get the rest off." She saw me hesitate. "Unless you want to freeze to death it's that or watch me try light a fire."

"Once was enough." I headed for the bathroom.

"Hand me your wet things. I'll dry them while you shower."

The bathroom hadn't changed. I stripped, turned on the shower, and climbed into the tub. The hot water was wonderful.

I had forgotten how fine thick, old silk felt on warm, freshly scrubbed skin. I tied the belt, and wiped my hand across the mirror to look at myself.

Spanner's reflection stared back at me from behind my shoulder. I was proud of myself for not jumping.

"That brown does suit you." She nodded at my hair,

then walked back into the living room. "Lotion and every-thing is still in the cabinet," she called.

I stared at the cabinet for nearly two minutes before I had the courage to open it. When I did, the breath hissed between my teeth in a combination of relief and disappoint-ment: no small glass bottle, half full of oily liquid. I closed the door, turned away, and realized the muscles across my belly were tight, my breathing hoarse. Even now, after months, I wanted to feel that oil under my chin, be kissed with its musky scent in my nostrils, surrender to it hungrily.

I went into the living room. From the kitchen came the lazy thump and tumble of my clothes in the dryer.

"I've made tea." Spanner was sitting on the rug, near the tin-topped table.

"I don't want any," I said brusquely. I was angry, angry that the drug had not been there. That I had wanted it so badly. That I had not been faced, at least, with a choice. I had wanted the drug, I knew that, but now I wouldn't know whether or not I could also have refused it.

"It'll warm you up. No? To business, then." She poured for herself. "I assume you've given some thought to how long your clip will have to stand up to scrutiny?"

"A standard thirty-second spot should do it. But most of the money that's going to be donated will be within the first ten or twelve. I've told you about Stella's friends, the ri-valry between them to give as much as they can as fast as they can. Judging by the society and celebrity gossip news, it's still fashionable to be the first to give to a new charity." I remembered Stella at Ratnapida, V-handing the screen scanner, laughing at beating out her friends. And the amounts had not been small. "So it all depends on how well the equipment from Hyn and Zimmer will perform—"

"Good for several minutes."

"—and where and how the money will be moved around." That was the sticking point. Now that Ruth

126

would no longer help with false physical ID, the bank accounts would be harder.

But Spanner smiled her narrow-eyed smile. "Since you've left I've become much more sophisticated. I have this program that will skip credit through the edges of slush funds—the ones no one dares to look at too closely, anyway."

"Like?"

"Like the accounts the various media use to pay their 'unofficial sources' at various levels of government; like the accounts the police use to pay their informants."

Programs like that were not easy to get. "Where did you get it?"

"A . . . client. And it's safe enough."

If, as I suspected, she had extorted it from a daisy chainer or cajoled it as payment from a sex client, then she was more than likely right. Still . . . "Have you tested it?"

"Once."

I could only accept her at her word. "I'll want my share in debit cards, immediately. The minute we can verify the money in our chosen account."

"Agreed."

I decided I wanted some tea, after all. "Hyn and Zimmer still think they can get us the equipment?"

"Any day. They sent me the specs earlier tonight." She stood, turned on her screen. "Come over here." I brought my tea. "Take a look. Fabulous stuff. If you could make a clip good enough, I could hold the net for six or seven minutes with these."

In the glow of the spidery schematics, her face looked softer. I had almost forgotten how appealing she was when she was alight with enthusiasm. I had to fight the urge to touch her cheek. I stepped back a little. "Where are you going to get the money?"

"I'll get it in time, don't worry." She couldn't take her eyes off the technical specs.

"But I do worry." She looked so happy, so vulnerable. "Look, Spanner, we could just forget this. I mean, I know I owe you money, but I could pay it gradually. A bit every time I get paid."

"Are you out of your mind?" The hard lines were back, grooved on each side of her mouth. She stabbed a finger at the screen. "Look at that stuff. It's hard to get, expensive, and already ordered. We can't just turn around and say, Oops, sorry boys and girls, we changed our minds! And how much do you earn a month, anyway? Not even enough to pay my expenses for two days! I need money now, not in dribs and drabs over the next few years. No. You heard what Hyn and Zimmer said about these people. There's no way out now but through."

I hated her then, for getting herself trapped in such a way that all she could do was dig herself a deeper hole, but then I laughed at myself. Wasn't that what I was doing? We stared at each other a moment. Whatever she saw seemed to satisfy her.

"Now, we still need information about the net nexuses."

Spanner might be the soul of impatience when it came to other people, but when she was planning something dangerous and illegal she could wait like a cat by a mousehole. I sighed. "All right. We could both name the locations of half a dozen stations without even thinking hard. And you're good with locks. So tell me why we can't just break in and use one of those."

She almost rubbed her hands. She loved displaying her skills. "Because everyone, no matter how security-conscious—in fact, especially those who are security types—adopts patterns of behavior. The systems that check for intrusion or piggybacking will have initially been generated randomly. But those results are subject to human oversight. And people always form habits. Patterns. If we can find someone to tell us the patterns, we find a hole."

TEN

LORE IS twelve. It is one of those rare days when both Oster and Katerine are busy at the terminals and she is free to do what she wants. It is July, and hotter than usual on Ratnapida; the constant hum of the air-conditioning drives her outside, to the carp pools. Tok is already there, lying on his stomach, dipping a blade of grass in and out of the water. His sketch pad blinks, forgotten, in the grass.

He looks up. "If you do this with the sun facing you, sometimes the fish think it's an insect or something, and try to grab the grass." Lore plops down next to him and watches while he dips the grass in and out, in and out.

"I can't see any fish."

"They're there. You probably scared them away." He throws the grass away. A breeze catches it and drops it in the center of the pool. They watch it turn slowly on the water. "So," Tok says finally, "Mum and Dad giving you some peace for a change?"

Lore nods. They watch the grass blade some more. It drifts into the tiny eddy near a stone.

"Hang in there," Tok says softly. "It'll get better."

Lore sighs, lies full length on the turf. "How do you cope?"

"It's not as hard for me. They leave Stel and me alone; maybe they see us as belonging to each other somehow." He shrugs, then smiles wryly. They both know Stella belongs to no one. No one has seen her for two months; they get occasional net calls from Macau and Aspen, from Jaffna and Rio. "And I've got my art. I can say, This is what I want to do with my spare time, until I join the company. They tend to leave me alone."

"I don't have anything."

"Find something."

Lore nods.

"So, what has Dad all hot under the collar?" Tok asks.

"Some emergency about patent law in the Polynesians," she says. "He thinks the government might disallow our proprietary rights on the *Z. mobilis* pyruvate decarboxylate gene."

"Dad's pet ethanol project." Lore nods again. She can no longer see the grass blade. It must have sunk. "Oh well, if Dad gets nowhere with the law, Mum'll send in the dirty-tricks department."

Lore sits up. "The what?"

Tok grins. "Didn't think you knew about that. The dirty-tricks department are the ones who do all the dirty jobs. Illegal ones. Off the record."

"You're making this up."

"Nope. Read about it for yourself. It's in Aunt Nadia's personal file—"

"How did you get into that!"

"I'll show you if you like. Anyway—"

"What does it say?"

"I'm getting to that. It talks about a bunch of boring stuff, accounts, company coups, that sort of thing, but it also talks about 'Jerome's Boys.' Remember Jerome Gladby?"

"The old man?" The last time Lore saw her grandmother's crony, an ex-COO, he was in a wheelchair, his booming voice reduced to a thin creak.

"He wasn't always old. Years ago he used to run a group of people who did nothing but fix things that couldn't be fixed by any other means. They carried guns, false ID, everything."

"You're kidding!"

"From what Nadia's journal says it sounds like they did anything necessary: spread disinformation, stole things, sabotaged rivals' plants. It was just getting interesting when Greta came on the net and kicked me out of the files."

"Greta?" Lore is astounded. "I thought she was in Hangzhou or somewhere."

"Zhejiang. She was just on the net, I guess. Anyway, she cut me out of those files clean as a whistle. Said little brothers who meddled in people's private business came to regret it. Then she was gone. And when I tried to get back in, the files were deleted. Or she'd hidden them somewhere."

Lore shakes her head. There is no point trying to figure out Greta's motives; she has always been unfathomable. Instead, Lore tries to imagine what it would be like to have Jerome Gladby's clandestine power. "Do you think that old man used to run around like a commando, pockets stuffed with knives and earwigging bugs?"

They laugh. "I bet all he did was sit in a secret room somewhere and issue coded orders over the net."

"Hey, maybe they took pictures of rival CEOs beating their dogs and blackmailed them?"

"Or planted government information in their bags and had them arrested by the police . . ."

"Or faked up footage of them doing things with children . . ."

They amuse themselves for nearly an hour with imaginary exploits that grow more outrageous. They laugh until Lore's stomach hurts.

She is still grinning when Oster finally emerges from his net conference and they go for a walk together along the beach. He rubs his eyes every now and again, and sighs.

"Everything go all right?"

"Mostly. But they've got some new hard-line government in power who want to throw away all international protocol and claim all foreign assets as their own, especially intellectual property."

"But you fixed it?"

"I think so. We've formed a loose coalition with other corporations—especially publishers and the entertainment business, who get all their money from copyright—and we hope that the threat of massive sanctions will cool the new government's ardor."

The sun is almost setting. Lore picks up a piece of driftwood and throws it as far into the reddening sea as she can. "But if that doesn't work you could always send in a couple of assassins, right?" she asks as they resume walking.

"Now there's a nice thought. It would solve a lot of problems."

Lore wipes sandy hands down her shorts. "Then why don't you? I don't mean actually kill people, but, you know, make sure that things don't go quite right with, oh, I don't know, the national power system or something."

Oster laughs as they walk, and Lore laughs along with him at first, but then she gets more serious.

"Is it true? I mean, could you do that if you wanted?"

He stops, looks at her closely. "Where on earth did you get that idea?"

"Tok was telling me about Jerome's old group."

Oster looks nonplussed. "But that group was shut down years ago, in my mother's day."

"So it did exist?"

"Yes. But it doesn't anymore, at least not in that form, anyhow. Now it's a legitimate troubleshooting team."

They walk on some more. A cormorant dives into a wave. "So why was it shut down in the first place?"

"It got out of hand."

Lore, imagination running riot, pictures grim men and women with drawn guns. "I don't suppose they liked that. Did they shoot anyone?"

Oster bursts out laughing. "Sometimes I forget you're only twelve." He ruffles her hair. She smoothes it back patiently. "Look, let's sit down a minute." They find an old, half-buried log and sit facing the sea. "The lubricant behind all corporate machinery is money. My mother didn't have to use threats. She didn't have to fire anyone. All she did was reduce the funding for the group and tighten their accounting methods. Illegal operations are very expensive: matériel is purchased on the black market, bribes have to be made in the right places, cleanup operations are time-consuming and delicate. They simply can't work without lots of liquid cash. No funds, no operation. So those who missed the glamour days went away and found some other kind of work, and those who are left have the souls of accountants. All that double-dealing stuff is history."

Lore feels relieved but vaguely disappointed.

Lore is almost thirteen. She has mulled over Tok's advice for several months. For her thirteenth birthday she asks for, and gets, a camera and edit board. It is not hard to use: point the camera and record; slide the disk into the edit board, chop out sequences, and paste it back together to make whatever you wish. Despite herself, she becomes interested, soon exhausting the possibilities of one camera and one board and largely unaware subjects. She adds a storyboarder with basic library. Now she has thousands of faces and voices that she can dub in over those of her family.

Oster and Katerine think of her films as a diverting hobby, and after Lore has shown them deliberately inane clips, they do not ask her what she is up to. So when she asks for new library cards for her storyboarder, they smile indulgently and buy them, not asking what she is playing with. In this way, she obtains several adult libraries.

She starts with Tok's subscriptions to art zines and parlays them into membership in all the on-line camera zines she can find, hanging silently in the net, soaking up all the tricks with camera, edit board, and storyboarder that professionals, enthusiastic amateurs, and self-labeled underground anarchists boast of to each other. She never leaves messages, never lets anyone know she has been there. She trades in one camera after another until she has a Hammex 20, with which she can make films as crisp and sophisticated as any net entertainment. She keeps learning and begins to enjoy her secret life.

She discovers that if she wanders the house and gardens with her camera, Katerine does not start conversations about bioremediation in Bangui or Luanda. If Oster starts talking about getting up before dawn to go game fishing, Lore casually mentions that she will be up most of the night, filming moonlight on water for her latest art documentary. Soon she carries the Hammex with her wherever she goes, but the films she makes are secret.

Her films are wish-fulfillment, for a while: Oster and Katerine eat romantic dinners together, kiss, hold hands, disappear smiling into the bedroom. Lore, whose body is beginning to wake, wonders how her parents look when they are in bed. She watches some of the standard pornography scenes from her library, then learns how to morph the faces of her parents onto the bodies of the library actors.

Before she goes back to school, she films the pond and the quay, every room of Ratnapida. When she goes back to her dorm room, she learns how to splice setting and character, and her films fill with porn actors wearing her parents' faces, fucking doggy-style on the copter pad, hanging upside down from the stone quay, thrashing in the carp pond. They cry out with her parents' voices, get dressed using the same habitual mannerisms. They *are* her parents. As her parents become more distant toward one another, Lore brings them flesh to flesh, sometimes inserting dialogue. It does not matter to her whether their words to each other are cruel or kind; they communicate. Her dreams become confusing.

Once she almost calls Tok, but then she gets scared. He will not understand. She watches her films, over and over, and wonders what sex is really like. She lies awake at night and listens to her school friends, wondering what they know, and what they do.

ELEVEN

THE NEXT day I plugged in my film library for the first time in months. I had to believe Spanner about the hole in the pattern; that was her job. My job was to create a short commercial that would be indistinguishable from the real thing; one that would persuade the rich to part with their money—and do it fast enough for us to get off the air, get the money out of the account, and disappear before net security could work out that their signal had even been piggybacked.

What would work best, I had decided, was an appeal based on charity to older people, those Tom's age or thereabouts.

Those born before 1960 had the hardest time adjusting to change. They were the ones who would suddenly stop in the middle of the street as if they had vertigo when some shopwindow flared and called out, or get that haunted, bewildered look when the PIDA readers changed again, or the newstanks swapped to a different format.

It was a very specific expression: hollow-cheeked, eyes darting, looking for somewhere to hide. I had seen that same look on the faces of war refugees, or the foreign-speaking parents of native-speaking children. Older people were immigrants in their own country. They had not been born to the idea of rapid change, not like us.

I needed a thirty-second feature—but the real punch had to be in the first eight of those seconds. I needed to know what was going on in the world of commercial net entertainment.

I took breakfast into the living room and ate while I flipped through the offerings: a two-hour docudrama about a woman and her child fending off urban predators in a burned-out Sydney tenement; a lot of breathy pseudonews; an interactive version of *The Thirty-Nine Steps*. I watched that one for a while, fascinated at how the original film was utterly destroyed by turning it into a game, then finally settled down to a modern version of Shakespeare's *Othello*. I only needed to watch about twenty minutes to see how visual fashions had changed in the months since I had left Spanner.

What seemed to be in favor was a kind of neomodernism, a fascination for details and emphasis on texture. What I had in my library would not be good enough. Oh, there were some tricks I could play: I could redigitize chunks of it, in effect reshooting frames to give the footage a "live" feel, enabling me to make the pans slower than the original, the focuses more lingering. But I would need to do some recording of my own. For that I would need a model.

I sipped at my tea. Maybe Tom would be interested.

I turned the screen off and stared out of the window. The sky looked the same today as it might have done a hundred years ago, or a thousand, or fifty thousand. I wondered what it must have been like to grow up in a community that stayed more or less the same, from birth to death.

To be able to reach ten, or twenty-five, or fifty, and think, *There, I'm not going to learn any more. I know enough to live my life.*

Magyar stayed out of my way for the next few days, but I caught her eyeing me speculatively once or twice and knew that this was merely an undeclared truce; she had not given up. With the systems back up and the two extra bodies, it was almost relaxing.

I whistled as I transferred the figures on the board to a slate.

Paolo came into the readout station. "What does that readout there mean?"

"I thought you were trimming back the rushes on forty."

"All done." I looked. They were. He pointed to the green numbers again. "What does that measure?"

His limbs were still stiff, still carefully nowhere near touching me, but the expressionless mask that usually curtained his face had parted, just a little. It was like watching an anemone uncurl and expose its mouth, delicate and beautiful. "Nitrogen. In various forms."

"What's the difference between the kinds?"

It would have been so easy to shrug, profess ignorance, and just go about our work routine, anonymous and safe, but he was leaning forward, peering, reaching out to touch. He might never ask for something so simple, so hard to give, again. And if those tentacles tightened once more they might never loosen. So I pointed. "Nitrites, free nitrogen, ammonia. Then various subdivisions. But they're not as important."

"Show me again. More slowly." I did. He nodded after each one. His lips moved as he repeated the names to himself.

"Paolo, do you want to learn?"

He shrugged guardedly. "Sure."

I had thought his eyes were soft, but they weren't. They

were hard, like the thick brown ice that collects over muddy puddles, the kind you think you can see through until you really look. *I don't trust you,* those eyes said. *I've been played with before.*

I shrugged back. "The more you know, the easier life is. I can teach you, if you like." I hoped I could, anyway. I had been the youngest child, smallest sibling; always the student, never the teacher.

I think he knew I didn't feel as casual as I looked; he wasn't stupid. But maybe it was the fact that I was willing to pretend that made him decide to take the risk. He nodded.

"After the break, then." When Magyar took her own rest.

After the break I took him into the concrete bunker. I pointed to the red button Magyar had used a few weeks ago, feeling a little self-conscious. "I can't slide back the floor to show you just how much water is pouring in here every minute, but believe me, four and a half million gallons a day is a lot."

The numbers obviously meant nothing to him. *You can do this,* I told myself. "Try to imagine a hose as big around as a pregnant woman squirting green or orange water polluted with all kinds of dangerous and unpleasant guck at high pressure into an empty swimming pool. When the pool reaches a certain depth, the water starts to pour out the other end, so eventually you get the water roaring out the other side as fast as it pours in. Now imagine that it's an enchanted pool, that somehow during its time in there, the water is changed from stuff that will kill you to clear, clean, crystal drinking water, and that water goes straight into the mains, where old men and little children drink it from the tap. It might not sound like much, but there are two things to remember. The water in that fat hose never, ever stops. And, most important, we—you and me and Cel and Kinnis and Magyar and all the others—are the magic. If we screw up or stop working, people die."

Shock, in Paolo, was a strange turning of his arms and a blank cast to his face. I watched him struggle with the idea of all that responsibility. "But what about the machines, the failsafes?"

"They work well enough, most of the time. But if the systems go down again, or if someone misreads the alarms, or there's an aberration so momentary that the sensors miss it at the influent point, then it's up to us. And that's just assuming that the problem is something the designers have anticipated. And that it's accidental."

"Sabotage?" He blinked. "How could someone sabotage this place?"

"Any number of ways, but the best place would be right at the beginning—close the whole train down."

"The influent?"

"Right here." I pointed at the floor, which shook very slightly with the vibration of the water flowing beneath us. "Put something big or lethal in there and, assuming the systems catch it in time, they'll close everything down. If they don't catch it at once, then the contamination will go on through to the whole of the primary sector and pollute four or five million gallons. And then there's human error." I showed him the spigot, the initial test readouts—all automated—the various lights that indicated what bacteria and algae were currently being used, their estimated biomass and suggested nutrients. "Depending on what's coming in, we add biomass, or change it, or decrease nutrients. So if we get an influx of something nasty that kills selected strains, we can re-add. Or if some strain is struggling, we can add preferred nutrients or decrease the nutrients of the strain that's proliferating too much and suffocating the desired strain. The initial readouts here, and then the ones I give to Magyar, determine what amount of which strain is needed."

I led him out of the concrete bunker. "It's important to understand the general principles." I stopped by trough forty-one. "Looks like the gravel here needs reraking. You start at that side." We pulled on our masks and got to work. I waited until we had both established our rhythms. "What did you learn from the orientation video?"

He pulled himself straight, as though this was a school test.

"Keep working. Magyar won't be on her break forever."

"Oh. Well, undifferentiated waste comes in there," he pointed with his chin back to the bunker, "where it's churned up to mix the solid waste into the liquid. Then the slurry is split into eighty treatment streams and piped into the troughs. That's where bacteria change some of the more poisonous nitrogen compounds into less poisonous ones."

I was impressed. "You picked up a lot from the orientation video. But the troughs do more than start the denitrification process. They also begin the biodegradation of some of the other substances. Go on."

"The surface water is siphoned off to the next stage, to those big tanks, the transparent ones, where it's busy and noisy and hot."

"The silos are kept at over forty degrees Celsius—forty-four to be exact—for the mesophilic bacteria that do all the work at that stage." It felt good to talk about specifics after so long. "And the water's kept in violent motion—spiral jet mixers, coarse bubble diffusers—to eliminate stagnation and prevent liquid stratification, always likely with heated water. And it helps to keep those solids suspended."

He pulled down his mask to get more air. It was hard to work and talk and get enough oxygen through the filters all at the same time. "You know a lot." Faintly challenging. His look around—at the rakes, the troughs, the stinking brown smear on my plasthene-coated thigh—was clear. *If you know so much, how come you shovel shit like the rest of us?*

I was not in the mood to play games. "You don't know me, or why I'm here. I don't know you. But I've decided to trust you, anyway. And you can learn from me." I needed him to trust me. I needed to help him. I needed, just this once, to feel good about myself.

My bluntness disconcerted him. He raked away at the gravel for a while. I was content to just do my work, too, and let him think.

Eventually, he stopped. I stopped, too, and waited. "I thought that water treatment was all about separating the sludge from the liquid. But . . ." He shrugged, and I noticed again how graceful he was, but how that grace stopped short of his arms and legs. A vague memory of some hotel room and Katerine on the screen scooted almost within reach, then disappeared.

"That's the way it used to work, when the solids were going to be buried or just spread around in fields to dry and decompose as best they could and be carted out to sea in barges. Here, they're actually used. Once at the tertiary stage and beyond, the algae, moss, and duckweed use the nutrients in the sludge. The moss is taken away and recycled for the heavy metals consolidated in it, but the algae and duckweed are eaten by snails and zooplankton. The snails are harvested and added to the next stage—where they're eaten by the bass and tilapia and minnows. The fish add to the solid waste, of course, but in a form readily used by the lilies. Except in the primary sector, where the air scrubbers take out some of the more toxic gases, everything that's produced is used to increase production of something else. That's the beauty of—" I broke off and pulled my mask back up. Magyar was heading our way.

Her stride was stiff and fast, and even from here I could see the muscles in her jaw clenching and unclenching. My PIDA might be safe, but something had obviously happened to make Magyar very, very angry. I steeled myself, but

Magyar walked right past. Her rage radiated from her like heat.

I wasn't the only one who had noticed. Kinnis looked over from his trough and shrugged elaborately. I wondered what was going on.

I spent the rest of the shift alternately looking over my shoulder and telling Paolo about the delicate ecological balance of the plant.

"The snails and the plankton reproduce at a rate directly proportional to the amount of algae available, but the zooplankton is far more susceptible to metals than the diatoms, so the proportions are constantly in flux. The algae have to be monitored very carefully, and in conjunction with the moss and metal uptake."

It was a beautiful system. Every time I arrived at the pseudo-Victorian monstrosity that was this building, I was amazed that such a pile of metal and stone and glass and electricity could facilitate such a miracle: fish and flowers and shrubs from sewage and deadly chemicals. Sometimes I wasn't ashamed of my family and how they earned their money.

I might be doing a low-grade job, but what I had said to Paolo was true: We made a difference. And it didn't have to be just in the general sense. By taking the risk of talking to Paolo, even just a little, I was making a difference to him and his life, teaching him things that he could use or take with him wherever he went. Seeing the change in his face, those unguarded moments, made a difference to me, too. It made me feel as though I was doing something worthwhile. I hadn't felt that way for a long time.

The only smudge on the horizon was Magyar. I wondered what had happened to anger her so much. My PIDA was safe. Spanner had fixed it. Hadn't she? But if Magyar was as smart as I thought, then no matter how my PIDA matched my height, weight and DNA, she would know I wasn't Sal Bird, aged twenty-five, the line-worker grunt from Immingham. She would keep checking, keep digging. And a PIDA could not protect me against a personal call to Bird's last job site, a chat with the supervisor . . .

If I could just explain to Magyar what the job meant to me. Tell her about Paolo, how good I felt to be teaching him. How much easier life would be for me, for all of us, if we just let down our guards a little and talked, helped each other. Maybe I should try trusting her the way Paolo was trusting me.

I waited for her outside. Fog condensed on the street-lights and dripped onto the pavement. Even here in the city, the night smelled of autumn: damp leaves mulching, wood smoke, wool coats slightly musty from six months in the closet. Ten minutes became twenty, then half an hour.

Then suddenly she was through the gates and five paces away, fog billowing around her.

"Magyar."

She whirled, pulling her hands out of her pockets. "Bird! What are you doing here?" We stood ten feet apart. The fog made everything feel enclosed, quieted, unreal. She put her hands back in her pockets.

"I want to talk to you." My voice was steady. How odd.

"It's too cold to stand around. You can talk while we walk." She set off, obviously not caring whether I walked with her or not. She walked fast, with big strides. Her shoes were soled with some soft, absorbent material; I felt as though I were watching a film with the sound turned off.

Try it, I told myself. *Just try.* "You seemed angry. Earlier."

"I was."

"I just thought we could clear the air between us." It sounded lame. She seemed to think so, anyway. She snorted. This was a mistake. "It's just . . . Look, you were angry—"

"I still am, Bird."

But the anger did not seem to be directed at me. "Is something wrong at the plant?"

She stopped abruptly, swung to face me. "Now why should I want to tell you?"

I felt a bit bolder. "Because it might affect me and everyone else who works on the night shift. I don't like surprises."

"You don't like surprises? What a shame. I don't much like being lied to, by you or anyone else. You want to know what's wrong with the plant? Then go to your bosses and get *them* to tell you what's going on."

"I can't. I'm not who you think I am." And I was stupid for thinking I could have achieved anything, risking myself like this.

"I know you're not Sal Bird."

"I'm the only Sal Bird there is."

She waited, hands clenching and unclenching in her pockets, but when it became obvious I wasn't going to tell her any more, she walked away.

〰️ THE WOMAN on the screen had dark brown hair cut in a sharp, shoulder-length line. "Spanner? Ellen. Sorry we missed your birthday. Thought you might like—"

A woman who knew when Spanner's birthday was. With brown hair. Lore hesitated, then sat before the video pickup and touched a button. The woman on the screen frowned. "Who are you?"

"Lore." She remembered to make the word slippery, in her new accent. They stared at each other a minute. Dyed brown hair, dyed red hair.

"No wonder we haven't heard from her for a while." Ellen smiled. It was an open smile, genuine, and Lore immediately liked her. "I was calling to invite Spanner for a drink. A belated celebration. You'll both come?"

They looked at each other some more. Lore wondered what Ellen saw. She almost asked her. Instead, she nodded.

"The Polar Bear, then."

"Who is it?" Spanner came through from the shower, drinking coffee, no towel.

"One moment," Lore said to Ellen, and turned off the video pickup. "It's Ellen," she told Spanner.

Spanner motioned Lore aside, slid into the chair. Lore was not surprised when she turned the video back on. "Hey. Did I hear something about a drink?"

"You did." Ellen grinned, looked Spanner up and down. "You seem in the pink."

They both laughed, and Lore felt like a child left out of a grown-up joke.

"Ten tomorrow?"

"Fine."

"We'll expect both of you," Ellen said, and the screen went gray.

"Who's 'we'?" Lore asked.

"Ellen and Ruth."

"The PIDA picker?"

"The same. Maybe some others."

"I feel like I'll be presented for inspection."

Spanner shrugged. "You know how it is. People always want to check out who you're with."

People, not friends. "Business?"

"Dilettantes. Ex-dilettantes at that."

Later, in the Polar Bear, as she sat at a table with Ellen and Ruth, and Billy and Ann, Lore thought she must have imagined the edge of disdain in Spanner's words.

Spanner was in high gear, drinking hard and dragging the others along in her slipstream. She smiled at Ellen and Ruth, bought them drinks until their cheeks were red and their eyes sparkled, until they laughed out loud and their bodies moved more freely. She drew the normally surly Billy into the circle until his pinched face relaxed and he stopped looking at everyone sideways; she listened attentively until Ann stopped punctuating all her sentences with a nervous laugh. Spanner's energy pulled them all together, made them relax and feel good.

Lore found herself being sucked in, despite herself; felt Spanner's attention like a small sun. She wanted to turn her face to that warmth, bask in it.

The late evening turned to midnight, then one. Ellen and Ruth made vague motions toward leaving, but Spanner waved them to sit down again and ordered another round. She made some joke about enjoying life while you can, even when you had joined the ranks of the faceless employed, and everyone laughed. And in that unguarded moment Lore saw Spanner's expression change.

It was a subtle thing: the raised eyebrows that had been full of concern and interest were now canted just differently enough for Lore to reread them as sardonic—contemptuous, even. She glanced around the table, caught Ruth's face, and realized that Ruth knew: Spanner was scoffing at them for joining the sheep; for no longer living on their wits; for being soft. She looked away, studied her beer.

IT WAS a bright, sunny morning, cold in the metallic-tasting breeze but warm where the sun bounced off sandstone and pavement. I stopped in one of those sun traps on the way back from the shops and enjoyed the warmth while I could. It felt like a moment, a bubble stolen from the summer, as though maybe while someone had been away for July and August with their windows closed, the sun had heated their room, made it warm and round and smelling of dust and hot carpet, and then the flat owner had returned from a long holiday and opened the window and let out this last, little bit of sunshine. I didn't want to go back to my flat and be alone all day.

I knocked on Tom Wilson's door. "I bought some Lapsang souchong."

"You'd best come in, then." His eyes were bright, but he walked stiffly. "Sit down, sit down. The kettle's boiled." I sat while he fussed with trays and teapots and cups. His slippers shuffled as he carried everything carefully to the window-side table. I poured. "Now, then. What's on your mind?"

"I need your help."

He smiled. "Well, that's gratifying."

"What I want you to do isn't exactly legal. That is, what I want you to do, here, wouldn't break any laws, technically, especially if you said you didn't know what it was all about—"

"You're planning to get caught?"

"No." I wished he wouldn't yank me to a standstill like that.

"Glad to hear it. Is what you want to do dangerous?"

"Not physically, no."

"Who will it hurt?"

Not *Will it hurt anyone?* but *Who.* He wasn't smiling, exactly, but his sandy-gray eyebrows were slightly raised, and the deep lines in his cheeks were deeper. "Some people's pride. A few very rich people who get their kick out of patronizing the poor, and the executives in charge of net security."

"And who will it benefit?"

For one wild moment I wanted to treat him like a father confessor, pour out my whole life—the kidnap, the years with Spanner, the trouble I was in and how this might, once and for all, get me out, but then I realized I was looking for forgiveness, absolution. "Me. It will benefit me, and a friend, and you. If you decide to help."

148

"Then tell me more."

"Spanner and I are going to piggyback the net signal with a thirty-second commercial of our own. No one will know that it's not genuine." I told him about Stella, the fashions of the rich Almsgivers. "So we put our signal out there and these ghouls send money, which gets electronically shunted up, down, and sideways and pops out in the form of anonymous debits which we then take and spend. End of story, except that we need some footage we can't get from the library. We . . . I need to film you."

"Nice to be needed. But as you can see," he gestured at his swollen knuckles, "I can't always get out and about. Could you film it here?"

I nodded. "And I can doctor the disk, make it look as though I shot through a zoom—maybe through a window or something, without your knowledge. Just in case."

"Good enough. What sort of things will I have to do?"

"The main thrust is going to be about how the elderly are feeling bemused by the world. I want to show how things have moved too fast for some."

"The more things change, the more they stay the same."

"Um," I said, noncommittally.

"You don't agree?" His hand shook a little as he put down his teacup. "Rape, murder, torture, it's all been done before. Loneliness, joy, love—been around for thousands of years. Clothes are different, but there's always been fashion. Food is different, but there's always been taste and fads. Oh, there may be new ways to read books these days, there's the net instead of radio and these silly PIDAs instead of a good leather wallet, but people don't change. Not really." He laughed. "The expression on your face! Live a few more years and you'll find out. Nothing really changes."

"But how did you feel when your money no longer worked and you had to get a PIDA?"

He shrugged. "It was twelve years ago. I was a bit uncertain at first: What if something went wrong in a computer and my account got tied up? How would I pay the rent then? But after a month or two I liked it. No more rushing to the bank. No more filling out bills. Everything's so easy."

"For some," I said. "I heard a story once about when the book reader first came out, a young man gave one to his grandfather. He turned it on, pulled up a copy of *To Kill a Mockingbird*, and showed grandfather how to change the pages. Granddad said, Thank you very much. The younger man left him happily reading. A year later, when he went back to visit, the young man found his grandfather reading the same book. 'Wonderful thing, this reader,' the old man said, 'but I wish they'd brought out some different stories.' The old man had no idea that there were nearly twenty thousand different books on that disk. That he could have bought hundreds of other disks, or simply downloaded others—anything at all—from the net. He was used to a book being immutable. The fact that the words on each side of the 'page' changed didn't make a difference: this was *To Kill a Mockingbird*, so how could it be anything else?"

We looked at each other thoughtfully.

"Anyway," I said, "that's what I want to look at. And don't worry about acting. All I want is some standard shots of you sitting, walking, talking, reading, eating. My programs can change your expression and put you in the street or whatever. I'll give you ten percent of my cut."

"When do you want to start?"

"How about now?"

TWELVE

LORE IS midway between thirteen and fourteen. It has been months since Oster and Katerine have spoken to each other about anything but business. Now it is late spring and all of the immediate family except Greta are gathered together at Ratnapida for the first time in almost a year.

"I've ordered a picnic," Oster tells them all. "We'll take in the grounds, sit in the sun and relax together. No," he says to Tok who is folding up his screen to take outside, "we're going to leave all the bloody paraphernalia in the house for a change."

They walk single file behind Oster, who is carrying the rug, to the pond, the ornamental one with the fountain. Lore assumes he has chosen this one, the first in a series that becomes progressively less formal, because Katerine hates the casual disorganization of nature. Lore knows they do sometimes think of one another, try to please each other, to find common ground, but they are like two planets following separate orbits.

It is a beautiful day; the sun is lemony and light, not too hot, and the grass is that particular lush bright green only seen when the first flush of spring growth is ending. Everything should be perfect, and everyone tries—lots of oohs and ahs about the food, some conversation about the two-year lawsuit against the company, which is nearing its climax in Caracas—but it is an effort. Lore watches Katerine stare into the distance, then reach to her belt for the slate that is not there before she remembers she is supposed to be relaxing. Tok sits on the grass, just outside the intangible circle of family on the rug. Every now and then he reaches to the plate in front of him and picks up some rice salad between his fingers, but most of his attention is focused on the pile of twigs and leaves and a pebble before him. Lore wonders what he is making, but Oster is in the way.

Oster is talking to Stella, who is sitting on the stone rim of the fountain, drinking straight from a bottle of vodka. This month, Stella's hair is layered: bruise purple on top and underneath—when she lifts her head to swallow—red, then ocher, then white. Unnerving, like splitting open a bruise with a scalpel, seeing blood, fatty tissue, bone.

"So, tell me how you managed to stay out of the scandal at Belmopan last month."

Oster's words suggest he is tolerant of and mildly amused by Stella's increasingly wild exploits with her set of friends, but Lore can tell—by the way his fingers are pick-picking at the cloth of his shorts and the glances he shoots up at Stella from under his brows when he thinks she is not looking— that he does not understand his daughter any more than he would if he had planted a potato and grown a rose.

"I wasn't there that night." She pauses to suck at her bottle. "I was passed out in my room."

Lore wonders about that. She thinks either Stella drinks less than she pretends to or she is extraordinarily lucky. For while Stella appears to go through the motions—driving recklessly while under the influence of various drugs, swimming with sharks while drunk—the accidents she has only ever seem to involve property or the occasional species of wildlife not on the endangered list.

"I assume you have at least six people who are willing to back you up on that," Oster says, trying for irony, but sounding waspish.

Stella laughs, and Lore wonders if the rest of the family understand how shrewd her sister is. In the last four years of wild behavior, she has never injured herself or another person, nor been the subject of any scandal that would have a negative impact on her character. Media-literate people on five continents probably know her name, but they speak it with a smile and a shake of the head, not with a spitting curse. Lore has always wondered why Stella does nothing with her intelligence and wit but travel from one party to another with as much fanfare as possible. She wonders for the first time whether or not Stella has a purpose, but cannot figure out what it might be.

It is getting hot. The sunlight makes Stella's upturned bottle sparkle. "I think I'll take a swim." She sets the bottle down on the rim of the fountain and stands up. She has unbuttoned half of her dress before Lore realizes she has no clothes on underneath. Oster is a little slower.

"What are you doing?"

"Preparing to climb into this nice cool water with the fish. Who probably have more feeling than some people." She glances over at Katerine, who pretends not to notice.

"But . . ." Oster seems to know he has missed something.

Stella pauses, dress halfway off her shoulder. "What's the matter? Don't you want to see what a fine figure your daughter has?"

Katerine simply ignores them.

"Stella! This is not appropriate—"

Stella laughs, a great, brittle shout. "Appropriate? Since when has this family ever been *appropriate*?"

Oster is looking confused and Katerine still staring at nothing when Stella lets her dress fall from her shoulders and steps into the fountain. The dress catches on the vodka bottle and as the material sinks, waterlogged, into the fountain, the bottle teeters, then falls toward the pool. Katerine and Oster dive for it at the same time. Lore is not sure who actually catches it, but the bottle comes up out of the water grasped by two tanned and streaming arms. Oster relinquishes it to Katerine. He wades into the fountain and shouts. "What are you doing? I don't understand you. Why are you doing this?"

But Lore is watching Tok, who is looking at Stella, and his expression is terrible, as though some huge revelation has fisted into his face and crumpled it like tin. He has a twig in his hand and Lore can see how white the skin is where he grips it. She wants to rush over there and cry *Tok! Tok!* but quite simply dares not. She thinks that if she calls him back from whatever horror he has seen he will return without some vital part of himself. She has read many fairy tales and understands instinctively that those who are dragged places unwillingly must find their own way back. She wonders what place he has found, what he has seen.

But then Oster slips and falls to one knee. He stands up making cross sounds, and sloshes his way back to the edge. "I'm going inside to change," he says to Stella, who has her face tipped up to the sky and seems to be smiling. "When I get back I expect you to be sobered up and decent." He stalks off. "I will not be mocked in my own house . . ."

Katerine is examining the vodka bottle, seemingly unperturbed. Lore glances back at Tok, who is now sitting still and sad by his pile of twigs. She catches his eye and he shrugs slightly. Lore does not understand, but she knows no one will explain; she does not even know the right questions to ask.

When Oster is out of sight, Katerine, still not looking at Stella's body, says, "Your father has asked you to be decent by the time he returns."

"Does my body offend you, Mother?" The words are a challenge, but the tone is tremulous, as though Stella has gone much, much further than she intended, and does not know her way back. Katerine turns slowly, deliberately, and looks at Stella.

Lore wonders what Stella sees in her mother's eyes. Her sister goes utterly blank. She steps from the pool mechanically and reaches for her dress. No one says anything while she fastens her buttons. She looks at the bottle, but Katerine is still holding it. Lore understands that Stella is unwilling to step any closer to her mother to reach for the vodka.

Stella, hair dripping, uncertain whether to reach for the bottle or leave without it, looks like a whipped dog.

"Your father will want to see you here when he gets back," Katerine says. She smiles, and Stella sits abruptly, leans back against the stone fountain rim, and closes her eyes. Just like that, she absents herself. Gone. Lore has seen Greta do that: just disappear. Tok returns his attention to whatever he is building from sticks.

Katerine lifts the bottle from the stone rim, checks to make sure the cap is secure, then looks at Lore speculatively. "Tell me," she says, "if Stella had dropped the bottle in the fountain and it was, by some miracle, both uncapped *and* full, how would you have gone about the remediation of the pond system?"

Water tinkles, the sun beats down, and Tok strips the bark from a twig while Lore tries to work out the approximate flow per minute in gallons from this fountain to the next pond and the next; the effect of about a pint of raw alcohol on the flora and fauna; the breeding rate of carp . . .

Tok makes some involuntary movement.

"What?" Lore asks.

He sighs. "It's a trick question, Lore. We were taught that the first thing to remember when faced with—"

"The first thing to remember when faced with a problem," Katerine interrupts, "is not to make the problem more complicated than it is. With this surface area," she gestures at the series of ponds, "and this heat, a pint of vodka would evaporate before it did any damage that would not remediate itself naturally in a week or two."

Lore digs a hole in the turf with her finger. She feels stupid, the idiot younger sister, the one who never knows what's going on, the one always left out of the joke. But when she looks up, Katerine is smiling at her and it's a nice smile, not cruel at all.

"You looked like you were working out some pretty complicated reactions. Had you considered and included the lethal-fifty dose for fish?"

"Yes," Lore admits shyly, "except I don't know the alcohol concentration L-fifty for freshwater fish so I was going on the figures I read in that report last year on the spill of ethanol in the salmon fishery in Scotland, so—"

"You read that?"

Lore nods cautiously. "I try to read as much as I can."

Katerine smiles. No, she beams, and Lore cannot remember getting that kind of approval from her mother before. She smiles back, tentatively.

"That Scottish job was complicated by the fact that the ethanol was contaminated by printers' ink." Katerine absently fills a plate, hands it to Lore.

"I know. I tried to compensate for that. But it was mostly guesswork."

"It often is, at least in the evaluation phase of a project." Katerine begins to fill another plate for herself. "Did you try for a differentiated flow rate or go for a median rate?"

Lore sits up straighter. "Wouldn't a median rate defeat the object? I mean, when Willem took me round the plant in Den Haag he said the whole point was to calculate and bear in mind the different rates at which living things speed up or slow down flow." She gets a nod and an encouraging smile for that. "And that's not even taking into account the different ways those plants act on the contaminant . . ."

And Lore finds that she is enjoying herself. Her mother is talking to her as an equal, not as the family pawn, the commodity to be traded on for points. When she is the center of attention she does not have to think about Stella, does not have to worry about Tok and what he saw. And she finds that while she talks of flows and systems, she has images in her head of bright water and cool colors, of sunshine and green plants. It is a miracle to watch phenol turn to carbon dioxide, to see metal absorbed by moss and made harmless, to see a natural ecosystem survive because someone, somewhere, bothered to sit down and think about a way to design a biosystem to augment it.

As the sun begins its downward slide and the blades of grass cast longer shadows, and she and Katerine continue to talk, she wonders if her grandmother—the rich one, the one who was stupid enough to spend money playing with their genes but smart enough to also tailor bacteria that made her family's company possible—ever saw whole systems shining in her head that way Lore does that afternoon.

When Oster gets back wearing his clean, dry clothes, Lore looks up and is about to smile at him, happy, when she realizes Katerine is grinning, hard, in triumph, as if to say, *See? Her heart is mine!*, and Lore's smile falters and she feels the shining systems in her head crack and tarnish.

Spring is long gone and the summer grows tired and hot and brown around the edges. Tok suddenly announces that he is ready to take on more responsibility and leaves immediately for Louisiana to take charge of the family's ongoing remediation project in the bayous. He has avoided everyone since the picnic, even Lore, and she suspects he wants to work harder not because he wants to assume the burdens and privileges of adulthood, but because he does not want to have time to think about the place he went to, the thing he saw, when he looked at Stella in the fountain.

Lore spends some time with Oster, trying to count the number of fish species in the azure and turquoise waters off the island. Her hair turns gray-white, like ash, and her skin darkens. Oster gets more pensive.

The water is as still as glass, and Lore is staring out at the distant horizon, thinking of nothing, when he asks, "Has Stella talked to you?"

Lore does not turn to look at him and does not ask what he means. "No."

"She must have said something."

"She didn't. She never talks to me."

"What about Tok?"

"What about him?"

"Don't be difficult, Lore."

Lore feels something rising up inside her, hot and empty, like an air bubble. "Tok hasn't said anything, Stella hasn't said anything. Nor have you or mother, not even Willem or Marley or Greta. No one ever really says anything." As she lists the family she notices how easily they slot into subsets, all but her.

Oster has the grace to look down at his feet. "It's just that I forget you're not little anymore. I'm used to you being the baby of the family. I think of you as being seven, of sitting up in bed demanding to know why your hair is gray. And it's still gray."

"What do you mean?"

He opens his hands, pleading for understanding. "Stella started dyeing her hair when she was eleven. Tok when he was twelve. Yours is still gray. I look at it and immediately think: Still too young to dye her hair, thank god."

Lore touches her white-gray hair self-consciously. Her youthful vow to never dye it now seems childish, as irrelevant as milk teeth.

Lore is fourteen two days before term begins. She arrives at school in Auckland with hair dyed in black and white flashes, like a head of lightning.

Lore is someone else and it excites her. She wonders why she didn't start dyeing her hair years ago. Now when she looks at herself in the mirror she sees a young woman who has designed herself. She can do anything she wants. She toys with the idea of wearing lenses but decides she likes the gray eyes and black and white hair. It gives her a cool, distant look, like the faces of dead heroes buried under ancient ice. It is a face that knows.

But what Lore knows is only through film. The time has come to discover with her body.

She calls up her anonymous friends on the net and asks about sex clubs.

The films Lore has seen and made are hard-core, not glitzy, romanticized versions of the truth, but, even so, the truth is more than she expected. The bar seems bright and friendly from the outside, as though there is nothing to hide, but the people Lore watches as they go in pay the cover using temporary debit cards, probably bought from one of the score of midtown dealers who convert PIDA credit to anonymous cards for a two-percent commission. Lore waits until they have disappeared inside, then offers her own card.

The hot, crowded bar smells. Beneath the high tickle of perfume and the raw throaty sting of alcohol lies the heavy, deep scent of bodies clothed and unclothed: leather, latex, the tang of sweat and excitement, and older smells, the kind that come from the stains the dim lighting is designed to hide. A thick bass line slides between and through the bodies standing at the bar, sitting at the tiny tables, dancing on the floor. It pushes against Lore's abdomen, like a hand.

She heads for the back room.

A woman at the door stops her, hands her something. A leaflet. In the back room it is too dark to read anything but the header: *Safer Sex Guidelines.* Lore puts it in her pocket and heads for the scene room.

There are about a dozen women there. Some are engaged in sex, some are watching. One woman with long hair and fashionably loose muslin clothes stands by the wall. She is petite but not frail and there is a bag at her feet. Lore knows what she should do: she should catch the woman's eye, walk over, and lay her hand on the woman's arm; she should look into the woman's eyes and say in a voice that means *Let's pretend,* "I'm Star," or Jade or Ellie, "a helpless, nervous virgin," and then they would just . . . do it. She has seen pictures of everything. She knows how it goes. But life is different from pictures.

She does not know what to do.

The woman sees her, smiles. Lore smiles back, then blushes. The woman pushes herself off the wall, hesitates. They both walk toward each other at the same time.

"I . . ." says Lore, and feels paralyzed.

"I'm Anne," the woman says, and takes her hand.

It is like the closing of an electric current, and suddenly Lore knows everything will be all right. They move off into a corner where a woman nods them to a stairway. Lore knows she climbs the stairs, but all she remembers is the feel of another woman's hand in hers. And there is a bed and some words but Lore barely pays attention. For years her want has been undirected, amorphous, aimed now at some figure on the net screen, now some character in a novel, but for the first time she knows exactly who will touch her, will kiss her, will make her sweat. *This woman. This woman* with her long hair and small hips will ease inside her clothes; *this woman* with the New Zealand accent will open her legs and smile conspiratorially when she finds Lore wet; *this woman* will slip her fingers inside Lore and talk to her and encourage her and fuck her until her tendons strain and she starts to thrash and then cries out until her throat is raw.

Lore feels her need boiling up inside her like lava in a bore. "Now," she says, "now," and pulls Anne to her, not knowing whether to laugh or cry with wonder when soft breasts touch hers and that beautiful mouth, soft as plums, fastens on her neck. She comes as soon as Anne touches her through her clothes, and feels a string of orgasms waiting to be told off, one after another like beads.

"Again," she says into Anne's neck. "Oh, again and again and again."

Lore is fifteen. It is summer once more, and she has been at Ratnapida for nearly five weeks. She is being driven demented by the constant push-pull of her parents. She wishes Tok were coming—but he is on a project on some island chain or other and will not be there for three or four days.

She digs out her camera again.

She has gone beyond putting her parents in fantasies, and now that she has the real thing, library sex is not much fun. So she uses the camera to make herself real. She takes it into the garden and films trails of ants moving endlessly as a stream between a fallen mushroom and their nest. At night, she plays the sequence to herself: only she has seen this. It is her vision, unique. No one else has seen these particular ants in this particular lighting. It is something to hang on to.

Something to hang on to becomes a genuine interest. She takes the camera down to the most secret of the carp ponds and finds that seeing through its lens makes her a more disciplined observer. She sees a frog, and films it carefully. Later that afternoon, she goes back, gets the frog in

her viewfinder, and realizes it is a different frog. It is a revelation: frogs are not all the same. This one has a dull patch
under its throat where shadows gather as it waits patiently
for a fly to pass by close enough to hook with its tongue.
She is fascinated by its eyes, the nictitating blink.

Hours later, when she turns the camera off and stands,
her knees are stiff, but she is happy. She has discovered a
whole new world: frogs and mosquito fish, caddis flies and
damselflies, cattails and duckweed and the slow, stately open
and close of water lilies. She smiles as she falls asleep that
night.

One evening Stella and a horde of her friends descend
upon the island, glittering with jewels, their clothes and hair
shimmering like peacock feathers. As far as Lore can see,
they do nothing but change clothes, party, and boast of who
has given how much to what charity. They watch the net,
and when charity commercials run, they transfer money via
PIDA to the charity accounts. And they do it fast. Seconds
count—microseconds, even. They have asked the charities
to provide official lists of who has given what to whom and
when, and the charities, being practical about money matters, have obliged. It is now chic to appear as the first donor
to any charity, even more so if the unknown fledgling organization grows into an international institution or becomes
popular with average people. Stella and her friends call
themselves the Almsgivers. Although no doubt various of
the agencies are glad of the largesse, Lore finds it mildly dis-
gusting that it is nothing but a game to these people. Sometimes it is hard to believe that Stella is Tok's twin, her sister.

She is glad when Stella leaves and takes her crowd with
her, but then there is nothing to come between Lore and
the rest of her family.

Six of them sit down to dinner: Lore, her parents, Greta,
and Willem and Marley. No one speaks while they shake
out napkins and servants bring bowls of cold consommé.
Fans turn slowly over their heads. Lore feels like an alien.

The others all seem to be in their own private worlds. Greta as usual is almost Zen-like in her invisibility. Lore often thinks of her as being gray and somehow shriveled, but her skin is fine and close-pored, soft, like a honey glaze. Her eyes are deep brown. Lore wonders if she gets that color from Katerine, or from her father, the man Katerine divorced ten years before Lore was born. Willem, too, has dark eyes. Lore decides that Katerine's eyes must be brown, but *brown*, she decides, is not enough. She is Katerine's daughter, she has a right to know.

Just as she opens her mouth to ask, the butler appears at her mother's elbow with a silver tray. "A letter from Mr. Tok," he says.

"He always did like to do things the old-fashioned way," Oster says as Katerine opens it. Across the table Willem picks up his spoon and sips at the soup. The others follow suit.

Katerine folds the letter carefully and tucks it under her plate. She picks up her spoon. "He's not coming." Her voice is steady, but Lore hears something, the slightly faulty note of a cracked bell, and is immediately alert.

Willem must have heard it, too. He leans and slides the letter free. He scans it quickly, then reads aloud. "Dear Everyone, I'm afraid I won't be able to make it to Ratnapida as promised, but I've taken an opportunity I wish I had taken years ago. Mother, I'm sorry, but I've resigned my job as project manager and don't intend to take it up again. Sahla is competent until you find a replacement. I'll be in touch soon." Willem puts it down. "It's just signed, Tok."

Everyone is looking at Katerine. She seems calm, but Lore understands that she is devastated. It means the world to her that her children work in the family business. For the first time in years, Lore feels something for her mother apart from the urge to please. She feels the need to protect her. Katerine looks so fragile.

Oster sighs. "He's probably decided to go study the flute, like he was always threatening to do."

"What?" Katerine looks dazed.

"The flute," Oster says again. "He has always loved music."

Lore is staring at the table, watching dozens of tiny fans turn the wrong way in the spoons, trying to understand. Music. Her brother, Tok, has always loved music. How had she not known this? She looks at her father. And how had he known? She looks at the family, at Greta and Katerine, Willem and Marley, and wonders what else she does not know.

Why did Tok say nothing? Why did Oster not tell her? Something inside her twists just a little.

". . . working on the phosphorus problem in the Lau Group islands," Greta was saying.

Katerine seems to have moved out of her daze. "Is Sahla up to that?" she asks Marley.

Marley shakes his head thoughtfully. "I don't think so. No."

Katerine wipes her mouth decisively and drops her napkin on the table. "Then I'll fly out there tonight."

"Katerine," Oster says. "For god's sake. You can call him instead. And he knows how to ask for help. He—"

"Who knows when Tok wrote that letter—"

"It's dated three days ago," Willem says.

"—how long Sahla's been out there alone, making who knows what kind of errors. Costly errors." She pushes her chair away from the table.

"It's not a big project. Not that important—"

But Katerine is already standing. "I'll fly tonight."

Lore finds herself standing, too. "I'll come with you." She tries not to see the hurt in Oster's eyes.

THIRTEEN

MAGYAR WAS not around when the shift started, and Paolo was as eager as ever to learn. We were scheduled to check the leachate barriers under and around our troughs, a tedious, time-consuming job. It seemed like a good time to start him at the beginning.

"There are all kinds of different ways to classify bacteria. There's temperature: thermophilic bugs prefer hot water, fifty-five to seventy-five Celsius; mesophiles like it medium; psychrophiles a bit cooler. They can be grouped by how they do or don't use oxygen. Aerobic bacteria only work in oxygen, anaerobic only work without it, and facultative bacteria work with *or* without. Beyond that, there's what the bugs eat. Heterotrophic bacteria feed on organic carbon sources, and autotrophic bacteria utilize carbon dioxide. Lots of those categories can be further divided into gram-positive and gram-negative, which is to do with the difference in the cell-wall structure." Paolo looked confused.

"You'll have to stop me when I talk about things you don't understand."

Maybe someone had told him to shut up at school. Asking questions did not seem to come easily. I just waited. "What's the difference between bacteria and fungus?" he asked diffidently.

Fungi, I thought, but now wasn't the time to correct him. I wasn't sure where to begin. "There are different ways to differentiate, but for our purposes, the difference is in how the microorganisms go about breaking down pollutants. Bacteria produce enzymes that break down the bonds between elements in a carbon chain. The enzymes are specific to certain types of organic compounds, and they're intracellular." He looked blank. "It means that the contaminant has to be soluble. It has to be able to enter the bacterial cell. So if the contaminant is a heavy organic, then a fungus is probably better. The enzymes they make also break down the carbon bonds but they're nonspecific and extracellular. So they need only close proximity, not solubility." His face was closing up. "Where did I lose you?"

"Everywhere." His eyes were hard and dry, but his voice shook. "I don't know enough to even learn. What's a carbon chain? Or organic? An enzyme? What does soluble mean? I feel like there's a whole world floating just out of my grasp, as though I'm blind and you're talking about colors. *Heterotrophic,* you say, or *enzyme,* and you may as well be talking about . . . about *flying* to a bird that's had its wings chewed off!"

He turned away and I wanted to reach out to him, put an arm around his hunched shoulders. I remembered just in time that he didn't like to be touched.

"I'm sorry. It's my fault for starting in the middle instead of the beginning."

"You just didn't expect me to be stupid," he said bitterly.

"You're not stupid." He wouldn't turn around and look

at me. "Paolo, listen to me. You're not stupid. Not knowing the right definitions is no different from not having the right tools to fix a burst water pipe. You can learn. I can teach you."

He looked at me over his shoulder for moment, then turned all the way round. "Can you?"

"Yes."

He studied me. By his expression, he didn't know whether he wanted to believe me or not. Hope could be dangerous.

He probably needed time to think. "We need to get all these barriers checked and that feed line on forty-two unclogged before the break. We can talk about it more then." He seemed relieved.

Paolo and I were the last into the breakroom. When we got there, both screens were off and the assembled shift was very quiet. Magyar was there, with Hepple. Her eyes were as hard as beryl.

". . . and so our acting shift manager—"

"Night manager, now." Hepple was smiling slightly and rocking up onto the balls of his feet.

Magyar forced a smile. "Mr. Hepple, recently promoted to night manager, has decided to take a look, in person, at our particular part of the operation. He'll be on duty with us this evening." So. That was what she was angry about. He was checking up on us and, by implication, her.

Hepple nodded at her, a patronizing, dismissive little gesture. It made me angry. "Thank you, Cherry." Oh, he was enjoying himself. "As you may know, I have long asserted that Hedon Road could be even more efficient than at present. I have been given this new position with a mandate to improve productivity. Toward that end, I have decided to pay closer attention to the on-floor management process."

Magyar's smile was brittle. We were *her* team, only she

could harangue us or praise us, and now Hepple was embarrassing her in front of us all. Judging by the way she kept her body turned slightly away from him, the stiffness in her shoulders, she wanted to stuff him in our dirtiest effluent and watch him swallow sewage. "And now we'll leave you to take your well-earned break in peace." She stressed *well-earned*, letting us know that this was not her idea, that she knew we worked hard enough as it was without being dogged every step of the way.

But Hepple had not finished with us. "I'm looking forward to watching you all in action. I'm sure I'll find— despite Cherry's protestations of understaffing—that you are a fully capable and hardworking team. That's all."

He seemed to be waiting for us to leave, then remembered it was our breakroom. He nodded at the room in general and opened the door. Magyar preceded him.

"Christ," Cel said. "That's all we need."

"I thought Magyar was going to pop him." Kinnis sounded as though he wished she had. "What do you think of that crack about 'Cherry's protestations'?"

Cel pulled a meat roll out of its self-heating carton and blew on it. "Means we won't be getting any more workers, and that he'll be looking for someone to fire and not replacing them."

"He's an ambitious little snot," Meisener said. There were general nods. One or two people wondered out loud if now might not be a good time to look for a job somewhere else. "I looked around before I signed on here," Meisener said. "Nothing. Tighter than a rabbit's arse. But I've seen these young turks get revved up before. Sooner or later he'll go too far, get too greedy too fast, and then things'll be back to normal. All we have to do is wait him out."

I wasn't so sure.

. . .

Hepple, immaculate in cliptogether over skinnysuit without a mask, came onto the floor half an hour after the break. I was at the influent station when he appeared, accompanied by Magyar. She explained the various readouts, and that "Bird here is on analysis."

He turned to me blankly, then snapped his fingers. "Ah, yes. Bird. New here. Three weeks, is it?"

"Almost four," I said.

"And how are you getting on?"

Magyar tensed.

"Very well, sir," I said. "I've found section supervisor Magyar attentive to the needs of both workers and process, which makes everything run very smoothly." *There, Magyar. What do you think of that?*

Hepple frowned very slightly, making his soft mouth pooch out like a baby's. "No doubt, no doubt. But we'll have things running even more efficiently soon enough."

If I had been Magyar I would have been insulted.

"Now, tell me. The viability of the bugs—" He pointed to the lines that fed the various species of bacteria and their required nutrients, if any, into the troughs. "—they're checked every two hours?"

"Yes." I looked at Magyar for some kind of clue. Her face was as stiff as a mask.

"Hmmm." Hepple turned to Magyar. "I think we should increase that schedule, don't you?"

"We will of course be happy to follow any of your suggestions." What else could she say?

"Indeed. Indeed." He sighed contentedly, like a cat contemplating a crippled mouse. "Yes. I think we'll have those readings taken every hour."

That was ridiculous.

"Sir," Magyar said smoothly before I could frame a reply, "I'm sure Bird would be more than happy to comply." She shot me a glance. I nodded earnestly. Slave and overseer ganging up on the plantation owner. "But she and I will need some input from you on our revised priorities."

I thought I saw where Magyar was going. "Yes, sir. That would help. I mean, at the moment the most important part of my job is monitoring the nitrogen and TOC levels. If I split my focus, mistakes will be made. Besides, the extraction and testing is routine and automated. Any significant deviation from the norm would activate the alarms."

"*Significant* isn't good enough now, Bird. From now on, any deviation, no matter how small, must be corrected immediately."

"Sir, might I ask why?"

"I want to run a lean, fit operation. Even small deviations lead to inefficiencies."

Out of the corner of my eye I saw Magyar open her mouth and then close it. I knew how she felt. Microadjustments were a waste of everyone's time. All of the strains used at Hedon Road were premium, genetically tailored van de Oest varieties, which bred true and, given the correct substrate and feeds, kept to a steady and reliable rate of growth. The automatic systems were finely tuned. Unless influent changes were sudden and massive, the system was capable of correcting itself.

In the overhead arc lights I caught the glint of sweat on Hepple's lip. He was worried about something. Worried people are not always rational. Best to acquiesce. "Sir."

"Good. Good."

I wondered why he felt he had to repeat everything. I was uneasy now. Insecure people could be dangerous.

He must have misinterpreted my expression. "If you can't keep up with the monitoring, then draft someone to help." He looked around vaguely, alighting on Paolo, who had just climbed from the trough with an armful of cut bulrushes. "You there! Yes, you. What do you think you're doing?"

Paolo, who was doing nothing wrong, stopped, uncertain.

I stepped between them. "He's new here, sir. I've—"

"Don't you have things to do, Bird?"

Magyar caught my eye, shook her head very slightly, then pointed to herself: *Protecting Paolo is my job.* She could probably do it better. I obediently turned back to the bank of readouts, but I listened hard, and kept them in my peripheral vision.

"As Bird says, sir, Paolo here is new, though he seems to be an excellent—"

"Yes, yes. Look, Cherry, I'm sure you have pressing duties elsewhere."

Magyar could do nothing but bow to the inevitable. Hepple turned to Paolo, and smiled. Paolo waited.

"Now, Paolo, is it? Yes, well, as you've no doubt heard, Bird here will be conducting hourly test sequences on our bugs. The results of those tests, and the monitoring numbers, will come directly to me instead of Magyar. And I want you to bring them to me. Personally. Every hour. No matter where I am, or what you might be doing."

That was ridiculous.

"Of course," Hepple went on, "this does not give you any excuse to slack off in your other duties. Is that clear?"

Paolo nodded, expressionless.

"When I ask you a question, I expect an answer. Once again, is that clear?"

"Yes, sir." His voice was thin and tight with anger. I moved around the instrument displays so I could see them both.

"Good, good." Hepple slapped Paolo on the shoulder, pleased with himself now that he had found someone to bully. I don't think he noticed the muscles bunch along Paolo's jaw. "Now, I want you to take me through your little part in our operation. Don't leave anything out."

There was no sign of Magyar. I wondered if she was somewhere grinding her teeth.

Eventually, Hepple got bored and left Paolo alone to pick up the pile of rushes he had had to abandon. I walked up behind him. The support strap that stretched between his shoulder blades was vibrating slightly, and I could smell his stress sweat. I wanted to lay a hand on his thin back, but did not.

"Paolo?" I said gently. "Paolo?"

"I'm fine," he said, stuffing rushes jerkily into a sack. He did not turn around.

"I'll talk to Magyar. She might be able to do something."

He whirled. "I said I'm fine." Something about his pale, thin face reminded me of Tok. A muscle at the corner of his mouth jumped. His eyes were almost black with anger and humiliation.

"I could—"

"I don't need a woman to fight my battles!" His voice was clotted and violent and I could not have been more surprised if he had hit me. We did not speak for the rest of the shift except when I monitored the viability of the microbes and gave him the figures to take to Hepple.

"He'll be sorry," he swore. "You'll all be sorry."

When I got home, it took me a long time to fall asleep. I dreamed of the loading yard at Hedon Road, of trucks screaming through puddles, trying to run me down.

LORE AND Spanner came back from the Polar Bear and the windows of the shop under their flat were bright behind the shutters.

"What do they sell there?" Lore asked, remembering the people coming and going that first night she had spent in Spanner's flat.

"Tired old porn. Want to see?"

They went inside. The lighting was bright and cheerful, as were shelf after shelf of plastic products: purple silicon dildos, bright pink things that looked like modern abstract art and took Lore a moment to recognize as artificial vaginas. Several screens were running two-minute demo loops. Lore watched one. Spanner was right. The porn was old and tired, almost laughable. The characters moved jerkily and in several frames the skin color of the man's body did not match his head. "I can do better than that."

"Yeah. Anyone who isn't blind could probably do better than that."

"Does this stuff actually sell?"

"I suppose."

"I want to see some more."

A woman with huge, meaty arms and several chins came out from behind the counter. "Then you have to pay for it."

"You're kidding," said Spanner. "No one would pay for this garbage."

"Lots of people do. You want it or not?"

Spanner looked at Lore. "No." The woman shook her head in disgust and lumbered back behind the counter.

"Look at this one," Lore said. Spanner glanced at it cursorily. "The sea in the bottom of the frame is a different color to that at the top. That's just sloppiness."

"The people who watch these things aren't looking at the sea."

"Maybe not, but it only takes a couple of minutes of programming to get the whole picture to mesh. I could do better than this with one hand tied behind my back."

Spanner peered at the screen. "He seems to be doing pretty well with both arms tied behind his back."

"And see that shadow on his thigh? Looks like it's noon. But the sun's setting."

Spanner looked. "I always wondered why these tapes seemed so odd."

"I was doing better work than this three years ago."

"You're serious, aren't you?"

"Of course I'm serious. Let's get out of here."

Later, in bed, Lore was just drifting off to sleep when Spanner spoke into the darkness. "What would you need to make those porn pictures?"

"More equipment than we could afford." Lore turned over, feeling sleep curling up along her backbone like a warm cat.

"Tell me anyway."

THE NEXT shift was even worse. Paolo was strung as tight as piano wire. Hepple appeared every forty minutes, asking about this or that, wasting our time, making everyone jumpy. My stomach began to ache. At one point, I thought Paolo was going to hit Hepple. At the break, someone turned the net volume up high, and what talk there was consisted of surly, one-syllable grunts. Everyone was tired and tense; I was almost glad to get back to work. I saw Magyar only once, two hours into the shift, and gave her a duplicate of the figures I was getting for Hepple. It made me feel better, somehow, that he wasn't the only one with the information. She looked as though she had not slept at all the night before. We didn't speak, but we nodded, like secret allies in enemy territory.

An hour later Hepple told us he was raising the water temperature several degrees. "I'm trying to speed up the through time. Faster throughput means greater daily volume, which will up our market share. This plant isn't working anywhere near full efficiency." I wanted to bang his head against the pipes. The only way to increase the throughput was to get a bigger work crew: keep the troughs clean and at peak efficiency. All the rise in ambient water temperature would achieve was a hotter work environment.

Why was he doing this? I considered, briefly, the Health and Safety Council, but once they found a reason to be interested in an operation, they investigated everything and everyone connected to it. I could not afford that.

I sweated in my skinny. The thick, humid air got thicker, more difficult to breathe. I felt trapped. The ache in my stomach reminded me of days with Spanner, unable to leave, unable to stay.

Paolo wore his rage like a cloak. He stumbled often, and seemed to be moving more slowly. While I was taking yet another set of readings, Hepple came across him in the far trough, struggling to balance a floating tray of rushes that needed rooting.

"Not there. Put them farther out, where they'll do most good."

Farther out was where the rushes were already most dense. Paolo shoved the tray ahead of him, shouldering aside the rushes, getting scratched. He took one of the stems from the tray, bent, came up again with the root still in his hand. He pushed the tray back toward the edge of the trough.

"Are you deliberately disobeying me, boy? I told you to plant these farther out."

"I can't."

"What do you mean, you can't?" Couldn't Hepple feel the rage and resentment burning behind Paolo's blank expression?

"The water's too deep. I can't reach."

"You mean, you'll get your face wet if you try too hard." Hepple smiled his soft-mouthed smile. "Get back out there and do it properly."

The tendons along Paolo's neck writhed like snakes.

"Well?" Hepple's voice was dangerously pleasant.

Paolo turned the tray around, pushed it back out. Hepple watched. I couldn't stand it any longer.

"Sir!"

He turned. "Yes?"

"Sir, Health and Safety regulations state that at no time is an employee required to let contaminated water come into direct contact with his or her unprotected skin."

"Is that so?"

I couldn't afford to lose this job, but I couldn't look at myself in the mirror if I stood by and let him do this to Paolo. "I just thought that for the good of the company you should be reminded, sir, in case something happened under your direct orders and Paolo decided to sue. Could be very damaging."

"It could, it could." He did not seem very perturbed. "Thank you for pointing that out." He turned back to Paolo. "Mr. Cruz, all of a sudden I find that you are physically unsuited to your task. We should never have hired you in the first place. People like you always bring trouble. You're fired. You can work the rest of the shift, then collect your pay at the office." He nodded at him pleasantly, then at me. "Thank you once again, Bird." Just like that, too fast for me to even think about it. He walked off, humming to himself.

Paolo's face was the color of milky coffee gone cold in the cup. I didn't know what to say. "Paolo, I'm sorry."

But Paolo wasn't listening. He was staring out at nothing in particular, and trembling all over. He walked toward the side of the trough. His mouth was moving. He climbed out, walked right past me, muttering through stiff lips. I had to lean in to hear him. He was repeating what Hepple had said: "People like you. People like you . . ."

"Paolo? Paolo, wait. Don't leave. Just keep working here. I'll get Magyar. We'll sort it out. He can't get away with this. He—"

Paolo turned; his eyes were completely black. "Yes, he can. People like that can get away with anything when it concerns people like me." His voice shook, and now there was a twisty bitterness mixed in with the anger. It scared me.

"Just stay here. Don't move." I went straight to the monitoring station and called Magyar. "Hepple's fired Paolo Cruz. No, nothing he's done. You need to get here." I was all ready to tell her I would talk to Kinnis and Cel and Meisener and all the others, that she would have a walkout on her hands if she didn't come, but I didn't need to.

"That's it, Bird. You tell Cruz not to budge. I'll be right there."

Paolo was still standing near the trough, muttering. He did not seem to hear me when I called his name. I didn't know what to do. I hesitated, then picked up some shears. At least I could keep an eye on him until Magyar got here. And I had my own work to do.

"Bird!" Magyar was talking and striding past me at the same time. "Come with me. Cruz, you stay right there." I don't think he even heard her.

I had to scramble out of the trough; she was not slowing down for anybody.

We found Hepple in the floor office, a clear-paned box twenty feet up with a view of the whole primary sector. He was sitting down, making notes on a slate. Magyar slammed the door open and was talking before Hepple had the time to sit up straight. "You have no right to fire one of my workers. Misconduct, if any, should have been reported to me, and I would have made the correct decision. You had no right to go over my head." I stood slightly behind Magyar, surrounded by reflections in the glass walls.

Hepple and his reflection laid the slate aside, carefully, as though his conversation with Magyar would take only a minute and he did not want to lose his place. "He was insolent. We would have had to let him go anyway when we downsized the workforce."

177

Magyar was momentarily thrown. "Downsizing? When was that decided?"

"This morning, I believe. So you see, it would have happened sooner or later."

"Wait. Just wait a minute. I thought you had grand designs to expand this plant, increase the throughput."

"I do, I do. But I persuaded the board that we don't need as many people to achieve that goal."

Magyar shook her head like a dog worrying a rabbit and I watched her reflection's hair shimmer back and forth. "This was the wrong way to do it. You tormented that boy. If nothing else, common decency should . . ."

Common decency. The phrase rippled back and forth like the reflection of Magyar's hair in the glass. She and Hepple were still talking, but I wasn't listening anymore. *Common decency . . .* I finally remembered, finally realized what it was about Paolo and the way he moved that bothered me.

All my fault . . .

Guilt, mine, my family's, stopped the breath in my lungs and pulled the muscles along my arms and legs rigid. But then fear—of him, for him, what he might do, *all that bitterness*—snapped me out of it.

"Sorry," I said jerkily to the air, and reached blindly for the door.

FOURTEEN

LORE IS fifteen. It is early March, and she is preparing to fly to Gdansk, where for the first time she will be assistant deputy project manager. An admin position, Katerine tells her, but a responsible one, nevertheless. Katerine will be taking charge personally.

Lore is up late the night before they fly, running over last-minute plans—so that she knows what is going on, so she won't embarrass herself in front of Katerine, or Katerine in front of others—when the phone rings.

She accepts the call. "Tok!" He looks different, but at first Lore can't pinpoint the change. Then she has it: his face has lost all trace of puppy fat. "How are you? It's—"

"I've been talking to Stella," he interrupts. "It's true. All of it."

"What—"

But he talks right over her. "Watch yourself. You might be next."

Lore is glad to see him, glad to hear from him, but she remembers how he had fooled her for so many years. How he had never talked to her. How she felt betrayed when he left. And now he is being cryptic.

"I haven't had any idea where you've been the last year or so, and now you . . ." She remembers she is fifteen; grown enough to take her first official job for the company. "It's late," she says, then—unable to help herself—bursts out, "Do you have any idea how badly you've hurt Mother?"

Tok looks momentarily blank; then, incredibly, he laughs. "How much *I've* hurt *her*? Lore, look," he shakes his head, "you don't—"

But the laugh and head shake are enough. She is grown now, no longer a child to be patronized, deceived. She cuts him off midsentence. She is tired, she tells herself. She has a lot of reading to do. When he is ready to apologize, he can call again.

It is early spring in Poland. The remediation site is slippery with mud; small pockets of ice crackle under Lore's boots when she takes samples for testing. The only wildlife she sees are worms, gray things that show a startling pink against the mud when a shovel cuts them accidentally in half.

It is a short job, but the weather and the work are brutal. Tok does not call. Lore is so busy she hardly ever sees Katerine, except one night when she is idly flipping through the net and comes across her mother, giving an interview to one of the national channels.

Katerine is smiling with that expert one-eye-on-the-camera-one-eye-on-the-interviewer stance Lore knows so well.

"—efficient job at the old Gdansk shipyards," the interviewer is saying. "How do you persuade your employees and team members to take on such difficult projects?"

"It's not hard," she says. "I throw myself on their mercy.

People love to be asked for help." *They actually like you better if you show some vulnerability,* Lore remembers her saying at a party once, *if you bare your throat and say please.*

Of course, Lore thinks. Everything Katerine does is for a reason.

It is April by the time everyone is satisfied the bacteria are doing their job and Katerine decides it is time to leave the shipyards in someone else's hands.

"It's autumn in Auckland," her mother says. "It'll soon be winter. I think we deserve a few days in the heat, don't you?"

They book themselves into a hotel in Belmopan, Belize. It is hot in the two weeks before the rainy season. Lore drives out alone to the beach every day to dive the reef, the second-largest barrier reef in the world, and the most beautiful. She tries not to think about Tok while she glides through the cool water with the blue tang and banded butterfly fish, through the aqua and rose of the coral. She rents a jeep and drives through the interior, stopping sometimes to film chechem and banak tree, sapodilla and blood-red Heliconia. There are leaves here the size of canoe paddles, and beetles as long as her thumb. All around her she can feel life—creeping, crawling, running, leaping from branch to branch.

The nights are warm and soft, black skies streaked with bright city light, laughter, and the scent of honeysuckle and cold cocktails.

Lore is in the shower when her phone rings. She ignores it. It rings again. She climbs out of the shower. It is her mother. "Turn on the news," Katerine says. "They're announcing the verdict on the Caracas class-action suit." The screen clicks off. Caracas . . . Lore, undecided, finds a news channel, but then turns the volume up high and gets back in the shower, only half listening.

". . . great disappointment this afternoon in Caracas . . .

181

Michel Aguilar, chief attorney for the plaintiffs, said earlier that this was a blow to all those who expected justice to ignore matters of privilege and influence . . ."

Lore hums to herself as she soaps her legs.

". . . Carmen Torini, former head of the project in Caracas that . . ."

At the sound of the familiar name, Lore turns off the shower and pads into the living room. Carmen Torini, surrounded by reporters and looking older than when Lore first saw her on Oster's screen, is talking to the camera.

"And we think it is an absolutely fair settlement. The van de Oest company has always maintained that it scrupulously obeyed the law and all guidelines of the federal government of Venezuela. We are not to blame for the terrible tragedy of twenty years ago. The project undertaken here, the bioremediation of groundwater contaminated by careless contractors in the past, should have proved faultless. It *would* have proved faultless if not for the greed of the government-supervised subcontractors. If greed had not motivated the substitution of the correct bacteria there would not have been the release of mutagenic toxins into the water table . . ."

Lore, still watching, punches in her mother's code. The news shrinks to a box in the upper left-hand corner of the screen. "When did you find out?"

"A few minutes ago. The judge just called."

"And our liability?"

Katerine laughs. Her eyes, green today, sparkle. "None. None whatsoever. We'll help, of course—that's only good PR—but at least we won't be suffering variations on this damn lawsuit for the next three generations." She punches the air in triumph. "See you in the bar."

Lore expands the news box. Now a mestizo woman is talking. She looks upset. ". . . got nothing! 'Oh,' they say, 'it's not our fault.' Then whose fault is it? The government can't afford to help. Look, this is my daughter . . ." She pulls a flat from her pocket, the camera zooms in. It is a picture of a limbless child, grinning. "She's dead now. My only child. And thousands of others ruined because someone thought they could make some money. Because . . ." She seems to catch sight of something offscreen. "Because of you!" She points and the camera pans wildly, picking up Carmen Torini, still talking to reporters. The reporters, sensing drama, part and let the two women confront each other. One, plump and weeping, beside herself with rage; one slim, well-dressed, patient.

"You're all so greedy! For the sake of making more money—"

"It was not our fault. If our design specification had been followed to the letter, this would not—"

"Fault! Liability! Just words! Does it matter to our children who is to blame? No. All they want is their lives back. Lives that were ruined because of the van de Oest patenting policy. What would it cost to set right? A few million? Hardly a drop in the company coffers. You should do what you can out of common decency. Who cares about who should have done what? We want to fix it. If guilt at your greed doesn't motivate you, then humanity, common decency should."

Carmen seems impervious. "The van de Oest Company sympathizes with your grief in the light of this tragedy. Although the suit for compensation and total grafts for all victims has been dismissed and we have been judged not liable, as a gesture of sympathy to the people of Caracas, the company has authorized me to offer prostheses to all who feel the need—"

The mother of the dead child is having none of that. "We don't want charity," she spits. "We want justice! We will not give up. While our children lie in their beds and look at us with their sad eyes we will follow you from country to country, crying 'Justice! Justice!' and we will be heard!"

Lore towels her hair dry. It was not Torini's fault that the locals had tried to cut costs and improve their profit margin by using a generic substitute for the specially tailored van de Oest bacterium around which the whole project had been designed. She thinks about the project in Gdansk and what might happen if, sometime in the next eight months, some greedy or stupid contractor swaps out one bacterium for another. Disaster. She makes a note on her slate to review the continuing supervision of this project and the others in which she has so far been involved. Mistakes happen, but they can be prevented. Then she turns off the screen, dismissing the matter from her mind. It has nothing to do with her and there is a cold drink waiting in the bar.

FIFTEEN

COMMON DECENCY. I pushed my way out of the floor office and began to run. It was difficult to breathe in the hot, humid air by the water, and by the time I reached the readout station, I was gasping. I ran from trough to trough. No Paolo.

I stopped a moment. Think. I had to think. How would he be feeling? What did he know about the plant? Where would he go?

"Sabotage? How could someone sabotage this place?"

"Any number of ways, but the best place would be right at the beginning . . ."

The influent. I ran.

There are times when the brain can't deal with what it sees, so part of it sits back and the rest looks closely at some irrelevant piece of information. I noted that the concrete under my feet was shuddering with the weight of water coursing beneath it; that when the huge trap in the floor was pulled back the air not only hissed and roared with the exposed flow, but that it tasted different.

And why, I wondered, were people who were about to kill themselves so compulsively neat?

Paolo's skinny was beautifully folded, collar top-and-forward the way shirts are sold in their cellophane packages. I had never been able to fold clothes like that. His limbs were piled just as neatly next to the skinny, all except one arm, which lay on its own to the side. I wondered idly how he had managed to take off that last arm, the right, I think. I supposed the designers had worked out a simple push-and-twist method.

Paolo was belly-down at the corner of the open trap, torso balanced over the chasm, lowering his throat toward the buzz razor jammed into the space between cover and floor.

"Don't," I said. *Don't, because it will please Hepple; because it will make a mess and I'll have to clean it up. Don't, because you won't be able to change your mind later; because if you do, oh, I'll feel guilty, so guilty, and I won't, ever, be able to make it up to you . . .*

He couldn't hear me, of course, but he saw me, saw my lips, and his muscles knotted long enough to hold his upper body away from the humming blade, a few inches above the point where he would fall, and I moved gently, not too quickly, and lifted the slippery, ugly razor free. I flicked it off. The muscles over his ribs were tight and absolutely still. He hung in the balance. I didn't think I could hold him up if he started to fall.

"Don't move," I said. "Don't move." I put the razor down carefully, not wanting to make a sudden move, a noise that might startle him out of his stasis. His skin gleamed with sweat. I knelt, braced one hand on the floor, and slid the other around his waist. If he wanted to, he could throw us

186

both off, and we'd be sucked away in seconds and drowned, if we weren't crushed first. *He doesn't know you're a van de Oest,* I told myself. I could feel him trembling.

I heaved him away from the edge.

He lay on his back, limbless, staring at the ceiling. I had the urge to apologize.

I got up and hit the stud that closed up the floor. I could hear his harsh breathing. I picked up the pile of limbs, carried them to his side. "Which one do you want first, right or left?"

"Right."

We were both very matter-of-fact. There was no other way to be. I reconnected the prosthesis to his right shoulder, then turned away politely while he snapped on the other arm and then the legs. When he had put his skinny back on, I squatted down beside him and handed him the razor. He slipped it under his left cuff with a practiced motion. Carrying a razor was a habit. I wondered how I would have felt, before, if I'd known that.

His eyes were brown, opaque. "You shouldn't have stopped me."

"Why?"

For a moment I thought he would not bother to answer. Then he looked at me for a long time, and asked, "Who am I?"

"Paolo Cruz."

"No. I'm nobody, a nothing." So bitter. "The only person who cares that I exist is my brother. He brought us, me and my sister, here from Venezuela, to lobby for our rights. But my sister died, and no one will listen to me or my brother. 'It was all settled long ago,' the courts say. They've given us nothing. Except these plastic arms and legs. And maybe that's all me and people like me are worth."

No, I wanted to say. But why should he believe me? Who had there ever been to tell him any different?

"To the courts and the medical industry, to those rich people who caused all this in the first place, I'm one of the disposable masses. Not even wholly human." He thrust his arm at me. "Feel that."

"I—"

"Feel it!"

It was soft and warm and dry. Pleasant.

"Just once, I thought, just once I wanted to *be* someone to those people, those Hepples and van de Oests. If I killed myself here, if my body fell into the water, they would have to turn everything off. They'd lose money. They would know who I was, me, Paolo Cruz, the man made of plastic."

I did not know how to tell him that all his death would have accomplished was a minor inconvenience to this shift: his corpse would have been caught on the sieves, easily fished out, and the blood would only have provided more food for the microbes. Unless, of course, he'd thrown in his prostheses, which might have been tough enough to foul the machinery.

We were quiet for a while, then I stood up. "Are you coming back to work? Maybe Magyar will find a way to get your job back."

"No. I don't want to be a nobody in this place anymore."

"But with what I'm teaching you, you could . . ." I shut up. I could not give him self-esteem. That was something he had to find for himself. "What will you do?"

"I'll think of something." He smiled humorlessly, walked over to the doorway marked EMERGENCY EXIT, and opened it. Alarms rang. "I hope Hepple thinks all the pipes have burst."

He left without a backward glance. After a moment, I closed the door behind him. The alarms shut off abruptly.

When I got back to the troughs, I found it had only been twenty minutes since I had gone with Magyar to Hepple's office. I went about my work mechanically.

Magyar appeared. She was flushed. "Who used that door?" She looked around. "Cruz?"

"He's gone."

She swore. "And I got him his job back, too."

"I told him you would." Though I hadn't believed it. "How did you manage it?"

"I put myself on the line, just confronting Hepple." She was trying to explain something. "I took a few risks. I put you on the line, too."

I suddenly felt very tired. "What have you done?"

"I told him he couldn't fire Cruz on such shaky grounds, especially since a government employee had witnessed the whole affair."

"You told him—"

Magyar's eyes gleamed. "I didn't actually say anything straight out, just hinted around. And then he said something about you spouting regulations at him, and got thoughtful. Then he said that, yes, maybe he had been hasty, and the downsizing would have to be looked at carefully and systematically. So Paolo is back in. Or would have been. And Hepple thinks we've got his balls in a press, so everything's back to normal."

It wasn't. It never would be, not when I kept seeing that slack, empty look in Paolo's eyes, hearing him say *I am nothing*.

"What's the matter? I mean, I didn't expect handsprings, but thanks wouldn't be out of order. Or are you just upset that I told Hepple you weren't quite who you seem to be? Which is something we still haven't cleared up."

"I'm not a government employee," I said wearily. "I'm not after your job. I don't mean anyone any harm at all. I'm glad you wanted to help Paolo, but as you can see, it's too late. All I want . . ." I felt dizzy for a minute. "I want . . ." I wanted to tell her that all I wanted was to do my job and be left alone, but I found myself crying. "He tried to kill himself. He took off his . . . and the razor . . ."

Magyar took my arm tightly. I thought she was worried I would fall into the trough, or run amok, or something, but she just said, "Don't rub your eyes. You don't know what's on your hands."

Very sensible. And then she was walking me somewhere while I rambled on about Paolo and his limbs and how he had tried to kill himself. I found we were in the breakroom. She made me wash my hands, then gave me a towel. Neither of us spoke. The eerie sense of déjà vu hit me, and I laughed.

"I wonder if Paolo felt like this when I was taking away his razor," I explained. "As though he was about five years old and being humored by a wise, kind person." And then I felt embarrassed.

She didn't launch into a denial. Of course she was humoring me. That's what you did with someone in distress. You patted them on the head, told them everything was fine, and waited for them to get back up to speed with reality.

I sighed. "We should get back."

Magyar looked at her watch. "Are you up to date in your readings for Hepple? Good. Then you may as well stay here. We break in ten minutes."

She seemed relieved to get away.

LORE WOKE up. It was five in the morning. She pulled a blanket around her shoulders and stumbled out of bed.

Spanner was at the workbench. Lore watched as she picked up a pair of delicate tweezers and opened up a PIDA, touched something inside, then inserted it into her box. She flipped it shut, hummed to herself at the readout, tapped a few keys.

"You're very good at that," Lore said.

"I know." Spanner turned. "What gets you out of bed at this hour?"

"Just wondered what you were up to." Spanner went back to her screen. "You know, you could get a job doing that."

Spanner turned again, smiling. "Now, why would I need a job?"

The first few times she had gone to the Polar Bear, Lore had not realized that Spanner was doing business. Spanner would share a drink and a few words, there would be a slap on the back or a nod, and occasionally something would change hands—illegal PIDAs, temporary debit blanks, information. They would go home and Spanner would unload her pockets. The next day she would spend hours at her screens, matching magnetic codes, stripping information; copying the corporate electromagnetic signatures on a stolen debit card, transferring them to a blank; or simply calling people and telling them she had what they wanted. Hyn and Zimmer figured a great deal in the blanks transactions— *"They're more or less untraceable, dear"*—but it was Billy who disturbed Lore the most. Every week or so he would cruise by, sometimes with Ann, usually without, and have a quiet word with Spanner, usually when they were at the bar and out of everyone else's earshot. Lore thought she heard them talking about *chickens*, but she tried not to listen.

It was around February that Lore noticed a difference in Spanner's bar dealings. She seemed to be talking more, and more urgently; there was more head shaking and less back-slapping, fewer things changing hands. And then one day Lore realized she had not seen Hyn or Zimmer for a while.

"What's going on?" she asked Spanner.

"Business is getting tight."

"Anything to worry about?"

"Not yet. There are always other ways to make money."

Lore did not want to ask about that. "Where have Hyn and Zimmer been lately?"

"Who?" Spanner laughed. "They're a couple of cautious old foxes. Whenever the police are cracking down they disappear for a while."

"Shouldn't you be more careful?"

"Oh, I'm too smart for the police."

Nevertheless, Lore noticed that Spanner went out later and for shorter periods, and once she lay low for forty-eight hours straight, wouldn't let Lore answer the screen at all. But then the next day she went out and came back grinning.

"Close your eyes." Lore did. "Now open them and look on the bed."

It was a Hammex 20. Lore picked it up, ran her hands over its familiar black curves. "These aren't cheap." She flicked the power switch, peered through the viewfinder. The drive hummed smoothly.

"Do you like it?"

"It seems in good condition." She put it back on the bed and looked at it for a while, remembering Ratnapida, her first pictures of goldfish swimming slowly through crystal and shadowed water. She turned to face Spanner. "How can we afford it if business is bad?"

Spanner shrugged.

Lore thought of Billy, his mean eyes and fast mouth. "Are we in debt?"

"No."

"Then how did we afford it?"

"I thought you'd like it." Spanner sounded irritated.

"I do, I just don't know how we can afford it."

"Well, we can."

Lore thought of Spanner's disappearances, how tense she had been when she came back. The skin on the back of her neck felt tight. "How?"

"Does it matter?"

It did, but Lore did not have the courage to push any further. She was not sure she really wanted to know how Spanner had come up with the money, who she was black-mailing about what. Or what else she might be doing. Spanner, as though sensing her acquiescence, smiled and slid an arm around Lore's waist.

"Do you like it? Really?"

Lore forced herself to smile. "You got exactly the right kind. They have the best lenses." And despite herself, she was touched. The old-fashioned Hammexes were not easy to find these days. She imagined Spanner going from one dealer to another, reading the trade bulletins, bargaining. How she got the money, who had suffered, was none of Lore's business. "Let's find a disk and take some pictures."

It was spring and Lore had the windows open. The soft breeze that blew across her editing desk smelled of new green. There were tiny buds on the branches outside—all the branches except one. She wondered how that had happened, why one branch would die while the others thrived. She supposed it just happened. Parts of things died. Nature.

The door banged open. She turned, smiling, expecting Spanner to tell her they had made a lot of money.

Spanner threw a bag on the couch. "They're not selling."

"What?" Lore's smile faded.

"The films aren't selling."

"You've been making a lot of copies."

"Oh, I can move the units, but not for enough money. Not as much as we need. People tell me they're tired of the same bodies in different situations."

Lore looked at the frame lit on the screen. She did good work, but her library was so limited. "I need some live action. Or a bigger library."

Spanner nodded and dropped onto the couch.

"You want me to stop?"

"No," Spanner said. "Let me think about it awhile."

Two days later, she disappeared for more than twenty-four hours. When she came back, she looked exhausted, but she was grinning.

"I've got something special." She held up a vial full of some clear, oily liquid.

"What is it?"

"You'll see. Come here." Spanner dipped a fingertip into the neck of the bottle, rubbed the finger along Lore's throat. She did the same for herself. "Just a little. It's very concentrated."

"It's a drug? What kind?"

"You'll see," she said again, and her voice was low and multilayered, her eyes dark. Lore wanted to trace Spanner's cheekbones with her fingertips, run her palm across her shoulders, reach down into her clothes, touch her, feel her moving under her hands. She wanted it urgently. She ached.

An aphrodisiac, then, a pheromone, but more powerful than any she had heard of, legal or illegal. This was unstoppable. Spanner began to unbutton her dress. Lore moaned.

"Anything you like, baby, anything."

There were about thirty people in the big room, spilling out into the kitchen, onto the steps. Lore introduced people, though most of them knew each other better than she did. Everyone was drinking very steadily. She brought out snacks, made sure the music never faltered. She avoided Billy, who just stood in the corner and watched everything with his small, flat eyes that reminded her of all the things she tried not to think about.

"I don't like him," she hissed to Spanner in the kitchen.

"You don't have to like him," Spanner said. "Just be civil. This is business."

Lore refilled her glass and went back into the living

room. Her wine was cold and aromatic, like sunshine at thirty thousand feet. The music was loud and insistent. Ellen was talking to someone at the other side of the room; they were laughing. Lore sat on the floor and wondered where Ruth was.

When Spanner came out of the bathroom she moved slowly from one group to another, smiling, shaking people by the hand, touching a cheek. The whole party suddenly seemed to Lore a gross parody of the business parties the van de Oests had occasionally hosted before Ratnapida.

"What's the occasion?" Ruth asked, and sat down next to Lore on the carpet.

"Hmm?" Lore was thinking about Ratnapida: long cocktail dresses, expensive jewelry, uniformed caterers. Always for a reason, to gain or cement advantages. Never for fun. From the other side of the room, Spanner's finger glistened just before she touched someone under the ear.

"The party. What's it for?'

"I've no idea," she lied, and nodded over at Spanner, who was still doing her hostess bit. "She just came home one day and said, party time. So it is."

Ruth looked at her curiously. "You know, you're nicer than I expected. Not like Spanner's usual—" She went red. "I mean . . ."

Lore wanted to tell her it was all right, but she knew that if she did, other things might come tumbling out—she would tell Ruth to find Ellen and run, now, before it was too late, before they were caught up in Spanner's web. *And mine,* she thought, *I'm the one with the camera.* "Did you know the woman Spanner was with before?"

Ruth nodded. "And the one before that, and before that. They don't usually last more than about six weeks."

Lore looked into her wine. What would she do, where would she go without Spanner? "Have you known her long?"

"Less than two years."

Lore wanted to ask more, but Spanner was heading toward them. "Ruth! Glad you could make it." She touched the back of Ruth's neck lightly. "Oh, there you are," she said to Lore. "Why don't you go get your camera?"

Spanner's pupils were tiny: the antidote, Lore assumed. Her own probably looked the same.

There were three people on the bed when she went to get her camera. They did not seem to notice her as she edged past them and lifted the Hammex. She checked the disk on the way back to the living room, where Spanner drew her aside. "Make sure you get everything. We need all the live action we can get." She nodded over to the corner where a couple was kissing.

No one took any notice of the amorous couple. It was not the polite ignoring of an inappropriate display of lust but, rather, that everyone was becoming engrossed in his or her own partner. Everywhere eyes were glazed, skin gleaming, lips moist. The air was thick with sex. While Lore watched, one woman started to unbutton the fly of the man opposite her.

Lore turned away, lifted the camera to her shoulder. A man was turning around his partner and pulling down her trousers. Lore cleared her throat, pointed to her camera. "It's switched on," she said to the air eight inches above their heads, "but I need your permission before I . . ." She trailed off. They completely ignored her. She licked her lips, remembering how it felt to be wrapped in the drug.

She saw Ellen with Ruth and hurried over, intending to stop them, get them out of there, but they were already kissing. From the other side of the room, Spanner was watching her. *Don't let Spanner see even a chink.* "Do I have your permission to film?" she asked dully.

"Just don't get in my way," Ellen said, and reached up under Ruth's dress.

Lore put the camera to her shoulder and filmed. Her face ached and her cheek, wet with tears, chafed against the eyepiece, but she filmed for hours.

When Lore edited the film, she swapped around heads and bodies, or used library heads. She needed these images—*they* needed these images—to make films that would sell for enough to feed them, at least until summer, but she could not bring herself to use her friends without some kind of disguise.

Weeks later she got a call from Ruth. "You bastard."

"What—"

"The film. I saw it. At a friend's. You bastard."

"Ruth . . . Ruth . . ."

"You think asking *permission* all nice and proper makes it *right*?"

"Ruth, I wanted to warn you—"

"I didn't see any pictures of you," Ruth cut in.

Yes, you did, Lore wanted to say. *You've seen pictures of me in far more humiliating circumstances; and my abductors did not even have the courtesy to swap my head for another's . . .* And all of a sudden, Lore did not care. What did it matter that Ruth was upset? She, Lore, had been through much, much worse. Ellen had given permission of a sort, hadn't she? And at least Ruth had enjoyed it while it was happening. Lore had not enjoyed one single minute of her ordeal.

She turned off the screen. Her mouth felt strange. She knew that if she looked in a mirror she would see her lip curling, like Spanner's.

THE FIRST people into the breakroom were Meisener and Kinnis. Meisener flicked a look in my direction but said nothing. Maybe he'd heard something. Kinnis either had heard nothing or didn't care. He went to the wall screen and V-handed the PIDA reader. He made a disgusted sound when the figures came up.

"Every month I check my wages—every month I hope someone somewhere made a mistake, or a program screwed up and I'll be a billionaire. Every month it says I made seventeen hundred."

"You should know better," Cel said, sitting down to unwrap her food.

"Hey, Bird. You think I should know better? No, and I'll tell you why. Hope is good for a person. You think I'd keep shoveling shit if I knew, really knew all I'd get was seventeen hundred?"

There were two other people waiting to use the reader to check their wages, so Kinnis moved aside. He sat between me and Meisener. "You got paid yet?" he asked Meisener.

"Na. Timed it all wrong. I'll have to wait until next month now."

"You?"

I blinked at him. Payday. Money. I nodded and joined the queue at the reader. Put my hand in when it was my turn, read the figures. Almost sixteen hundred. I had earned money, in my own right, without family help, without hurting anyone else. I drew my hand out and looked at it. I wondered if Paolo would get paid.

When I woke up the next morning the sun was bright and I lay in bed a few minutes, smiling. I was alive. I had the next two days off. I had been paid.

Sixteen hundred was not much, but it was manageable. I still had a chunk left from before—nine hundred, maybe—and the scam would net tens of thousands. I felt rich.

I took breakfast onto the roof and watched the clouds, the glints from the river. There were several barges on the water. I wondered what they were carrying today. Steel from Scunthorpe, maybe? I closed my eyes and let the breeze blow soft against my lids. People had been using the river for thousands of years. Wheat during Roman times. Clay before that. Maybe blue beads and young, scared slaves; a tun of beer. And before then, in the days when boats were hollowed-out logs, scraped goatskins, dried fish from the coast, dyed feathers for a religious rite. What had the weather been like then, and how had the air smelled? Maybe life had been more simple. Maybe it was possible to sit high up every day of your life and just sniff the breeze. Maybe not.

When I climbed back through the window, the sun was shining full on the west wall, adding yellow to the already acidic green. Very ugly. I turned away from it, then turned back. This was my flat. I could change the color. I didn't have to tell anyone, or ask, or take them into account. I could spray everything purple and orange if I wanted. I laughed, delighted. Mine.

Perhaps something neutral, alabaster or beige. Or linen. No, not warm enough. Maybe peach? The possibilities were overwhelming.

I sat down at the screen and pulled up the inventory of a couple of decorating shops. There were little tables that showed you how to work out how much paint you'd need. I did that. Decided I could afford it quite handily. Except I'd forgotten all the brushes and dustcloths and cleaning fluid and trays . . . I added it up again. Still manageable.

But then I looked at the walls again, at the kitchen, the bathroom, the steep stairway and complicated gables over the bed. I'd never picked up a brush or spray gun in my life. Where would I start?

Maybe Tom could help? But he was old. The only other people I knew were Spanner, and my shift at Hedon Road, and I couldn't, wouldn't, ask them.

Or there were Ruth and Ellen.

I remembered that interview with my mother on the net.

How do you persuade employees or team partners to take on such difficult projects? the interviewer had asked.

Easy, she said. *People love to be asked to help.*

Easy.

It took twenty minutes pacing the living room before I could bring myself to tap in their number.

Ruth answered. The tendons down each side of her neck tightened for a second when she saw me, but she managed a guarded smile. "Lore. What can I do for you?"

"I just got paid. And I know we agreed to have dinner sometime, the three of us, but I wondered if I could impose on you for some help instead. My flat needs decorating and, well, I don't know how. I thought maybe you could give me, ah, some advice. If you've ever done it yourself. I mean, I've never even bought paint before."

She was looking puzzled. "You want me and Ellen to come help you choose paint."

"Essentially, yes."

She smiled, and this time the skin around her eyes stretched. "You're settling down, then?"

"Yes. The flat's nice, except for the color. And the temperature. I think it'll be cold in a month or so."

"Then you'll need Thinsulate paper for all the outside walls. Have you thought about colors?"

"You'll help, then?"

"Of course we'll help! Why don't you bring the measurements and samples and things round and we'll have dinner."

Dinner. "When?"

"The weekend?"

I grinned at her so hard I think there were tears in my eyes. "The weekend would be wonderful."

SIXTEEN

LORE IS seventeen. Her final exams are done. Two weeks before the end of her last term at school, her mother calls.

"Are you ready to leave that place yet?"

Lore grips the table beside the screen. "You've decided? You'll let me do it?"

"I've decided. I'll let you do it."

"Complete control?"

"No. You'll be Marley's deputy."

"But—"

On-screen, Katerine holds up her hand. "Marley has graciously agreed to let you co-lead, unofficially, but I can't justify giving you complete control of such a high-profile project."

"High-profile? The Kirghizi project?"

"It is to the Kirghizians."

And now Lore grins. Second-in-charge of a huge project. The one she has been waiting for. "When are we scheduled to start?"

"Our contract with the Kirghizian government is valid as of this afternoon. I suggest you talk to Marley. And Lore, don't screw up."

Lore packs, hands shaking—partly from a fierce exhilaration, partly from nerves. Ever since the company started bidding on this project she has had her heart set on it. She has disk after disk of plans, all ready to go. Working with Marley will not be too bad; she usually gets on well with her uncle's husband. He'll let her use some of her ideas, surely. She leaves without a backward glance for the school, but she takes a taxi ride past the sex club for old times' sake. She thinks briefly of Anne, the first one. She will never come here again. She will probably never use a sex club again. There is no need.

Lore makes several overflights of the Kazakhstan region three hundred miles north of the Aral Sea. The area is suffering from the Soviet Union's disastrous attempts in the middle of the last century to turn the sun-drenched deserts of Uzbekistan, Tajikistan, Turkmenia, and Kirghizia into a vast cotton monoculture. The Aral Sea, once the largest body of water in Central Asia, is beyond immediate salvation. The Soviet regime drained the inland sea of two-thirds of its volume, diverting its sources, the Amu Darya and Syr Darya, into thousands of miles of irrigation canals and ditches crisscrossing the new fields of cotton that stood where once there had been only arid steppe. Muynak, once the Aral's largest fishing port, now stands forty-five miles from the water's edge. Rusting hulls of abandoned vessels and barges line what was once the shore. When Lore orders the copter lower, she sees that many of the hulks have been scavenged for the metal.

The family has won the first of the multilevel, forty-year programs: to clean up the water table of Kirghizia and route the clean water back to the Aral. Marley has suggested that her initial brief should be the fertilizer, pesticide, and defoliant pollution resulting from wholesale crop spraying throughout the nineteen sixties, seventies, and eighties. He will deal with the biological contamination—bacteria, viruses, parasites, and algae. If she has any questions, all she has to do is ask. And he, of course, will have to approve any requisitions over ten million.

They are sitting in Marley's project tent, which is actually a collapsible three-room stretch dome. Marley is drinking green tea, looking as sleek as a spaniel. Lore is impatient to get started. "What's our plant and equipment budget?"

"One hundred and twenty million."

"That's not enough . . ." She thinks hard. "Labor?"

Marley smiles. His teeth are beautifully white. "I wondered how quickly you'd catch that. Almost one hundred million."

Lore laughs out loud. "Then all we have to do is swap sixty or so from one to the other. Once we've got everything functioning, we don't need much maintenance. Labor costs will be minimal."

"Ah, but don't forget that projects like this, for small countries, are as much about politics as pollution." He raises his eyebrows, sips.

"I don't understand."

"Jobs."

Lore sighs. Jobs. People. Votes. Much harder to deal with.

"However, that does not make the problem insurmountable. If you take the time to examine your budget sheet—"

"I've only just got here."

"I wasn't criticizing. If you take a look, you'll see there's a two million set-aside, labeled 'misc.' Some project leaders will use that as an emergency reserve, some will use it as a carrot in the form of bonuses to their labor force, others will use it in discreet bribes to local officials. Whatever is most expedient."

"And you know some amenable local officials?" Lore is realizing that reality is not the same as designing systems on her screen. She is glad she is only the deputy.

"Let's just say I know of them."

"And you'll . . . soothe their worries and smooth their palms?"

"No. You will."

Lore knows she has asked for this responsibility. She also knows that her mother would not have given it to her if she was not ready. She does not feel ready, but she grits her teeth and begins.

She sweeps the minister for labor and the commissar of the treasury up in a whirl of lunches and dinners, gifts them with the latest in personal transport technology, and even gets one of her assistants to find the male minister a female companion. All the time that she nods and smiles and soothes and explains, while she dabs at her mouth or takes another sip of champagne, she frets. She wants to be working, to be building something, seeing her ideas take shape.

It takes nearly three days to get them both to sign off on the budget changes, and even then she has to promise to "forget" to post the changes with the relevant Kirghizi departments.

"Is it always like this?" she asks that evening in Marley's tent.

"Usually worse," he says. "It's impossible to get everyone to agree. To get things to move and change, we need to bend the rules a little. Some of us enjoy it."

"Do you?"

"No, but your uncle Willem—"

"Just call him Willem. You know he hates being an uncle."

"—but Willem, I think, gets a secret pleasure from the wheeling and dealing. As does your sister Greta."

"Greta?" Lore is astonished. "She always seems like such a . . ." She hunts for a polite synonym for nonentity.

"Greta is a much more powerful force in this company than most people realize," Marley says seriously. "Your future might be smoother if you bore that in mind."

Lore knows that Marley is trying to tell her something but she has no idea what. "What about the rest of my family?"

"Katerine does not wheel and deal. She cuts to the heart. That's her enjoyment."

"And my father?"

"I don't know what your father enjoys." Nor does Lore, these days.

Although she is up the next day well before dawn, she does not want to be perceived as inexperienced and over-eager. She spends an hour walking the desert. She hears no birds, sees no rodent tracks, senses no slither-and-hide of lizard or snake. Here, the desert is barren.

When it has been light for nearly an hour, she calls together her managers.

The solution is easy enough in theory—they will use an advanced oxidation process, a combination of ultraviolet, hydrogen peroxide, and titanium oxide to break the dioxins down to relatively harmless weak acids and carbon dioxide, which can then be further remediated with biological agents—but in practice, the task is massive. There will be factors unanticipated simply because of the scale. Lore reminds her managers of this and tells them that every detail, no matter how small, must be overseen, whether by them or by trusted assistants. Meticulousness might not eliminate problems, but it will reduce them. She outlines the preliminary schedule of shifts and leave for the next few months, but warns them this may have to change when they hit snags. She orders herself a new project tent, one with more amenities; she does not mean to leave the project HQ until everything is on-line.

It takes five months to get the vast UV-reflecting troughs built. It should have taken two, but the glass coating on the contractors' first load is substandard, and has to be done again. Then there is some kind of ethnic conflict between the Muslim Kirghizians and their Orthodox neighbors, and many of the local workers are conscripted. Lore has dinner with the minister and manages to get her labor force exempted from the draft.

"Is it always as bad as this?" becomes Lore's standard question.

"Usually worse," comes Marley's smiling reply. He is always ready with advice, both theoretical and practical, and Lore sighs and goes back to negotiating, or drawing, or simply shouting, whichever is most expedient. Half a year later, the pipeline is done, stretching south across the Kirghizi desert mile after mile to the Aral Sea. Lore is fascinated by it. She watches the first water hiss through the special glass tubes along the center of the troughs and begin to bubble as the absorbed UV changes the toxic dioxins to aldehydes, then carboxylic acids, and finally carbon dioxide. It will take forty years, but she has begun it.

"Did you know," she tells Marley that night, "that all this, this mess, the ruin of a whole ecosystem, a whole generation of people, was practically for nothing? About eighty percent of the water carried by the original canals away from the Syr and Amu Darya never even reached the cotton fields! They were criminally inefficient. The canals were made of unlined sand. Can you believe that? Sand!"

The grandiose insanity of the initial scheme to turn a desert into cotton fields outrages Lore. She forces herself to read every study that has been made of the suffering population. The water minerals are running at 1.5 grams per liter, thirty-four percent of adults and sixty-seven percent of children suffer respiratory illness, and seven out of ten inhabitants have hepatitis. All because some maniac thought that climate, geography, and ecology were amenable to ideology.

The sheer scale of that idiocy prods her into a fever. She has to find some way to make a statement, create some monument to remediation as powerful, as awe-inspiring as that lunacy. So she squeezes the budget and builds tower after tower—artificial waterfalls. Water falls hundreds of feet, brilliant with the reflected light of bank after bank of alien-looking heliostats that focus on the cascades the power of sixty suns, enough UV energy to initiate the reaction of organic pollutants to CO_2 in less than forty-five seconds, the time it takes for the water to fall from the top to the bottom.

Mile after mile of these artificial waterfalls glitter in the desert, carbon dioxide fuming from their bases like smoke. Lore dreams of them at night, and wakes in the morning filled with their imagery, satisfied in a way she has never found before—not from sex or food, not from exercise or books or making films. From her mind, her planning, has come this scheme to change a tiny portion of the world. In forty years these rusted hulks will be gone, the birth pathology rate will fall from its current horrendous forty-one to something more normal, and people will fish again in the Aral Sea.

SEVENTEEN

RUTH AND Ellen owned a tiny house in a row of sixteen, all painted bright, primary colors. They faced what had once been a brickyard. The yard had closed down unexpectedly four weeks after they had signed the mortgage, making their home instantly worth thousands more. The yard, Ellen told me as she took my coat, was being converted into a seed nursery by one of the big garden-center chains.

Ruth showed me the living room—small, but with ingenious shelving—then led me into the big kitchen. Ellen followed but said nothing.

There was a bathroom extension, compact and rather chilly, and a back door that led out onto several square feet of concrete.

"We're going to turn it into a patio or something, but we need to get the inside of the house fixed up first."

"It looks fine to me." And it did: clean, bright, open.

"You should have seen it before. Upstairs is still a bit of a mess."

Ellen handed me a big glass of cold white wine. I drank it as I followed Ruth to look around upstairs. Ellen filled it again for me when we came down.

We sat in the bay window of the living room, at an old table with scarred legs covered with a cheerful cloth. Handmade stained-glass shades colored the lamplight, dimming it enough so that I could barely see the thin patches in the chenille curtains. The room felt warm and vibrant and jewel-like, and I wondered if they knew how much I envied them.

Ellen brought in soup. We started to eat. I did not know what to say. I had hurt these two a while ago, yet here I was, eating their food.

I cleared my throat, waved my spoon at the walls. "Do you think these colors would suit my flat?"

"Tell us what it's like." There were rich shadows under Ruth's cheekbones, along her jaw.

"Empty. I mean, bare. Long and narrow, low ceiling. Strange angles at the roof and corners." My soup was gone. I refilled my wineglass, just to have something to do with my hands. "A high window, but wide. From my bed it looks like the horizon a long, long way off." That surprised me, but they weren't giving me funny looks. I was encouraged. "In the late afternoon and early morning, the light slants in and sort of washes the walls. Sometimes it's like stumbling out of a dark tent to desert sunshine, to sand stretching away in the distance." I held my wineglass up until the light turned it gold. "I want the air to feel as though it's this color. Sunshine on sand." I felt very pleased with myself. "Yes. A sort of sandy peachy color."

Ruth got up and went to the bookshelf that ran along the long wall over the couch. She brought back an old book of photographs. We pushed aside glasses and bowls.

"How about this?" Dunes, blue sky. Camel prints into the horizon. "Or this?" Sunset, sand the color of orange and caramel. "If you find the right color, they'll match it for you."

Ellen brought back a tray with two covered dishes and we had to set the book aside. We spent a moment spooning things onto our plates: some kind of spicy vegetable casserole, with roasted potatoes and baked parsnip and carrots.

I tasted the parsnips cautiously. They were light, sweet like fresh pastry. "These are good." We ate quietly, looked at some more pictures. Ellen said nothing much. I drank steadily.

"Thank you," I said, and gestured to my empty plate, the book of photographs. "I'm grateful."

Ellen leaned back in her chair. "You should be." Ruth shot her a look but she ignored it. "I'll be honest. I didn't want you to come. What you did was unforgivable, except that I did a few things I'm not very proud of while I was with Spanner. She has that effect on people."

"She didn't exactly hold a gun to my head." I wondered why I was defending Spanner. Or maybe I was defending myself; I wasn't a child to be told what to do. At least not anymore.

"True."

Ruth was utterly still. Ellen seemed to be waiting for something. Something from me. I emptied the wine bottle into my glass, took a hefty swallow. "How did you meet Spanner?"

"In a bar," Ellen said. "She was playing pool. I couldn't keep my eyes off her. You know how she is." Oh yes. "She was losing. Not very gracefully." I could imagine: the glint in her eyes, hair thrown back, anger flushing her cheeks, her strides around the table getting more and more like the stalk of some hunting animal. "One thing led to another." She picked up a fresh wine bottle and gestured at Ruth's glass.

"That's the third bottle."

"I know."

Ruth sighed and pushed her glass across the table. I was getting drunk, but I nodded when it was my turn. Ellen filled her own last.

"So, how about you, Lore? How did you meet Spanner?"

I thought about how to answer, because the question wasn't only *How did you meet her?* but *Who are you, where are you from?* They didn't need to tell me their backgrounds, because they were Ruth-and-Ellen and Ellen-and-Ruth. Their coupledom said *We're nice people, otherwise we wouldn't have lived together so long, wouldn't be capable of love.* But I had lived for over two years with a woman they both stepped around very carefully, which made me suspect in itself; and now I was alone. They wanted a pedigree, a provenance, a way of knowing what to expect in the future. I understood it and resented it at the same time.

"I was naked and bleeding, left for dead in the city center. She found me." I didn't look at them. "She took me—" I swallowed; I had nearly said *home.* "She took me back to her flat on Springbank. I had to stay with her because I couldn't use my real name. For fear my parents . . . for fear . . ." Even though I knew what they must be assuming, this felt too close to the truth for comfort. "Anyway, I was a babe in the woods. I had no idea how to support myself. Spanner showed me how." Now I met their eyes. "And, yes, I did some things I'm not proud of. You don't know the half of it."

"But you didn't know any better," Ruth said, trying to excuse me, trying to make everything all right.

"Yes, I did. I think I always did. Just as I'm sure Ellen there knew at the time. We can tell ourselves that we had to, we had no choice, until we're blue in the face, but how many days did I starve while I tried to find other ways to make money? None. I had food, shelter, access to the net. I didn't *need* to do those things." I wanted her to understand. Poor Ruth, or lucky Ruth, who had never had to look inside herself and face what stared back.

"But you mustn't feel guilty."

"Why mustn't I? I *am* guilty. But you know what bothers me? I don't *feel* guilty. Not really. Sometimes I feel this heavy weight in the pit of my stomach, but it's more like an acknowledgment of stupidity than guilt. I was so stupid."

"And young," Ellen said.

I hadn't looked at it quite that way, maybe because I hadn't felt young since I was about seven years old. "You might be right. But I knew, all those nights when I lay awake, trying not to think about what I had just done that evening, or afternoon, or morning, I knew that what I was doing was wrong. Oh, most of the time I didn't care that I hurt others—"

"Not even us?"

It would be easy to lie. I sighed. "Not even you. I was more concerned with how low *I* must have sunk to do that, what it meant for *me*, not how you felt. I'm sorry."

Ruth touched my hand briefly.

"I wonder if Spanner would have corrupted me if I'd spent more than five weeks with her," Ellen said thoughtfully.

"She didn't corrupt me." She had just showed me what was there, pointed me inward to all the seams and twisted paths. "That's something you can only do to yourself." It was hot. I was thirsty, but I didn't want to get up in the middle of this to get a glass of water, not until they understood. I drank more wine. "We all have wounds. We all get hurt. But self-pity, lack of courage, leads to a sort of . . . mortification of the soul. Corruption. And then it takes more courage, costs more pain, to clean it up afterward."

I drank more cold wine, thought about the heat in Belize, how I had been cool in my hotel room, cool and unconcerned about the fate of those people in Caracas. "I was in the jungle once. I lay on my back in the middle of a clearing while insects crawled over my hands and under the small of my back, and looked up. Up through the endless greenery." I spoke slowly, remembering. "The jungle isn't just one place, you know—it's a dozen, all in layers. And the animals and insects of each layer are utterly oblivious to what's above them, or below. They don't even know anything outside their world exists. So I lay there, covered in bugs, and tried to imagine what the world looks like to the white hawks and harpy eagles soaring over the canopy hunting for their food—troops of howler and spider monkeys. A green carpet, maybe. Something flat, anyway. They float about up there and have no idea that lower down anteaters ramble about, clinging with their prehensile tails to thin tree trunks, leaning down and licking out termites from the high-up nests. Sloths live there, too." I had seen them, fur slimed with algae, hanging upside down, creeping from bough to bough. "Did you know that the sloth's claws are so well adapted to hanging upside down that if it fell off, to the forest floor, it would die because it couldn't crawl away from predators?" I had been born to soar above the canopy, oblivious. But humans were adaptable, weren't they? "The eagles don't know the sloths and anteaters are there. The sloths and anteaters don't know that underneath them are other layers. Little, quick things that flit from bloom to bloom, like bees and hummingbirds. And kinkajous and geckos and insects. All scampering about, oblivious." The layers I had seen that day were endless. "The bottom layer is the forest floor. Big things, slow-moving. Heavy. Jaguars, herds of peccaries, tapirs. Where things squeal and run." Bright crunch of blood. Shrill screams. "Layer after layer, each separate, each teeming with life . . ."

They were looking at me oddly.

"Don't you see? Everything works in layers: jungles, cities, people. Each layer has its predator and prey, its network of ally and foe, safe place and trap. Its own ecosystem. You have to get to know the land." I wondered if I was making sense. "We don't always know what we're getting into. And we don't always know how to get out. We can't understand everything. We each have a niche." I remembered Paolo, saying, *I'm nothing, a nobody.* Thought of Spanner, her amusement when I had suggested a job: *Now, why would I want a job?* "If we fall out of it, like the sloth, we're not equipped. We can die. Others can see it happening, but they can't help. They can't climb down the tree and help us back up. We have to do it ourselves." I was crying. I couldn't seem to stop.

≈ INTEREST IN the porn films lasted until early summer, but then their money began to dry up again. They swapped their PIDAs often—though her middle name always remained *Lore*—but their stock began to dwindle, and there were no more PIDAs from Ruth, and no more money to get them elsewhere. Hyn and Zimmer stayed out of sight, and Spanner went out more and more often on her own. She came back restless and irritable. One evening after they ate, she stood behind Lore's chair and rubbed her shoulders.

"We're going out tonight to meet some new friends. Wear that black thing I bought you before Christmas. The dress." She went into the bathroom, and Lore heard the click as she opened up the cabinet, the *chink* as she dropped the tiny glass vial into her pocket with her razor.

It was a warm night, and Lore's dress clung to her body. Her shoulders and neck felt exposed as they rode the slide to the bar. It was a new place, built only a year or two ago on a patch of land that had been a park until the city ran out of money. Inside, it was all rounded angles and glass just a little too thick to see through. The floor was some kind of clay tile. There was no bar, just table service, and the clientele had the tight, jerky look of people who were on display, or desperately wanted to be. Their nervousness was catching. For the first time since Lore had known her, Spanner—her hair up in a twist, wearing a formal tunic—

did not order beer. Lore followed her lead and got a cold vodka cocktail. It felt peculiar to be wearing a black dress and sipping a cocktail.

The ceiling was mobile and made of glass, thick chunks tinted aquamarine and azure, indigo and electric green that moved slowly, occasionally showing Lore sliding reflections of another table, her own hand, the floor.

"They're here." Spanner stood up and waved.

Afterward, when Lore thought about that evening, she was sure Spanner had introduced them all, but she could never remember their names. The man was in his early forties, in cotton trousers and soft shirt. He was tall, and stooped all the time, though Lore was not sure if that was from habit or because he was uncomfortable. The woman was a little younger, late thirties, and plainly excited. She smiled a lot. Her hair was thick, black and glossy, about shoulder length. They bought another round of drinks. Lore noticed that, like herself and Spanner, they paid with anonymous debit cards.

Spanner, as she could so easily when she made the effort, was charming them, telling tales of riding the freighters at night for no charge, of the more colorful regulars at the Polar Bear, of the night she and Lore had tried to burn their own front door in the fireplace, only to find out it was definitely noncombustible. They ordered another round, then another. The waitress seemed to be always at their table with a tray of frosting, clear drinks. Each time, the couple paid.

The woman talked about her job. She did not say what she did, exactly, but hinted that she worked for the executive branch of the city council. "Very dull," she said, but her coy smile suggested it might be anything but.

There were rings on every finger of her right hand. They flashed and sparkled as she talked, tapping neatly manicured nails on the tabletop. She leaned forward. Lore could feel the heat of the woman's skin on her own bare arm. The man hardly spoke.

Lore's glass was empty. So were the others. "Shall we have another?"

"Well, no," the woman said, suddenly diffident. Lore was watching her hand again. It had been a while since she had seen such expensively manicured nails. "I could do with something to eat. Perhaps you would both like to join us?"

"We'd love to," Spanner said. Lore nodded. She had no choice, not really. She knew what was happening.

"And then perhaps a film afterward."

Outside, the night was very immediate. The man misstepped in the doorway and swayed. The woman laughed and slid one arm through his, another through Lore's. "We probably all need support."

Instead of heading for the slide pole, the woman stopped by a small black car. Lore realized she was not surprised. "Yours?"

The woman nodded. "We're here," she told the car. Lore heard the locks click back. There was one driver's seat on the right-hand side, and three other seats arranged in a triangle. "Take us home," the woman said once they were all inside, "and let's have some privacy." The windows polarized to black. The man sat in the driver's seat but appeared to go to sleep.

The drive took twenty minutes. Lore had no idea in which direction they were going. In the close quarters of the vehicle, Lore could smell the woman's perfume, a surprisingly light fragrance, one she found familiar. She wondered if this woman had ever attended one of the low-voiced dinners with family representatives, where crystal flashed and deals were made between one course and the next. Crystal, Lore thought fuzzily, like silverware, reflected a distorted version of reality. Look in a spoon or into the bottom of a glass and what looked back at you was swollen and grotesque.

The car pulled into a driveway. The wheels crunched on old-fashioned gravel. It was too dark to see the apartment building as they were led inside, but Lore got the impression it was big. She smelled the close greenery of a formal shrubbery; a brick wall enclosed the courtyard.

Food was already laid out on the low table in the living room. They sat down, Lore and Spanner on the outside leather couch, the woman and man on chairs opposite each other. They ate and talked. The man seemed almost not to be there. Gradually they stopped paying attention to him. There was icy, sparkling wine, dry as carbon dioxide.

Then the food was gone, and the woman was pushing the table aside. Her cheeks were flushed. Even in her thin dress, Lore was hot. Spanner looked serene and detached, untroubled by the heat.

"The film now?" the woman asked, ignoring the man. Lore, pleasantly heavy-eyed, nodded. Whatever the woman wanted: she was paying. Or Lore assumed she was.

The screen unfolded from the ceiling, opposite the couch. The woman dimmed the lights.

There were no titles, and the music was lush and eerie. Figures walked and ran and whirled in various locations— beach, moor, desert—and Lore began to wish she had not had so much to drink. She could not make sense of anything.

"I'm a little warm," she said.

"I would rather keep the temperature as it is," the woman said softly.

"Why don't you just unbutton your dress if you're uncomfortable?" Spanner asked. "I'm sure no one will mind." She raised her eyebrows at the man and the woman. The man was staring at the carpet. The woman shook her head.

"No, please go ahead. Make yourself comfortable. No one minds a bit of flesh if you don't." And she turned back to the screen.

It felt like a suffocating dream. This was it. Spanner, and

the woman, wanted her to take her clothes off. She wanted to jump up and scream, demand to know if anyone else would be naked. *I have been naked too much!* But she knew she would not do that. This time she had a choice.

On the screen, the characters were talking, then eating breakfast. Half of them were not wearing clothes. The scene changed, and one woman was lifting a teenage boy onto what looked like an altar.

"Unbutton your dress," Spanner whispered. "I won't let either of them touch you, or take pictures."

The woman was watching the screen, rapt. As Lore watched, the woman took off her jacket and laid it aside, not glancing back at the couch The man seemed to be asleep.

They needed the money, and it was just a dress. In a dream, Lore unbuttoned her dress and pulled it down to her waist. She sat back in the couch. The leather was cool against her naked back. On the screen, the woman was positioning herself over the naked teenager, and the onlooking audience—or chorus, or whatever they were—were touching each other slowly. The heat, the alcohol, the film all made Lore feel as though she were under water. A trickle of sweat rolled down between her breasts.

"You still hot?" Spanner asked. "Why don't you take the dress off?"

"Aren't you hot?"

"No." Spanner smiled. "Come here." She held out her arm. Lore slid over next to her. "It'll be fine. Just take the dress off." Spanner kissed her on the forehead, stroked her neck. "It's dark in here anyway."

Lore shook her head, trying to clear it, and wondered when the drug would start to work, when she would stop caring. The heat decided her. She stood up, pulled off the dress, then her underwear, and dropped them on the carpet. The woman turned briefly, nodded, then turned back to the screen. Lore snuggled back next to Spanner. Spanner had said she would protect her.

Spanner turned, smiled, ran a finger under her chin, then turned back to the screen.

As if being naked had freed something, all of a sudden Lore could smell the shampoo in Spanner's hair, the musk of her skin. She kissed her neck below the ear. Spanner's hand, resting on Lore's shoulder, began to stroke her neck absently. The woman was still watching the screen. Lore laughed quietly and slipped her hand under Spanner's tunic.

"Kiss me," Lore whispered. Spanner turned away from the screen. "Kiss me," she said again.

Spanner put her hands on both sides of Lore's face and kissed her very, very gently. "More . . ." Spanner did it again. Her lips were like fruit, soft and ripe and very slightly moist. Lore leaned forward, pushing, wanting Spanner to kiss her harder, wanting to feel the warmth of Spanner's body. Her breath was harsh and rapid.

"Sshh, quietly." Spanner glanced over significantly at the rest of the room. The man was asleep. The woman was still watching the film. She would notice nothing if they kept very quiet. It was a game.

Spanner turned to face Lore, stroked her shoulders and upper arms, across her throat and the top of her chest. Lore tried to sit up, so that the stroking hands would brush her breasts. Spanner smiled and put a finger to her lips. Then she unbuttoned her tunic. Lore climbed right up onto the couch and reached for her. Spanner held up her hand: no. Lore sat still, knees hunched under her chin. The leather was warm now, and soft, like skin. Her hairless vulva felt swollen and slippery. Spanner stood up, got off the couch carefully, slowly, so that the woman would not see them in her peripheral vision. She got back on the couch behind Lore. Hard nipples rubbed Lore's back below her shoulder blades. A hand came around and cupped one of Lore's breasts.

"Ah." Lore was moving now, unable to keep still. Her belly was full of lava and blood ran thick and heavy under her skin, making her feel slow and liquid.

"Yes," whispered Spanner, "yes. Oh soon, soon." Her hand was running down Lore's ribs now, cupping her hipbone, running back up to her breasts. Then it began to move slowly, very slowly down the center of her body. It held her stomach, pressed. On the screen, bizarre images of red and purple flowers shimmered; the music was rising to a deafening crescendo.

Spanner had both arms around her now, both hands moving rhythmically over her body, belly, flank, thigh, inside her thigh, back to her belly, over and over, "Please, Spanner. Oh, please," and Lore no longer cared whether or not the woman heard, no longer cared whether or not she saw. She writhed in Spanner's arms, trying to thrust herself onto Spanner, any part of Spanner, just so that she could feel hot, live skin between her legs. And the room was thick with her own smell, sweat and need and sex, and Spanner's, and she wanted to spin inside her need forever, without touching, but now Spanner was urging her, turning her to face the back of the couch, belly against the leather, breasts over the top, legs apart. She heard the soft *zzt* of Spanner's zipper and felt breath on the back of her neck, Spanner's thigh pushing between her own. She arched backward, trying to make the connection, but then Spanner's hand came around the front to dip slowly, teasingly, through her labia. "Ah . . ." She shuddered. "Please Spanner, oh please." But Spanner was positioning herself, wet and hot against Lore's moving buttocks, and suddenly the couch cushion sagged to one side as the woman, naked from the waist down, climbed onto the couch. She touched Lore's hair with one hand. The other was between her own thighs. She was looking at Spanner.

"Now," she said, and Spanner slid her finger deep inside Lore and Lore's muscles were clamping down around it, she was straining, humping, and Spanner was gasping behind her, pulling herself up and down, leaving hot, wet trails, and the woman was flushing deep deep red and laughing and crying out and their triple need tore up inside Lore, right up into her guts until she screamed and every muscle in her body went rigid and she slid sideways onto the cushions, Spanner still inside her.

It was still hot. The man snored gently. The screen was blank.

THE HARDEST part of the shift for me was always half an hour after the break, when there were still nearly four hours to go and my blood sugar was low. Today, I felt restless and tense and hot. At the readout station I pushed the hair off my face with the back of one hand and just hoped there was nothing toxic on my glove. Hepple, though he was keeping a low profile since Magyar had hinted I was a Health and Safety spy, was still demanding hourly readings.

The readings were normal, absolutely normal, but something nagged at me. Maybe it was just the fact of Hepple's demands, but something seemed not quite right. I checked everything I could think of, even the enzyme levels and secondary by-products like dichloroethylene. Everything on the button. It must be the heat making me tense. I waited for my neck muscles to relax. They didn't.

I missed Paolo, wondered what he was doing now, but it wasn't that. I was waiting for something to happen. I just didn't know what, or why.

I downloaded the latest results onto a slate and went to find Hepple. He was in his glass office.

Instead of motioning me to put the slate on his desk, he reached for it immediately. He was looking the numbers over thoroughly when I left.

Maybe he was expecting something, too.

I went back to trough forty-one, decided to replace some of the rushes, just because I was restless, then changed my mind and went back to the readout station and checked the monitors. Everything was fine. So why wasn't I happy about it? Think. Start at the beginning. The plant and equipment itself? Everything seemed in order. The influent? No. Nothing wrong with that. Nothing wrong with the bugs, either; they were standard tried-and-true van de Oest series. Guaranteed, as long as they were supplied with . . .

And then I remembered. *The puddles, the truck, the driver calling, "Sorry about that!" The logo: BioSystems.*

I swore, ran a sample on the bug food. Took down one of the slates and after a few minutes' fiddling managed to access some old records. Compared the two. Just as I thought. I picked up the phone. "Magyar, I need to talk to you."

"What's happened?" Even over the line I could hear her tension. She was waiting for something, too.

"Just get here."

I felt savage. If Hepple had appeared right then I think I would have kicked him until he bled. Four million gallons a day, straight into the city's mains, and he was risking it all for the sake of shaving half a percent from the plant's operating costs.

Magyar arrived, breathless. "Tell me."

"Hepple. Stupid bastard." I was so angry I could hardly speak. "The bug food. Hepple bought the cheap stuff. Generics."

The folds around her eyes seemed to swell slightly, making her eyes look smaller. "How bad is that?"

"Right now, not very, but I don't know how long it will stay that way. I can try adjust the nutrients by hand until we can replace it. The system should catch any big swings—ones that are within known parameters, anyway—but the van de Oest proprietary nutrients have got to be restored."

"How much time do we have?"

"Hard to tell. These bugs are genetically designed to fail without exactly the right ingredients, but given the mixture of microbes and varying substrates available here, I couldn't begin to predict when or what form that failure will take."

"But you're sure they'll fail."

"Yes."

A beat of silence. "Give me your best estimate of how much time we've got."

"A week? It depends on what we get down the line." All it would take was one big spill . . . "I can't believe Hepple's done this."

"Oh, he's probably got some very plausible-sounding reasons." She sounded vicious.

"Then you'll need to go over his head."

"I'll try."

"Try hard. Meanwhile . . ." I started pulling down all the slates, feeling about on the shelf. Empty.

"If it's the manual you're looking for, I've got it. Oh, don't look so surprised. I knew Hepple was up to something. I just didn't know what. I decided to prepare for disaster."

I felt foolish for underestimating her.

She read my expression and gave me a tight, amused look. "What do you know about emergency and evacuation procedures here?"

"Not much." Which is why I'd wanted to take another look at that manual.

"We've got just about enough sets of emergency escape breathing apparatus, if you include the SCBAs and the moon suits. But I haven't had the chance to check them and find out if they're properly maintained. And I don't know how many of the shift know how to use them. Which is why I need you. I don't know who you are, or why you're here, but I'll use you if I can."

·   ·   ·

I took the manual home. There were two messages waiting. The first was from Ruth; she was smiling. "Hope you enjoyed the dinner the other day. Let us know when and we'll come and help you redecorate."

The second was Spanner: "It's just before midnight. I'm on my way out. I should have the money we need by morning. I'll call you."

I ate, and opened the manual at random. I would not worry about Spanner and I would not feel guilty that it was her taking the risks. I would not.

After an hour or so, I pushed the manual aside. Rules and regulations were not enough to distract me from how Spanner might be earning the money for our scam. She *chose* to take the risks, I told myself. It was she who had suggested the scam in the first place. I was doing my part, too.

Maybe she was back already, safe. I called. No reply.

I turned on the edit box. Tom appeared on the screen. If I wasn't going to get any sleep, I might as well do something useful.

At six in the morning I was playing the short video of Tom over and over again, obsessively. I called Spanner's number for the tenth time. Nothing. I ran the video again. By the magic of digital imaging, Tom stood at a slide pole, looking bewildered; faced the image of his bank-account representative and wept; threw a book against the wall in frustration. Text drifted across the pictures: *You can help. Send money now.* The account numbers would be inserted later, when I got them from Spanner.

I tried her number again.

I had started out taking notes: shave a frame here, a pan there; add a zoom focus and fade. Now I was just watching, over and over.

It was after seven. This time when there was no reply from Spanner, I knew there was something wrong.

• • •

There were no lights shining around Spanner's door seal; no reply to my knock. I tried the handle. It swung open.

"Spanner?"

No reply. I went in.

"Spanner?"

No one in the living room. I put my head in the bathroom, the bedroom, the kitchen—and stopped abruptly.

She was standing very still by the kitchen counter, profile to the window. "I was worried to death! Why didn't you—"

She turned her head very, very slowly.

"Oh, dear god." She tried to smile and I felt my face stiffen in shock. I reached out to hold her, support her, but stopped short of touching her. She was standing rigidly and her face was a grayish, doughy color. Pain. Pain would do that.

"Is the medic's number on your system? No, don't try to nod. Just . . . just blink if the answer's yes." She blinked. I raced into the living room, punched in his number. It was his service. I told him to get here right away, then, worried I might be garbling my words in shock, told him everything all over again. I ran back into the kitchen. Spanner was still standing there, helpless.

"Don't worry, I won't touch you. Do you need to lie down?" She blinked twice.

I couldn't touch her. She wouldn't lie down. She couldn't seem to talk. We stared at each other. Her breathing was stertorous. I smiled. I didn't know what else to do.

"You'll be fine. The medic's on his way. He's very good. But you know that. Remember how he fixed me? You'll be fine."

I don't know how long I kept up that inane chatter, but when the medic banged on the door my throat was beginning to feel sore. I didn't dare take my eyes off Spanner. "In here!" I called. "The door's open."

He came in in a blast of cold air and had his coat off before I could even say hello. "Tetany," he said to no one in particular. "Saw that in a horse, once." *A horse?* "It's the pain." He had his bag open. "Have you tried to touch her?"

"No."

"Any idea where she hurts?"

"No."

"Can you talk?" he asked Spanner. She blinked twice.

"That means no."

He grinned at me over his shoulder, and it occurred to me that he thought we were some kind of comedy act. *No. And she says no, too.* My legs started to shake.

He held up a spray hypo.

"No!"

He looked at me, raised his eyebrow. "Allergic?"

"Yes. I mean, no. I am, but she isn't." He waited patiently. *This is not the past!* "No, I'm sorry. It's all right. She's not allergic."

He reached up to touch Spanner's shoulder, but she flinched visibly so he sprayed it into her left buttock instead. "Watch."

She began to shudder like a dog, and sweat. Her breathing came in great gasps.

"Help me get her to the bed."

Between us, we shepherded Spanner into the bedroom.

"She won't want to lie down." She balked at the bed. "I can give her one more shot, but it'll put her out. Can you authorize payment?" I nodded. He squirted the stuff into her right buttock this time. "Catch her!"

She fell as I imagined a robot might: arms and legs stiff and not swinging quite right.

"We need to get her clothes off."

I think the worst thing was that I couldn't see anything wrong: no burns or cuts or rashes. No bruises or welts. Nothing.

We had her clothes off and he was palpating this and that, bending knees, thumping her chest, nodding to himself.

"She'll need watching for twenty-four hours." He laid out six hypos. "Painkillers and antibiotics. One every four hours. Then I'll come back." He had pulled on his coat, held out his reader for me to V-hand, and was opening the door before I realized he hadn't told me anything.

"What's wrong? What's happened to her?"

"All her limbs have been dislocated and then snapped back in. Several times. She's the second person I've seen with this in three days."

"Dislocated . . ."

"There's some maniac out there who seems to get their kicks from hurting people severely. I'm tempted to ignore my Hippocratic Oath and report this to the police. Oh, your friend there will be fine, if she rests, and if no infection sets in, but people like the one she met up with last night shouldn't be allowed to go free."

I was taken by a sudden, low impulse to tell him *I don't live here! I don't do this kind of thing! I'm not like her!* but I had, once. And I had been, no matter how unknowingly or unwillingly, complicit in this.

"How long will she need to stay in bed?"

"Up to her. The danger of spontaneous redislocation and infection should be past in about forty-eight hours." He nodded once, shortly, and left. I felt terribly ashamed.

At four that afternoon, Spanner woke up and managed to drink some water.

"Go home." Raspy, but perfectly clear.

"The medic said—"

"Just go away."

"You shouldn't be left alone."

"What about. That job. Of yours."

"I'm not going anywhere while you need me."

"I don't want you. In my flat. You left it once. I won't have you staying. Here. Out of pity. Go away."

"You need—"

"Go away." Her eyes were so wide that white showed all the way around the irises. She meant it.

"There are four hypos left. I'll set the system to wake you every four hours. You must use them. The medic says there's danger of infection. He's coming back tomorrow morning. I'll lock the door behind me, just the mechanical lock, and give him a message about where the key is."

Silence, apart from her breathing. "I got the money."

"I don't care about the money!"

"I do. I earned every. Single. Penny." Her face was gray again. "Shit. Shit. Hurts."

I wondered if she had laughed and come while he had been popping out her joints. I turned away, swallowing bile.

She laughed, very softly, so as not to shake her arms or legs. "You never could. Face reality. Go on. Go back to your job. Earn your. Respectable money. But don't forget. Me and you. Have a bargain."

"I'll call you when—"

"Don't. I'll call you. When it's time. About ten days."

Tom was leaving the building just as I got back. He asked me something about the fake ad I was making, then peered at me.

"You look terrible."

"I'm fine." I tried to smile and push past him.

He grabbed my arm. "Leave him," he said bluntly. "Or her. Find someone who'll care about you."

"I'm fine," I repeated tiredly. "I need to get some rest before work."

He sighed and let me go.

I called Ruth and Ellen's. Both out. No forwarding, as usual. "This is Lore. Spanner's hurt. She won't let me help her. She might let you, Ellen." I told her where I had left the key. "Please. Help her."

I went on shift that day as though everything were fine. Nothing happened. The readings kept showing normal. It was easier to concentrate on the job than to think about Spanner and her pain.

The next day, and the day after that, I went to each equipment locker on my list and tested oxygen tanks, meters, foam canisters. The moon suits, the level-A protective gear, were good quality stuff: flashproof as well as fitted with two-stage regulators. The battery telltales were green when I tested them, and the radios were in working order.

"Everything so far is in surprisingly good shape," I told Magyar.

"Good. Keep checking."

I made sure that the EEBA by the readout console was working, then checked the portable eye showers, the emergency lockdown valves, the reverse pumps. There was fresh oil on one of the pump works. I rubbed it thoughtfully between finger and thumb. The oil felt strange, almost tacky, on the plasthene gloves. After I'd checked the exits and the sprinkler system I called Magyar again. "I'm puzzled."

"You surprise me, Bird."

I ignored that. "I found fresh oil on one of the pumps."

"Good. Or isn't it?"

"It's just puzzling. None of the maintenance logs indicate any attention in the last few months. But I find all the batteries are charged, all the pumps freshly greased, all the air tanks full. That last is especially unusual. A good snort of O_2 works well on a hangover."

She caught on fast. "Then who's been topping everything up?"

"I was hoping you could tell me that." But I was more interested in *why* than *who*. Someone was making sure the emergency gear was in good condition. Whoever it was knew enough to understand we might be heading for trouble. "Who here knows how to use all this stuff?"

"I doubt if anyone does. I can use the moon suits, but the others haven't clapped eyes on an EEBA since their orientation video, assuming they were shown it, or bothered to watch it if they were."

"They need to learn."

"Training will mean a drop in productivity. Hepple won't authorize it." A moment of silence.

"If you're thinking of asking them to stay behind on a voluntary basis, they won't like it."

"But they'll do it." She looked offscreen at her watch. "Still twenty-five minutes of break left. Lots of time to spread the good news."

I was right: they didn't like it.

"Why?" demanded Cel.

"First reduced productivity pay because of the masks," grumbled Meisener. "Now this."

Kinnis just looked surly. "I don't understand."

Cel folded her arms. "We're already shorthanded, worked half to death. I think we need a good reason to go along with this as well."

"How about this," Magyar said pleasantly. "One week from today there will be a test of emergency procedure know-how. All personnel who fail will be dismissed without notice and without pay in lieu. Good enough?"

Kinnis sighed. "What's the pass rate?"

"I'll be fair. Anyone who attends all sessions and spells their name right passes. Lessons start tomorrow. Enjoy the rest of your break."

I was beginning to appreciate Magyar more and more.

EIGHTEEN

IT IS five weeks before Lore's eighteenth birthday. She is at the party of a young woman called Sarah. Sarah's family owns half the real estate in Montevideo. The party is being held in what is sometimes called an aesthetics research institute, but is really a pleasure resort, dug into cave complexes beneath the Río Negro.

Lore and Sarah and about a hundred other invited guests are standing, bare-armed in their finery, in a vast underground auditorium. The walls, which are more than three hundred feet high, are tiled with white ceramic; the floor is paved with milky brick; the corners and doors and lights are sealed with white enamel. The air is frigid.

Sarah, whom Lore has known for only a week, has beautiful, satiny beige skin and black hair cut longer at the front than the back. Her hair is blowing this way and that in the cold breeze coming from the tunnel that leads into the cave from the right. Although the tunnel is prob-

231

ably ninety feet in diameter, it occupies only the top corner of the wall.

People are talking and drinking, but they have been promised a surprise by Sarah, and there is a current of tension under the conversation. They are waiting.

It is hard to say when it actually begins. Over the tinkle of crystal and the susurrus of silk Lore hears, no, feels, a change. A vibration. The breeze falters, resumes differently. Something is skimming toward them down the tunnel. Others feel it now, too. Heads turn this way and that; Lore catches the anxious glitter of diamond earrings. It is coming.

There is a whispering from the tunnel, and Lore can feel it against her skin: the approach of something huge. Everyone watches the dark hole. No one is talking. Lore thinks of beasts and their lairs, the tunnels they make. But what animal would make its home in this kind of cold?

Suddenly warmer air comes boiling, frothing from the tunnel, and she can see something approaching, something so huge and black it fills the opening of the tunnel. It is so big her mind quails, and it is gathering its muscles to leap.

God! she thinks, because this is not a projection. She can *feel* the heat radiating from the beast; she can *feel* the air moving. And there is an animal smell, dusty and hot, and the electric tension of the hunter's mesmerizing gaze. Someone cries out, and there is a burst of muscle-straining panic: people throw themselves to the floor, pearls breaking, stones ripping from jeweled chokers. Lore catches a glimpse of eye-white and feline green, and ivory yellow reaching claws as the beast pours smoothly from the tunnel.

And then Lore wonders if time really does slow to molasses when one is in fear for one's life, because the beast doesn't fall upon them in a snarl of sleek pelt and glinting teeth, it . . . stretches.

She blinks, thinks perhaps she is a little mad as the huge panther thins and seems to shudder before her. And then it bursts, exploding into thousands of small birds, all soaring and swooping and twittering at once. The air is filled with bright avian song.

"They're birds!" someone shouts. And Lore is laughing, climbing to her feet, unable to turn away from the swoop and flutter in the air.

Birds.

Sarah is holding out a glass. Champagne. Lore takes it. Her hands are shaking. "Electromagnetic control," Sarah says. But Lore doesn't want to hear the mechanics, just savor the wonder. She gulps the champagne, holds it out for a re-fill from one of the passing waiters. Sarah slides her arm around Lore's waist. Her fingers are very warm just above Lore's hip. The birds wheel twice, then begin to pour back into the tunnel.

The water room is sixty by sixty, tiled in an intricate pat-tern of blue and azure with walls of aquamarine and tur-quoise glass block. Vitrine sculptures of fish and mermaids stand in the corners. There are fountains everywhere, and water runs down the walls. The air is damp and full of the music of liquid. The tank, about twenty feet square, is sunk into the center of the floor.

Lore takes off her dress, kicks off her shoes, then peels Sarah out of her green silk sheath. Her stomach is not flat but slightly rounded, with the side ridges and sliding mus-cles of a belly dancer. Her navel looks naked, as though an emerald should glint there. Lore dips the tip of her little fin-ger in. Sarah tilts her chin up: *Take me.*

"In the pool."

She wants to soar and swoop and mate on the wing, gulp at the medium that buoys her, like a bird.

Lore is nervous and excited. She takes Sarah's hand and they step to the side of the pool. The heavy pink liquid laps idly at the tiles. The first ledge is about three feet deep.

They step down, slowly, and the liquid, body temperature, slides up their ankles, their calves, and behind their knees. Up, further.

Sarah bobs a little, letting the surface tension rub between her legs. Lore moves behind her, circles her waist, and throws them both in. She keeps hold of Sarah as she kicks for the bottom, twenty feet down. She wraps one leg around the ring there and waits, shuddering with fear that she tells herself is anticipation.

It is not water, of course, but perfluorocarbon, and when Lore has no breath left in her body, she opens her mouth and breathes in. It is like breathing a fist.

Her body shoots toward the surface, ancient habits demanding that she cough up the liquid and breathe air, but her lungs are full long before she reaches the silvery pink of the surface, and she can still move, still think, and the panic recedes. She is alive! She laughs, a strange, gushing affair, and experiments with pulling the perfluorocarbon in and out of her lungs. The liquid moves in and out, in and out, like a sliding arm.

She swims down and Sarah up; they meet near the middle, porpoising over each other, belly to belly. Even their skin feels different: rubbery and resilient, like that of marine mammals. Lore strokes back over Sarah, turns her face down, covers her, belly to back, and cups the small, cool breasts in her hand. Sarah dives. Clinging like limpets, they swerve at the last minute, then turn this way and that along the smooth bottom. Lore imagines they are seals diving after agile fish. They part by mutual consent, enjoying themselves, playing like children. But they swim around each other, always each other's focus, like dolphins courting. Lore is exhilarated. Partly the champagne, partly moving in three dimensions, partly the fact that the perfluorocarbon supplies two to three times as much oxygen as air. She swims all the way to the top, until her back and buttocks poke out into the air, and floats, like a hovering hawk, until Sarah is directly beneath her. Then she stoops.

The liquid pouring into her lungs is like a river running through her. She feels as though she could be hauling herself along a rope, a line made of water, the rope running through her, tight, taut, fiercely singing. She catches Sarah and clamps an arm around her waist, a mouth at her throat. Sarah keeps swimming, laughing, until Lore traps Sarah's legs in her own and thrusts a finger inside her.

They make love for nearly an hour. Each time they come they thrash like fish.

NINETEEN

IT HAPPENED just before one in the morning, and there was nothing anyone could have done about it.

I was walking away from the readout station with the latest figures when something in my peripheral vision made me turn back. The numbers on the volatile organic counters were rocketing. All the alarms went off.

It was like a stun grenade: red lights on the ceiling rotating; a mechanical clanging; an electronic shrilling. All designed to pump adrenaline into the system and make you move *fast*. A computer-generated voice came over the sound system. "Attention! This is not a drill! Attention! Evacuate the premises in accordance with emergency procedures! Attention . . ."

I pulled off my filter mask, grabbed the emergency-escape breathing apparatus from the shelf, and snapped the mouthpiece over my face. Air gushed, cool and clean. I held the mask in place while I slipped on the head straps and clipped the minitank to my belt. My suit would protect most of my skin, and I had five minutes of air.

Beyond the glass people began to run. I looked at the readouts.

System already locked down and isolated. Influent diverted. Bright amber numerals ticking away the seconds since the alarms kicked in: fifty seconds. Gauges for holding tanks beginning to show increasing volume as the line pumps reversed their flow. Good.

Good, I thought again, and wished my heart didn't feel squeezed between two plates.

I waited, and waited another ten seconds before I realized no one was giving orders. The emergency-response coordinator had evacuated the plant. Job finished. The rest was up to the regional fire department's response teams, and the expert system. But that would take too long.

I pulled the microphone free from its hook, switched it to MANUAL and PRIMARY SECTOR. "This is Bird. Attention Magyar, Cel, and Kinnis—stand by. Attention everyone else." My voice was blurred by the EEBA mask, but not too badly. "Emergency escape breathing apparatus available in hatches six, eleven, and fourteen. The air's good for five minutes. Leave immediately. Attention Magyar. There are two moon suits at hatch six. Suit up, bring the second suit to me here at the monitoring station. And hurry."

I checked my tank—four minutes left—and the readouts. The system had still not identified the volatile organic compound. I did equations in my head. Protection factor, threshold limit value, maximum use concentration. Worst-case scenario: There were maybe three minutes left before the fumes would be dangerous to someone without a mask. Air for one minute after that. I checked the clock: *2:18.*

I was shivering. *Run,* my body was saying. I began to wheeze. Psychosomatic—it had to be.

"Cel, Kinnis. When your EEBAs are secure, go to locker . . . Go to locker . . ." But my mind was blank. What locker, why?

You're panicking.

Red light skimmed the white concrete floor as the ceiling lamps outside went round and round. Think. Where was the self-contained breathing apparatus stored?

Think! No good. The afterwash of the panic had wiped the memory away.

"Attention Magyar, Kinnis, Cel. I can't remember which locker the SCBAs are in. Cel, Kinnis: You have four minutes' air left. Go to drench shower two and wait. Magyar: Find the SCBAs, take them to Cel and Kinnis at drench shower two. Cel, Kinnis: If Magyar isn't there in three minutes, leave. Otherwise, I want you all here, on the double."

3:40. It seemed strange to be in the middle of such a brightly lit emergency. In my imagination there had always been smoke, no power. Thick black murk. But everything looked normal except for the flashing red and the howling noise. The clock trickled seconds like sand: *3:58, 3:59.*

The troughs were draining into the holding tanks. Microbes and their nutrient flow had also been diverted. I checked the concentrations: the system was compensating well, sending the correct ratios of bacterial strains.

I imagined the pollutant: smoky and sickly, an oily stink that curled around my mask.

Tetracholoroethylene, the readout said now. PCE, a short-chain aliphatic. Not as dangerous as some. If Magyar wasn't panicking I would have plenty of time to get into the moon suit before the bugs started to metabolize the PCE into the more dangerous vinyl chloride and dichloro-ethylene. Skin-permeable, flammable, toxic. I switched radio frequency on the microphone.

"Magyar, can you hear me?" Maybe she had overestimated her proficiency with the suits. Maybe the real thing had been too much and she had fled with the others. "Magyar. Magyar, report!"

"I hear you, I hear you." Her breathing, harsh in the enclosed environment of a level-A protective suit, came over the station's speakers. "Don't lose your marbles."

I grinned under my mask—despite the smell, despite the danger, everything. There was never any way to tell who would panic in an emergency. "I wasn't."

"Hold on." Some noises. "Kinnis and Cel now have their gear. I'm on my way. Tell me what's happening."

I briefed her on the PCE; it was the metabolites—the vinyl chloride and dichloroethylene—that would be most dangerous. "But the weakened bugs mean the system is unreliable. There are a score of things that could—"

The door opened: Magyar, huge and clumsy in her silver flash-coated moon suit, lugging a large case. "Your suit."

It was strange to see her in front of me but hear her voice from behind. I took the case, put it on the floor, snapped it open, lifted out the equipment. The tank and two-stage regulators were heavy. I swung them out upright on the floor, then squatted to check the tanks and valves. I turned on the air, felt it cool and steady against my palm. A quick glance at my minitank. Reading empty. I slung the harness of built-in air hoses over my shoulder, then ripped off my EEBA and fitted the larger, silicon face piece over nose, mouth, and jaw. The air was cool and slightly metallic. The face piece fitted tight and clean. I chinned on the radio. "Keep your eyes on the vinyl chloride while I get into this thing." I stepped in the heavy neoprene boots and pulled the suit up to my waist. The bat-winged upper half was awkward, but I managed. Hood next. It cut my peripheral vision a bit.

Magyar studied the board and flipped a switch, then pushed a button. The noise and flashing red lights stopped abruptly.

Cel and Kinnis came in. "What happened?" Kinnis asked, at the same time as Cel said, "Tell us what to do." They both looked uncertainly from Magyar to me and back again.

"For now, we all do as Bird says. Except when I disagree. Kinnis, help her on with that thing."

I was already done, just checking that all the zips were

fastened. Everything felt very unreal. I couldn't make out Kinnis's expression from behind two layers of metallicized PVC, but he moved tightly, tensely.

"I asked you both to stay because I trust you, and Magyar and I may need your help. In the present concentrations you should be safe enough with SCBAs and skinnies—but give each other a quick visual check for tears or weak spots in your suits. If conditions change, I'll ask you to leave." They both nodded. "Here's the situation. Somewhere upline there's been a massive spill of PCE. It got into our pipes. It's killed everything in the troughs. Right now, everything's being pumped back out into the holding tanks. Influent has been diverted to other plants, but we're monitoring it. As soon as it runs clear, we can take it again."

"Only if the troughs have been cleaned," Cel said.

"That's your job. And Kinnis's. Even if you get only three or four back up, it'll keep the system moving. First, a warning. PCE is toxic, in liquid and vapor form. First signs are dizziness and nausea. Either of you two feel dizzy, leave immediately. The gas will irritate your eyes and burn your skin. Check your masks carefully for a tight seal. Do that by turning off your air for three seconds and trying to draw a breath. If you can, you're leaking. Do it now, before the fumes get bad. When the fumes get concentrated enough—though they shouldn't, especially where you'll be—you could suffocate without your respirators. So don't remove them for any reason whatsoever. Once the bugs start to metabolize the PCE there'll be vinyl chloride and dichloroethylene." I hesitated, then decided there was no such thing as too much information. And I didn't know exactly how much Magyar did or didn't know. "Vinyl chloride and dichloroethylene are much meaner than PCE. Carcinogenic, recalcitrant, and very flammable with a low flash point. Neither of you have flash suits. Once the concentration of those chlorinated aliphatics reaches a certain point, you leave. Got that? Good. Now, either of you know how to program by remote?"

They both nodded. Kinnis remembered his radio. "Yes."

"Kinnis, you stay here and reprogram the rakes for removal of reeds. Cel, I want you to start hosing down the troughs. The two of you will coordinate pumping out the tainted swill." The members of the emergency-response team were probably only just arriving and climbing into their gear. "Kinnis, keep an eye on this number at all times." I pointed to the vinyl-chloride readout. "If it gets above two-fifty, evacuate immediately. Stay on this radio frequency—" I glanced down. "—frequency A. Magyar and I will be on B."

"Where are you going?"

"The holding area. At the emergency station."

The emergency station was set up like the readout station. Magyar and I ran through the checks. Amber numerals at the top of the console ticked from 14:04 to 14:05.

It was hard to believe it had only been fourteen minutes.

"All strains on-line," Magyar said.

"Check."

"The emergency-response crews will be arriving about now. Lights flashing, lots of shouting."

"Decon zones being set up," I agreed. "No one knowing what they're doing." A zoo. But we were here, on the spot, and if we did everything right we could keep the system from real shutdown time.

"Everything reads fine except the PCE. Still climbing."

What a mess. I didn't envy whoever had the job of explaining what had happened to the press. "Who's the designated media liaison?"

"Who do you think?"

"Not Hepple . . ." It was funny, really. I wondered if he even knew that some of this was his fault. "How's the PCE doing now?"

"Still climbing."

"Vinyl chloride?"

"Steady."

I swore.

"I take it that's not good."

"It should be rising rapidly as the bacteria process the PCE. How's the dichloroethylene?"

"Steady."

We had a problem. I queried the system: the bugs being fed into the tanks were viable. That wasn't it.

16:04.

I began working the board.

17:16. 17:18. 17:19.

There. "It's the substrate. Conditions are too anoxic— probably electron deficient. The bugs need electrons to fuel their metabolism. Without them they don't reproduce. But that should have been compensated for by . . . Ah."

I stared at the numbers.

"What? Tell me what it is, Bird!"

"The system should have automatically delivered glucose to enrich the mixture. It didn't." I showed her the screen trace I had run.

She followed the green and blue lines carefully to the red bar. "Looks like the drum is blocked."

"Yes. But I've never heard of a glucose drum clogging before."

Silence. "Are you saying this was deliberate?"

"It's very possible." I would bet on it, especially given the filled air tanks, the greased pumps.

Silence again. It was hard to tell what she was thinking in the bulky suit. "I'm going to unplug that drum." The radio flattened her voice. "Keep me informed of changing conditions."

I switched to Kinnis and Cel's frequency. "You're going to have longer than we thought. How are the troughs?"

"Give us another twenty minutes and we'll have four troughs cleaned out and ready for restocking," Cel said.

"More now that I've finished the reprogramming and can help," Kinnis added.

"Keep the channel open, and keep me informed. Out."
Back to B frequency. "Magyar?"

"Here. I've found the problem."

"What is it?"

"A closed-head drum lock." *Locks, always locks.* She grunted. "Damn gloves are so clumsy."

"Be careful, there's—"

"Sparks, I know. But whoever did this was smart enough to use a nonsparking lock bar and what looks like a bronze alloy lock body. Polyethylene gaskets." Another grunt, then a sigh of satisfaction. "Electronic locks might be fancy, but not much stands up to a simple crowbar."

But monsters don't use force. They don't dare. Gray Greta. What would she have done in this situation?

There was more noise over the suit speakers. On my board, figures began to move.

"Glucose should be running now," she said.

"It is."

"You know, Bird, you're going to have to get over this impression you have that I'm dumb."

"I know."

I switched frequencies. "Cel, Kinnis—with any luck you can stay there a while longer. The next strain of bugs should kick in and metabolize the chlorinated aliphatics well before they reach a dangerous concentration."

"If you say so." Cel sounded impatient, as though she just wanted to get on with what she was doing and leave the thinking to someone else. I wondered how it would be to trust like that.

The vinyl chloride and dichloroethylene concentrations climbed steadily. I waited for the methanotrophes to start working. The numbers kept going up. Something was going wrong.

"Cel, Kinnis, I want you out of there, now. The concentrations are getting too high. There's danger of a fireball."

243

"We only need another minute or—"

"Now. Acknowledge that."

"Acknowledged."

Magyar came back, still hefting the crowbar. She watched while I checked one readout after another.

Nothing was responding the way it should. The readout kept climbing. In desperation, I turned up the thermostat. Maybe heat would kick start the methanotrophes.

"What's going on?"

"No methane monoxygenase."

"This one time, assume I'm dumb."

"Methane monoxygenase, MMO, is the enzyme secreted by the methanotrophes as they metabolize the vinyl chloride. No MMO means something's wrong." The nutrient lines were clear and open, feeding steadily. "I don't understand it. They got their food, they've . . ." Except they might not have the right food. Hepple had replaced the correct, van de Oest nutrients. Time for desperate measures. I knew, in the final analysis, what methanotrophes ate. "Cel, Kinnis. Are you out?" No reply. "Cel—"

Click. "This is Decon One. Be advised that your team has been taken to Decon—"

They were safe. That was all I needed. I switched back to Magyar's channel. "Brace yourself. I'm bringing on line methane."

Magyar froze. Her gloved fist tightened on the crowbar. If she dropped it, there might be sparks. I imagined a hiss as the methane started to jet down the lines.

"What's happening now?" Magyar asked after a minute.

The MMO numbers were not moving. "Nothing."

"Talk to me, Bird. What should happen?"

"The methanotrophes will use the methane as their primary substrate, the vinyl chloride as secondary . . ." Still nothing.

"Come on," Magyar muttered.

The amber numerals ticked. *41:33. 41:34.*

"There!" It was a slight change, and sluggish. "Yes!" The MMO counter was climbing faster now. The vinyl chloride stopped. Began to decrease. "It's working." I watched for a while, just to be sure.

52:07. 52:08.

Everything was working. Running perfectly. "I'm going to reduce the methane." I did, slowly, cautiously. The numbers remained steady. I nudged it down further. Fine. I stretched, inside my suit. "You can put that crowbar down now."

She laid it flat on the floor. Always careful. She leaned over the readouts. Her head moved inside her hood, which I interpreted as a nod of satisfaction. I watched the incident clock for a while, feeling drained. "Now what do we do?"

"Now we wait."

I was hoping she would say that. I would hate to have left before the end, before the influent ran clear and we could switch everything back.

There was no conversation, no lowering of barriers now that we had worked shoulder to shoulder or any of that nonsense. We were too busy watching readouts, checking lines. Now that the immediate danger was past I realized how hot it was inside my suit, how the sweat trickling down beside my ear alongside the silicon mask seal itched. I pulled my right hand carefully out of a batwing sleeve, ran a finger around the seal, and put the hand back.

"There." Magyar was pointing. A light on the board switched from red to green. Volatile organic carbons were back down to preincident levels.

I beamed at Magyar through my faceplate, though I doubted she could see it. She did not seem to smile back, anyway. "Let's check the numbers prior to accepting influent," she said.

I looked at the board. "We have . . . nine operational troughs in the tertiary sector."

"Nine? Kinnis and Cel did a good job."

I nodded. I didn't want to think about them, where they

SLOW RIVER

were now. I didn't want to think about the debriefing.
"What percentage of influent should we accept?" The larger
the percentage we had to turn away at this point, the
greater the damage to our standing in the industry. All the
plants were built with overcapacity. Even though our reduction might only last a day or two, the impact on our market
share might be permanent.

"We'll take forty percent."

I nodded. If everyone went on bonus, did double shifts,
and doubled up on the troughs it might work. "You want
to do it?"

She waved me back to the switches and cleared her
throat. Although everything we said would have been inter-
cepted by Department earwigs and snooping hams, this next
bit would be the part of the record that got replayed most
often. "It's oh-one-hundred forty-one. Influent reads VOC
at seven parts per million. Taking pipe locks off-line."

"Check."

"System reinstated."

"Check."

"Holding tanks locked down—"

"Check."

"—and negative air pressure enabled."

"Check."

"That's it, then." She reached up and punched the black
button beneath the steadily ticking amber numbers. They
froze at *69:23*. Just over an hour. It felt like a week. "Emergency declared stabilized at oh-one-hundred forty-three."
She stretched. "Lock it down."

I entered the commands to seal off the holding area.

"Let's go take a look at the damage."

The vast space of the primary sector was very strange,
full of the hissing sound of filling troughs, without the usual
overlay of rake whine, aerators, and people sound. I wondered if Magyar was as tempted as I was to crack open her
hood and breathe deep.

"No one died," she said. "But they could have. I want the bastard who set this up." She stumped along the concrete apron, closing flapping locker doors, stopping to pick up the occasional abandoned filter mask, fingering the gleaming joints of a drench hose. "What I don't understand is the elaborateness of it all. All those topped-up tanks and new batteries. Why? What was the point?" I had heard a woman on the street sound like that, a woman who had been on her way to the grocery shop, when a man had shouted at her, called her an ugly bitch. More bewildered than angry: What had she done to deserve such malice?

I was more interested in what was going to happen next. "Magyar, when we go out there, I don't want any credit."

"You mean you don't want the attention."

"That's right."

"There's nothing I can do about what Kinnis or Cel might have said."

"I know that."

Her sigh sounded like the hissing of a flat tire over the suit radio. "I'll do my best to keep the cameras off you. And I won't mention your name. Good enough?"

"Yes."

"Right. I'm doing this because I think I can trust you, and despite everything I like you, but one day you're going to tell me what this is about." I nodded. Time to worry about all that later. "Let's get it over with."

Decon One was waiting in the shower room with hoses and secondary suits. There were no cameras, so I just did as I was told, and stripped and showered, and let Magyar yell and fume and tell them they were idiots, that there wasn't any danger, thanks to herself and her team . . . She was still arguing when we were passed along to Decon Two.

Another shower, this time being pestered by two tech specialists and the recon team leader who insisted on radio-ing everything, verbatim, to his first Go Team. Everyone more or less ignored Magyar's protestations that the plant was now safe. My name had only been mentioned once, just so that Operations could stand down the rescue aspects of its Go Teams. They sent a medical team, which hustled us into a small room draped with plasthene sheets and filled with the paraphernalia of high-tech medicine.

Cel and Kinnis were sitting on two of the beds. "Hey, Magyar, they won't let us out."

"We're following procedure," the medic with the most flashes on his epaulets said smoothly. "Regulations—"

Magyar was like a controlled explosion. "You're in charge here? Good. I want to talk to the operations chief, now."

"You can't—"

"Then you do it. Verify the following: one, that Decon can confirm that I and my team maintained air integrity at all times; two, that our medical exam shows no ill effects of the PCE; three, that we obeyed all emergency procedures to the letter, that our conversations are on the record for analysis and discussion, and that therefore our presence is no longer needed. And when you have all that sorted out, I want to add to the record my opinion that if you attempt to keep us here any longer against our will your behavior will be not only unethical but illegal." She folded her arms. The medic gradually wilted under her stare and went to the phone.

Magyar sat down next to Kinnis. He grinned. "I'm glad they'll listen to someone."

She grinned back, and I realized she was not angry, but pleased with herself. She was planning something.

The medic finished on the phone. "You," he pointed at Magyar, "you're wanted in Ops for debriefing. You three," to me and Cel and Kinnis, "you can go. You're instructed to avoid the cameras."

"Don't worry," Cel said shortly.

He nodded at one of his assistants. "He'll escort you to the gate."

"I know the way. Besides, I have to get my gear from the locker room."

"It's already been removed to zone three." The cool zone. The edge of the contamination perimeter. "But—"

Magyar stood up. "Better do as they say, Cel, and just be glad they're letting you go. Looks like I'll be up all night."

Cel agreed eventually, and the three of us trooped out behind the medic's assistant.

Outside, it was as bright as day: emergency-response trucks sat in a circle with arc lights burning into the black sandstone building. Camera teams, with anchors talking into their own spotlights. Dozens of groups in flash suits and air hoses, protective helmets, radios . . . I could almost smell their adrenaline, and wondered how they would work it off now that they wouldn't be needed. While I watched, two ambulances turned off their flashing lights and drove away. There were probably about two hundred people watching and waiting for survivors. While most of them would be the next shift waiting to go in, many were media.

"Cel." She turned. "Wait."

"What's going on?" Kinnis asked.

They had trusted me earlier, with their lives. "I can't afford to have my face seen on the net, or my name mentioned. I need to avoid them."

Cel shrugged. "I don't see how we can help you."

"I thought that if everyone was swarming to talk to one of you—or both of you—I could get away unnoticed."

She narrowed her eyes at me. She didn't relish the idea of a media feeding frenzy, and I didn't blame her.

I had a sudden inspiration. "Kinnis, won't your wife be worried?"

"Christ, yes. I hadn't thought about that."

"One quick way to let her know you're safe would be to get on the net. You, too, Cel."

"I don't know," she said slowly.

But Kinnis was looking at the cameras happily. "Being on the net would make me a hero to my kids, Cel: the guy who saved the city. And like she said, it would let my wife know I'm safe."

"I don't know," Cel said again, then sighed. "I don't know why I keep doing what you say." *Because I ask it. Katerine was right.* "Come on, Kinnis. You head for those teams over there, I'll take this side." She walked out, waving. "Hey!" Lights swung her way.

Kinnis stepped out after her, to one side. "Me, too!"

I slipped into the shadow left behind by the piercing light and hurried away.

≋ IT WAS almost dawn by the time they were dressed and outside. The woman and Spanner stood in the doorway, murmuring. Something changed hands. Lore looked around, ignoring them. The apartment building was a converted warehouse, made of the long, thin bricks manufactured before the eighteenth century: they were in the center of the city, surrounded by trees and a high wall.

They found a café. Lore stirred her coffee aimlessly. Her body felt hopelessly confused: whenever she thought about what had happened she felt a flush of arousal followed quickly by shame.

"I don't want to do that again," she said quietly, not looking at Spanner.

"You enjoyed it."

"Yes. That makes it worse."

"It would have been better if you hadn't liked it?"

"Yes. At least then I would have felt more like me. More in control." She stirred the coffee some more. It slopped over into the saucer. "I just feel so . . . used." No, she *wanted* to feel used, but she did not. She felt as though it did not matter, and that frightened her. She stared blindly across the river, broad here, and slow moving.

"Anyway, it's done now. And you did enjoy it. You can't tell me it wasn't good."

And it had been; it had been very good. What did that say about her?

"When did you drug me?" Her voice sounded surprisingly calm.

"Who says I drugged you?"

"Just tell me when."

"After you had already taken off your dress."

After you had already taken off your dress. So she did not even have that much of an excuse; she had already unbuttoned her dress. Some part of her had been willing, even without the drug.

Spanner squinted at the rising sun, sipped from her coffee. "So," she said casually, "do you want me to tell you when I'm doing it, next time?"

Next time.

Lore watched the sparkle of morning sunlight on the river. It looked so bright, so optimistic, on the surface. But underneath there were river reeds, and pikes to eat smaller fish, and the rich river mud was made of dead things, including the bones of thousands of people.

Next time. "There's no sign of business improving?"

"No." Spanner waited for a waiter to refill her coffee. "This is more profitable, anyway."

How many times had the river accepted victims? The river did not care whether those who slid under its surface were women or men, victims of murder or heroes trying to save a drowning child. It was all the same to the river. Death was all the same. Just as it did not matter what kind of person Lore felt she was inside: if there were many more times like last night, she would become someone else, someone who did those things.

But Spanner and the temporary fake PIDAs were all that held the implacable, uncaring river of her past from pouring in on her head. With Spanner she might drown; without her, she certainly would.

THE MESSAGE tone woke me minutes after I had gone to bed.

"Lore? Ruth. I heard about the plant. Are you all right?"

I staggered out of bed. "I'm here." I found the ACCEPT button. "I'm fine."

"Oh. I woke you. Sorry."

"It's all right. What time is it?"

"Half past four. Listen, about Spanner." I sat up straighter. "Ellen's been with her. She called and left a message saying the medic's been back and there's no infection. Ellen seems to think the pain's still pretty bad, though. Do you know what happened?"

"No." If Spanner hadn't told them, it wasn't my place. Maybe one day. I was too tired to care if my lies were convincing.

"Well," Ruth said uncertainly, "I'll let you get back to sleep. You look exhausted."

"Thanks. And thanks for calling." I meant it. It was good to have someone who cared.

I was dreaming about a fire when the screen woke me again. This time it was Magyar. She must have got my number from the records.

"Hey, Bird, you there?"

"I'm here." I scrubbed my eyes. "Time is it?"

"After five. They've just let me out. Kept asking me over and over what had gone wrong. And how I'd known how to fix it."

"You didn't tell them?"

"I told them part of the truth: that I'd been reading the manual a lot lately because I was worried that Hepple's idiotic games were going to hurt the plant somehow."

"What did they say?"

She laughed. "Not much. Then they sent Hepple from the room."

"He was there?"

"Not for long." When she smiled her eyes wrinkled upward, like a cat's. She stretched. "I feel good, Bird. I don't think he's going to work in this city again."

"You told them about the bugs, the nutrients?"

"Everything." She yawned. "Thought you'd like to know: Someone from the command-post staff, the documentation people, said they've traced the spill up-line to some off-road drainage in the north of the county. Well away from any manufacturing complex *and* off the usual transport routes. The official opinion is fly dumping."

"Right."

She nodded. "As far as I'm concerned, this was planned." She yawned again. "Before I forget, tomorrow's shift is twelve hours: four till four. With overlap."

"That'll be fun." I tried to imagine the chaos of overlapping shifts, with both shifts overtired and irritable.

"Yeah. But the pay's good: time and a half for the whole twelve hours." Another yawn. "Gotta go. Those leeches sucked me dry. You'd think it was my fault things went wrong. 'So tell us again why you think the glucose line malfunctioned, Cherry.' Over and over. Jesus. And I hate it when they call me Cherry." She reached to the side to cut the transmission, then stopped. "I didn't tell you earlier, Bird, but I think between us we did a good job. It was hard to not tell them what you did. I hope you know what you're doing."

"I do."

"Good, because it's too late to change your mind without making me look like an idiot. I'll see you at the beginning of the shift."

No one had ever said to me before, *See you later, at work.*

TWENTY

WHEN LORE gets back to her suite after swimming with Sarah, she is exhausted and has the faint beginnings of a hangover. The light on her screen is red: she has a message. She ignores it. All she wants is a shower and several hours' sleep.

She is climbing into bed when the phone chimes. It takes her a moment to recognize the family-emergency override tone. She drags the sheet from her bed to wrap up in.

"Yes?"

"Lore . . . Lore . . ." The screen remains blank and whoever has called her is sobbing. "Lore . . ."

"Tok? Tok, is that you?" The screen suddenly flashes into color: Tok's face is swollen and ravaged with grief.

"She's dead. Those bastards. Oh, Lore, she's dead . . ." He says more, but his tears thicken the words beyond sense.

"Tok, please." Who was dead? "Take some deep breaths. Tell me—"

"She was trying. God, she was . . . She killed herself, Lore. Can you imagine that? Feeling so bad you don't want to wake up ever again and eat breakfast, you don't want to look up ever again and see tiny white clouds in the sky. Just wanting to forget. That bastard. She . . ." More weeping.

Lore's heart feels so big she can hardly breathe. "Tok, who's dead?"

Tok looks up, astonished. "Stella. She killed herself. She . . ."

Lore does not hear the rest. She is flooded with relief that it is not Katerine. Tok is looking at her. "Why? Why did she kill herself?"

"Because of what that monster did to her. Almost every night. She only started therapy six months ago, Lore. She was finally facing it. But then I think it just got too much, I think she looked ahead and saw this thing, this black swamp inside her, this cloud that looked like it would stain her life forever, and couldn't face it. Well, I can face it. I'm going to make that monster pay. Come back home, Lore, wherever you are. I need you. We'll do this together."

Lore just looks at him, horrified. What is he talking about?

"I'll contact you in a day or two, tell you where I am. I'm going to put a stop to it. This has gone on too long." He reaches to the side and his picture blips out.

Lore stares at the blank screen, unable to move. What is he talking about? *Stella is dead.* What does he mean? Who is the monster? A quick image of Greta and a locksmith glide through her memory. She shakes her head. *Stella is dead.* She has a sudden image of Stella and her friends standing around the net screen, drinks in hand, vying to send money to some amateur charity. *Stella is dead.*

She does not know how long she sits there, but when someone knocks at the door and she gets up, she finds she is stiff. She expects Sarah, and opens the door without checking the peephole.

Two masked figures burst in. One takes her arms and the other points something at her face. There is a funny smell, and the floor comes up to hit her.

TWENTY-ONE

I OPENED my eyes again at eleven in the morning and thought it was the message tone that had woken me. I was halfway out of bed before I realized it was the door.

Someone was knocking on my door.

This was the first time since I had lived alone that anyone had knocked. It made me think of Uruguay.

"Hold on." I found a shirt, padded to the door. "Who is it?"

"Why, who're you expecting?"

Tom. Even so, I made sure both chains were fastened before I opened the door a crack. "I'm not dressed."

"We don't mind." He held up his hand. I saw it was attached to some kind of string. "Brought you a present." A leash. And a dog. A black, stocky-looking thing with a startlingly pink tongue.

"No. I can't—"

"Don't get your knickers in a twist," he said cheerfully.

"He's not to keep. Just to borrow for an hour or two every day. Can we come in?"

I opened the door and the dog dragged Tom in. "Sit down while I dress."

"I'll put the kettle on."

"Fine."

I went into the bathroom and showered quickly. I could hear the dog's claws clicking on the floor as it padded about, sniffing things. When I came out of the bathroom, rubbing my hair, it sat down and panted at me. Its entire hindquarters shuffled back and forth as it wagged its tail.

I patted it cautiously on the head. It wagged harder. "It looks young."

"He. He's eight months old. His name's Gibbon."

"As in *The Decline and Fall of the Roman Empire?*"

Tom smiled. "Knew you had an education. Now, hurry up and comb that hair, tea's ready." I did, then checked to see if I had any messages. Just one, a notice from the plant, reiterating what Magyar had already told me: tonight's shift had been extended. *For the next three days,* the notice said. No *please* or *thank you*, just an assumption that we would all cooperate.

We sat at the table by the window. The dog sat on the carpet, watching me carefully.

"I got him yesterday. From the pound. I thought to myself, 'Tom, you're getting old. More to the point, you're thinking you should *feel* old and lonely. You need something to look after.' I decided a dog would be just the thing."

"But . . ."

"How am I going to walk a young, healthy dog like this every day? That's where you come in. I saw you dragging yourself in the other night, and I said to myself, 'That lass needs a bit of fresh air, something to take her mind off things.' And then I heard about the bit of bother at the plant last night and thought a walk by the river would do nicely."

I thought Tom thought entirely too much. And then I wondered how he knew I worked at the plant, and realized too late he'd been guessing. I smiled wryly. "By the time I get him to the river we'll both be exhausted and it'll be time for me to head back."

But Tom had evidently been thinking about that, too. He actually folded his arms in satisfaction. "Bet you didn't know you could reach the river not two minutes' walk from here."

I acknowledged defeat. "You'd better tell me how."

I got to work early. Twelve hours was a long time to spend in a skinny, especially when there was cleanup *and* overlapping shifts arguing about jurisdiction, and I wanted to be prepared.

Tom had been right about the walk. The fresh air and exercise had stretched the tension kinks out of my shoulders and put vigor back in my veins. Although I knew it was all in my mind, I felt cleaner, as though the breeze had blown away the stain of aliphatics and aromatics from the spongy tissue of my lungs.

I sighed as I took my time sliding on wrist supports and strapping on my waders. Now I was going to clog everything up again.

"It's going to get worse," Kinnis said cheerfully. He hadn't even sealed his skinny yet. "Lot of work to do."

"I hear these daytime jerk-offs have only got a few more troughs up," Meisener agreed.

"Less than forty is what I heard," Cel said as she started stripping off her street clothes. "Hey, Kinnis, you were dumb as a rock on the net last night."

"Yeah? At least I looked good, not like you, you ugly cow."

I stepped out of the line of fire. The next stage would be thrown gauntlets, goggles, raucous laughter. It always made me feel out of place, the way the rest of the shift familiarly insulted each other, threw things, played jokes. They knew it, I think, but I never got the sense that they might gang up on me and herd me out. They could have done, in the beginning, but they hadn't. Maybe I had been as strange to them as they to me. They wouldn't do it now; I might be weird, but I had worked with them, helped them. I had been adopted and my difference was now taken for granted—like the slowness of a younger sister who is defended fiercely on the school playground. All of a sudden I liked these people, liked them a great deal.

The shift was hard, but we were used to that, and the two shifts meshed together more smoothly than I had anticipated. There was no sign of Magyar, but without any discussion, our shift took on the heavier, dirtier work. The day shift seemed content to let us. I wondered how many more centuries it would take to break the physically-stronger-equals-morally-superior equation, then shrugged and concentrated on the job.

Once the day shift had left, the work was faster and smoother. An hour before the break, we had almost fifty troughs up.

"Maybe we should slow down," Cel said from behind me. She was leaning on her rake, surveying the progress. "Time and a half is a hard thing to lose."

"I wonder how Magyar got that for us."

"The way I read it, she can get what she wants right now. Did you know she's been in executive land all night? Rumor has it they gave Hepple's job to the day-shift supervisor—Ho? Hu? something like that—and offered Magyar his job."

"On the day shift?"

"Yeah," she said, misinterpreting my expression. "What would she do with those soft wankers?"

"Do you think she'll take it?"

"Maybe."

. . .

We broke as usual after four hours. For the first time in a while, I sat by myself in the breakroom. I didn't like the thought of a new shift supervisor. Magyar and I understood each other. It would be annoying to have to go back to being careful all the time about what I was and was not supposed to know. And Magyar was smart. What if the new one was mean, or petty like Hepple?

The second third of the shift seemed harder than the first, despite the fact that we were on our own. By the second break, Cel's rumor had gone round and there was intense speculation. No one seemed to doubt that Magyar would take the job—the interest was all about who would take Magyar's place. I watched the fish and spoke to no one, then went back to the troughs and worked like an automaton.

Finishing at four in the morning felt different from two. Bleaker. Or maybe I was just tired. It was one of those strange, warmish winter nights, when the air is full of moisture and you can hear the wind.

"Bird." It was Magyar, waiting for me. "I expect you've heard the rumors."

"Yes."

We walked in silence.

"You won't ask, will you?"

"No."

"I didn't take the job!" She seemed angry. At herself, or me.

I didn't know what to think, or how to feel. "Why not?"

"I don't know. It just . . ."

I smiled, I couldn't help it. "Cel said you wouldn't know what to do with those soft wankers."

Magyar grinned back. "Work their asses off."

We walked some more. I had no idea where we were going.

"It seemed like a good idea at the time: better hours, more money. No Hepple. Then they asked me who they should give my job to. I thought about you. You know more about that place than you've any right to. You'd do a good job. But . . . I don't know . . . you're not who you say you are."

"You could have suggested someone else. Cel, maybe."

"Don't think I didn't consider it. But the more I thought about you, the more I thought we had some unfinished business. You lied about your identity to get a job you're way, way too qualified for. I can't trust a person who does that."

"I wouldn't cause trouble."

"Maybe not, but how can I be sure?"

I did not point out what I had done last night.

She made a soft sound of frustration. "I like you, but I don't trust you. Who are you?"

"I can't tell you that."

"Then tell me why you took this job."

"Because it was something I knew how to do. And it's inconspicuous enough to avoid attention."

"From the police?"

I nodded. We walked some more. We were in the dock-side area now—the real docks, not the tourist arena.

"What did you do?"

"I think I killed someone."

Five dangerous little words. They hung there like gnats. If I could I would have leapt and snapped them back, like a dog. For a split second I thought about running. Magyar would not follow me.

Instead, after a brief falter in my steps, we kept walking.

"That's not everything, is it?"

"No."

"But it's all you're going to tell me."

"Yes." I was cold and tired. I stopped walking. "What will you do?"

261

"Nothing." I couldn't see her face, just her breath, pearly against the dark, industrial sky. "You helped me last night. You helped all of us. And I'm a patient woman."

You'll tell me eventually, she meant. It wasn't a threat. Not quite.

"Get to bed. Bird." *Or whoever you are.* "You look worn out."

I went to the Polar Bear.

THE DATA-SLATE business stayed tight, and more and more Lore woke up with restraint marks on her wrists, or arms sore from paddling some flabby-legged sixty-year-old. Once, toward the end of summer, she woke up in their flat with a butt plug still strapped inside her, and she rushed to the bathroom and vomited. Afterward she hung limply over the bowl and whispered to the water, "It wasn't *me,* it wasn't *me* . . ." But even as her gorge rose again, her skin flushed with remembered heat. She wept.

Sometimes all Spanner would have to do was show her the little bottle and she would nearly come.

By November, they were tricking six nights out of seven, and sometimes more than once a night. They usually took it in turns: one to perform, one to guard. On the nights or afternoons when she was the one watching Spanner fucking some spoiled teenager or limp old man, she felt powerful: she was in charge. She was the one who made sure there were latex and antivirals; she was the one who pulled Spanner off when the client had had enough; she was the one who took the money. She was in charge; she had choices. This might not be love, but she was not being lied to.

They earned a great deal of money, but they always seemed to need more.

The holiday season came again. Lore wandered the

streets, ending up by the medieval gate that had been exca-
vated thirty years before. She stared at it, then out at what
had once been a dock, long ago. A huge shopping mall,
tawdry with age, floated there now. She wondered why
modern creations became uglier faster. It was raining. Something about the gray sky and the sturdy shoes splashing
through puddles reminded her of Den Haag, of her hand in
her father's as they ran, laughing, from the chauffeured car to
the brightly lit store. She had bought Tok an art program for
his slate that year. Her father had helped her choose presents
for everyone. And she had felt so lucky. Her father was a
busy man, with meetings to run and schedules to keep, but
here he was, running through the rain with her, choosing
presents as though the future of van de Oest Enterprises
rested on their decisions, queuing up like an ordinary person
at the store café for hot chocolate while they gloated over
the presents all snugged up in the bags under their chairs.

Lore smiled to herself, caught sight of that smile in a
storefront window, and faltered. It was all a lie, because *he*
was all a lie. All her memories of him were tainted, soiled
by what he had done to Stella. How could someone do that
to another, and smile and smile and pretend love?

She found herself huddling against the cold armored
glass of a clothing store. She could not think of a single
thing to buy Spanner that would not be a lie, because all
their money was a lie.

I DON'T know why I went to the Polar Bear—to
exorcise some ghosts, maybe; maybe I just wanted
some beer; maybe I couldn't face being on my own—but I
did not expect to see Spanner.

She was holding court at one of the center tables, gestur-
ing with one hand, laughing, pausing to drink.

Just go, she had said last time I saw her. She would rather have suffered that terrible pain than have me in her flat. Yet here she was, waving me over. And here I was, sliding into a seat, nodding pleasantly at the woman and two men I didn't recognize at the table.

"Lore!" She twisted her head over her shoulder and shouted at the bar, "Bring Lore a beer."

Judging by the smears on the table and the flush on their cheeks, they had been there a few hours. Spanner's color was high, too, but I noticed that although she lifted her glass often, she drank slowly, and there was a stop-start quality to her movements. I guessed that as well as the enormous dose of painkillers floating through her bloodstream she must be popping with stimulants.

After a few how-are-yous which meant nothing, I was left out of the conversation while Spanner laughed and glittered some more. It was warm. I settled into a half-lidded somnolence, sipping now and again at my beer, more tired than relaxed. Then Spanner and the others were standing up, shaking hands.

"The weekend? No problem. Yes, it *was* good to talk to you. No, no, I'll stay and have a chat with Lore here."

Then it was just us.

"What are you doing out of bed?"

"I'm fine."

I let it pass. If Spanner could walk, she was *fine*. It didn't matter what that walking would do to her, how it would damage her for the future; it didn't matter how many drugs, or how much, it took; if she could walk, she was just fine. It was not my problem anymore. It wasn't.

"Is your video ready?"

"Yes."

"Good. Then we'll go tomorrow night. Four-thirty."

"I can't." I cast about for an excuse. "I'm working until four."

"How long does it take you to walk half a mile?"

"But the equipment—"

"It's ready."

"—and the information . . ."

"I've got it. I've looked at it. We're ready. And tomorrow, at four-thirty, at a switching station here in the city, is our hole."

"No." The idea was ridiculous. "Look at you. You couldn't even lift that pint without a shot."

"So? The fact is, I *can* lift it."

"And how sharp will you be, full of drugs? No. We'll wait."

"We can't wait." She pushed her beer away. "I can't wait. The information and equipment cost money and favors. I owe several people. By now they'll have heard . . ." She spread her fingers in a fan, indicating her body, the way it had been injured. I could see the faint glimmer of powder under her eyes where she had covered dark circles. She had already owed money before all this. Now, to get the equipment, she had pulled in favors. The people she owed would be getting worried: it was why she was out and about. Counteracting the rumor that she was finished. In the game Spanner played, worried creditors were lethal.

I hesitated. There was a lot at stake. If Spanner was just a microsecond slower than she had to be, the alarms would ring. If the alarms went, odds were they would get us. We'd be hauled in. She knew what that would mean for me: my family, the public humiliation, the possibility of a murder charge. I could only guess at what it would mean for her.

"Can you do it?" *Tell me the truth. Just for once. Can you do this with all those drugs coursing through you?*

"Yes."

She could have left me that night in the rain, just pretended not to hear me, and walked away. I could have died. "All right, then. Tomorrow."

We didn't shake hands.

．　　．　　．

It was raining, but I didn't feel it. I was wrapped in plasthene: hood, long coat, booties over my boots, hands sprayed with a transparent layer of plaskin. I crouched on the pavement, shielding the open pack with the waterproof coat. Spanner cursed in the darkness. I waited. The switching station's lock was standard design; it should not be too hard. Not usually. I could feel words welling up my gullet like fish on a rising tide: *Let's go back. It's not too late to change our minds* . . . But then the lock clicked, and Spanner slid the door open, and I was handing her one pack and carrying the other inside. I pulled the door shut. It was pitch black until I found the lights.

The station was ten feet square and low-roofed. Digital relays switched soundlessly, lightlessly. It was cold. There was one chair on casters. The floor was smoothed concrete. We shook ourselves to get rid of the worst of the rain, but didn't dare take off the coats. We were clean for this job: no stray skin or hair for the security snoops to read for DNA.

"Do you want the chair?" I asked.

Spanner was already unfastening her tool roll. She shook her head.

The stillness and silence were unnerving. "Why aren't there any console lights?"

Spanner reached up and touched something and then there were soft reds and ambers and greens, an occasional pink and turquoise.

I unfastened my own pack and began handing Spanner things one by one: the disk that had taken me hundreds of hours to put together; the matte, featureless box that had cost so much; a flatscreen; connectors . . . Spanner had spent hours earlier, cleaning everything with ultrasonics where she could, a toothbrush where she couldn't. No stray hairs or skin or oil to be left behind for analysis. I sat back and watched her work.

With tools in her hand and a job to do, she was transformed. Each gesture was gentle, precise as she set up the diagnostic flatscreen, watched the waveforms, nodded, reached for her tone pad. I remembered those hands touching my back, the spaces between my ribs, stroking. I remembered the whites around her eyes, the way she had trembled with the effort of not moving, not jarring her dislocated joints before the medic came.

I swallowed convulsively.

She pushed the disk into its drive, watched the screen, frowned, sucked air through her teeth.

"Trouble?"

"Um? No. Take a few minutes."

I was distracting her. It was time I prepared myself for my part.

The access window was flat to the wall behind and to the right of Spanner. I pushed the chair until it was opposite, then sat down with a board on my lap. I thumbed it on, maneuvered myself and the chair until the green ALIGNED panel lit up. All the other panels came up amber one by one: the station's security systems were all on-line, doing their job, checking and rechecking access. They would flash red one by one as Spanner piggybacked the net signal, but we had a program to override the alarms at source. As long as the human overseer did not check during the dozen or so seconds we were working the signal, we should be fine. And according to the information bought along with the hardware, they shouldn't check. *But they might.*

There was no way to know whether or not the program would do what its writers claimed; there was no way to make sure the handshake box would successfully mimic the net's signal, which was changed on a random basis. Spanner had looked over the code—I had even taken a look—and as far as we could see it was the real thing, but there was only one way to be certain.

I looked over at Spanner. She was working smoothly. A soft tone seeped through the room. "Box has the hand-shake," she said. "Now we just wait." She reached up and turned on the station screen.

The schedules had listed a rerun of an old, fashionably cult-status sitcom on the assigned channel, and the net was nothing if not efficient. Nevertheless, I found myself breathing hard with relief when the star appeared with her trade-mark grin. If that was as planned, maybe everything else would go smoothly. I wondered what people would be watching on the demand channels: films, live sports, live sex, dog shows, cartoons . . .

"Commercials in two minutes eleven seconds."

Usually, commercials were tailored for the viewing audience, but we were going to hit everyone with the same thing. As Spanner had said, "Look, we may be going after the rich and stupid, but the kind of people who regularly watch the net at four in the morning—the depressed, the sleepless, the drunk, people who've been up fucking their new love all night—we can pull them in, too." What she meant, of course, was: Let's take from the defenseless, the ones who don't really have anything to give, or who will give to anything because they are about to end their lives.

"Hope the damn handshake doesn't change in the mid-dle of the commercial," she muttered. I didn't ask what would happen if it did. I didn't want to know.

"Is the account program on-line?"

"Yes. Commercial in fifty seconds."

My hands were tight on the board, going purply white at the joints. We were going to wait until the end of the first advertisement; probably thirty seconds. At that point there was less chance of the security snoop noticing—they weren't paid to guard the advert signal. We had no idea what the commercials might be, but Spanner had watched dozens of the most likely candidates, and written interrupt programs for them. If it was something we didn't recognize, though, she would have to do it by hand.

"Twenty seconds. Nineteen. Eighteen. Seventeen . . ."

My board was amber all the way.

"We're synchronized." We would ride silently for a few seconds.

Still amber. "All clear."

"Four seconds. Three. Two. One."

The screen cut to a brilliant green. *"This is—"* and Spanner swore. The screen suddenly dulled to brown and red: the ruined floor of what had once been rain forest.

"What's happening, what's happening?"

"Minimercial," Spanner said briefly. "They'll take the whole commercial spot."

We had less than three minutes to decide what to do. "Board's amber."

"And the signal's very sweet," Spanner said. "I'm going to do it." Her voice was sharp, decisive. "I'll cut in when it's done. Steal program time."

"You know this commercial?"

"No, but a windup's a windup."

She was right. You could always tell the last few seconds of an ad. "Do it," I said.

It was dangerous, much more dangerous than we had planned. Viewers never timed adverts, but after years of always getting the same number of seconds their bodies would be tuned to it. Inside, they would think, *Hey, there are a lot of ads today . . .* And maybe one of those viewers would be the security snoop. Maybe he or she would be fast, would flip the trace before we cut.

"Here's the windup."

"All clear." No going back now. If the drugs had affected Spanner in the slightest, if she made one millisecond's mistake, the cut would be obvious. Adrenaline tightened the muscles around my eyes; my breathing got shallow.

She was perfect. The white lettering faded out and then in to the bright red and yellow that was the first frame close-up of Tom's tie.

I looked at the board. "Ten-percent red. Twenty." The security program had started to trace our signal. It wouldn't find us until the whole board lit.

"Come on, you babies, come on," Spanner muttered. I wondered what the account program was telling her.

"Twenty-five percent. Fifty!" The sudden flicker of red across the board made my heart leap sideways. "Seventy!"

"Taking us off." My board went blank. She started stripping down the screen, unhooking the box.

I found I was kneeling on the floor, stowing things in the backpack without knowing how I got there.

"Nearly twelve seconds," she was saying.

"Cut the account," I said.

"Money's still coming in—"

"Cut it!" I didn't care how much or how little we had. We needed to cut and run. A nanosecond could make a difference to a security program.

She touched a key, pulled a lead free. "All closed down."

And then we were standing outside in the rain, pulling the door closed, leaning against the wall, laughing. The rain ran in my ears, my mouth, down my neck, but I didn't care. We should be running, but I didn't care. Adrenaline exhilaration could do that. I laughed and laughed: we were free, safe. I had forgotten how sweet it felt to operate outside the law, how good, how *big* it made me feel . . .

Reluctantly, I pushed myself away from the wall. "We have to hurry."

"They didn't trace us." But she was already sobering, looking from left to right. Information technology and its finer points did not matter much to the crocodile brain. It wanted some physical distance. We hurried.

I started to feel safe when we were about a quarter of

a mile away. I slowed, stopped, started stripping off the plasthene protection. Spanner followed suit. "How much did we make?"

She grinned. "Guess."

"A lot." I started to fizz again. A lot of money. For a few minutes' work. "Tell me."

"A hundred and four, maybe a hundred and five thousand."

I laughed out loud, incredulous.

"Shut your mouth," Spanner said, "you might drown in this rain."

I was suddenly glad of the rain, glad to be getting wet. It was real. All that money. I felt dizzy. It made a mockery of what I earned at Hedon Road.

The Polar Bear was quiet, only half a dozen people in the place. Spanner had ordered us whiskey. I rolled the glass around in my hands, content to sniff at the fumes. Spanner was on her third drink in thirty minutes. She probably should not be drinking at all with the painkillers she was on. Now that the adrenaline high was fading, I was too tired to care.

"So, what will you do with your share?"

"I don't know." I sipped, enjoying the hot, smoky taste. After taking out start-up expenses and paying Tom his share, I'd have more than thirty thousand, tax free. I could drink this stuff every day. Live in a bigger apartment. For a while. "Maybe I'll give it to someone." Magyar might be willing to get Paolo's address from the records. I tried to imagine his expression when he found he was thirty thousand richer. I stared into my glass. Such a warm, welcoming color.

Spanner reached over and covered the glass with her hand. "Who?"

"What?"

"Who are you giving it to?"

Giving the money to Paolo was a stupid fantasy. It wouldn't help him or me. But I needed to talk—and who was there but Spanner? So I told her about Paolo. About him coming to Hedon Road, about his youth, his strangeness. About his eyes, the way they seemed to open when he realized I wasn't mocking him, that I would teach him. How young he was, and vulnerable. How he had tried to kill himself. How I felt guilty.

She sipped at her drink. "You didn't exactly cut off his arms and legs with an axe."

"No. But I should have done something when I could. So should my father, my mother. Willem. Everybody." I wanted her to see, to understand. I told her about the hotel room, the judgment in the Caracas case. How, when I had heard, I had shrugged in my air-conditioned hotel room and climbed back in the shower. "But how could I have known then, when I was only sixteen?" They had just been pictures on the screen. Somewhere inside I had thought the dirt on their faces to be makeup, their anguish an act.

But Spanner wasn't listening. "Money means so little to you that you can afford to just give it away?"

"It's not the money."

"Of course it's the money!" *What else is there?* She was scared, I realized suddenly. Money was all she had. If I didn't think much of that, what would I think of her?

"Spanner . . ."

But she was almost hissing. "You make me sick, you know that? You're an arrogant bastard. You think the world cares what you feel. You think you can make a difference, but you can't."

I had never seen her scared before. It made me uneasy. Something had changed. It had always been the other way around. But I wasn't afraid anymore. She could not make me do anything I didn't want to do, ever again. She had rescued me, and taught me to stay alive, but I had paid and paid and paid. I had paid enough.

I think she saw that, and I think it frightened her even more. I wanted to explain to her that I wouldn't hurt her, that I wasn't like everyone else she knew, but I didn't know what to say—and I wasn't sure if it was true.

She saw my indecision. "Poor little rich girl!"

"No." I was too tired for this. I finished my drink and stood up. "Not anymore. I work for my living. I work hard. I do a good job. It means something."

"Shoveling shit means something?"

"What does *your* job mean?" I was suddenly blazingly angry: with her, with the world that had shaped her, at myself and all the things I had done or neglected to do. "What does it mean to you that people pay to use you like a disposable tissue? Does the money make you feel good, worthwhile, even when you can't move because of the pain and you're all alone because you don't have any friends? Does it make you feel good that you might have died if this poor little rich girl hadn't decided to take pity on you? Does it make you feel good when you wake up in the morning hating yourself because of the things you did to make a quick hundred? Does it?"

I have never seen a snake in the second before it strikes, but I think I know how it would look. It would move its head back a fraction of an inch, it would close its nictitating membranes partway, and the sunlight would slide across hard gray fangs, dry as ancient bone. And then its expression would go blank as all the muscles but those it would use to strike, to drive the venom home into soft mammalian tissue, relaxed.

But then Spanner just picked up her drink, tossed it back, and smiled.

TWENTY-TWO

Lore is eighteen. It is her birthday, or it might be. She is sitting in a tent erected inside some kind of warehouse, or maybe it's a barn. The smells are certainly rural rather than urban: wine and garlic and oil, the occasional hint of grass too long in the sun. The Mediterranean, perhaps, or the South of France. She wonders how they got her here from the resort; she remembers nothing after the two men drugging her in the room.

She has been inside the tent for nearly three weeks, as far as she can tell. They keep her sedated. To begin with, they put it in her food, but because she does not always eat everything, they keep getting the dose wrong. One time, they gave her so much that she slept for over two days, or so they said. Now, though, her system is so saturated that they simply hand her a pill and stand over her while she puts it meekly in her mouth and swallows. But she thinks it is probably her birthday.

The tent is empty but for a sleeping bag and a bucket.

274

The bucket is emptied every twelve hours. Sometimes the tent stinks. She is humiliated. She is kept naked though not, she is sure, through prurience. There are two men; one, the taller, wears clothes that always seem to smell of something frying, like fish; the other, shorter than Lore, moves fast and slightly sideways, like a crab. When they bring her food trays or empty her bucket or hand her the pills, both wear gloves, and hoods like ski masks. She has no idea what they look like, of their race or age, but she feels she could tell them apart even without the height discrepancy. The tall one, whom she thinks of as Fishface, seems nice. He always averts his head when he enters, almost as though he is ashamed of what he is doing. The other one, though, Crablegs—she does not like him. He is the one who talks, the one who tells her to eat her pills or she will have to be tied up; the one who wakes her up and shouts at her that her family is refusing to pay the ransom. It was Crablegs who brought in an old folding chair and a camera one time, along with a copy of a news flimsy.

"Sit on the chair," he said, "and hold this in front of you, so they can see the date."

Who? she wondered, but could not quite make her mouth shape the words.

He fiddled with the camera and brilliant light flooded the tent. "Talk. Tell them you're scared for your life."

She was not scared. The drugs made everything seem distant and somehow irrelevant. Lore just sat there, blinking. "Light's too bright," she slurred.

"You don't like it?" He moved closer, shone it directly in her eyes.

She tried to hold up her hand to shield her face, but her fingers felt like bunches of sausages, and the flimsy got in the way.

"In front of you, I said. So they can see the date. So they know we haven't killed you yet."

Yet. She thought about that. She should be scared, but

all she could feel was the smooth wood under her buttocks and the slick flimsy against her stomach. *Naked,* she thought, *naked and vulnerable.*

"Talk," Crablegs ordered, and turned up the light.

She just wanted the light to go away, to go back to her cotton-wool dreams. She whimpered.

"That's it, that's better." He filmed for a moment, then adjusted something near the microphone. "Now, tell them how much you want to get out of here."

She wanted the light to stop. She wanted to lie down and sleep. "Please," she said. A tear slid slowly down beside her nose, under the curve of her cheekbone, across the corner of her mouth and dripped off her jaw. "Please," she said again. "Please . . ."

"Tell them."

"I want to go home." It didn't matter that she slurred, it didn't matter that after all she had been through to be an adult in the eyes of her parents they would see her like this: naked, vulnerable, weeping. "I want to go home. Please . . ."

He turned off the light. "You can stop now."

But Lore couldn't stop. Her weeping turned to wet heaving sobs, to hiccoughs.

"Oh, shut up. And get off the chair."

She slid to the floor, clutched at his trouser leg.

"Get *off* me. Jesus." He wiped at the slime on his leg. "Jesus." He threw something at her—a handkerchief. "Clean yourself up."

He left, carrying the chair and camera, still wiping at his trouser leg.

Her sobs steadied. She cried in a low monotone for hours and hours, until they gave her more drugs, and she slept.

But today is her birthday, at least it might be. Today, she can think a little.

The day began unpleasantly, when the pill she was handed with breakfast half dissolved in her mouth before she could swallow it. Afterward, when Fishface left, she spat clots of soggy white power into her hand, and wiped her hand on the floor. She ate nearly all the food on her tray in an effort to get rid of the taste on her tongue. Some time later she noticed that the leftovers on the plates were sausage, and croissant, and juice. Breakfast. It must be morning. And that was when she started to think, to try count the days, and realized it was her birthday.

Eighteen. She now owns her share of inherited stock in the family corporation. She is rich.

When Fishface brings her lunch tray, she is alert enough to slide the pill under her tongue and pretend to swallow. She can feel it dissolving and wonders how much will get into her bloodstream before she can spit it out.

Fishface's hood moves slightly in what Lore interprets as a smile. She stares blankly at the floor, hoping he will not notice she is more alert than usual. She catches sight of the white smears on the floor and her heart jitters. She forces herself to look away, look at anything but the floor, and after a moment, he leaves. She waits, listens. Hears a door opening somewhere, then closing. She spits the pill into her hand. Where can she put it?

There is bread with the meal. She tears off a crust and pokes a hole in the dough, then hesitates. Maybe they give the scraps to a dog. They might notice if it fell asleep. She searches the floor of the tent, finds a tiny tear in the plastic. Underneath, she can feel the long, scratchy grain of old wood. She pushes her finger one way, then another, finds a crack between the planks. She squeezes the pill through the hole and into the crack.

By now her lunch, soup and bread, is cold. She looks at it and remembers: Stella is dead. For a moment, she wishes she had the pill back, wishes she could just drift here, not thinking, until her parents pay up and she can go home. Then she will find it is all a nightmare. She never went to the resort. Tok never called. Stella isn't dead.

All of a sudden she is angry with Stella. *You have no right to make me grieve!* she thinks. Her situation is difficult enough without grief—she needs to be able to think, to plan, not to feel leaden like this, awash with memory. When she gets out of here, she will tell Stella exactly what . . .

But Stella is dead.

Grief is more terrible than she ever thought possible. It is as though there is a hole right through her. She shakes, her muscles spasm and ache. It's hard to swallow because her throat feels too tight, and her heart jumps and skitters. She is sweating. And then she understands. It's the drugs. Lack of drugs. She's withdrawing.

Over the next few days she works out a way to taper off the sedatives. The sodden lumps she spits from her mouth aren't easy to divide, and sometimes she takes too much, but after six days, she is back to nothing, and no longer shakes.

She makes more holes in the bottom of the tent and explores the floor, a few splintery inches a day. On the fourth day of exploration, she finds a six-inch nail. It is old, rusty black iron, and bent at one end, but it comforts her to hold it between the fingers of her left hand, let it poke forward when she makes a fist. While she has a weapon she is more than a helpless victim. She can think, she can plan. At night, before she falls asleep, she tucks the nail down by her feet inside the sleeping bag. In the morning, she holds it in her fist and smiles.

The nail becomes the center of her universe. Her fingers begin to smell of rust, but for Lore, it is the smell of hope.

TWENTY-THREE

I WAS still thinking about Spanner's hard gray smile in the breakroom as the shift started draining their hot drinks, picking up masks, and standing, ready to get back to the last third of the night. The news was showing on the screen, but as I fastened my neck seal and strapped on waders, that dry-bone smile was superimposed on the changing pictures. The sound was off, but the female anchor was nodding at something the male anchor had said, her face composed in that caring expression they always affect when they talk about someone or some cause the listening public will want to take to their hearts.

I should not have said those things to Spanner. They should not have been spoken aloud. It was the kind of thing Spanner herself would have done, not me. Not Lore. And the snake would strike, sooner or later.

A close-up of the male anchor cut away to a second screen: a picture of a teenaged boy with the kind of feather cut that always looks so good on dusty black Asian hair. He seemed vaguely familiar. Perhaps it was the chair he was tied to.

My muscles went rigid, as though my hands were tied to my sides. My body seemed in the wrong place, the wrong position, as if I should be sitting down.

The picture on the screen changed from the boy to me, sitting on the same chair. My body felt confused, in three places at once: sitting in a tent, in bright light, weeping and slurring; naked and bleeding on the cobbles, bathing in the light of images of myself tied to a chair; standing clothed—uniformed, anyway—in a hot breakroom.

The bell signaling the end of the break rang, but I just stood there, stupid and still and alone, while the pictures of me played. Eventually, the screen cut to the male anchor speaking soundlessly, and then back to the sixteen-year-old boy. Then a man, old enough to be the boy's father, hurrying down some steps on a narrow street, the kind found in the centers of some Asian cities, shielding his face from the sun and bright camera lights.

I could move again. I turned up the sound. "—tape was given to the net an hour ago. Although the family refused to comment, a spokeswoman for the Singapore police department tells us she suspects the Chen family have known about the kidnap of Lucas Chen for over a week."

Cut to female anchor. "And this isn't the only similarity to the van de Oest abduction over three years ago." Another picture, this time of a young Frances Lorien. Solemn-faced, arrogant. I wondered when it had been taken. I didn't remember it.

I turned the sound off, and sat down. I stood up again, quickly. Sitting made me feel vulnerable, made me remember the light, the camera.

Not again. Not all those pictures running, over and over.

I looked at the screen again. The boy wasn't me, but the chair was the same, and the tent, the light. Everything.

Probably the same kidnappers. *Kidnapper,* I told myself. Fishface was probably three years dead.

"Bird!" Magyar. Hard-eyed and cross. "Break finished more than—"

"I know. Five minutes ago." I felt unreal. Suspended somewhere between *then* and *now.* Between *Frances Lorien* and *Bird.* "I'm Lore," I whispered to myself. "I'm Lore."

Magyar stepped closer. "What are you mumbling about?"

"You want to know who I am? Take a look. Up there. May as well look now as later. They'll be playing it for days." Poor Magyar, she didn't understand. "What do you think—is it me?"

"What?"

I nodded at the screen. She glanced at it, then back at me, then, almost unwillingly, back at the screen. Her face began to change, muscles moving as her brain processed the information. I suppose it was a shock. She jerked her arm up and out to the volume switch.

"—*with Oster van de Oest, live from Auckland.*" The fountain was buttery with summer sunshine. Oster, used to cameras, had made sure the sun was behind him so he wouldn't squint.

"*We empathize with the family of Lucas Chen. We know how we felt when Frances Lorien was taken. We know that somewhere, someone knows where she is. Even after three years. We're prepared to offer two hundred and fifty thousand for information leading to the discovery of the whereabouts of our daughter.*"

He looked different. Older. And so formal. He thought I was dead.

I turned the sound off. "It's not Auckland, you know." Magyar looked at me blankly. "The house. Ratnapida. The family has an agreement with the news services not to reveal where we live." They were showing more pictures of me. Magyar was looking back and forth from me to the screen. "Not that easy to see at first, is it? But you'd have spotted it eventually. It's there, if you think to look."

She was turned away from me now, studying the bright pictures, but she watched me from the corner of her eye.

"That's me. Frances Lorien van de Oest. The real me. Or it was." I didn't know who I was now. I had an eerie sense of multiplicity, of staring down at my reflection in the water and seeing three faces instead of one.

Magyar was very still, and her eyes looked odd. Slitty. Sunk back into their epicanthic folds. I knew I should be wary of her strange expression, but I felt oddly dispassionate. Unreal. The pictures on the screen kept moving, mute. The three reflections in my head rippled. *Who am I?* Magyar still didn't say anything. She was clenching and unclenching her plasthene-gloved fists. Her mouth was a straight line.

"You aren't supposed to be angry," I said calmly, from a great distance.

"No? Tell me, Bird, how am I *supposed* to react?"

Like everyone else reacted to the van de Oest name: shock, awe, then a closing off as the person they were dealing with changed from *human* to *van de Oest*.

"I don't understand. Why are you angry?"

"Because I feel like a fool." Her nostrils were white. She was breathing hard. In, out. In. Out. Abruptly, she jerked her arm around, looked at her watch. "We've already lost shift time. Time is money. Unless you've decided you've had enough of playing at poor little miss worker bee, I want you on-station in three minutes. And I'll expect you to make up the time you've lost."

Just like that. Dismissed. "But . . ."

"But what?" Hand on hip.

But I'm Frances Lorien van de Oest! Didn't she know what that meant? She couldn't just *dismiss* me, as if I were anyone else . . . *But she had*. Which is what I wanted, wasn't it—to be treated as a real person?

"We're not done with this, Bird. Not nearly done. We'll talk after the shift. After you've made up your time."

She waited. I waited back, then realized she had the upper

hand: I was the worker, she the supervisor. The fact that I had told her who I really was didn't change that. I left the break-room. As though my movement had disturbed the surface of a river, the three faces shivered and blurred together, indistinct.

I don't remember walking to the troughs, but found myself there, trembling, looking at my face in the slick black water.

Who am I? What would I say if I opened my mouth?

We ordered loc, the hot chocolate liqueur. Magyar took a big gulp of steaming liquid and burned herself. She swore, called to the man behind the counter for some ice, then scowled at him when he shoved an ice bucket her way. Her eyebrows were very dark against her pale skin.

She put a cube in her mouth, crunched, sucked.

I said nothing. I did not even want to breathe too hard, in case the single blurred reflection in my head separated out again.

"So. We're here to talk about the way you lied to me."

I spoke carefully, uncertain of my voice. Of my accent. Of the language. Of my own tongue. "It's hard."

"Do it anyway." Utterly unsympathetic.

"Tell me about your family."

"Why? We're here to talk about you, not me."

"Do you have brothers? Or sisters?"

"Both." She swallowed her ice and took another exper-imental sip of loc.

"I have—*had*—two sisters and a brother. But one is a half sister, Greta, my mother's daughter, and she's so much older than me she's more like an aunt—"

"Is this relevant?"

"—and the other brother and sister are twins. Were twins. Stella killed herself." Now she was listening. "In some ways I was like an only child. And my parents should have di-vorced fifteen years ago. I am used to hiding things that mat-ter to me, keeping them close. It's what I do. Who I am."

"Tell me why the fuck I should care about that! You

think that just because you can buy me and Hedon Road, probably the whole city, a hundred times over I'll nod and say, Fine? Just like that? Without even an explanation of why you've been hiding, lying to me? Lying to everyone."

There was no way to deal with her anger. I ignored it. "This job, Hedon Road, isn't a game to me. I need it. I have less money than you do." *Not true, not true. What about the thirty thousand?* The faces shimmered, each with their own secrets.

The muscles in her jaw had relaxed a little, and her pupils were returning to normal.

"I was kidnapped. You know that. When they, when I escaped, I couldn't go back." The rest stuck in my throat like small polished pebbles.

"Why? And why did you lie?"

I sat there, mute.

"I feel like such a fool. Do you have any idea how *used* I feel? All that time I was ordering you around, telling you to bring me this readout or that, treating you like an apprentice. Making you work like that. All that time, you knew, you *knew* . . ." She swirled the remains of her loc around the glass. "You know something? You've made me feel ashamed of myself. Of how I bullied you. I don't like that."

"You didn't bully me."

She wasn't listening. "But *why*? That's what I don't understand. You say you need the money, but why? Why aren't you back with Mummy and Daddy—"

"Don't." Sharper than I intended. "Please, don't call them that."

"Fine. Your family, then. Why aren't you with them, in your fancy house, or estate, or whatever?"

"Ratnapida."

"What?"

"The house. It's called Ratnapida." Stella in the fountain. Oster. Then, later, Oster and Tok, standing side by side. Tok looking beaten.

"Whatever. You could be in the sunshine, doing nothing. So why are you hiding? And what happened to the real Sal Bird?"

I think I killed someone, I had told her. "I never met her. She died in an accident." I waited for her to decide whether or not to believe me. I knew I looked calmer than I felt. Years of training at the dinner table.

She absorbed that, nodding. Still expressionless. "Go on."

"The man I killed . . ." I swallowed. *The man I killed.* "It was one of the men who kidnapped me." I told her about the tent, the drugs. About Crablegs and the camera. About finding the nail.

"This is hard. I haven't thought about it. It was . . . So when they took me outside, after they'd told me my family hadn't paid . . . I thought . . . it just . . ." Another swallow. I looked down at my hand on the bar. This was not something I wanted to think about. I stared at my fingertips, the way the skin curled pinkly around the nails. She put her hands on mine, warm and dry. I still couldn't look up. *Try,* that hand said. "I had the nail hidden in my fist. When we got outside I hit him in the neck."

She lifted her hand from mine and picked up her drink. "Was he dead?"

"The other one, Crablegs, he said I'd killed him. "But . . ." But of course Crablegs would want me to think that. Keep me confused, docile. "I don't know. I just assumed."

"Then that's the first thing we do tomorrow."

"We?"

She just looked at me, indecipherable.

I felt strange. "I need another drink."

We were quiet while the drinks arrived.

"When did it happen, the kidnap?"

"September. Three years ago." Crisp clean air like the scent of apples. The cobbles, blood. Only he might not be dead after all. And Magyar had said *we.*

285

"September. Right. So we'll look at all the murder reports from three—"

But I wasn't listening. I might not have killed him after all. "Do you have any idea what this means to me?" I said suddenly.

Her voice was soft. "Why don't you tell me?"

I put my hand on hers, the one still wrapped around her glass. Neither of us said anything. We both pretended our hands weren't warm and soft together, palm to back, finger on finger, the hair of her forearm touching the underside of my wrist.

"I want to tell you something. About my family. Why Stella killed herself. No one else knows." Not even Spanner. *Do you know what I'm entrusting to you?* I think she did. "My father loved me. That's what I thought. But then I found out my sister Stella had been . . ." I couldn't say it. It was as though there were a clothespin crimping that part of my mind together. I had to talk about it. "I had bad dreams about a monster. My older sister, Greta—she was already grown by the time my mother married my . . . Anyway, she understood what was really happening. She gave me a lock for my door, so . . ." *the monster* "my . . ." *the monster* "so Oster couldn't come into my bedroom when I was alone. Stella went into therapy. Tok said she was getting better, but then she killed herself. And I hadn't known. Anything. All that time, he was doing that to her. Had been. And then when she got older, when she wasn't a helpless child anymore, he tried it on me. But Greta knew." Greta, always gray and stooped, hesitant as though something was about to come around the corner and get her. "I think it had happened to her, too. What I can't understand . . ." The air in the bar seemed too thick all of a sudden, the oxygen all used up. I wanted to go belly to the ground, where it was safer, where it was easier to breathe. "What I can't understand is why no one told me. Tok knew. Stella knew. Greta knew. I didn't. I should have guessed. There were all these clues. He even . . . He even took me for a walk and asked me what I knew, what I had been told."

What did Stella say? he had asked.

No one tells me anything, I replied.

But Greta had tried. Or at least she had got me the lock.

Magyar was frowning. "I'm trying to understand some-thing. You said you thought Oster turned to you when Stella was too old . . ."

"Yes."

"But you think Greta was abused, too."

"Yes."

"Lore." Her eyes were soft, trying to tell me something, but I had no idea what. She sighed. "Tell me about the time . . . Tell me about the night the monster came to you."

"I dreamt. At least that's what Katerine said when I woke up with her hand on my shoulder."

"Katerine was there when you woke up?"

"Yes." I was puzzled.

"Lore." She took both my hands in hers. "Just think a minute. You dreamed about the monster, and when you woke it was Katerine who was there." I looked at her blankly. "You say Greta had been abused, too. But she was an adult by the time your mother and father mar-ried."

"Yes . . ." I said slowly.

"Then if the abuser likes them young, it couldn't have been Oster."

Absurdly it was Tok who came to mind, his laugh of dis-belief when I shouted at him about being mean to Katerine, demanded to know if he realized what he was doing to her: What *I* have done to *her*?

"It's too hot in here. I have to go outside." The air was so thick I felt as though I was swimming toward the door, fighting for breath. I leaned against the wall outside, gasp-ing. I had forgotten to bring my coat. Through my thin shirt the bricks were hard against my shoulder blades.

Katerine on the bed, fully dressed. "It's a dream," she said to Oster. Oster, who was just stumbling into the room.

Magyar came out, our coats draped over her arm. She held mine out silently.

"But she's my mother," I said finally.

"Yes."

My mother, the monster. Which meant Oster wasn't a monster after all. This time I had to bend forward, head nearly to my knees, before I could get air into my lungs.

My mother, the monster. And Oster—he could be my father again. The one I thought I'd lost.

I started pulling on my coat. "I have to go."

"Go where? Are you all right?"

"I don't know. But I need to think."

The air above the wharf was heavy with damp, the scent of timbers softened and swollen with rain and river water. I slipped down the right alleyway, found the panel set in the pavement, and levered it open. I laid my fingers lightly on the switches, then flipped them. The lights went out.

There was no moon and the stars hid behind soft black clouds; nothing to reflect from the water. Just me. I sat down on the wharf, careless of the cold. I could feel the river rather than see it: distended by the rains of the last two days to a thick, dark tongue feeling its way blindly to the sea. Somewhere downriver a barge bumped hollowly against its moorings. Water lapped softly at the timbers.

An old river made old sounds. The water at Ratnapida had never sounded or smelled like this. There, it fountained in the sunshine, tinkled on stone, plopped when a fish surfaced for a fly. Even the rain sparkled—fast showers, followed by rainbows and glistening grass. Young water, and lighthearted. Maybe that was why Stella had chosen the fountain as her backdrop . . .

It all seemed so different now: Stella desperate and pleading, begging for Oster to *notice*, to do something. Giving him—and me—clues that we couldn't see.

Katerine had watched the whole scene so calmly. Too calmly, I saw now: What mother should be able to watch her daughter like that, half naked, drunk, obviously in some pain? Why hadn't I thought about that before? Because that's just how Katerine was: closed up like a lacquered fan.

But not always. Something, some feeling I had never seen, never even caught a glimpse of, had prompted her to steal into her children's room at night—Greta, Stella, me—and . . . and . . . I felt again the heat of the monster's breath on the back of my neck and the fear, the creeping flesh feeling that something was terribly awry in my seven-year-old world.

How many times had Stella had to lie quietly through that? A mother was a foundation, a cornerstone, a touchstone, not a monster. Not the reason to kill oneself.

All the time my mother had been doing that to my sister I had wanted her to love me, had ached for her approval, had wanted her to believe I was *like* her.

I had to lean forward with my weight on my palms, I was so dizzy. Did the fact that I knew, now, what she had done make her a different person? Was I a bad person because I still wanted to be like her? And I still did. On some level I always would. It was what I had grown up with, that image of the calm, competent woman.

I didn't want to think about it. I stared down at my hands, at the drying cobbles, the miniature riverbeds that formed between them. Here and there were discarded remnants of the tourist trade: beverage cans, a torn disk wrapper. It would all be cleaned up by midmorning.

Katerine had always liked things clean and orderly. Efficient. *That monster,* Tok had called her. *That monster can't be allowed to get away with it.*

Tok and Oster talking to the camera. Tok looking—not beaten, I realized, but exhausted. What had they done to her? Where was she? Why hadn't they said something, anything on the net?

My mother. I imagined her carefully: tidy hair, concise conversation, economical gestures. She had never gestured much, come to think of it. And her hair was always cut the same way, though she did occasionally tint it varying shades of blond, as a concession to fashion. Her eyes . . . I had never known the color of her eyes. Did she hide them in a subconscious attempt to hide her soul?

My mother, who was all too human. She had got away with hurting her children because she was so . . . acceptable. But someone must have known. Tok had. And he had tried to tell me. Why had he taken so long to speak out?

My father should have *known*! But so should I. No: I was a child. *Not really.*

Had Oster known? I tried to remember how he had behaved that afternoon with Stella in the fountain. He had known something was wrong. He had even asked me what I knew . . .

He should have known. I couldn't get away from that. He was my father—Stella's father—and he should have taken some responsibility, some interest in us apart from that absurd competition with his wife to make us love him more.

He should have known. But he wasn't a monster. And I missed him. I wanted to have him back. I'd spent the last three years believing him to be something he was not, and I wanted to touch him, maybe have him ruffle my hair, anything, just to make contact again with the father I had thought I had known.

A barge hooted from downriver, a burly morning noise. Almost dawn.

I stretched and stood, feeling strange: wobbly and light-boned. So much had changed. I had my father back, and had lost my mother. And Magyar knew who I was. She could see through the obscuring reflections. To her I wasn't *van de Oest*, I wasn't *Criminal*, I wasn't *Bird*. I was just me, Lore.

LORE'S BIRTHDAY came and went. Twenty. She went out in the blustery September wind with the cat's daily ration of leftovers. As usual she knelt to push the plate under the bushes without really looking, but this time the plate bumped into something soft. She peered into the tangle of dry wood and old, dead leaves.

It was a kitten. Dead. Probably about two weeks old. Skinny. Fur the color of sand.

She looked at it a long time, then went inside to get her work gloves and spade. It weighed nothing.

Kittens should be round, she thought. It struck her as terribly wrong for something so young to look so used-up. It should have had warm milk, and spring, and a skyful of butterflies to chase. Not a short, hard life and an end on the cold ground.

It was wrong. All wrong.

Spanner was reading. "I don't really see what the difference is, whether you enjoy it or not." She barely looked up from the gray book screen in her lap.

"Because it's a lie." *Because kittens should be round.*

Spanner switched to the next page. "It's flickering again."

"What?" Lore was confused for a moment; then she realized Spanner was fiddling with the screen contrast. "Turn that book off and listen to me."

Spanner turned it off, put it down on the cushion next to her. "I was listening. You were saying that if you enjoy yourself it must not be real."

"You're being obtuse."

"No. It's a job, just like any other. You don't begrudge Jamaican cane cutters a smoke to make their work less monotonous, do you? Or Chileans a good chew of coca leaf to get them up the next mountain trail where the air's too

thin for anything except their goats. So why deny yourself?"

"Because I hate what we do."

"You just said you enjoyed it."

"I do, at the time."

"Then you'd rather not enjoy it?"

"I'd rather not do it at all."

"And you'd rather not eat, too?"

"There has to be another way! We could use a fake
PIDA, a good one, to get a job. We could—"

"We have a job."

"I hate it! It makes me feel ashamed, and I'm sick of being ashamed."

"There's nothing to be ashamed of. You haven't hurt
anyone."

"I've hurt myself. This is *my* body, *my*—"

"Temple, right?" Spanner shook her head. "It's not a
temple, it's a sack of meat." She slapped herself on the thigh.
"A tool made of muscle and skin and bone, to be used the
same way we use any other tool."

"No." Lore was horrified. "Your body isn't just a tool
like a . . . a screwdriver. It *is* you. What it does and feels
makes you who you are. Don't you see that?"

"You are who you fuck?" Spanner's eyes were challenging. "Then who does that make you?"

"Someone I'm ashamed of." And Lore understood with
blinding clarity why Stella had killed herself. To be used like
a receptacle, a commodity, and to *know* it, to be helpless before it, and then to see that helplessness reflected back at her
every time her eyes met her abuser's across the table, every
time she saw herself in the mirror. There would never be
any way to escape that kind of shame. She looked at Spanner, who was waiting with her eyebrows raised. "What happened? What happened to you, to make you feel you have
to do this?"

"Nothing had to *happen*. I'm not some pathetic victim, reacting instead of acting." She folded her arms. "I'm simply a realist."

Lore stared at her, then shook her head tiredly.

"You don't believe me?"

But that was not what Lore had meant by the head shake. How could she argue against someone's reality?

She looked at Spanner for a long time. At the hair that needed combing, the light blue eyes she had seen cry only once, at the beginning of the wrinkle on the left side of her mouth, where the muscles pulled when she laughed. She wanted to hold Spanner close, stroke her hair, tell her it was all right, she didn't have to be a realist all the time; she, Lore, would let her dream, let her stretch and reach and *try*, and if she failed, then it wasn't the end of the world.

But Spanner's pupils were tiny and her arms were still folded and her face was like a mummy's: thin, drawn too tight, used up too early. She had never had the chance to play, to laugh without calculation, without looking over her shoulder. *Kittens should be round.*

Lore was suddenly very, very tired. "I'm going to lie down."

She went into the bedroom and drew the curtains against the lights outside. The close, dark air reminded her of the tent. She felt trapped. There had to be a way out. For both of them.

She fell asleep and dreamed of Stella, surrounded by her friends at Ratnapida, laughing, watching the net charity commercials, thumbing her PIDA into the base of the screen and sending thousands to some aid organization Lore had never heard of. Then jetting off to some other island paradise to do the same thing. Always traveling. Running, running, but never getting away. Stella, who had escaped by dying.

When Lore woke it was dark, and she knew how they could escape.

I slept for nine hours and woke up feeling stiff and sore, as though my body had tried to rearrange itself physically to fit three people inside one skin. I felt denser, more closely packed. Solid and strange.

There was a message on the screen from the plant: shifts were back to normal. I had received four other calls, all aborted without leaving a message.

The flat was stuffy. I went down to Tom's. "I brought you a recording of the . . ." I was suddenly embarrassed. *Scam,* I thought, *fake commercial,* and was ashamed. I held out the disk. He took it. "This is yours, too." I pulled the small packet of debit cards from my pocket. "We got more than I thought. There's about five thousand here." It was more than the share we had agreed upon, but he needed it more than me. Now it was his turn to look embarrassed, but he took the packet. "I thought Gibbon might want a walk."

We walked along the canal, the dog at the fullest extent of his leash. A stiff wind pushed the clouds along at a tilt and slapped water up against the banks. The air smelled of weeds and wind and Gibbon's coat. We saw two Canada geese landing in a wide dike. Gibbon ran for them, barking and dragging me behind him, but the geese just ignored us. He wanted to run some more, so we did, feet thudding on the densely packed dirt of the towpath, mouths open.

For a while, it seemed that I ran through the fountains with Tok, that I ran through the city streets with Spanner, that I ran on my own in an older skin. I felt as though I swam through the swirling meeting point of three rivers, each at a different temperature, each tugging me this way and that. Then it was just me, and Gibbon, and a windy afternoon.

Tom was watching the net when I got back. Not the scam. Soup was heating.

"You didn't watch it?"

"No. I didn't want to see myself looking old and useless."

He was old, and arthritic, and lonely—but his eyes were not heavy-lidded and ancient and used up, like Spanner's; they weren't dull and eaten-away and dead like the kitten's. How did he watch the net for hours and keep eyes like that?

I wondered if he had seen the video of Chen's kidnapping, of me; what he might do if he had recognized me and seen the reward posted; whether he would turn me in . . . and if I would blame him if he did. A quarter of a million would change his life.

He looked at me a long time when I handed him Gibbon's leash. I met his eyes. *Not like Spanner's at all.* I patted Gibbon. "The walk was a good idea," I said.

I got to the plant a little before six. Magyar was waiting at the gates. Her relief was obvious.

"Was it you who called and hung up? Thought I wouldn't show?" It had occurred to me while I dressed, sweating, remembering the look on Tom's face, my own doubts. I didn't want to tempt friends, or those who might become friends. I could have run, disappeared, just another tiny rodent in the undergrowth of the city . . . But if I ran I would be alone again, never knowing who I was when I bent to look at my reflection.

Being near Magyar made me feel known and understood.

We walked into the locker room very close but not quite touching. We caught a few slantwise glances, coming in together, and Kinnis even slapped me on the back, grinning hugely.

I wondered why I wasn't telling them that their obvious assumption was wrong. I wondered why Magyar wasn't, either.

"Later," Magyar said, "at the break."

We went our separate ways.

All through the first half of the shift, Cel kept watching me, raising her eyebrow at me when I caught her gaze. Annoyingly, I kept blushing.

Five minutes before the break Magyar came to find me. I watched her striding toward me, loosening her mask, frowning. The different lights ran across her hair, which looked very clean and soft. When her right leg moved forward, the skinny pulled taut over her left breast. The plasthene would feel warm under my hands.

"Bird."

"Magyar."

"We need to talk."

"Anywhere but the breakroom. I'm beginning to feel like a trophy wife." I just blurted it out, and she blushed, which meant I did, too, imagining what she might be thinking, and I couldn't take my eyes off her lips, which were very red. And then of course Cel was there, raising her eyebrow at us both.

Frowning ferociously, Magyar led me to the glass-walled office where we had faced off with Hepple. She went around the desk and sat in the comfortably upholstered chair. She was angry again. "Feels good. Want a try? No? Well, I suppose you've sat behind big desks a lot. You were probably used to chairs like these by the time you were seven."

I thought we had gone through all this rich girl–poor girl stuff yesterday. "What's bothering you?"

"Have you checked the police records yet?"

"No." I should have. Of course I should have, but I had been sleeping, exhausted and confused.

"I did. Or my friend did. She works in the county records office. I called her this morning, asked her to check."

"And?"

"And nothing. At least not from this part of the country."

There was a large dry patch high up in my throat. "How about hospitals?"

"Also nothing."

The dry patch was getting bigger. "I don't understand."

"Nor do I, frankly."

I didn't really want to ask her. "Do you believe me?"

"I wonder if you're telling me everything."

"You've heard the high points. There are some things I don't want to talk about. Some of them are a matter of public record," like the net video, "some are things only I know about." And Spanner. "But I haven't lied to you. Except about my name."

There was another chair on my side of the desk. I took it.

"So, what do we do from here?"

I didn't have any suggestions. She was the one who didn't trust me. I was tired of dancing to other people's tunes. Somewhere below, water gushed loudly through a pipe. It was hot in the glass box.

Eventually, she sighed and put her feet up on the desk. "You're a van de Oest. But you won't go back to your family because your mother abused your sisters and might have abused you. And because you think you killed someone. But there's no record of a dead body. No body, no murder, no crime. And if your mother did abuse anyone, it's not your fault, so why should you suffer? Why not just go back and get her arrested?"

"She may already *be* arrested." I told her about Tok and Oster, the strange appeal they had made two years ago. "But there's more to it than that."

Magyar folded her arms in satisfaction. "Thought there might be."

"My ransom wasn't paid for a long, long time. I thought the delay was deliberate."

"Thought or think?"

"I don't know." Did the fact that it was Katerine and not Oster make a difference? No. "I was in that tent for weeks. The ransom demand was thirty million." I ignored the way her pupils dilated. "They wouldn't actually expect thirty million, of course. That's just a negotiating tool. But they would expect about ten."

"How do you know that?"

"It's the kind of thing you learn growing up."

"*You* might."

I supposed it might seem odd, to grow up understanding the mechanics of abduction. "Ten million—even thirty million—means nothing to my family. Just on my own I'm worth more than that." Talk of millions was doing what mention of my name yesterday had not. I could see the shutters start to come down in Magyar's head. "Don't. Damn you, Magyar, don't go away, don't pretend I'm not real. There's nothing I can do about the money. It's what I was brought up with. But I don't have it now."

"You could, though."

"I could. But I won't."

"We'll see." But she smiled. It was just the corner of her mouth, but she was trying.

"At those prices, my release should have been negotiated within a week. Ten days at the most. I was in that tent six weeks. Why?"

"Bad communications?"

"No. They had excellent lines of communication. Think about it. Someone knew where to abduct me from. I'd been in Uruguay less than twenty-four hours, but they were ready: transport, masks, drugs. And they even knew I was allergic to subcutaneous spray injections. How?"

"I don't know."

"Someone told them. And the only people who knew were family members, and those close to the family." I gave her a minute to absorb that. "So if my family, or someone close, set the whole thing up, the question has to be: Why? The family doesn't need money, nor does the corporation."

"Maybe it wasn't money they were after."

"That's what I'm afraid of. Maybe they just wanted me out of the way."

"But why? And if it was the family, for family reasons, why the Chen kidnapping?"

"I don't know."

Silence. "So you changed your name and hid." I nodded. "Well." She did not seem to know what to say.

She knew I had been in danger, maybe still was. She knew I was rich but would probably never claim the money. She knew I thought I had killed a man. "Magyar, will you help me?"

"Yes."

Yes. "Just like that?"

She lifted her feet off the desk, gave me a crooked smile. "Murder, money, high intrigue. It's just getting interesting."

Another silence, this time longer. "Magyar, why?"

"Why do you think?" she asked softly.

It was not a rhetorical question. But she had known what Kinnis and Cel and all those others had been thinking, and she hadn't contradicted them. "Because . . . Damn it, Cherry, you know why."

"Maybe I do. But I need to hear it. I don't think I can take any more surprises from you." She got up, came around to my side of the desk. We stood about twelve inches from each other. The hairs on my neck and the backs of my hands tried to rise. It was like being in a strong magnetic field. I felt very exposed in my skinny.

"I like you," I said suddenly. Which was not quite what I had intended. "I like being near you. And I admire you. What you think matters to me." And I had made myself vulnerable. She was the only person in the world apart from Spanner who knew who I was.

I could see every pore in her face, the way the creases around her eyes deepened when she smiled. "Why didn't you start trusting me a bit earlier?" She moved closer, nine inches, six.

I could feel the heat of her body through the plasthene of my suit. Our hipbones were almost touching. I imagined the feel of her skin under my hands.

The end-of-break Klaxon sounded. Down below there was movement as the shift came back to the troughs.

"Shit." I started to turn away.

She snagged my hand. Plasthene on plasthene. Safe and erotic. She did not seem to care about the glass walls. She moved her hand to my wrist, tugged until my arms came around her waist. She laid my palm against the small of her back, pressed it in place. My belly was an inch, half an inch, from hers. Heat swarmed up my legs, down my spine. "Is this what you want?"

I nodded.

"Say it."

"Yes. This is what I want. You are who I want."

What was between us swelled suddenly, and was almost tangible: ceramic and smooth, rounded as an egg.

We stepped apart by mutual consent. Magyar did not sit behind the desk again, but perched on one corner. I hovered uncertainly by the door. "We have a lot to do," she said.

"Yes."

"And I'll have to split my time between this"—she gestured at the space between us, *the possible murder,* she meant—"and the sabotage."

"Yes." I turned to go, got as far as touching the door handle, turned. "Magyar, were you ever loved by your family?"

"Yes."

So sure. "I don't know if I was. I know that no one else ever did. I'm not sure what love is, but I want . . . I want to be real." I wasn't sure what I was trying to say. "All the people I've slept with, none of them knew who I really was." None of them had whispered my name, sent me love notes. Told me they couldn't live without me. "I've never had any romance, ever. But how could I? I've been so many people, I never knew which ones were real. I want to find that out before you and I . . . before we go any further. I want to see what that's like. Do you understand?"

"No," she said softly, "but I'm trying."

Good enough.

TWENTY-FOUR

THE SEVEN hours between lunch and dinner are the longest part of the day. She tries to stay fit by doing stretches and sit-ups and resistance exercises, but she does not have the strength to work out for more than thirty or forty minutes. The rest of the time drags. She weeps often: for herself, for Stella, for Tok. She wonders why her family has not ransomed her.

Something is different. Both men come into the tent together. She sits at the far end of the tent while they stand at the entrance. They fill the tent, breathe all her air. She must not look scared or they will know she is no longer drugged.

"Your family is stalling," Crablegs says.

Lore looks from one to the other, not sure if she should say anything.

Fishface squats down until his hooded face is only a foot

or so higher than Lore's. "We've asked for thirty million," he explains, "which isn't much."

"They say ten is all they'll give. We think maybe they don't care whether you live or die."

Fishface stands. "If they don't give us the money, we can't give you back. You do understand that, don't you?"

He sounds genuinely regretful. Lore wants to reach out and pat his arm, let him know she understands that he is really trying.

"Think about what you want to say to them, to persuade them to pay." They leave without another word.

Ten million. What can she say that will make them pay if they don't want to? And why wouldn't they want to?

She thinks of Katerine, and Oster. Perhaps they are still competing for her.

Then why haven't they paid?

When Crablegs brings the camera again, what will she say to convince her parents that she is worth thirty million?

Lore looks inside herself and finds only a vast space. Who is she? Her father would recognize the Lore who goes with him to count fish in the bay, and talk about the silliness of their ancestors. Katerine, on the other hand, knows and cares only for the Project Deputy, the efficient young woman who designs huge systems and suavely courts the Minister for This and the Commissar of That.

But what of the girl who would lie in Anne's arms and swim with Sarah, the child who dreams of monsters and still sometimes gets up in the middle of the night to check the lock on her door? Who will recognize her? No one but herself. She has shared none of these things, told them to no one. She has been so alone.

TWENTY-FIVE

I WAS on the roof, nailing planks together to make a planter big enough for a tree, when my phone buzzed. I scrambled back in through the window, picked up a handset. "Yeah."

"Meisener," Magyar said.

"What?" I put my hammer down on the table.

"It was Meisener who sabotaged the plant. Had to be."

"Hold on." I climbed back through the window with the handset and sat down. The slates were cold through the thin material of my trousers. "Go on."

"Four people with enough know-how to jam the glucose line and ready the emergency equipment started work at Hedon Road in the last three months: you, a day-shifter, and Paolo and Meisener." She added dryly, "I assumed you didn't count."

"Thanks."

"The day-shifter joined just the day before the spill. Not enough time to fix things."

"No."

"So that left Paolo and Meisener. And apart from the fact that Paolo left before it all happened, I don't think he was capable, do you?"

Paolo had neither the knowledge nor the focus. "No."

"Right. So I had a look at Meisener's records—"

"Which will be false."

"Yeah, they read like yours: plausible dates and places— names of plants and supervisors, family, even vacation dates—but something just doesn't add up."

"Go on."

"Even if you only believe part of his records, he's had enough experience to know what he's doing."

"Where was he when the spill came in?"

"I'm getting to that." She sounded annoyed. "I back-checked with Incident Documentation. He was one of the first out."

"Nothing incriminating about that."

"No, but he apparently helped half a dozen people into EEBAs before leaving."

"That's significant?"

"*I* think it is," Magyar said. "He already knew where everything was. Which means he was expecting something to happen."

"It could." It could also just mean he was an old hand, like me, like Magyar herself, and knew a badly run plant ready for an accident when he saw it. "If he's guilty, he'll be moving on soon." To whatever his next job was, for whomever paid him. Meisener, the cheerful, bandy-legged little man.

". . . little bastard."

I was thinking, irrelevantly, of sea and sand and sitting on a log. Then of my last van de Oest project in the Kirghizi desert. Of a truck driving through a puddle, and Hepple. "What?"

"I said, I want to strangle the little bastard. He could

have killed my people. All for money! But why? That's what doesn't make sense. Who benefits? The whole thing smacks of organization, which takes money. Even if we *had* shut down for several days and managers lost their profits, it doesn't mean anyone else would have *made* money. Unless it was a matter of market share, and even then—"

Market share. Hepple. A tent, wind singing along the dunes outside. Marley, saying something about . . .

"—divided up among several rival plants, so it wouldn't be worthwhile."

Silence.

"Are you there?"

"Um? Yes. Sorry." The wisp of memory faded.

"Well, what should we do? Apart from beat the bastard to pulp."

"Watch and wait." A dissatisfied, incredulous silence. "We need more information." There was something missing. Something important. *Hepple. A truck. Tok. Marley.* I shook my head. "We don't know for sure that he's responsible."

"True." Grudging. "He might not even know we know it's sabotage."

"If it is him, he'll know what the plant managers know."

Her sigh was loud and long. "Meet me outside the plant at half five?"

"Yes."

I picked up the hammer and a mouthful of nails and went back to building my planter—one of five. I was going to make an orchard. Me, the sky, some trees. Maybe bees would come up here after all.

The wood was new, still sappy and white against the silvery glint of the nails. Difficult to saw, but less expensive. On a water worker's pay, I couldn't afford any better.

But there's that thirty thousand tucked away.

I tried not to think about that. If I didn't spend the money I could pretend I hadn't been in that bunker with

Spanner. I could ignore that awful dead-bone smile she had given me, the things I had said. The things I knew because of what I had done.

I thought about Magyar's words: *managers' profits.* Hepple wouldn't be getting any this quarter. His own fault. His greedy attempts to shave expenses could have cost people their lives. *Market share.*

The hammer slipped and caught the edge of my thumb. I spat the nails out of my mouth and swore. Carpentry wasn't my forte. Tok, now, he could have taken these bits of wood and banged them together in a second. Very practical and workmanlike. He was the kind of person who could take two twigs and a piece of string and make something interesting and sturdy. He had done; beautiful things made of found objects dotted the grounds at Ratnapida. He had never been able to just sit, empty-handed. And then he had gone to study music. So hidden, after all. Close-minded. I suppose it ran in the family.

We had shared things, though. And he had helped me. Like that time by the pond when he had told me to find something to do, something to use as a shield against our parents' interest. I hammered the nail home, set another in place with a tap. That afternoon had been sunny, like most Ratnapida days I remembered. Throwing grass stems for the fish. I hammered the nail in. Set another. Smiled as I remembered Tok telling me about sneaking a look at Aunt Nadia's files. Lifted the hammer.

It came out of nowhere, a metaphysical hammer blow between the rise and fall of the real tool: *Hepple. Market share. Jerome's Boys.* And it all fell into place.

Magyar was waiting for me in the locker room. The shift would not change for half an hour and everything was quiet. We sat next to each other on the wooden bench, not too close. "Jerome's Boys," I told her. "They were a dirty-work team run directly by the van de Oest COO, forty years ago. They enforced the company monopolies, before the courts got around to it. Any means necessary. Which is why they were supposed to have been disbanded. Maybe they were, but someone's had the same idea." Magyar was staring at me as though I was crazy. "Look at when Meisener joined. Just a few days after Hepple started cost-cutting."

"Hepple? This bunch of enforcers tried to wreck my plant because of that useless idiot?"

"No. Or, rather, yes: because of what Hepple *did*. In a way you were right. It's about market share."

"I'm trying very hard," she said, "but I don't see what Hepple's got to do with it."

I started again. "My . . . the van de Oests originally made their money by genetically tailoring bacteria and then patenting them. Every time their bugs were used, they got a cut. Then they retailored the bugs so that they don't work unless they're supplied with special proprietary bug food—which is where they make their real profit these days. Treatment plants need the bugs, the bugs need the food. The van de Oests license people to supply both and earn a lot of money for doing nothing. They have a monopoly. When Hepple canceled the food order in favor of generics, he was breaking that monopoly. Someone stepped in to protect it."

"They would risk all this, thousands of lives, to protect a monopoly?"

"They didn't intend anyone to get hurt. Except in the pocket." They wouldn't risk another Caracas. "And even if people died, the van de Oests would have come out of it smelling of roses. It's happened before. After all, they would say, if their instructions had been carried out and the proper food used, nothing would have gone wrong. The finger will point at Hepple, and the people who were stupid enough to hire him."

"Which is what's happened."

"Yes."

"So," Magyar said slowly, "this group, Jerome's Boys or whatever they're called now, is responsible. But they're illegal. They're not supposed to exist. So where do they get their money?"

The lubricant behind all corporate machinery is money, Oster had said. *No funds, no operation.*

Ridiculously, I felt too ashamed to tell her. *It's not your fault,* I told myself, but they were my family. I shared the same genes, the same upbringing. I might have had the same values. "It . . . They . . ." I looked down at the floor, then back up again. "Kidnap is a great source of income."

"Kidnap is . . . ?" She stared at me. "Tell me if I've got this right. Someone assembles a group to protect the company. But they don't have access to legitimate corporate funds. So they kidnap the heir, you, and get—how much, ten million?"

"Tax free."

"—ten million tax free, to fund them. Their purpose is to insure corporate market share by doing things like illegal information gathering and plant sabotage. The point of insuring market share is to keep up van de Oest family income . . ." She shook her head.

"I know, it doesn't make sense."

"It doesn't make any *kind* of sense! Whoever's in charge of these people has to have a mind like a corkscrew."

"And access to everything that goes on." Corporate records and strategy. Marketing. Research and development. Personal family records. "They had to know I was going to be in Uruguay. They had to know I was allergic to spray hypos. They had to have an organization. Just like the organization that sabotaged the plant. And look at who's been kidnapped now: Lucas Chen, heir to another bioremediation family. The kind of person the dirty-work group would be collecting information on. Don't you see? It makes perfect sense." Someone in my family had had me kidnapped. Had put me through all that humiliation and fear and guilt. Had put me in a place where I might have killed somebody. Someone in my *family*. "Have you heard any more from your friend in county records?"

"More of the same: nothing, nothing, and nothing. She'll keep checking, but either you didn't kill him, or someone doesn't want anyone to know that you did."

She didn't say: *Which is the same thing.* It wasn't.

She stood up, looked at her watch. It was almost time for the shift change. I had a sudden picture of Magyar in my kitchen, making coffee, talking about nothing in particular. I wondered if it would ever happen.

"So, what are you going to do now?" she asked.

"Help you watch Meisener."

She made an impatient gesture. "Don't you think you should tell someone what you know? You should take it to the police. You haven't done anything wrong. Or at least call your father. The poor man thinks you're dead."

"I want it to stay that way for a while."

"You're punishing him for something you once thought he did. But he hasn't done anything wrong, either."

"He's done plenty. Ignoring problems isn't that far from creating them."

"Yes, it is. Especially if he's trying to fix things now."

"Two hundred and fifty thousand will not fix anything! And all it would have taken three years ago—three years ago!—was a single sentence. One sentence: 'I won't let your mother hurt you again.' But he didn't."

"I don't know whether he truly tried then or not. But I think he's trying now. He's trying to find you."

"Well, I don't want to be found."

"Why not?"

"Because I'm ashamed!" Because kittens should be round. Because still sometimes I felt as though I might cast three shadows in a bright light.

From down the corridor came the sound of voices. Some laughter. The sudden slush of a shower.

Magyar gave me a quick, hard hug. It was so fast I hardly

realized what she was doing until she let go. "Just think about it. You can always phone in some anonymous information to the police. But you have to do something."

"We'll watch Meisener."

≈ THE GARDEN lay fallow. Lore only left the flat when Spanner forced her out to make money. Instead, every time a charity commercial came on the net, Lore downloaded it. After discarding the big, established organizations, she had twenty-three examples. She began to compare: the pitch, the age of the live spokesperson in relation to the charity, the vocabulary used, the background scenery.

She was sure she could create a short commercial at least as good as any of the ones she had seen. But she had no idea which were the most effective in terms of bringing in money.

After some thought, she accessed net archives, downloading charity commercials that were two or three years old. She analyzed them for the same trends she had spotted in the later adverts, then brought up the tax records of those organizations that were still alive enough to be filing.

"It *will* work," Lore said, but Spanner was putting on her jacket. "It will," she went on more calmly. "We have a few minutes before we have to be there. Just sit down and listen." Spanner zipped up the jacket. She was pulling gloves out of the pockets while Lore talked fast. "Look, you've seen what I can do. And you've seen the commercials. They can't afford anything more expensive than library shots with maybe one live head. No interactives. Nothing I can't handle. True?"

"True."

"Then all we need is a false account, and maybe twenty seconds break-in time."

Spanner shook her head. "We can't even replace our own PIDAs in this climate."

"We can get an account set up by getting Ruth's help. She works at the morgue, remember."

"I hadn't forgotten. But she's not likely to help us, not after the film."

Lore swallowed. "Maybe if we explained . . ." And there was always that film, with the right head attached to the right body: there was always blackmail.

"And what about breaking into the net transmission? Ruth can't help us there."

"No." Lore tried to smile. "Actually, I was hoping you would be able to think of a way to manage that."

Spanner frowned. "I suppose . . . No. The equipment would be too expensive. It wouldn't be cost-effective."

"How expensive?"

"I don't know. A lot."

"Five hundred? Ten thousand?"

"More." Spanner was still frowning, still thinking. "But maybe not that much more. It would be difficult to get hold of, though Hyn and Zimmer would be able to help . . ."

"But we don't know where—"

"I can always find the old foxes. How much do you think we could make?"

Lore thought about lying. "I don't know," she admitted. "It depends how good my tape is. If I could count on ten seconds, say, then maybe . . . thirty thousand?"

Spanner nodded. "We'd more than break even after the second run."

Assuming we don't get caught after the first, Lore thought, but said nothing. She was feeling odd, almost excited, a little scared. It might work, it might. This might be a way out. She was finding it hard to breathe.

Spanner pulled on her gloves and tapped her breast pocket where the vial nested. "Meanwhile, we still need money. Even more if we're to get that equipment."

Spanner's eyes were very blue, Lore thought, very beautiful. And there was no choice. They had to get their money from somewhere. For now. She nodded, and the motion spilled the tears that had been gathering in her eyes.

Spanner took off one of her gloves and gently brushed at Lore's cheek. "Don't cry. We'll just do this for a little while longer. Just until we have the money for the equipment. Then I'll make everything all right. I promise." She smiled, but Lore just cried harder. She had seen that half curl of the lip: Spanner was lying.

After Lore had set out the cat's food, she sat on the damp earth by the rockery she had made of broken bricks and lumps of concrete with the steel still stuck through it. The worst of winter was over. There were two snowdrops poking bravely from the scraggy grass. It had rained earlier; the earth smelled freshly turned. She felt utterly blank. She watched the sky, a beautiful, cold, clear blue that made her ache. It reminded her of the Netherlands, of being six, of being looked after, protected from the world.

A faint mewling brought her back to the present. It came from under the bushes. She moved her head very slowly. Slight movement. Something—several somethings— small. She stayed very still, trying to breathe quietly, evenly. Heard it again, this time two thin squeaks. Kittens.

Lore thought about the thin, pathetic thing she had buried just a few months ago, the kitten that had died of utter starvation. Nothing, probably, had improved for the feral mother, but she did not know the meaning of giving up. Giving up got you nowhere. Nowhere at all. She would keep trying, keep giving birth, until she had a soft, round kitten.

MEISENER CAME in, talking to Cel, while I was wriggling into my skinny. I watched him covertly while he took off his coat, folded it up and bundled it into his locker, and unhooked his slate.

His slate. It would be so simple. If I dealt with Spanner again. No. Not that. Not again. *But you have to do something,* Magyar had said, and she was right. Lucas Chen was strapped to a chair in a tent, somewhere, or shivering in a sleeping bag, naked and afraid. I had to do something.

I worked through the first half of the shift, thinking, then ate my food at the break while staring unseeingly at the fish loop, still thinking. Near the end of the shift, I found Magyar. "Is there any way you can stay here after the end of the shift? Pretend you need to do some office work, or something?"

"I don't need to pretend. There's a lot to do."

"Would they notice if you uploaded Meisener's records to me at home?"

"I could find a way to disguise it. What do you have in mind?"

"A records search. Between your official status and the things I've picked up in the last couple of years, we can learn a lot about Nathan Meisener."

The flat was cold when I got home, but I opened a link to Magyar before I even turned on the heat so that she could start uploading Meisener's information. I asked her to also call each of the previous employers he had listed, and get from them several things: a picture, a DNA scan if available, biographical data—age, height, family and so on—and the references and employers he had listed.

I turned on the heat and lights and made some tea while she started on that. It was going to be a long night.

When the information began to come through, I kept Magyar's link in the top left corner while I scrolled through the data.

The preliminary data from his last listed employer,

EnSyTec, checked out. "It says he worked for these people nearly eleven years," Magyar said as I sipped and read. "It looks kosher to me."

"How about the résumé he gave them—does it match the one he gave when he applied for this job?"

"I don't know. All I could get immediately without bumping up a level was his performance records, which match what he gave us when he arrived."

"See if you can get the rest."

"It's three in the morning."

"Not in Sarajevo."

Her picture box at the top of my screen went blank. I scrolled through the résumé that had got Meisener the Hedon Road job: EnSyTec, eleven years; Work, Inc, a placement agency, for three; Piplex, a manufacturing plant, for six years before that. It just didn't feel right. Meisener did not strike me as the kind of man to stay in one place for eleven years. For all his competence and outward cheer, he struck me as a person who would one day simply not show up for work. Rootless. But he said he was married, with children.

I went back to the biographical information: Sarah Meisener, a chemist with a local government lab. Number listed. I called Magyar at Hedon Road and left a message. "When you get off the phone to Sarajevo, try calling Sarah Meisener." I gave her the number, and went back to the list.

I finished my tea and was debating between soup and toast when Magyar came back. "I wasn't talking to Sarajevo," she said. She looked pleased with herself. "It was Athens. Meisener's ex-supervisor. 'I didn't think he would be working anymore,' he said when I told him we were thinking of promoting Meisener to shift supervisor. 'Is his heart better now, then?' 'Heart?' I said, 'are we talking about the same Meisener?' 'I know,' he said, 'built like a bull, doesn't look like there's anything wrong with him.' 'A bull,' I said, 'yes, indeed.' Apparently he was retired early.

Planned to go to Israel. The supervisor in Athens is making sure I get the full record. 'Old Nathan deserves every chance.' Best buddies, it seems." She grinned. "Would you call that bandy-legged little man a bull?"

"No."

"No. I think we've got him."

I wasn't so sure. He could have just assumed an ID, the way I had. But I had been aiming for the long term, for something that would stand up for years, forever, if necessary. It could have happened. If I hadn't met Magyar, if she hadn't made me take a good look at myself, I could have been trapped at Hedon Road, as a drudge, for the rest of my life. My bones felt as though they were shrinking; the thought was appalling. Meisener, though, would only have been working for the short term. Four or five weeks. *You got paid?* Kinnis had asked. *Nah. Timed it all wrong.* But he had timed it perfectly: employers often did not check too rigorously until money had changed hands. Which meant that maybe Meisener, or whoever he was, had taken a shortcut. "Did you try his wife?"

Magyar snorted. "At four in the morning? What would I say: Did Nathan get home all right?"

"Just call, and hang up. Tell me what you get."

I decided on toast. Easier to eat at the screen. The smell of scorching bread reminded me of being five, the sun hot on the courtyard stones in Amsterdam, Tok shouting *How do you know it's clean?* How did anyone ever know anything was clean? I was no longer hungry, but I forced myself to eat one of the slices, with a thin spread of baba ghanouj. I wondered what Lucas Chen was doing, if he felt *clean.*

The screen signaled that Magyar was calling. Her face was smooth; she was not happy. "She answered on the first ring. A cool blonde. Young. And the video pickup was fuzzed around the edges."

"Did you say anything?"

"I got off the line as soon as she came on. Gave me the creeps. But that's not all. I'm downloading that information from Athens. Interesting reading."

She stayed on line while I read. "No army experience listed," I said.

"I noticed that."

"And no Work, Inc." Magyar was nodding: she'd noticed that, too. "I wonder who owns that company."

"Difficult?"

"Tedious. I'll be a while." For a trace like this, you didn't need genius, or hot equipment, or special codes. All you needed was patience, obstinacy, and a certain feel for reference and information systems. I had watched Spanner often enough to know how it was done.

I accessed phone information, and after twenty minutes found the number for Work, Inc. Another half an hour told me who that phone account was billed to: a Juno Satuomi, whose bank account was maintained by the Filament Corporation. The Filament Corporation had three listed board members: C. Santorini, an anonymous representative of Ketch Lighters, and the CEO of Allman Znit Associates. The first two were dummies; the third had four corporate officers. I backchecked them all. Three seemed ordinary enough, but the fourth was called B. Grimm. B. Grimm was the owner of a small company called Hansel & Gretel Designs, which turned out to be nothing but a post office box, a bank account, and a single employee. The employee was Michael Meissen. Checks were paid into the H&G account regularly by Montex, a charitable organization.

A charity.

Back to the library. A request for the Montex donor hierarchy from the register of charitable organizations. There were one-off donors, who were mostly anonymous; the Supporters; and Patrons. Patrons were divided into Silver, Gold, and Platinum. There were one hundred and sixteen names on the Platinum list—people who gave more than seventy thousand a year. There, near the end of the list was G. van de Oest.

Wind whistling along the sand outside the tent. Marley nodding seriously. "Greta is a much more powerful force in this company than most people realize. Your future might be smoother if you bore that in mind."

And Tok, years earlier, telling me: *"It was just getting interesting when Greta came on the net and kicked me out . . . she cut me out of those files clean as a whistle."*

I waited outside the conservatory in Pearson Park. It was eleven in the morning. I had not slept at all. My face, drawn and gray as the clouds scudding overhead, was reflected in wavy lines by the slightly flawed glass. Magyar, when she finally arrived, did not look much better.

It was warm in the conservatory, bright with bird noise. We were the only people there.

"She must know as much about rival business families as she knows about the van de Oest operation," I told Magyar. "Information is power." Something Greta had learned from Katerine early on, no doubt. "And Greta would need to feel powerful." Poor Greta, who always looked as though she was expecting something or someone to swoop upon her from around the corner.

"You have to go to your family and tell them this."

I stared at a mynah bird, grooming its wing. Purple highlights reflected from the black feathers. "No."

"Yes. Greta has to be stopped."

"She knew," I said, "all that time ago." The bird's beak was very orange. "She helped me."

"All she did was give you a lock!" Magyar, I realized, was protective of that seven-year-old child who had not been able to look after herself. I loved her for it.

"But the lock stopped it. Greta stopped it."

"She didn't help Stella."

The bird looked at me, cocking its head this way, then that. "Maybe she thought, I don't know, that Katerine was unstoppable. If it happened to her early enough, and often enough—"

"Who knows what she thought? Who cares! You were hurt! She had you kidnapped, humiliated!"

The bird, disturbed by the noise, flew up to the roof of its aviary. Greta had given me the lock that had saved me. "Maybe she didn't know I was the one they'd take, maybe . . ." Of course she would have known. But they weren't supposed to try and kill me. What had gone wrong?

"And what about poor Lucas Chen?" I said nothing. "Lore." She took me by both arms, above the elbow, tight. "Stop looking at the birds. Listen to yourself. Just listen. You're making excuses for her. Abuse is never an excuse for tormenting others. Especially a sister. She has to be stopped. You have to talk to your family."

"I can't."

Magyar let go of my arms, laid her hand along my cheek. "Lore, love, you can't hide forever."

Why not? The mynah bird was flying this way and that, trying to find a way out. "I can't go back. They're too strong." Katerine's Lore, Oster's Lore . . . They would break me to pieces again. "I'll be the youngest again, the baby, the pawn . . ." I trailed off. She was looking at me oddly.

"It wouldn't be the same," she said gently. "It couldn't. Katerine would go to jail. Greta would go to jail."

I stared at her. They were my family.

"Lore, you've had your life stolen away. You have a scar more than a foot long on your back. You think you killed someone—you suffered night after night of believing you took away a man's life. Lucas Chen is probably scared for his life, right now. Stella is dead. You can't go back."

It was a terrible litany. "No," I said, and I didn't know whether I meant *No, I can't go back* or *No, you're wrong.* I didn't want to go back, but knowing that it was not there to return to was terrifying.

"Tok. I could call Tok." And then it would all be over. I could get rid of the false PIDA, get rid of poor, dead Sal Bird, let her finally rest in peace. I could reclaim my identity. Be Lore again. No more hiding, no more lying; no more dealing with Spanner except to buy her a drink if she hit hard times. Move away from the tiny flat, the cramped bathroom where I banged my head every morning . . .

"What would happen to us?"

"What would you want to happen?"

"I wouldn't see you every day at the plant. I'd be living . . ." I floundered.

"Where? Where would you be living that I couldn't see you if I wanted, or you couldn't see me?"

I had been about to say *Ratnapida*. But I could never live there again.

"Getting yourself back doesn't mean going back to everything the way it was. Or would you want to leave me behind like your tired old identity?"

"No."

"Then what? You think I won't be able to cope with the change? You think that just because I was brought up poor I wouldn't be able to adjust? No? Good. Because I can. I always knew you weren't who you said you were. At least now I know who you are. It might take me a while, and there might be some bumpy times, but I can adapt. Don't throw me away."

She was looking at me. Her eyes were steady. I could see things reflected in them, too small to make out. The reflections seemed to be changing shape. Her eyes were wet.

I held out my arms. She stepped into them. To my surprise, she was an inch or two shorter than me. We stepped back half a pace. I kissed her. She blinked and tears spilled. I kissed her again. Then she held me. We stood like that a long time, my face hidden against her shoulder, while the

world changed, while the sodden weight of the last few
years evaporated from my head, my shoulders, my calves,
until my arms felt light enough to rise into the air of their
own accord, as in those childhood games where a friend
pins them to your side and you struggle to lift them, then
the friend releases you, and the muscles remember the
struggle, and the arms move away from your ribs as though
floating on a tidal swell.

"Look at me," I said. "I am Frances Lorien van de Oest.
I have a job. I have a place of my own. I have friends." I
knew who I was. Lore. And when I forgot or became confused, Magyar would know. "I have a future."

Magyar squeezed me tight, and released me. She wiped
at her face, then grinned. "You also have lots of money."

The mynah bird screamed at us, but from close by, like
a mother scolding her children.

We walked around the pond. I was hungry but I didn't
want to leave the park. I didn't want to have to talk to anyone who wasn't Magyar. And there were too many decisions to make.

"You're sure that nothing's turned up on that body search?"

"Sure. I checked again before I left to meet you."

"The records might be being withheld. Because my family's involved."

"Who would know?"

"Greta." *But she had given me a lock.* We walked in silence, feet hitting the pavement at the same time, hips
moving together. "I'll go ahead anyway. Even without
knowing. I can't hide forever. I'll call Tok first, and then my
father. He could probably find out if the police are holding
anything back."

"Do you want to tell him everything?"

"I don't want to hide anymore."

"Privacy isn't always the same as hiding."

"I think it will be hard for me to tell the difference for

a while." We stepped over the gnarled roots that twisted over the pavement. It was the second time we had passed the tree. "Once I'm fairly sure I won't be arrested for anything, I'll reclaim my identity."

"How long will that take?"

"I don't know. Depends if I've been declared legally dead." I could have been dead. Because of Greta. Crablegs had tried to kill me with that nasal spray. I could have been a skeleton at the bottom of the river, along with all the tens of thousands who had died here since humankind had been able to swing a rock. But I knew Oster wouldn't have had me declared dead. He wouldn't want the publicity. "When Oster is here, when I'm sitting across from him, face-to-face, when I can smell him, see the wrinkles in his shirt, I'll tell him about his wife, and Greta. I'll give him time to get used to it before I go to the police."

"Not too much time."

"There's Chen, I know."

We were going past the tree again. "When, then?"

"Tomorrow. I'll tape a statement for the police, have it all ready to hand over. We'll get them all: Katerine, Greta, Meisener, Crablegs. All the others." I was shaking. "They have no right! Years they've been playing with people, as though we were just chess pieces. I don't even think Greta knows that other people apart from her really exist. Thousands of people have suffered. Tens of thousands." And she had suffered because of Katerine. As I nearly had. As I had.

I wanted to see Katerine alone on a chair in a windowless room. I wanted her to weep. I wanted her eyes to turn red and sore. I wanted her to beg, to plead for some water, her contact lens case. "I want to see the color of her eyes."

"Who?"

"My mother. I want to see her suffer." No, it was more than that. "I want her to see me. I want her to look up at me and see me. I want to be able to look into her eyes and see myself reflected there. I want her to see that I see the

321

world through my own eyes, and not hers. I want her to acknowledge me. See that I'm real, I exist. I'm grown, my
own person. That I'm finally free to become who I might
be." I linked my arm through Magyar's, pulled her to a halt.
"Tomorrow. I promise. This time tomorrow."

"Tonight. Right now would be better."

"But tomorrow I'll be ready. I'll—"

"Lore, if you wait for the right moment, you'll wait forever. There *is* no perfect time. You just have to do it anyway. Things won't be any better tomorrow."

"But what's the hurry?" I had waited three years. "If it's
Lucas Chen you're worried—"

She made an impatient, chopping motion. "I'm sorry for
what he's going through, but it's you I care about. Tell me
honestly—will it be any easier to talk to your father tomorrow than today?"

Me and Oster. I took a deep breath, let it out again. "No."

"Tonight, then."

I nodded reluctantly. "Tonight. But I'll make the tape
first. And after tonight's shift . . . What?"

"You're doing it again. Not facing things. Tell me, why
wait until after the shift?"

"It's my job . . ." But, of course, she was right. I would
never work there again. There was no more Sal Bird, aged
twenty-five. Done with, all done with. Tonight, during winter dark in this part of the world, I would call Ratnapida. A
blaze of light, clear water. Limpid reflections. No more obscuring the truth. No more shadows and lies. Tonight.

"Do you want me to come home with you?"

"No. Tonight will be soon enough. I need some sleep.
And I need to tape that statement. I'll call you at the plant
when . . . when . . . I'll call you."

I held her again, for a long time. I could feel the shape
of her through her coat and mine, the hard bone, pliant
muscles. I wanted her with a hard, deep ache. Tonight.

TWENTY-SIX

THE NEXT day in the tent passes slowly. Lore gets her breakfast, but long after her internal clock tells her it is early afternoon, there is still no lunch. She begins to worry. Why haven't they fed her?

Why feed someone you are going to kill?

Thirty million. It isn't much. She has no idea what the family's total holdings are but she knows it adds up to tens of billions. Thirty million. She had requisitioned more than that herself for the Kirghizi project.

It must be Oster. He must have found out that she and Tok know about Stella, know what he has done to her. Maybe he has already killed Tok, somehow. Maybe he is deliberately stalling negotiations so that her kidnappers will kill her, then no one will know what he has done. But how is he stopping Katerine from paying? Her mother is smarter than Oster.

Lore shakes her head. She has to understand, has to work it out, find a way to make them pay.

The afternoon ticks on. She does stomach crunches, leg lifts, push-ups, and stretches. She is hungry. For the first time in nearly two weeks she finds herself longing for one of the pills she has hidden under the tent. She takes out her nail, holds it, puts it back in the sleeping bag, takes it out again.

The afternoon turns to evening. No supper.

When her body tells her it is time to sleep, she isn't tired, but she lies down in her sleeping bag because it makes her feel less naked. She holds the nail tightly and breathes slowly, evenly, trying to relax her muscles one by one, from the feet up.

Bright light floods the tent from outside as someone rips open the flap. "Up. Now." It is Fishface, but Lore hardly recognizes him, his voice is so harsh. "I said now." He steps menacingly toward the sleeping bag and Lore wriggles out hastily, nail tucked in her left fist, out of sight. He grabs her arm. "We're leaving."

"Did they pay?"

He does not answer.

Lore looks around her as they head across the old floorboards she has only been able to feel with her fingertips. It is a barn, very old. Hundreds of years old, probably.

Outside the night is cool and clear. The smell abruptly changes, and she knows she is in a northern European country—England, perhaps, or Ireland—and that the scents of garlic and sun permeating the inside of the barn are a trick. So much planning . . .

She shivers as Fishface marches her across a cobbled yard toward a pair of headlights. Some sort of vehicle. Lore moves slowly, docilely: she is supposed to be drugged, and she needs to think.

They are now only forty yards from the vehicle. It is an off-track van, the kind with doors that open at the back. The doors are open. She does not want to climb in.

They are going to kill her. She is sure of it. Old farm equipment lines the stone walls of the yard. She can smell the rusting metal.

They are almost at the van now. She can see someone inside, programming directions into the instrument panel. Crablegs. The floor of the van is covered in plasthene. To catch the blood? She maneuvers the nail into position in her fist.

They are at the van. Crablegs is standing at the lip, holding out his arms to her. Fishface is behind her. He moves his hands from her arms to her waist, not gripping now, just getting into position to boost her up and inside.

Lore pretends to stumble. As she knows he would, Fishface reaches to catch her. She turns fast, nail in fist.

His eyes are brown. The look that flares behind them is part shock at her speed, part fear, part a strange kind of acceptance: she will kill him. That nearly undoes her. But her fist is already swinging in its short arc. He doesn't move. The nail rips into his neck and blood fountains. They tumble into metal. Something sharp. Bright pain. Blood splashes on her face, her arms, her throat, in her hair. She is screaming. Crablegs is screaming. Fishface is silent.

Shock makes all the rest hazy, unreal, underwater slow-motion: the van, the shouting, then silence as the van rumbles through the night. The long sigh, the hissing nasal spray creeping across the air between her and Crablegs molecule by molecule, deadly.

And breathing it in, sucking it down, tumbling backward out of the van while it's still moving is a rite of passage. She could have died. She should have died. She moves from one life, from Frances Lorien van de Oest, to another, arriving—as all newborns do—naked and covered in blood.

TWENTY-SEVEN

I set the Hammex 20 up on its tripod and sat opposite, in the chair beneath the window. The camera lens was like a cold fish eye, unblinking. I stared at it, forgetting what I was supposed to say. The reflection of a bird flying past my window flashed in the glass eye and made me jump.

I cleared my throat. "When I was seven, someone tried to sexually abuse me. I think it was my mother . . ."

I talked for hours, occasionally sipping water from the glass next to me. I told the camera about Greta helping with the lock, about Stella killing herself, about Tok calling me in Uruguay. I told the camera everything I could remember about my kidnap; about Fishface and Crablegs and the tent; how they had known I was allergic to spray-injector drugs; what they had said and how they had said it. I talked about the nail.

When I found I was talking at great length about the qualities of the nail—how it smelled, how it felt in my hand, how big it was—I turned the camera off, used the bathroom, made myself some tea. When I resumed, I was much more terse. "So when they took me outside, I thought they were going to kill me. I tried to escape. In the course of that escape attempt, one—the one I called Fishface—was seriously hurt. Then I was bundled up into a van." I described the van as well as I could. "Crablegs threatened to kill me. He tried, with some kind of nasal spray. I got away. I was hurt, naked, alone. I was helped by a stranger."

That's what Spanner still was: a stranger. One with a dangerous smile and skillful hands. I wondered what she was doing, right now. I wondered if someone was hurting her for money. It was getting dark outside. The sun went down early on winter afternoons.

"I illegally took the PIDA from the corpse of a woman called Sal Bird, who had died, I was told, in a swimming accident in Immingham. I worked at Hedon Road Wastewater Treatment Plant." I gave my address and phone number. I explained about the sabotage; about Meisener; about Montex and the van de Oest corporation and Greta. "I think Lucas Chen has been abducted by the same persons as myself three years ago."

I thought about saying more, but there wasn't any point. This was only to give them enough to start with while I was dealing with my family and dodging the glare of publicity. No doubt I would spend hours closeted in some grim-looking police station while being politely interviewed by the officer or officers in charge. For all that I had done, I had never seen the inside of a police station. The idea frightened me.

On the other side of the window, neon in shopwindows and the sodium of streetlights were blinking on. The flat was gray and shadowy beyond the camera flood. I should really stand up and make some calls: tell Ruth and Ellen the truth before the net caught the story; let Tom know that the building would be swarming by this time tomorrow. Maybe he had a relative he could stay with for a day or two.

I just sat there, hands and feet getting cold, watching the

camera light grow more sharp-edged as the shadows in the flat turned from gray to black.

~~~ IT WAS spring again. Lore had been prostituting her body for more than a year. All that money. She lay there for a long time, stroking the quilt, thinking, finally admitting to herself what she had known, on some level, all along.

That evening, as they were preparing to go out to meet more customers, Lore sat down on the rim of the bathtub.

"How much does it cost?"

"Mmn?" Spanner was facing the mirror. She continued to brush her hair, but Lore knew Spanner was watching her.

"The drug. How much does it cost?"

Spanner paused in midstroke, then shrugged. "What does it matter? We have enough money."

"We've been earning an average of six thousand a week for more than a year. That's more than three hundred thousand—"

"I can count."

"—and where has it gone?" Lore stood up, took the hairbrush from Spanner's hand, and shook it in her face. "I want your attention, and I want the truth. Why, exactly, have we been selling our bodies for the last year?"

"To earn—"

"The truth!"

"That *is* the—"

"But not the whole truth, is it? Yes, we've been letting old ladies watch while you sodomize me; you've tied me up while some executive jerks off because it's his birthday; I've had to watch while you piss on some jaded couple. For what?" Lore was pacing up and down now, hairbrush still in her hand. "And don't tell me money. It's the drug. I thought the drug was to make our lives bearable while we made money the only way we knew how. But that's not it at all, is it? I got it all backward. That was never the point. The whole *point* was the drug. The whole *point* was what you and I did while we took the drug. Because you like it. Deep down inside, you like it."

"You do, too. Otherwise you wouldn't be doing it."

That wasn't true. Was it? Lore shook her head. "Just tell me how much we've been spending on that drug."

"A lot. Everything." And Spanner smiled.

Lore hit her. An open-handed slap that sent her spinning across the sink.

"Why?" She was panting. But Spanner said nothing. "I should have figured it out sooner. Why hadn't I heard about this drug? Why didn't anyone else know about it? Because it's new. Who steals it for you? You make me so angry! We could have earned more selling it than using it. Couldn't we? *Couldn't* we!"

But if they had merely been selling it, Spanner would not have had the same power; she would not have known something Lore didn't.

Lore wanted to hit Spanner again, hit her over and over, blame her for everything. But something held her back. She was already the kind of person who sold herself, who humiliated herself on a regular basis. She did not want to become the kind of person who enjoyed hurting others.

Spanner had turned her back on Lore and was examining her face in the mirror. "It's swelling already. I'll have to use a lot of makeup to cover it before we go out."

Lore felt cold and sick. She had hit Spanner. She could not understand why Spanner wasn't reacting to that. "We can't go out. Not now. We—"

But Spanner whirled, teeth bared and tendons standing out in her neck and shoulders. "We have no choice! You think the drug's expensive? You have no idea!" She barked with laughter. "We *owe* money, you fool. And they know where we live. They're not forgiving types, either. So you get your body into that dress and come with me, because if we don't earn some cash tonight, tomorrow you won't be in any position to worry about what kind of damage this stuff will be doing to your health."

Lore's mind went terrifyingly blank. She was beginning to feel that the whole world was out of control. She closed her eyes. *Think fast.* "They know you. Not me. You need the money more than I do."

"They won't take long to figure—"

"But for now, you're the one." Lore made her voice hard and flat. "So you need my help, for a change. So I'll make you a deal. We'll go out tonight, and tomorrow, and the next day. For as long as it takes. But we won't use that drug anymore. And we'll save the money."

Without the drug, it would be unbearable. At least, she hoped Spanner would find it so. And then maybe she could be persuaded to look at the possibility of a net-commercial scam.

"Is there any left?"

Spanner held up a vial, still half-full.

"Then you can use it." She no longer trusted Spanner to look after her while she was in throes of hormonally in-duced ecstasy. And maybe the effects of the drug would not be lasting if she stopped taking it now.

Without the drug it was terrible. Lore felt like a recep-tacle, one of those plastic vaginas she and Spanner had both laughed at in the sex shop. But she stayed with it grimly. And she stuck to Spanner's side like a burr.

"I won't let you run up any more debt," she told her. So they earned their money, and they saved, and after six weeks Lore decided it was enough.

Lore prepared the garden for a long absence. That's how she thought of it, a long absence, not a permanent one; she did not want to examine why. She just pruned and aerated and clipped. She had hoped to see the cat one last time, but it stayed away. It would always be wild, coming and going unbidden. Like hope. She hoped Spanner would feed it. Probably not.

Afterward, she cleaned her spade and shears and clippers carefully and wrapped them in oilcloth. Then she waited patiently for Spanner to wake.

When she did, Lore called her into the living room. She gestured at the two piles of debit cards on the table. "Choose one," she said. "They're roughly equal. You can check them if you like."

Spanner looked at them, and at the two suitcases against the wall. "Does this mean what I think it means?"

"Yes." Lore sat on the couch. She had meant to be businesslike, but the lost look on Spanner's face brought back memories of all the good times they had had: the exhilaration of riding the freighters; packs full of stolen slates; champagne at four in the morning. "Yes," she said again.

Spanner squatted on her heels by the table, examined the pile thoughtfully. "You know, there's enough here to bankroll that scam you were talking about earlier."

And Lore couldn't leave without one more try. "We could both start afresh," she said. "You've got skills. It wouldn't be hard. We could move, find another flat. Somewhere where Billy and the others couldn't find you." Spanner said nothing. "We could take new names. Get real jobs. You have skills. It's never too late to start again."

"Isn't it?" She looked up, and Lore was reminded of the ancient look, the soft pain she had seen that first night on Spanner's face when she had seen how badly injured Lore had been.

"No," she said, but even to herself she did not sound convinced.

Spanner laughed, but it was a sad laugh this time. She scooped up the nearest pile of cards. "Well, it lasted longer than I expected that October night, and it was more fun."

"Please, Spanner . . ."

"No. We're different. This may not be what you feel you deserve from life, but it's the level I've found, the place I call

331

home. It's where I belong."

"No. It's where you think you belong, because you believe you don't deserve any better. But you do. We all do.
There's a chance here, with this." Lore nodded at her own
pile. "Don't dismiss it."

But Spanner was already getting up, flipping the switch
on her screen, pulling up a swirling graphic in vibrant colors. Lore picked up a suitcase in each hand, paused. "I've
entered my new address in your files."

Spanner said, without looking up from the screen: "I'll
see you again. You'll always need me."

I STOOD and stretched, turned off the camera light,
looked at the clock. Eight-thirty. Morning in Ratnapida.

A bath first.

The tub took a while to fill. I don't remember thinking
anything in particular.

I climbed in but felt no urge to use the soap. Gradually,
the water stilled. My face came into focus on the surface, between my bent knees. I looked at the reflection curiously:
brown hair, gray eyes, good bones. The gray eyes watched
me back. This was me. I didn't need Sal Bird anymore.

This is what my father would see when I met him tomorrow. What would I say? How would I explain how I
had lived the last three years? I wouldn't, not right away. It
would be enough that I was here. At last.

And then I was filled with a sudden energy, the need to
call, to meet Oster and show him my real face, to wait for
Magyar outside the plant afterward. I reached for the soap.

I was toweling myself dry when the screen chimed. I
wrapped the towel around myself and took the call.

"Magyar!"

"You haven't called yet, right?"

"No, but as soon as my hair's dry—"

"Too late. Your father's here, demanding to know where you are."

That couldn't be right. I hadn't called him yet.

"Look, if . . . if you need more time, I can foul up your employment records to hide your address."

"No." It came out crisp and decisive. "I mean, yes, hide my address. I'm coming in to see him."

"Now?"

"Right now." My hair could dry on its own.

I don't remember getting dressed, or whether I took the slide or walked, but I do remember the sheen of Magyar's hair in the street light outside the plant, and I remember walking through the gates next to her, carefully, as though my body were built upon bird bones, hollow and light. And I remember the door.

It was pale wood: ash, something like that. Very pale. There was a nameplate: P. RAWLIN, SUPERINTENDENT. I stood in front of it, my face about four inches from the grain, long enough to worry the assistant. He shifted slightly behind me, and Magyar gave him a look. I closed my eyes. My father was behind that door. Whom I had loved, then hated, and did not know at all. I took one last look at Magyar, who nodded.

The handle was one of those old-fashioned knobs. Brass. Slippery under my sweating hands. It turned easily.

Dark red carpet. A desk, a big slab of some dark wood. A man climbing to his feet as the door shut behind me— the plant superintendent. To the right, a woman in a brown suit. A quick glance from her pale eyes to me and then from me to the man sitting on the left side of the desk. A strange, eerie silence. Then the superintendent, Rawlin, saying something at the same time that the door swung shut with a click and my father jumped to his feet, face eager, hands open: "Lore! Oh, thank god, Lore!"

His words were like solvent on cheap varnish, stripping

away my comforting glaze of unreality.

"—god. Lore. When I heard, I came as fast as I could. We've just land—"

The world was painfully bright and real. I held up my hand, making him stop. "Who told you? Was it Meisener?"

Oster dropped his hands. "Who?"

"Meisener. Or that's what he calls himself. He works here."

"Wait a minute," the superintendent said, coming out from behind the desk. "One of our workers knew you were here?"

"Oh, he's not yours."

Rawlin frowned at that, then ignored it. "But if he knew you were here, why didn't he claim the reward?"

"It wasn't Meisener?" I asked Oster. But of course it wasn't. And then all my adrenaline had boiled away and I felt old and sad and tired. They were all staring at me. I sighed. "Let's start again." I nodded to Rawlins. "Superintendent," I said, then held out my hand to the woman. "I'm Lore van de Oest."

She responded automatically, as people do. "Claire Singh. Director of City Sewage."

I smiled the polite smile I had not had to use for a long time. "My father and I haven't seen each other in a while. We would like some privacy." It took her a moment to understand; then she flushed. Perhaps it was the smile, perhaps she remembered that Oster could buy her and her city from his daily operating budget. "Rawlin," she snapped. "We'll leave father and daughter to themselves for a few minutes."

I watched them leave, refusing to meet my father's eyes until the door was closing behind them. I tried to imagine what Magyar would make of their exit. I felt better knowing she was there.

Then there was no way to put it off any longer. I turned to my father.

He held out his arms again, but more cautiously this time, and that caution, almost timorousness, undid me. He was my father.

"Oh, Papa . . ."

I threw myself into his arms. But I wasn't six anymore, and he couldn't keep out the world. And he seemed smaller than he had been. We moved apart a little to look at each other, hands still wrapped around biceps and triceps.

"Lore . . ." Long and drawn out, as though it was new in his mouth. "Lore, I thought you were dead."

"I was, in a way."

He reached up, seemed about to ruffle my hair, then touched the ends gently. "Brown suits you."

We held each other at arm's length in silence, measuring. Still daughter and father, but changed. "Come for a walk with me. By the canal."

"In the city?"

His surprise and distaste amused me. "I've lived here three years. I'm one of the people I used to be scared of. We'll walk by the canal and no one will bother us. Assuming the media doesn't have this already."

"It's tight as a drum. That won't last past tomorrow morning, of course."

"Unless your informer takes it to the net for extra money."

"No. That was one of the conditions of receiving the reward."

It made sense. "Will you come for that walk? You can have a bodyguard follow us, if you like."

I opened the door. Magyar was there, trying to look bored, succeeding only in looking fierce and alien in her green skinny with its red and black strapping. I stood aside, gestured from one to the other. "Magyar, this is my father, Oster. Dad, this is Cherry Magyar." I put my arm around her waist briefly, so he would understand, and said to her, "My father and I are going for a walk. I'll be back. After the shift, outside."

I hadn't meant it to be a question, but of course it was. My father was here in the flesh. Everything was real. This was her chance to back away from Lore van de Oest. All she said was, "Don't be late," and gave my father a piercing look.

· · ·

It was wet and cold and windy. The towpath was surprisingly light: the water reflected the city's glow. We walked in silence for a while.

"Did you fly straight from Ratnapida?"

"Yes. Private plane from Auckland to Bangkok, then on to Rotterdam. Then here."

"I imagine you feel cold." It was summer in Ratnapida. Mid-eighties on a cool day.

"The carp are bigger," he said. "Even in just three years." More silence.

"Lore, will you come home?"

I didn't know what to say.

"She's gone," he said softly. "Your mother."

"What happened?"

"It was terrible."

I took his arm as we walked, and he told me: Tok arriving in the middle of the night, shouting, "making all these accusations. He was wild. Shouting, almost screaming." He wouldn't wait until morning. He had waited too long already, he said. Stella was dead, Greta was a twisted shadow of what she should be, because ever since they were very small Katerine had been going into their rooms and . . . using them.

"Did you believe him?"

"I didn't want to."

"But you did, didn't you?" Accusatory. "Because you already knew."

The arm in mine tensed. I thought he would pull away, but then he sagged. "I didn't know. I mean, I was never sure. But I think I've suspected . . . That night when you screamed and wouldn't be left alone without a lock . . . But she was my wife! Your mother. Mothers don't . . . they don't *do* that sort of thing."

"Stella is dead. I nearly died. Tok ran away." I had a sudden vision of myself as a mechanical bird, parroting: *Stella is dead, I nearly died, Tok ran away. Stella is dead, I nearly died, Tok . . .*

"It's so easy, Lore, to ignore things. To pretend that what's there is your imagination."

"Do you know, do you have any idea, what your . . . your *pretense* cost me? Do you?"

"Tok said . . ." His voice was low and brown with grief. Maybe I should have felt sorry for him, and I did, in a way, but I was too angry. "Stella died. I didn't even get to go to her funeral. I don't even know where you *had* the funeral. Katerine was there, and not me. Katerine and Greta. And why? Because you didn't pay my ransom! Because—"

"What do you mean, we didn't pay your ransom? Of course we did. Greta handled it. She told me so personally."

"Greta," I said. "Greta. Good old gray Greta. Greta will get the job done. Give it to Greta." I hardly recognized my own voice, it was so twisted up. Oster looked sick. "Don't you like who I've become, Papa? I've been through some hard times, staying alive. But I'm not a bad person. I don't hide from the truth." *You're doing it again, hiding from things,* Magyar had said. Well, not anymore. "Let me tell you some things about Greta, Papa. Are you listening? Because I will follow you and speak until you do hear. Gray Greta, efficient Greta, is running a group like Jerome's Boys."

"But—"

I was implacable. "One of them, who goes by the name of Nathan Meisener, was almost responsible for the deaths of thousands and thousands of people. I could have been one of them. And she's risking the deaths of thousands every day. She had me kidnapped. Yes, my own sister. She probably kidnapped Lucas Chen."

Oster looked bewildered.

"You're not asking why, Papa, but I'll tell you. She took me because I was an easy target. And she saw me as being the favorite, of you *and* Katerine. Maybe you would *both* pay the ransom. And she needed the money, because she needs to control things, have secrets, secret power. Only she didn't know what to do when Tok started making the accusations. Everything got confused. Maybe she thought Tok knew about her. Maybe she panicked and tried to get rid of me: I stopped being a person and became a liability. People aren't real to her. Why? Because my mother made her crazy." I was trembling with rage, only now it was not only at Oster but at Katerine. Katerine, who had ruined the lives of untold people. Who had nearly ruined mine. Katerine.

"Where is she?"

"What?"

"Katerine. Where is she? Where did you send her? She's not in jail. It would have been on the net."

"Tok said we should get the police. But I couldn't. She's your mother."

She's a monster. "She should be in jail."

"I couldn't . . ." He seemed unwilling to continue. I just waited. I was scared, I realized. What if she was somewhere nearby?

"Don't you see? Not having control, not knowing what was going on hurt her." Not enough. Not nearly enough to make up for Stella, and Tok, and me, and Lucas Chen. "I made her leave. Divorced her. Divested her of her holdings." It all sounded impossibly military, like a court-martial. "She's watched. We get reports . . ."

He trailed off. I had a sudden, sickening feeling in my stomach. "Who sees to the reports?"

"Greta."

Greta. She was everywhere.

Oster was still talking to me. ". . . don't understand why she would want to hurt you. She's your sister. Are you . . . are you sure?"

He was hunched up, like a dog expecting a kick. I felt sorry for him. "I'm sure. And I don't think she does want to hurt people. She doesn't think about that. What she's thinking about is the family. The business. Control. The patents, the intellectual property, the profits. It's her life. The way she's found to not think about being small and held down by her sweating, crying mother . . ." I was the one who was crying. *Greta, who had got me a lock. My mother, lost . . .*

He stared at me. His eyes were bright with city lights. "How do you know all this?"

"Oh, Papa, *you* are the one who should have known!"

He reached out and touched my tears, found a handkerchief. "We can't be everywhere, and know everything at once," he said sadly.

But you didn't even try! He had removed himself from the responsibilities of ownership. He had been happy to leave it all to his wife and her family. He had delegated himself right out of the command chain, and gone off in his boat to count endangered fish.

"The business carries your name. You're responsible."

I didn't know how to make him understand. *I met a man called Paolo, I wanted to say, whose life is ruined because you didn't care enough to oversee the business. The money comes in, and you take it, you don't care how it's made, you don't care that we still rake in tithes on every patent use, that we preside over a monopoly that we don't need anymore. We already have so much money we don't know what to do with it.*

But even when I was seven years old I had known he preferred to leave the real work to others. He wasn't a termite on the forest floor, organizing the building; he was a brightly colored bird soaring up, up above the canopy, unconcerned with what went on below, as long as the sun still shone and there was nectar in the orchids.

There was too much for me to explain, and I didn't have time.

"I have something to do tonight," I said. "Something that won't wait. I've made a tape. I'll give it to you. You must make Greta give back Lucas Chen." I hesitated, then decided not to threaten him with taking it to the police, making the whole sordid business public. "And I want your help. I want you to speed up the formal reclaiming of my identity. I want a copy of my PIDA."

He knew there were things I wasn't saying, but he merely nodded. "I have it." They had probably sent it to the family as proof that they had me. "I'll get it messengered over first thing tomorrow. Will I see you then?"

He looked old and frail. "Oh, Papa, yes."

We walked farther. We had been walking awhile.

"I have to go."

We held each other again. Longer this time, and harder. I had my father back. "Tomorrow," he whispered. I hurried down the towpath.

Spanner was in the Polar Bear, drinking alone. She saw me in the mirror and watched me thread my way to the bar, the way a well-fed snake will watch a young pig: trying to decide whether it should kill now, or wait for its prey to grow a little and make the attraction, the mesmerizing gaze, the final strike worthwhile.

I didn't bother to sit down. "Why did you do it?"

She shrugged, looking down at her drink. "Why not? You always said I would do anything for money."

"And will a quarter of a million make you feel good about yourself?"

"Money always helps."

"That's what you've been waiting for all along, isn't it? A reward. For your prey to finally get big enough, worth the risk. Worth lunging for, pumping full of poison."

Her eyes seemed dry and blank. No reflections there. No clues about how she felt, or if she did feel anything anymore. I doubted she understood a word I was saying.

"Did you hate me right from the beginning?" She said nothing. "Why did you hate me? Because I had what you didn't, self-respect?"

She stirred. "You didn't *have* any self-respect when I found you naked and bleeding and nameless. No, what I hated was that you had choices. You *chose* to not go back to your family. I had no choices. I've never had choices."

"That's not true. There is always a choice."

"Easy to say when you're a van de Oest."

Perhaps she was right. I would never know. I was not her, and I was glad. "What do you want me to say? That I hate you? I don't." And I didn't. I didn't feel much of anything except sorrow that she could not and would not see the chances and choices and possibilities of change I felt everywhere about me. And it wasn't just because I was a van de Oest. Stella had been a van de Oest, and she had killed herself. Greta had been brought up as one, and she had twisted and stayed twisted. You had to allow change, you had to want it. You had to believe you deserved it. Spanner did not hate me; she hated herself.

I left her sitting there alone, looking at her reflection in her beer. I wondered what she saw.

The medic had a clinic in the center of town. I had to offer him a triple fee to open up for me for a nonemergency.

There was no nurse. He cleaned my left hand himself, worked on it quickly and efficiently, and closed up the incision with a plastic staple. He sprayed it with plaskin. Put a small sticking plaster on the top. "That's to remind you it's stapled. Otherwise, you might forget and try to use it."

I wondered how many times he had saved people's lives, or how many times he had tried and failed, without notifying the authorities. His eyes were very tired, down-drooping, like a bloodhound's. He was exhausted. What would happen if there was a gunshot wound, or a serious stabbing to attend to, and he was too tired?

"Doctor," I said on impulse as he collected his instruments in a tray, "if I made a donation, would you give me some information about one of your past clients?"

"No."

"For thirty thousand?" He hesitated. "For thirty thousand now, and a yearly stipend—enough to hire an assistant for the night shift? I'll put it in writing if you like."

He put the tray down and looked at me steadily, his eyes more like a dog's than ever. "What's the question?"

"Did you treat a man, just over three years ago, with a wound to his neck? A man about six feet tall. The wound would have been about here." I pointed to the left side of my neck, at the carotid.

"What kind of wound?"

"Puncture. Tear. Made with a long, rusty nail. And if you did treat him, did he die?"

He said nothing for a long time. "Let me ask you a question instead. You know I need the money—the clinic needs it. If I refuse to give you confidential information, would you withhold it?"

The man had saved my life. He knew it, I knew it. I sighed. "I'm sorry. I shouldn't have asked." That wasn't enough. The thirty thousand was stolen, anyway. "You can have the thirty thousand. No strings attached."

He went to his terminal and for a moment I thought he was going to pull the information I needed, all the case notes, because I had made the selfless choice—like the child in a fairy tale being rewarded by the old witch in disguise. But life isn't a fairy tale. He was making up my bill.

He held it out.

"Thank you," I managed, and headed for the door.

At the wharf, the lights were still out from my last visit. The surface of the river was choppy in the wind. I watched it awhile. The riverbank is the one place in the jungle where an animal is visible from the air and the ground.

The grate in the pavement was hard to lift one-handed, and I got a bruise on my wrist when it fell the first time I tried. It seemed appropriate. This should not be too easy and painless.

Turning on the lights was like stepping out into the open. "My name," I said to the wind, to the river rolling to the sea, "is Frances Lorien van de Oest. I live here."

I would spend the rest of my life by the river, being visible.

. . .

I got to the plant just as the shift was leaving. Magyar was the last out. Maybe she had been waiting as long as she could, giving me extra time, or putting off the possibility that I might not be there. Her shoulders were hunched against the wind, her face pinched and worried. Her head turned this way and that, searching.

I stepped into the light. "Magyar."

When she saw me she smiled. It was like opening the door of a furnace: a blast of light, fire, warmth. For me. This woman's eyes were bright and lively, full of herself and her vision of me. I could see myself there, if I looked.

I held out my hands. She took them, then lifted my left hand to the light. "What happened?"

"I had the false PIDA removed." For a while, I would be nobody but the Lore I had made. We stood in the street, wind howling around us, Magyar's hair streaming behind her. I imagined her in my kitchen in the morning, skin warm and smelling of sleep, that beautiful hair tucked behind her ears, making coffee, talking of this and that. "Come home with me."

"Yes."

We walked hand in hand down the street. When I met my family again, I would introduce them to both of us.

AUTHOR'S NOTE

THERE IS a disturbing tendency among readers—particularly critics—to assume that any woman who writes about abuse, no matter how peripherally, must be speaking from her own experience. This is, in Joanna Russ's terms, a denial of the writer's imagination.

Should anyone be tempted to assume otherwise, let me be explicit: *Slow River* is fiction, not autobiography. I made it up.

ABOUT THE AUTHOR

NICOLA GRIFFITH was born in Yorkshire, England, where she taught women's self-defense, led creative-writing workshops, and was the singer and songwriter for a band. She now lives in America with her partner, sf writer Kelley Eskridge. Her short fiction has been published in the United Kingdom and the United States and has been translated into several languages. Her first novel was *Ammonite*, for which she won a Lambda Literary Award and the 1993 Tiptree Award. *Slow River*, her second novel, was written with the aid of grants from the Georgia Council for the Arts and the Atlanta Bureau of Cultural Affairs.

DEL REY® ONLINE!

THE DEL REY INTERNET NEWSLETTER (DRIN)

The DRIN is a monthly electronic publication posted on the Internet, GEnie, CompuServe, BIX, various BBSs, and the Panix gopher. It features:

- hype-free descriptions of new books
- a list of our upcoming books
- special announcements
- a signing/reading/convention-attendance schedule for Del Rey authors
- in-depth essays by sf professionals (authors, artists, designers, salespeople, and others)
- a question-and-answer section
- behind-the-scenes looks at sf publishing
- and much more!

INTERNET INFORMATION SOURCE

Del Rey information is now available on a gopher server—gopher.panix.com—including:

- the current and all back issues of the Del Rey Internet Newsletter
- a description of the DRIN and content summaries of all issues
- sample chapters of current and upcoming books—readable and downloadable for free
- submission requirements
- mail-order information
- new DRINs, sample chapters, and other items are added regularly.

ONLINE EDITORIAL PRESENCE

Many of the Del Rey editors are online—on the Internet, GEnie, CompuServe, America Online, and Delphi. There is a Del Rey topic on GEnie and a Del Rey Folder on America Online.

WHY?

We at Del Rey realize that the networks are the medium of the future. That's where you'll find us promoting our books, socializing with others in the sf field, and—most important—making contact and sharing information with sf readers.

FOR MORE INFORMATION

The official e-mail address for Del Rey Books is

delrey@randomhouse.com

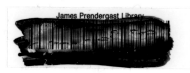
Griffith, Nicola.
   Slow river

	DATE DUE		